PRAISE FOR *THE MASK COLLECTORS*

"In *The Mask Collectors*, Ruvanee Pietersz Vilhauer brilliantly connects traditional Sri Lankan exorcism ceremonies, a sinister pharmaceutical company, mysterious deaths, infertility struggles, and the tensions within a marriage into a sophisticated and utterly unique thriller. I have never read a book quite like this very special one—it kept my heart racing right up until its powerful and satisfying end."

—Caroline Woods, author of *Fräulein M.*

"Ruvanee Pietersz Vilhauer's *The Mask Collectors* is a fascinating culture-clashing tale of superstition and human desire, of evil and corporate intrigue. A mind-blowing premise artfully transformed into a veritable feast of suspense."

—Anjanette Delgado, award-winning author of *The Heartbreak Pill* and *The Clairvoyant of Calle Ocho*

ADDITIONAL PRAISE FOR RUVANEE PIETERSZ VILHAUER

"Mesmerizing, tranquil, and worldly, these stories kept me transfixed. Each is a long, beautiful excursion into the difficulty and suspense of human relationships. One emerges from the book believing life to be more peaceful and more intense than before. A wonderful, masterful work of art."

—Rebecca Lee, judge, Iowa Short Fiction Award

"With a steady hand, soft heart, and sharp insights, Ruvanee Pietersz Vilhauer miraculously balances the precarious beam of identity and cultural displacement. The stories in *The Water Diviner* speak straight to the soul, its universal aches and voids, and we are better for getting to know these characters."

—Nancy Zafris, author, *The Home Jar: Stories*

"Full of richly drawn characters and empathetic inquiry . . . *The Water Diviner and Other Stories* investigates many aspects of Sri Lankan culture, including the long-term effects of colonialism, ethnic and religious differences, caste and class systems, colorism, racism, immigration, and more. A deep humanity drives each story, with the quest for answers always undertaken by inhabiting another's skin."

—*Foreword* (starred review)

THE MASK
COLLECTORS

OTHER TITLES BY RUVANEE PIETERSZ VILHAUER

The Water Diviner and Other Stories

THE MASK COLLECTORS

A NOVEL

RUVANEE PIETERSZ VILHAUER

Text copyright © 2019 by Ruvanee Pietersz Vilhauer
All rights reserved.

Published by Little A, New York

www.apub.com

Amazon, the Amazon logo, and Little A are trademarks of Amazon.com, Inc., or its affiliates.

ISBN-13: 9781503903678 (hardcover)
ISBN-10: 1503903672 (hardcover)
ISBN-13: 9781503903661 (paperback)
ISBN-10: 1503903664 (paperback)

Cover design and illustration by Philip Pascuzzo

Printed in the United States of America
First edition

THE MASK
COLLECTORS

AUTHOR'S NOTE

The representations of *thovil* and *hooniyam* in this novel are informed by many, sometimes conflicting, anecdotal accounts, as well as the writings of the anthropologists Nandadeva Wijesekera and Bruce Kapferer. The practice of hooniyam is often shrouded in secrecy, and it encompasses many types of rituals that are intended to cause harm to a selected victim. *Yak thovil* are healing ceremonies performed to exorcise demons believed to be responsible for causing illness and other unfortunate circumstances. In yak thovil, exorcists wear masks representing particular demons, which are summoned and then banished through symbolic performances. Thovil are enormously elaborate events that include drama, dance, comedy, impersonation, incantation, and music. Costumes, masks, and many symbolic structures and objects are used, which vary according to the specific purpose of the ritual. I have taken liberties in describing these practices, in order to make them more digestible and comprehensible to the general reader, and to serve the purposes of my story. My descriptions in this novel cannot hope to do justice to the complicated cosmology in which the practices are embedded, or the rich historical, social, and religio-spiritual contexts in which they occur. I refer readers interested in learning more to *Deities and Demons, Magic and Masks* by Nandadeva Wijesekera, and *A Celebration of Demons* and *The Feast of the Sorcerer* by Bruce Kapferer.

1

DUNCAN

Saturday

By late afternoon, all the searchers had returned to the camp pavilion. Everyone knew that Angie Osborne's body had been found, but still no one knew how she had died.

Lunch seemed so long ago, Duncan thought. The food had all been put away. The two long folding tables in the pavilion were bare except for a desolate tin vase of daffodils near a handwritten cardboard sign that said **Sorry, no finger bowls! Use tap at back of pavilion.** The yellow banner emblazoned with the words **HAPPY 23RD REUNION TO THE KANDY INTERNATIONAL SCHOOL CLASS OF 1993!** looked incongruously bright above the tables.

Duncan put an arm around Grace's shoulders, for the familiarity of it. Her body stiffened against his. "Mo and Suki got to her first," Duncan said, turning away from the flashing lights of the police vehicles beyond the pavilion. "I was right behind them." He was thankful for the sturdiness of the picnic table on which he was perched. He had been feeling shaky since the discovery of the body. Everything felt dreamlike.

Grace shrugged off his arm and turned to face him. "Are you sure about the blood?" she said, gripping his hand. Her fingers were cold.

"Positive. I looked. We all looked."

"Poor Mo. Look how hard it's hit him," Grace said.

At the time they'd heard the scream, only ghostly blurs of figures and tables had been visible outside the small pavilion, but now the fog, which had been unseasonable for May in New Jersey, had completely dissipated. Duncan looked over to where two of Grace's old schoolmates were hunched at another picnic table: Mo, with his head in his hands, and Suki, saying something into Mo's ear.

"He was much worse before. He kept trying to revive her, even though it was obvious she was gone. Suki and I had to pull him off." Duncan shuddered as the sound of Mo's sobbing came back to him.

"I just can't believe it," Grace said, her knuckles pressed against her lip. Her eyeliner was smudged, accentuating the dark sheen of her cheeks. "How could she die just like that? Someone our age?"

Duncan shook his head, running over the scene in his mind's eye. He was finding it difficult to get over the shock of seeing Angie lying there in the woods. Her arms had been flung wide, and her plaid shirt had been rucked up on one side, exposing a tanned, muscular portion of her belly. The skin under her navel had been marked with a prominent white scar that disappeared into the waistband of her jeans. It had been the flies that had tipped him off. There'd been two small clusters of them settled too close to her eyes. When Mo and Suki rushed forward, the flies had ascended in a buzzing mass and zipped away. Angie's eyes, blue and empty, had been fixed on the dead leaves scattered by her head.

"I don't know. She looked almost like she was resting. The only weird thing was . . . well, I don't know. Maybe I imagined it. Or exaggerated it in my mind. That happens with stress." Eyewitness accounts were frail. Didn't witnesses—to bank robberies and car accidents—often misremember what they'd seen? They would think they'd seen someone pointing a gun, or a car speeding, when in fact those things had not really happened. The mind played tricks in traumatic situations.

"Weird how?"

"Well, her tongue," Duncan said. He ran his fingers over the table surface, feeling the crevices in the weatherworn wood. "When I got there, behind those two, I thought I saw her tongue sticking way out of her mouth."

"Maybe that's normal," Grace said.

Duncan took off his glasses and rubbed his eyes. They felt gritty, from fatigue maybe. "I don't know. Her head was turned sideways like this," he said, demonstrating the angle. "Her mouth was open. I could have sworn her tongue was lying on the ground. It looked too long to be real. Like a long slice of pink banana." He rubbed again, wishing the grittiness would subside. He wanted to lie down somewhere and close his eyes. "But we were all so emotional. And then after Mo tried reviving her, shaking her and pulling her up, you couldn't see the tongue quite as much." He wished the image of the tongue wouldn't keep coming back to him. He had only ever seen a tongue that long in a woman who was supposedly possessed, in Sri Lanka. That had been years ago, during an exorcism ceremony he'd been watching.

He saw Grace's anxious expression and realized how insensitive he was being, going on about the death scene. They may not have been close, but Angie had still been her classmate.

"Are you sure she wasn't shot?" Grace said.

"Then where was the blood? And anyway, I don't know if the shots had anything to do with her. Remember how close they sounded, over that way? That's where we all went initially. We stayed on the trail. That's why it took so long to find her. She was farther off, due north, and off the trail." Suki, Mo, and Duncan had trudged along a creeping stream for several hundred yards. They had crossed a rickety wooden bridge before coming to the fallen tree beyond which they'd found Angie, on a patch of flattened grass that was still brown from the harsh winter.

"But why the shots—?" Grace started to say, when a man appeared beside them. He was wearing a navy-blue suit and a gray tie, but Duncan knew he was a policeman because of the way he had been hobnobbing with the uniformed officers.

The officer was easily six or seven inches taller than Duncan, who, being five feet eleven, was not particularly short. He bent his head toward Duncan, the gesture increasing the slight stoop of his shoulders. "You are Duncan McCloud?" he said. His eyes drooped downward a little at the corners, which gave him a melancholy air. His mouth was wide, and a prominent soul patch nestled above his chin, as if to compensate for the close crop of the blond hair on his head. His voice was deferential, and so soft that Duncan had to lean toward him to hear what he was saying. His breath, faintly minty, wafted across Duncan's cheek.

"Yes," Duncan said, sliding off the table.

"Mortensen," the officer said, reaching out his hand to shake theirs. "Detective Washington Mortensen. Correct me if I'm wrong, but it was you who found Ms. Osborne?" he said to Duncan. He slipped a pen and a small spiral-bound notebook out of his jacket pocket. His hands, square palmed and long fingered, dwarfed the notebook further.

"Along with two others. Mo and Suki," Duncan said, looking around for them.

"Mohammed Hashim and Itsuki Watanabe," Grace said, her bulky silver watch slipping halfway down to her elbow as she pointed. "They're over there, by the keg." Duncan, looking over, saw that Mo and Suki had joined a group of the Kandyans who were huddled by the side of the pavilion in two tight circles, clutching paper cups. Mo had a cup as well. The guy was a teetotaler. An orthodox Muslim. Had grief made him revert to his high school ways?

"I just have a few questions, if I may," Mortensen said, his eyes cast down at his pad. "What time would you say it was when you found Ms. Osborne?"

Duncan rubbed his head, trying to remember. The chronology of the afternoon was oddly blurred in his mind. They'd tramped around in the foggy woods for God knew how long, barely able to see where they were treading until they got to higher ground. "Not sure about that. The last time I looked at my watch was at 4:05. We were searching for twenty, thirty minutes after that. Maybe four thirty or so?"

Mortensen wrote on his pad in tiny letters that looked impossible to read, his jaw moving, apparently chewing gum. "I don't want to take too much of your time, Mr. McCloud. But perhaps you could tell me about what exactly occurred." He turned the pages of his pad, read something on it, and turned to a blank page. "What did you notice about Ms. Osborne when you came upon her?" he said, his eyes still downcast.

"When I first saw her, I thought she was asleep. She was on her back with her head turned sideways. But then I saw her mouth and eyes were open. Her tongue was hanging out." Duncan wondered if he might be making too much of what he thought he'd seen. But every time he thought back to the moment they'd found Angie, the tongue was what jumped to mind. Almost everything else seemed hazy now.

"Did you see a gun, Mr. McCloud?"

"No, no gun," Duncan said. After his initial frenzied efforts to revive Angie, Mo had been too distraught to do more than sit by her body, crying, and Suki had just stood there in shock. Only Duncan had scanned the ground for anything unusual among the layers of twigs and decaying leaves. "We all heard shots earlier, but that was before two, maybe around one thirty. And they seemed closer than where she was. Somewhere around there." He pointed toward the northwest.

2

GRACE

Grace's old school roommate, Marla Muller, was sitting slumped at a picnic table. The side of Marla's T-shirt was ripped, revealing a sliver of her pregnant belly. Her face was puffy and dusty, streaked with trails of tears. "I just can't believe it," Marla said. "I should have felt it last night if she was going to die. But there were no vibes, nothing. All she was doing was typing. Nothing was wrong. How could she have died?"

Grace smoothed Marla's matted hair, trying to ignore the knot of worry in her own stomach. Should she mention that Angie had called her? But then Marla would wonder why she had not said anything before. Marla would want to know whether Angie had been in touch with her previously, what the missed call had been about. There was no way Grace could answer those questions.

"I should have gone with her," Marla was saying. "Maybe then she wouldn't have fallen."

"You couldn't have gone hiking in your state. You shouldn't even have gone searching," Grace said, rubbing Marla's back, trying to push Angie's words out of her mind. She wished more of Angie's message had been audible. *Keep it secret.* What had Angie meant by that? An image came to her, of the last time she'd seen Angie, in Palmer Square. Angie's face had been flushed under the bloodred lamps, her eyes watery and a little bleary. Grace pushed the image away and hugged Marla closer.

"How long has it been since you ate?" she said, when Marla finally stopped crying. "You have to take care of the baby." As if she should be talking. She shook off the thought. "I'll get you something from the kitchen."

The kitchen building next to the pavilion was a squat structure whose crumbling brick exterior was streaked with ivy vines. Inside was an army-green kitchen smelling of burnt coffee, with an outsize fridge in one corner. Grace took out some leftovers from the buffet lunch they'd had before the day took its ugly turn. As she placed the plate of food in the nearby microwave, a low voice reached her ears. There was such urgency in the tone that she craned to listen. It appeared to be coming through a door that led outside.

A small glass pane was set in the door, and through it she could see dark trees outlined against a dusky-pink sky. She stepped to the door and saw it was slightly ajar.

"Because I'm not a fool." It was Bent, Grace realized. "This has to stop here . . . Well, the whole thing's going to blow up." There was a pause. Bentley Hyland came briefly into view as he walked past the window. "No, that won't cut it . . . Yeah, there will . . . That isn't good enough . . . Look, I'm telling you." He glanced in and saw Grace. She heard him mumble something unintelligible into the phone, and then the door opened.

"Hey," he said. His clothes, like those of the other searchers, were dirty. His hair had rumpled across its parting, and his widow's peak was clearly visible.

"Is there a problem?" Grace said, although she already knew. So many years had passed, and he hadn't changed.

Bent straightened his back and put his phone away. "Work crisis," he said, his voice hoarser than usual. "It never stops." He jerked his head at the door. "I have to go out there to call them. The only place I can get phone reception." *Even in the middle of this tragedy,* Grace thought. Even though he had known Angie intimately. Even though her death had to be affecting him terribly. Work came first. How ambitious he'd always been. She'd given him a present once, for his nineteenth birthday, to salute his ambitions. It had been a squat little resin figurine with upraised fists that she'd bought from a Hallmark store, with lettering that said **WORLD'S GREATEST SALESMAN**.

"Are you doing okay?" Bent said.

How formal they were now with each other, almost as if they were strangers. Back when she'd been in college in Chicago, she'd used to watch through the window, waiting for him to show up at her apartment. She nodded. "I should be asking you. Are you? Do you want to talk about it?"

His body sagged, as if he'd deflated. "What is there to say?"

"You knew her so well," Grace said. A new alertness flickered in his eyes for a moment. He didn't know how much she knew, she realized.

"You mean . . . ? Well, yeah. Most of us knew her better than you did. You never did like her much."

Grace flinched at the bluntness of that. It sounded wrong now that Angie was dead. And it wasn't really true, in the end. But Bent didn't know that.

Bent was watching her. "Thanks for bringing Duncan," he said. With a strained half smile, he added, "We didn't want him to quit before he starts."

Grace nodded. "He seems more comfortable now. You were right about the informal setting."

"Cinasat's big on informal settings," Bent said. "Hammond's dinner is all about that. I would normally go, except I have things to attend to."

"Right . . . but after all this, I don't think we'll be going either," Grace said.

Bent frowned. "You have to. Hammond's expecting you. Duncan's starting on Monday."

That's why he should relax, Grace thought, *not waste the evening talking to a bunch of strangers at a company party.* Duncan had only met Hammond Gleeson, Cinasat's chief executive officer, a few times.

Bent eyed her pursed lips, still frowning. "Really, Grace. Don't skip it, yeah?"

The microwave beeped. "I have to take this to Marla," Grace said. She pulled the plate out and left the room without looking back.

The police inquiries took hours. Mortensen seemed to speak to everyone. Whenever Grace looked around from where she was sitting, he was hovering near one of the picnic tables scattered around the pavilion, his head bent deferentially toward another of the Kandyans. She never saw him extracting individual people from the tight clusters here and there. He seemed to have a knack for making himself unnoticeable, even with his extraordinary height.

"If you don't mind me asking, Mrs. McCloud," Mortensen said. "Where were you when Ms. Osborne was found?" Earlier, when Mortensen had been talking to Duncan, Grace had slipped away, murmuring about the need to tend to Marla. Now there was no avoiding him. He had led Grace to the northeastern edge of the clearing in which the pavilion stood. The piney scent of the woods drifted toward them, driven by a recurring breeze. Night had fallen, and the darkness under the trees beyond was thick. Only a few fireflies pierced it, flickering on and off as if they were trying in vain to defeat the night.

"Here. I was babysitting a kid. Janie, a nine-year-old," Grace said. "She's Bentley Hyland's daughter. He asked me to stay with her while he was out searching."

"Just you and her here?" He bent toward her, and she smelled his minty breath.

"No, Sofie Tittleworth was here with her four kids." What if he saw that she was hiding something, she kept thinking. What if everything came out?

"How long were you here?"

Grace shrugged, trying to look at ease. "Since before lunch."

"You heard shots?"

Grace nodded. "We couldn't have missed them. They were loud." She rubbed futilely at the stain on her sweatshirt. The sweatshirt was hunter green, with a yellow *KIS* logo across the front. Each of the alumni had received one of the sweatshirts the evening before. When the first shot sounded, she had been at the buffet table, serving herself a spoonful of chicken curry. She had jumped, jerking the serving spoon. Now the top of the *K* had a red curry stain on it. "There were three shots. Later on, we heard a scream. It was loud, really shrill. It got cut off very suddenly." She shivered, remembering. There had been something creepy about the high-pitched quaver of it, the way it had come to an abrupt stop. "That's when people went searching."

"For Ms. Osborne?"

"Not for her specifically, although everyone had been wondering where she'd gone to. People just went to look, because of the scream. It was really foggy earlier. You could barely see anything out here."

She watched him scribble in his book. "Angie fell, right? That's how she died?" she said. Her voice sounded too strained, she thought.

"I understand you being upset, Mrs. McCloud. You and all your friends." He paused, chewing his gum thoughtfully.

"I didn't know Angie very well in school," Grace said. "I ran into her once about twelve years ago, but other than that, I hadn't seen her since I left Sri Lanka." She hesitated, not sure how much he knew. "That's where we all went to school. In Sri Lanka. At an international school there. Kandy International School. This is our—"

"Twenty-third reunion. Yes, I gathered," Mortensen said. "Did you see her this morning?" He moved his jaw again. The gum chewing seemed incongruous, given his deferential manner. Somehow it made her feel more on edge.

"No." Grace tried to keep her voice steady. "I didn't even know she was going to be here. She travels a lot, I think, on assignment.

Traveled, I mean. She was a journalist for the *Washington Post*. She wasn't on the list of people who had signed up to come. I heard she showed up really late last night, unexpectedly. She stayed in Marla's cabin. Marla Muller—she's over there. Some of the others met up with Angie in Marla's cabin. Not me. My husband and I had already gone to sleep when she got here. I don't think anyone saw her this morning. Marla said Angie had already gone when she woke up. Hiking, Marla thought."

Had she explained too much? Crickets were calling all around them, rasping in the darkness. They seemed loud, and Mortensen's silence seemed unduly long. His eyes on her face were unblinking. Was he wondering why she seemed anxious if she hadn't been close to Angie? It occurred to her suddenly that the police must have found Angie's phone. Why had that not occurred to her before? That was why Mortensen was watching her. He wanted to see if she would bring up the phone calls. "I guess I should tell you," she said, trying to make her tone casual. "Angie called me and left a voicemail message. She said she wanted to see me, meet my husband. I thought it was a bit odd because I hadn't seen her for twelve years. I didn't know her very well, as I said, and we didn't keep in touch."

"When did she call?"

"Around eight this morning," Grace said, checking her watch involuntarily. "At 8:19, actually. I saw the time stamp."

"Do you have the voicemail?"

"No, I erased it," Grace said. She could feel the corner of her eye twitching. She pushed at the skin with her fingers, grateful for the distraction.

Mortensen cocked his head. "Why did you do that, if you don't mind my asking?"

"That's what I usually do." She struggled to keep her tone even, still rubbing the corner of her eye. Would he ask to see her phone? Could he do that? Then she remembered it was probably dead by now. There had been only a little charge left in it at lunchtime.

"Did you call her back?"

"Several times," Grace said. "To find out why she wanted to meet. But I couldn't reach her or leave a voicemail."

"You have no idea why she would want to see you?"

Grace shook her head. *But speaking of that, listen, I really want to talk to you.* Why had Angie wanted to talk about what had happened in Palmer Square? "No. As I said, I'd completely lost touch with her." Mortensen was watching her closely. She managed to look him briefly in the eye.

"The others don't know that she called me," Grace said, and then wished she had not blurted that out.

Mortensen's gaze sharpened, his jaw stopping in midchew. "Was there a reason you didn't tell them?"

"I didn't think it was relevant," Grace said. "She didn't say much. The message kept cutting out. I couldn't make out most of it."

"The one you erased," Mortensen said, his voice grave.

"Yes." For a moment, there seemed to be absolute silence. Then the crickets started their raucous rasping again.

Mortensen made a note in his pad. His eyes skimmed over her face. "And you haven't mentioned it even since you heard about her death?"

"Not yet. It just didn't seem relevant." *Sure Duncan knows,* Angie had said. But how could he?

Mortensen was still watching her. "It's such a terrible thing to happen," Grace said, "when we've come here to celebrate." She added, "Those shots had nothing to do with her? I heard she fell? Is that what happened?"

Mortensen closed the cover of his notebook with the utmost care. "That I couldn't tell you, Mrs. McCloud." His voice was barely above a whisper. "That's for the medical examiner to determine, you see. Our usual examiner is out of town. We're waiting for another one to show up."

Grace watched him amble away, dread jumbling her thoughts. Surely she'd had no choice but to tell him that Angie had called. But what if he mentioned it to the other Kandyans? Should she say something to them? But would they wonder why she had not said anything before? And what if Mortensen could find out what Angie had said in the voicemail message? Was that what the police did in cases like this?

She took a deep breath. She was making too much of it. Even if Mortensen did manage to listen to Angie's message, it wouldn't mean anything to him, and she could just say she had forgotten exactly what Angie had said.

3

DUNCAN

Saturday

Watching Grace approach, Duncan was struck, as he often was, by how deceptively fragile she looked, with her bird bones. Like the rest of her family. At their wedding, her relatives had stood out from his own large-boned family, quite apart from skin color. The bird people among the behemoths. No one would guess how tough minded Grace was, how pigheaded she could be, by looking at her. She was too thin, thinner than she'd been when he'd met her. The bulkiness of that eternal silver watch of hers made her wrist look as delicate as a twig. The fixation on her work was what kept her that way. No time for a proper lunch most days. No sense of priorities. He shrugged off his irritation, seeing how pinched she looked now. For once, she didn't look like she was thinking about her work, her lab flies. She seemed so tense, almost frightened.

"Did the cop tell you when we can leave?" he asked, moving closer to Mo to make room for Grace at the table. A faint odor of sweat hung around Mo; the cologne scent that had enveloped him at lunchtime had dissipated. He was clutching a bottle of beer. The keg had run out, and pizza and beer had been ordered from Ridgeville, the nearest town. Someone had put out the lunch leftovers on a table in the lighted pavilion, and a few people had put scraps of cold curried vegetables or chicken on their plates along with pizza.

"I didn't ask him. But sounds like everything's up in the air. He won't even say if she fell," Grace said. Duncan heard her stomach growl. She had probably not eaten since lunch. The pizza had come while she'd been talking to Mortensen, in festive red delivery boxes that seemed terribly out of place, given the situation. It was cold now, but Duncan put a slice on a plate and handed it to her.

Grace picked it up listlessly.

"Suki says she had to have fallen," Marla said. She'd washed the streaks of dirt off her face, but she looked too tired to be sitting up. Duncan wondered if she knew what stress could do to a pregnancy. Or was she like Grace, refusing to admit that she might be under stress?

"You fall on the backa your head, right here." Mo slapped the back of his neck with his hand. "You don't stand a chance. Your brain right there . . . that controls your breathing." His words were slurred.

Bent reached past Mo for another beer. "No blood, though." He knocked the cap off the bottle with one sharp tap against the table edge and drank deeply. Duncan thought he'd had as much as Mo had drunk, but on Bent the beer seemed to have had no effect. Bent had calmed down a lot over the course of the evening. That said something about his capacity to deal with unforeseen circumstances, Duncan thought. He rubbed the thin silver ring on his finger, looking Bent over surreptitiously. This guy was going to be his superior, although they were the same age. He had the kind of blue-blooded good looks Duncan associated with young politicians: a thick head of light-brown hair, small, almost pouty lips, an unusually long jaw, regular features marred only slightly by faint pouches under his eyes. But according to Grace, he was no blue blood. His family's wealth had been made through the furniture company his grandfather had built from scratch.

"They'll be able to tell. A bruise even if there's no blood," Suki said, using his Hawaiian print shirt to wipe the moisture off his beer bottle.

He was the plumpest of Grace's old classmates. He looked like an over-grown adolescent, except for his beard, which partially camouflaged his double chin.

"Apparently the medical examiner decides that," Grace said, her voice tight. "I don't know if that means later or now."

The bench wobbled as Bent swung his legs around and rose to his feet. "I'm going to ask the guy how long this is going to take." Duncan watched him stride off, the beer bottle swinging from his hand. Clearly a man who could take charge. No wonder he'd risen to the top at Cinasat.

"I just can't wrap my head around it," Marla said. "Angie, of all people."

"She could have . . . lived forever," Mo said, gesticulating. Beer sprayed out of his bottle, splashing onto the table and soaking Grace's sleeve.

"Never mind," Grace said. She tugged her sweatshirt off and tossed it under the bench.

Mo glugged more beer. A trickle ran down the side of his chin, and he rubbed roughly at it. His shirt was crumpled. The light from the pavilion revealed how stained it had got. This was a far cry from the pressed, primped Mo of that morning. How many beers had the guy had, Duncan wondered. Poor sod. He could still see Mo in his mind's eye, the way he had wailed when he had seen Angie lying there, how he'd shaken her, not seeing the futility of trying to wake her up. This was such a different side of Mo. None of the usual sarcastic polish. He had seemed down in the dumps when he had been talking about his financial troubles the night before, but this was something else. He was crumbling.

"Remember the junior field trip?" Mo said, leaning across the table. "When the bus went off the road at that . . . hairben . . . hairpin bend? How Angie crawled out the window . . . like that withougetting hurt?"

"Yeah, that bus driver was shouting," Suki said, a grin starting on his face. "Remember? '*Aney, aney, baba,* wait, wait!' He was more shocked at seeing her knickers when she was climbing out than anything else."

Duncan watched them giggling. They needed the release. He relaxed himself, letting their reminiscences fade into the background of his consciousness. He directed his attention toward the woods, beyond the wall of darkness that surrounded them. He closed his eyes, listening to the crickets. He loved the sound of them, their collective enormity, their uninhibited clamor. In the woods, everything seemed possible.

He didn't know how much time had passed when he opened his eyes again.

"Thawoman . . . wasn't afraida anyone," Mo was saying. Tears were streaming down his cheeks.

Marla and Suki had teared up again too. Turning to Grace, Duncan saw something that wasn't just sadness. Was it survivor guilt? That was the problem with Grace. Even growing up more or less Catholic himself, he had never known anyone with such a propensity for guilt. *What childhood does to you,* Duncan thought.

He squeezed her hand. "You need to sleep," he whispered. "Everything will seem easier in the morning."

"Did Bent find out if we could leave?" Grace said.

Mo raised his head. "That . . . that fucker is the root . . . doesn't care about anyone," he said.

Marla put her arm around him. "What are you talking about, Mo? You're too drunk." She tried to pry the bottle from his grip, but he pushed her hand away.

Duncan peered around, searching for Bent, but he wasn't in sight. Mortensen was alone in a corner of the pavilion, his head bent, talking into a phone. As Duncan watched, he slid the phone into his pocket and ambled out of the pavilion toward two uniformed police officers standing by a portable floodlight, which they'd set up to illuminate the path to the trailhead. A lengthy conversation took place. *Some controversy, from the arm waving and head shaking,* Duncan thought. Eventually, the uniformed officers fiddled with the floodlight, turned it off, and carried it away. Mortensen emerged from the darkness and wandered toward where they were sitting, his shoes crunching the gravel.

"You are all free to go," he said, his large hands adjusting the lapels of his jacket.

"For tonight you mean?" Duncan said. "Or we can take off?"

"The investigation has been completed," Mortensen said. He sounded as if he were reading aloud from an instruction manual, Duncan thought. There was no expression in his voice.

"So you know what happened?" Grace asked. "Angie fell?"

"Then what about the shots?" Suki said.

Mortensen raised his hand in a gesture that was almost priestly in its gentleness.

"We have been informed . . . about the cause of death. Ms. Osborne died of a heart attack." In the light from the pavilion, his face looked rigidly composed. A muscle twitched in his cheek.

Grace said, "What?" just as the others broke out simultaneously.

"Heart attack?"

"Wait . . ."

"She didn't fall?"

"Are you sure?" Duncan said.

"She had a medical history," Mortensen intoned.

"Of what?" Suki said.

"A hystec . . . ectomy, not heart attack!" Mo's slurred voice was shrill.

"Her medical records were obtained," Mortensen said stiffly. "The medical examiner . . . he said the cause was clear. And the risk of heart disease was plain."

"What about the shots?" Suki said again.

"And that horrible scream? Was that Angie?" Marla said.

Mortensen bent his head as if in prayer. "The shots were poachers, possibly. The scream—maybe a wounded animal. There's no physical evidence of shots being fired, you see, only reports. It has been concluded there is no connection between the shots and Ms. Osborne's death."

"So thassit?" Mo said. "Now we go off and have . . . live . . . happyeverafter?"

Mortensen's glance brushed over Mo, the table littered with bottles, and the half-empty bottle in Mo's hand. "Ms. Osborne died of natural causes, Mr. Hashim," he said, his voice only a murmur. "We have to go by . . . the medical examiner has to make the call. He has determined that there is no evidence . . . that the death is due to natural causes. I understand how difficult this is for everyone." He indicated the darkness with another of his gentle gestures. "It's late. Sometimes rest helps."

He slipped away to where a few of the other Kandyans were huddled.

"She didn't think she had to worry about a heart attack," Marla said. "After the hysterectomy, she made changes. Organic food, biking to work . . ."

"I don't fucking believe it," Mo said.

"Any of us could go," Suki said, looking at the veins in his wrist as if a clot were suddenly going to appear.

By the time Duncan and Grace left the area, it was close to eleven o'clock. The police had left, and the pavilion had emptied. The lights had been turned out, throwing the place into deep shadow.

There was only a bit of moon out, and it did nothing to light their way. They trod cautiously back to their cabin, feeling their way with their feet, trying to stay on the graveled path beyond the kitchen building.

Gravel scattered ahead, and a point of light pierced the darkness.

"Who's there?" Bent's voice said sharply. He scanned his penlight over them. Duncan wondered where he'd been; surely he'd not been around when Mortensen announced his news.

"Thank God the cops finally figured it out," Bent said. He sighed heavily. "We all have to try to be at peace with it, yeah? But in the morning. Now I'm too exhausted."

"No one's back there in the pavilion," Grace said.

"Gotta get Janie's sweatshirt," Bent said. "She's asleep, but she'll want it in the morning."

"Forgot mine under the bench back there," Grace said.

"I'll drop it at your cabin," Bent said. The patter of his feet crunching the gravel and the bobbing light indicated that he had broken into a jog. *Even now, he has the energy to run,* Duncan thought.

"He was in his cabin working, I bet," Grace said. "Even with all this, he can't put his work aside."

4

GRACE

Sunday

"Some weekend," Duncan said as he steered their old Volkswagen Jetta out of the lot.

Grace rolled down the manual window, turning the wonky handle carefully. She leaned against the headrest and breathed in the smell of damp grass.

Duncan took one hand off the wheel to smooth her hair. "You're doing okay?"

"At least it's behind us," Grace said. The flies in rack thirty-seven were waiting, their ovaries ripe for the picking, but she was in no mood to resume her work. Once she got to the lab, she'd have to settle down. So much to do, and so little time. A normal lifespan was short enough, but there was no guarantee anyone would have even that.

They drove in silence through Ridgeville, which seemed oddly deserted for a Sunday morning. Grace watched the trunks of silver oaks pass by in a blur, then a vast cemetery studded with rows of somber headstones, like outsize teeth. A scarecrow loomed in a neighboring field, raggedy black robes flapping from its outstretched arms.

Angie's voicemail message kept digging into her thoughts. She wished she could tell Duncan the whole story. Or what she remembered of it. But that couldn't happen. Certainly now wasn't the time, when he was already demoralized. It seemed like ages ago, but it had not even been a month since he had been so unexpectedly laid off from St. Casilda College. The arbitrariness of the layoff had been the hardest part of it for him. Grace knew he had to be thinking of the value of the sacrifice he'd made for her career, but he would never bring that up. Not directly at least.

All she could do was make sure he had a shot at a good career now. "What time do we have to be at the thing tonight?" she said.

He turned to look at her, the sun glinting off his rimless glasses. "You still want to go?"

"We should," Grace said. "Because you're starting tomorrow. Bent seemed to think it was important."

"I think it's a big party. No one even knows who I am."

"Apparently this Hammond cares about entertaining his employees."

Duncan sighed. "I hope the job's going to be okay. At least Bent seems a decent sort."

"He's got his pluses," Grace said.

"Not even a flicker there?" Duncan said, his eyes on the road ahead. "A long time ago maybe, but still . . . He's a charismatic guy."

"Give me a break," Grace said. "That would be like me asking you about Lara."

A faint grin appeared on Duncan's face as he looked over at her. His eyes looked more green than blue in this light. His tan had deepened over the weekend. "Not quite the same. Bent doesn't look thirty pounds heavier than he is in your college pictures. And Lara and I didn't go back and forth, on and off. That was strictly a high school romance." He cleared his throat. "And also." A sigh. "You're not about to start a job working with Lara."

"You're not working *with* him," Grace said. "You don't even know how often you'll set eyes on him." She lay back against the headrest. "On and off . . . Well, a couple of times maybe, but I did get out the

24

second year of college, don't forget. Anyway, I was thinking yesterday, watching him. I didn't really know him well at all. I mean, I spent all that time with him, but it seems pretty superficial in retrospect. I don't know if he was too self-absorbed, or if I was."

He was silent. She closed her eyes and tried to focus on the whoosh of the tires, the roar of displacing air as they sped toward home.

When she awoke, they were at a gas station off Route 23. A wind had sprung up, chilling the car a little.

"Just need some water," Duncan said, getting out.

Grace reached into the back seat for her sweatshirt. It was only when she pulled it on that she noticed something stiff in its pocket. Sticking her hand inside, she found a cream-colored business card. Written on it in an expansive blue script were the words "Meet me— first bridge, northwest trail. 9 a.m." On the other side of the card was the silver Cinasat Pharmaceuticals logo, the *t* in the word suggesting a caduceus. Bent's name and title were embossed in somber black:

Bentley Hyland III
Senior Vice President of Marketing

A familiar feeling of irritation rose in her chest. Bent was still acting as entitled as he'd always been. He must have stuffed the card in the pocket the previous night before hanging the sweatshirt on her cabin door. Clearly he'd wanted to press her again to bring Duncan to the party. It wasn't only the peremptory tone of the note that annoyed her. Hadn't it occurred to him that she might sleep late after what had happened? And this was only a party, after all, work related or not. Duncan would be annoyed if he knew Bent had insisted he attend.

Duncan emerged from the station shop, a bottle of water tucked under his arm. Grace stuffed the card back into her sweatshirt pocket, leaned back, and closed her eyes again.

5

DUNCAN

Sunday

"I wonder where my wife is," Duncan said, hoping to break away from the conversation. The couple he was with, Cherise and Ray, were both in the sales division at Cinasat. He was getting tired of their bragging. For the past fifteen minutes, they had been bombarding him with the minute details of their extensive wine collection, something he couldn't care less about. They both seemed to be in their sixties. He couldn't help wondering what they were going to do with all that wine. They spoke as if they planned to live forever. "Ah, there she is," he said, sidling away. "I'll catch up with you in a bit."

He wound his way through the gaggles of people in their trim tuxedos and flimsy finery, past the open-air bar and the linen-covered table bearing hors d'oeuvres. Grace was in a corner of the garden by a stone bench whose back was a towering eagle, its outstretched wings looking oddly muscular. Standing there, she made a striking figure, with her back ramrod straight and her black hair curling onto her shoulders. She was in a short cherry-red sleeveless dress that she hadn't worn for years. It looked good on her, he thought, admiring her slender limbs. She worked too hard. She should get the chance to go to more parties like this—but of course, she probably wouldn't want that. She didn't look like she was enjoying herself much. Her lips, painted with a redder lipstick than she normally used, were pursed.

When he got to her, she raised her martini glass, her watch sliding down her arm.

"How many million, do you think?" she murmured.

"This place?" He shrugged, looking around the meticulously landscaped grounds, with their blooming magnolia and cherry trees, crimson rhododendrons artfully shaped to look riotous, and clumps of ornamental grasses. Foliage peeped from the crevices of rock walls, and even this early in the year, beds were packed with vivid flowers. The house was a colonial with a pleasant stone facade. He'd seen little of the inside when he'd been escorted along a shadowy hallway into Hammond's study to sign the last of his employment forms. Mostly he'd passed by closed doors, but he'd caught a glimpse of a dimly lit sitting room with twisted sculptures in dark metal and somber oil paintings. Only one gooseneck desk lamp had lit the study, throwing the odd assortment of objects on the walls into shadow.

"Drug money," Grace said, rolling her eyes.

"Very funny," Duncan said. He rattled the ice in his whiskey glass. Could he really do this? Work for a pharmaceutical company?

"Come on, Duncan," Grace said. "Take a joke."

"Everyone's full of jokes," Duncan said. "You know what Dad said when I called him about the job? 'You're leaving devil dancing to dance with the devil?' Funny. Ha ha."

"You're going to be fine," Grace said. "You're not leaving anthropology. You're still going to do the same research. Just for real money."

"This whole thing is a show, isn't it?" Duncan said, looking around at the expanse of the lawn, the expensive cut of the men's jackets, the bar with kinds of whiskeys he had never thought he'd drink. Their dilapidated green Volkswagen had stood out in the line of luxury cars parked in the long driveway. "That's probably why they invite new employees to these things. Isn't that what Bent said? They like to show people what they can have if they stay with the company."

They picked tiny canapés from a tray a passing waiter offered and sipped their drinks. "I haven't talked to Hammond except for those two minutes in the beginning," Grace said. "Did you, when you were inside?"

Duncan nodded. "Yes, a while. He seems a bit of a hard-ass, but interesting. Well traveled. All over South America, the Middle East. The Indian subcontinent. And Sri Lanka. He even speaks a little Sinhala. Hard to believe, huh? Not fluent, but enough to get around. He's been to Sri Lanka several times, apparently."

"He reminds me of a gecko," Grace murmured, thoughtfully.

Duncan grinned. "You say the weirdest things. The GEICO gecko?"

"Not the cartoon kind. A real house gecko, like the ones back home. That see-through skin. And the shape of his body. The way he moves his head."

Not a bad comparison, Duncan thought, remembering the slithery beige lizards with translucent skin that flitted along the walls of Sri Lankan houses.

"He's not as colorless as he looks," he said. "Seems very interested in devil dancing, for sure. You should see the devil masks on his study wall. Quite a collection."

"Typical tourist," Grace said.

"No, not those gaudy ones they sell to tourists. These are all the real thing. Unusual ones. But definitely Sri Lankan. A few I hadn't even seen before."

"Like the one you said was in the Cinasat lobby?"

Duncan nodded. "He said he got them from collectors. I can't imagine how the collectors got them. People don't give them away. They seem old, probably from the time the British were there. They look like they came from actual rituals."

Grace twisted her lips. "What's with the Sri Lanka fascination anyway?"

"Not just from there," Duncan said. "He has a couple of Indonesian masks. And some other things from other countries. Daggers and etchings and statues. From Nigeria, Brazil, Mexico. Same as in the Cinasat lobby. I think he's just interested in other cultures. That's apparently Cinasat's big thing. Not just multinational, they keep saying. They have multicultural partners. I still couldn't get a straight answer about the job, though. No shoptalk, he said." He rubbed his ring, trying to smile. Every time he tried to get ahold of a clear job description, he got the same message. Later. Always later.

"I've only met salespeople here so far," Grace said. "And two doctors. Medical doctors."

Duncan bit into a date wrapped in bacon, wishing he didn't feel so uneasy. Just outside his comfort zone, that was all, he reminded himself. "I'm the only anthropologist here, as far as I can tell."

"Well, you are," a voice said, the southern accent thick.

Duncan looked up to find a middle-aged woman standing before them. Her smiling face was framed by wisps of short ash-blond hair. An elaborate necklace that reminded Duncan of a Thai Buddhist temple lay against the heavily freckled skin above her black-and-white floral dress. She was holding the dregs of a martini.

"Duncan, right? Ada, Hammond's wife. I'm sorry it took me so long to find you," she said, the bracelets on her wrist jingling as she gestured at the chattering groups scattered around the garden.

Duncan shook her outstretched hand. He could feel little calloused nubs on her palm. "This is my wife, Grace," he said.

"Well, I'm so pleased to meet you both," Ada said, her hand on Grace's back. "Having a good time, I hope."

Duncan nodded dutifully, although Grace just smiled stiffly, as they both took more canapés from a waiter Ada waved over. "I hear you're from Sri Lanka," Ada said to Grace. "And of course, you"—turning to

Duncan—"are going to be our new Sri Lankan anthropologist." She laughed, a high, tinkling sound. "Listen to me! Our! I mean Cinasat's, of course." She leaned forward conspiratorially, and Duncan caught a whiff of vodka. "I don't work for Cinasat. I make jewelry, not drugs!"

Duncan slid his eyes away from Grace, who was looking a little nonplussed. "Was there another anthropologist at Cinasat before I joined?" he said. "I mean, I know there are others who are experts on other countries . . . but Sri Lanka specifically?"

Ada nodded energetically, but her smile faded. "Maybe you know him." Her face fell further. "Knew him. He was a lovely man. Just lovely. Frank Salgado." She hailed another passing waiter and replaced her empty glass with a glass of wine.

Duncan stared. "Professor Salgado? University of Peradeniya? I thought he had retired years ago. I knew him way back when I was in Sri Lanka. The last time I talked to him was maybe thirteen, no, fourteen years ago." He wouldn't have described Professor Salgado as lovely. *Cantankerous* was the word he would have used. Salgado had a reputation for being outspoken. At least one person at the university had seemed afraid of him. "He was working here in the US? In New Jersey?"

Ada's forehead wrinkled. "Well, he was a consultant," she said. "He came here a couple of times, for dinner." She shook her head, touching the temple ornaments at her neck. "He brought me some lovely stones. From a city called Ratapoorna."

"Ratnapura," Grace said. "That's where a lot of our gems come from."

Ada turned to her. "That's what he said. He was going to plan a trip there for me. But now . . ." Her voice trailed off.

"He retired? That's why Duncan was hired?" Grace said.

"He died, the poor man," Ada said. "Drowned."

Duncan stopped in the middle of biting into a shrimp toast. "Whoa. When? Where?"

"I know, it's too terrible to think about," Ada said. "Somewhere in Sri Lanka. They found his body washed up on a beach. A few weeks ago." She sipped from her glass, shaking her head. "Very sad."

"Are you mourning the cat again?" Hammond said, appearing beside her. He rubbed Ada's back. "Ada was close to that cat. But she was old."

Duncan was struck briefly by how incongruously austere Hammond looked next to his wife, with the close cut of his graying hair at the sides of his narrow, balding head and the pencil line of beard edging the transparent pallor of his lean face. He was a slight man, half a head shorter than his wife.

Ada turned to him, her glass clutched to her chest. "Not the cat, dear. I was telling them about Frank Salgado."

Hammond's eyes sharpened, flicking over the wineglass in her hand. "I'm sure they don't want to hear about that," he said.

"I didn't know Salgado was working with you," Duncan said.

Hammond turned to him abruptly, his gray eyes piercing. "You knew him?"

"Back in the day," Duncan said.

Hammond paused, swirling the whiskey in his tumbler. "Who would have thought. A coincidence," he said.

"Not really," Duncan said. "Not many anthropologists there. And very few who've written anything on devil dancing. Even Salgado's work in that area was a long time ago. Back in the seventies. What was he doing for Cinasat?"

Hammond held his whiskey up to the light. "A good man," he said. "I'm sure you'll hear about his contributions once you start working. Bentley can catch you up." He turned away from them to scan the deck leading to the house. "Speaking of Bentley . . . I have to go and see him."

"He's here?" Grace said.

Hammond glanced at her. "We have a matter to attend to. You'll excuse me, I hope." He clasped Ada around the waist. "Bentley has his daughter with him, dear. Maybe you could bring her outside for some treats while we finish up."

Duncan watched them walk toward the house, Ada tottering on her high heels. Hammond guided her off the lawn and onto the stone path that led up to the deck. "I thought Bent wasn't coming to this?" Duncan said.

"That's what he said," Grace said. "At the reunion, I mean." Duncan saw a flicker of apprehension and realized she was remembering Angie. The image of Angie lying in the woods flashed into his mind again. That tongue. He shivered, remembering the woman he'd seen long ago in Sri Lanka. His memory of that exorcism ceremony was vivid. He could remember the electric atmosphere of it, the way his pulse had raced in his throat, how the hairs had risen on his arms. An elderly woman, a relative of the patient being exorcised, had begun convulsing, tense in her upright chair, the tongue dangling out of her mouth impossibly long. Everyone at the ceremony had claimed that was because a demon from the patient had entered her body.

"Another drink?" Duncan said, shaking off the image and taking Grace's arm. "And then maybe we can leave."

They crossed the springy grass to the bar and ordered their drinks.

"Who'd have thought—Frank Salgado?" he was saying, when he felt a tug at his sleeve.

"Hi!" Bent's daughter, Janie, bounced up beside them, a lock of her dark-brown hair swinging over her shoulder, the last of a prodigiously frosted cupcake in one hand. Her eyes, large and slightly slanted, were raised toward him.

"Hey!" he said. He furrowed his forehead theatrically. "Don't I know you from somewhere?"

Janie giggled. "From the camp, silly!"

Duncan wondered how much she'd heard about Angie's death. How well had she known Angie? Better not to ask.

"I bet you don't know Grace," he said, pulling Grace forward.

Janie giggled again. "Yes, I do! She sat with me!" She pointed a frosting-smeared finger at Grace and then Duncan. "You went to school with my dad."

"No, not me," Duncan said. "Just her."

"My middle name is Grace," Janie said.

"Really," Grace said. Duncan sighed at her awkward expression. She must have barely talked to Janie when she'd babysat her at the camp. She always seemed to get tongue-tied around kids.

Janie helped herself to a chocolate tart. "I like these. But this is a boring party," she said. "Do you want to play a game?" She caught Duncan's wrist, her grip surprisingly strong for someone so ethereal seeming.

How simple life was for kids, Duncan thought. "Well, I don't think we can," he said, wiping a streak of frosting off Janie's cheek with a napkin. "We have to be going soon."

"Daddy said *we're* going soon," Janie said. "But he's in there"—she jabbed her fingers toward the house—"talking and talking."

6

GRACE

Sunday

Duncan seemed a little more comfortable about the job now after the informal context of the party, Grace thought, although he still kept rubbing his ring, the way he did when he was worried. She was glad Bent had called her a few days previously, to ask her to bring Duncan to the reunion—although she hadn't told Duncan that. And Bent had been right, after all, to insist they go to the party. "Bent said they didn't want you to quit before you started," she said as Duncan pulled the Volkswagen into their driveway. "He was making a joke, but I think they really need you on board."

"In Salgado's place, apparently. Drowned . . . Can you imagine? You should ask your parents if they heard about that in the news in Sri Lanka," Duncan said, opening his door.

Grace stepped out of the car, the driveway gritty under her bare feet. She was reaching inside for her shoes when she heard a car door click shut nearby, and then the sound of deliberate footsteps.

In the weak light seeping from their neighbor's windows, she saw a tall figure looming.

"Detective?" Duncan said, sounding as surprised as she felt.

"Sorry to bother you both," Mortensen murmured.

Grace glanced involuntarily at her watch. It was almost eight. Why was he here?

"I know it's late," Mortensen said. "But I wondered if I might have a word."

"About Angie?" Duncan said.

Was this about the voicemail message? Grace's heart began to thump. What if he said something to Duncan? What would she say?

"Just some routine inquiries," Mortensen said. "Some clarifications."

We could just say we're too tired, that it's too late, Grace thought. But Duncan slung his suit jacket over his shoulder and said, "Come on in, please."

Inside, Grace watched Mortensen sweep his eyes around the living room, at the books that overflowed off the IKEA shelves onto the old kilim rug, the magazines strewn across the glass coffee table, the Sri Lankan batik wall hanging, and the framed sketches of woods she had drawn for Duncan.

Mortensen set himself in the striped armchair by the sofa and slid his notepad out of his jacket pocket. It was going to be fine, Grace reassured herself.

"Was Angie . . . Did you find something?" Duncan said, leaning forward from his position on the sofa.

"The medical examiner ruled that Ms. Osborne died of a heart attack," Mortensen intoned. "This is not about Ms. Osborne." He adjusted the collar of his shirt. "Per se. There were some details we were just following up on. Regarding the gunshots."

Grace perched on the arm of the sofa, relieved. He wasn't here about Angie. No need to worry.

"You went hiking that morning, I believe you said, Dr. McCloud?" Mortensen said, his eyes on Duncan's tanned forearms, exposed below his rolled-up white shirtsleeves. At the reunion, Mortensen had called Duncan "Mr. McCloud," Grace remembered. Had he done some research on Duncan? On her?

"But I was back well before lunch," Duncan said, his voice rising a little. Mortensen was putting him on the defensive, Grace thought. She saw Duncan frown as he said, "The shots were in the afternoon."

"You said earlier that you returned from the trail with your husband," Mortensen said, turning to Grace. "But Dr. McCloud mentioned he hiked alone."

"I slept in," Grace said, trying to keep her breathing even. When she'd woken up and heard Angie's message, she'd jammed her feet into her sneakers and run out to the trail in a panic, terrified that Duncan would run into Angie on his own.

"When I woke up, he'd already left for his hike. I thought I'd see if I could join him. I didn't go very far. I met him coming down the trail, and then we went back to the pavilion together."

Mortensen's eyes ran over her and then fell to the notebook in his hand. "The shots were fired, you both said, early in the afternoon." He consulted his notebook. "Around one thirty. Who was with you at the time?"

"I was at the buffet table in the pavilion," Grace said, remembering how she had jumped, splattering curry on her sweatshirt. "Only the kid, Janie, was there."

"I was just going to get more plastic cups from the kitchen building," Duncan said. "For beer."

"You two weren't together?"

"Not when the shots were fired," Duncan said. "A bit later, we both sat down to eat at one of the tables outside the pavilion."

"How much later?"

"I don't know," Duncan said. He took off his glasses and polished them on his shirtsleeve. "Maybe fifteen minutes? Twenty? I had to find the cups and take them to the keg by the pavilion, and then I served myself from the buffet."

"Who was around when the shots were fired?"

"I couldn't see," Duncan said. "You probably heard. It was very foggy at the time. The fog started just before lunch. We could barely see a couple of feet."

Mortensen turned to Grace. "Did you see who was around at the time of the shots?"

Grace shook her head. "Janie and I went out to a table. Then Duncan showed up. And later, Mo and Marla."

"We were all there when we heard the scream," Duncan said.

"How much later was that?"

"Maybe an hour," Grace said.

Mortensen flipped the pages of his notebook and scanned his tiny handwriting. "And all of you know each other from high school?"

"Most of us," Grace said.

"There were a few spouses and kids," Duncan said. "My connection's only through Grace. Although I am about to start working with Bentley Hyland."

Mortensen scrutinized Duncan. "At Cinasat Pharmaceuticals? My report . . . I believe it was mentioned . . . that you and your wife are college professors?"

"I'm a former professor," Duncan said, turning the ring on his finger. Grace's heart sank at the sadness in his voice. "I just signed on to a new job at Cinasat. I begin tomorrow, actually."

"I see," Mortensen said, looking him over. "But you knew Mr. Hyland previously."

"I only met him briefly when I interviewed," Duncan said. Grace could hear that this line of questioning was making him a little uncomfortable. "Grace didn't keep in touch with him, so I didn't meet him before."

"The others you did know?"

Duncan nodded. "Sure. Over the years, a little. What is this all about? What were the shots . . . Why are you asking? Are they connected to Angie's death? Did something else happen?"

"Based on the medical examiner's report, it is not a criminal matter." Mortensen's voice was stiff. "The shots are. This is not deer season. Hunting is illegal," Mortensen said. "We are investigating that . . . and a related matter."

Duncan opened his mouth to say more, but Mortensen turned to Grace. "How well do you know your classmates—Mr. Hyland, Mr. Hashim, Mrs. Muller, Mr., er, Watanabe?"

Grace frowned. He was being too opaque with these questions. "Very well. I've known them all since high school. Seventh grade, when I started going to the school. They were at the school longer than me, although obviously, they're not Sri Lankan. Kids from all over go there. Mostly diplomats' kids, but not only." She hesitated, wondering how much to say. "We all went to college here in the US. I didn't really stay in touch with Bent after my second year in college, in Chicago." Duncan was looking at his fingernails. "The other three I've kept in touch with all along, although I don't see them much. Just emails or calls once in a while. With Mo and Marla, occasional visits."

"What do you know about their work?"

"What do you mean?" Grace said, confused. "Who?"

"All of them," Mortensen said.

"Mo is a real estate developer in Philadelphia. Suki manages a comic book store—in Boston. Marla used to be a math teacher in South Jersey, but now she doesn't work. Bent is a VP at Cinasat. Why does what they do matter?"

"These are routine inquiries, Dr. McCloud. We just need to know how well you know them." He paused, contemplating his notes. "Have any of them started a new job recently, or had any problems at work?"

"Nothing I know about," Grace said. "Mo said he's having some problems with a building he's leasing to some pharmaceutical company. And Marla stopped working. For the pregnancy. Why is this related to anything?"

"When's the last time you talked to any of them, before the reunion?"

He could bring up Angie's call any minute, Grace thought. "I don't remember exactly," she said, rising. "Look. It's getting really late. I have work in the morning, and Duncan is starting a new job tomorrow."

"Of course," Mortensen said, rising to his feet, his face inscrutable. He paused in the act of tucking the notebook in his pocket. "Did you, by any chance, see Mr. Hashim with a gun?"

Grace stepped back. What was he talking about?

Duncan's mouth had fallen open slightly. "Mo had a gun?"

"I doubt that," Grace said. She paused. "Do you mean if we ever saw him with one, or at the camp?"

"At the camp," Mortensen said. "Did you know he purchased bullets in Ridgeville?"

"Whoa," Duncan said.

"What? You mean like for hunting?" Grace said.

"Two different kinds of bullets. For a rifle and a handgun. Have you ever seen him with a gun, Dr. McCloud?"

Grace stared at him, confused. "No. I . . . I mean, he could have guns, right? People do." Now that she thought about it, it seemed like something he would have done in the old days. Buy a gun. Or two. Just for the hell of it. But Mortensen was making it sound more sinister.

"Why in Ridgeville?" Duncan said.

"That we don't know," was all Mortensen said. Then, after a pause, "What about Mr. Hyland and Mrs. Muller. Did they have guns there?"

"Are you kidding?" Grace said. "Bent had his daughter with him. And Marla certainly didn't go out there hunting. She's pregnant! Seven months!"

"Of course, I'm sure she wouldn't," Mortensen said. "This is just routine, you understand. Simply a matter of getting corroborating information. I didn't mean to alarm you." He slid the notebook into his pocket as he glided toward the door.

7

DUNCAN

Monday

Duncan leaned back in his chair, trying to appreciate the room before
him. It was certainly nothing like his small, disheveled office at St.
Casilda College, which had had mismatched bits of furniture and ratty
blue carpeting that the harried janitorial staff rarely vacuumed. Here,
the floor was charcoal-colored hardwood. On one side, two gray leather
armchairs stood on a sternly patterned rug, which was shot here and
there with flammeous streaks. The silver-gray wood of his desk was so
smooth that he couldn't help running his hands over it. And he could
always spin around in his desk chair to look out the picture window at
the expanse of lawn below.

He needed to get some of Grace's sketches in here, he thought. He
found the large black-and-white photographs on the walls, of shadows
snaking across sand dunes, too forbidding. He would have preferred
photographs of woods. In high school, he had spent many Saturday
mornings in the foggy woods near his house, away from his mother's
suffering and the cloying smell of grease his father brought back from
work. It had been in the woods that he'd first dreamed up a new vision
of his life, a life that moved beyond grease into the kind of worlds Ms.
Logan, his former teacher, had described to him.

He wondered again at the number of light fixtures in the room. There was enough light in the room with just the two bright lamps standing like sentries in the corners. What darkness was there for all the other lights to fight? A lamp on the coffee table. Track lights across the ceiling. A chrome desk lamp peering at his computer screen. A shaded bulb suspended above his chair. He shrugged, sighing. It was a room designed for nighttime work. That probably meant long hours would be the norm.

"Come in," he called, hearing a knock.

Bent slipped in, his hands in the pockets of his trousers. "Settling in?" His eyes were a little bloodshot, Duncan noticed, the skin under them puffier than it had been during the weekend.

"It's a good office," Duncan said. "Not really what I'm used to."

"You'll be happy to have got out of your college," Bent said. He settled in one of the two wooden chairs in front of the desk. "It was going under, anyway. Those old buildings are all falling to pieces. They'll never find the funds to renovate."

Bent spoke as if he knew a lot about St. Casilda. Duncan wondered if Cinasat had done some research, to find out if it was true that he had been laid off because of financial exigency. There was no need to feel bothered by that, he decided. Companies probably did routine checks of employment history.

"You had a good time at Hammond's, yeah?" Bent said. "I dropped by for a few minutes. On the way to my ex-wife's . . . Janie's mother's house." He adjusted the sleeve of his pinstriped shirt. It was rolled up, exposing a sprinkling of light hair and an elegant gold watch. "Hammond mentioned you knew Frank Salgado . . . Did you . . . Were you in touch with him recently?"

Duncan shook his head. "I just met him a few times, way back when I was working in Sri Lanka. He wasn't exactly a friend. He didn't think I should be studying Sri Lankan rituals. Because I'm not Sri Lankan."

He shrugged. That was something he'd struggled with once. Being an outsider. Now he'd come to terms with it. "What happened to him?"

"We don't know the details," Bent said. "An accident. They think he'd been swimming. He drowned, apparently. Tragic." Bent shook his head. "He would have kept working for us, I'm sure."

"What was he doing for you?" Duncan said. "Something related to rituals?"

"Mostly he helped us find local contacts," Bent said. "And he worked on the initial phase of . . . It won't make much sense to you yet. I'll explain more later, yeah? First we need to get you started." He rubbed his eyes. He looked tired, Duncan thought.

"Are you dealing with everything okay?" Duncan said. "The weekend . . . It was hard enough on Grace, even though she hadn't seen Angie for decades."

A grimness slid over Bent's face for a second, but then he brushed his hand across his face as if to fan away the memory. "Let's not go into it," he said. And then, "I'm flying down to Texas tomorrow. Angie's parents' place. The funeral's on Wednesday morning. A memorial service. The body was cremated, you know." His eyes passed over Duncan and came to rest on the chrome pen holder on the desk.

"I'm sorry for your loss," Duncan said. "The loss for all of you." He watched Bent pull the pen from the holder. He started twirling it in his fingers, turning it around and around with practiced skill. "All Grace wanted to do was get back to work. Her way of dealing with the loss. I think she feels guilty."

Bent fumbled a twirl, dropping the pen. "How do you mean?"

Duncan hastened to explain. "Survivor guilt. Isn't that what they call it? The questions death brings up. Why Angie had to be the one to die, in the prime of her life, her career."

When Bent straightened up from picking up the pen, his lips were pressed together. "We all have that guilt."

"But you know how it is with Grace. The whole thing with her father."

Bent frowned.

"The bribe," Duncan reminded him.

"What bribe?" Bent said, his forehead furrowing further.

Here he was, assuming that Bent remembered everything about Grace. He felt relieved. It was true, what Grace had said. Their relationship really was a thing of the past.

"That bribe he took when she was a kid. To pay for her to go to KIS."

Bent shook his head, still frowning. "She had a scholarship."

"A partial scholarship. You know her father had a good government service job. But it wasn't enough to pay the fees. He took a bribe," Duncan said. "That was when he started working in the private sector— after he lost the government job." Looking at Bent's confused face, he realized that Grace had not told him any of this. "She never told you?"

Bent shook his head again. "Makes sense, though. Why she was always so determined to succeed. So driven, yeah? Wanting to make every minute count."

"Her way of paying him back. At least, that's what I think. Because she felt like it was her fault. Even though that's absurd." Duncan was feeling uncomfortable now. This was an odd conversation to be having. Would Grace mind that he'd told Bent? Why would she? But even if she didn't, should he be talking about his wife with her old high school boyfriend? How had he got himself into this awkward situation? The weekend had forced a kind of intimacy into his interactions with Bent. He had to remember Bent was a coworker. Maybe even his boss. "Anyway," he said. "Not quite sure how I got into that."

Bent put the pen back in the holder and leaned back, taking his cue.

"All your books came in?" he said, looking at the floor-to-ceiling ebony bookshelves. Some unseen lackey had already arranged Duncan's books there. "Checked out our online library yet? We can get any journal you want, just name it. And anything else you need, just holler. You'll find we keep our employees happy."

"Holler, hmm . . . ," Duncan said, trying to lighten the atmosphere.

Bent grinned wryly. "You met Geri, yeah? She acts like that, but she's incredibly efficient. All you have to do is ask."

Duncan had not said much to Geri Trikefalou, the administrative assistant who guarded the reception area of the marketing division. She was a massively built woman with stiff waves of mauve-tinted hair who had regarded him with the grim expression of someone who would not give an inch. "I'll be sure to ask her," he said, thinking that she probably wouldn't answer. "Although I don't know what I could possibly need. I don't have anything specific to do yet, other than read this, I guess." He gestured at the folder he had found on his desk. It was tagged with a gray Post-it note that said "For Dr. Duncan McCloud" in small precise handwriting. Inside the folder's thin blue plasticized cover was a stack of sheets titled "The Placebo Effect: A Summary." It was a lengthy document, eighty-three pages of small print.

"It'll get you started," Bent said. "Things are moving along quickly on our end. We had hoped you'd start a week ago, really."

"From my perspective, it's all been so quick," Duncan said. A recruiter for Cinasat had contacted him barely a week after he had received his layoff notice from St. Casilda. The interview with Hammond Gleeson had followed a few days later. The recruiter had sent Hammond the book Duncan had written, *Exorcism Rituals in Sri Lanka*. Duncan suspected that Hammond had only skimmed it. How could such a busy man have had the time to read three-hundred-plus pages of dense anthropological discourse? In the interview, Hammond had been eager to hear about Duncan's research in Sri Lanka. The job offer had been extended at the end of the interview. The nondisclosure training workshops and paperwork in the subsequent days were the only parts of the process that had been time consuming. The last of the forms had been signed only the evening before, at Hammond's house.

Bent nodded, businesslike. "We're happy to have you. But we need you up to speed on the basics of the placebo effect." He tapped the blue folder on the desk. "Most people think that means the good things a sugar pill does, but of course, you understand it's something broader."

"Well, sure. The effect of believing a treatment's going to work," Duncan said. "Whether the treatment is a pill, or something else. Surgery, acupuncture, whatever. Even just a meeting with a doctor. Or a healing ritual."

"Exactly," Bent said. "That's where your work on exorcism ceremonies is going to come in. What was it you said in your book? An exorcism ceremony is all about illusion?"

Duncan had written about illusion right in the introduction section of *Exorcism Rituals*. The introduction would have been an easy enough read, even for a busy person.

"Well, that's how exorcists see the rituals," he said. "Demons are masters of illusion. That's precisely what gives them their power—their ability to influence humans, by tricking them. The exorcism rituals are designed to turn that power on its head. To trick the demons, and at the same time to expose the demons' trickery for what it is. To lift the veil from the patient's eyes."

"Very well put," Bent said, although Duncan detected a note of derision in his voice. "So what you mean is that these rituals work through illusion, yeah? They make people believe they're going to get better. In other words, the placebo effect."

"That's one way of thinking about the rituals," Duncan conceded. "I'd say that's our view. The exorcists wouldn't say that. Or their patients." The faint buzzing sound of a fly reached his ear. He looked to his left, but there was nothing there. How could there be a fly in here, in this perfectly climate-controlled room?

"Yeah, yeah, of course. But obviously, what we're taking is our view, yeah?" Bent said. He took the desk pen out of its holder again and twirled it, his dexterity mesmerizing. "One thing we want you to do is write an article connecting these rituals to the placebo effect. That has to be done very soon. Cowrite an article, actually, with Derek." He nodded, indicating the blue folder on the desk. "He'll explain the details."

"Derek Weinberg?" Duncan said. He had noted the author's name and august institutional affiliation on the document. "Why would someone at one of the best medical schools in the country want to collaborate on an article with an anthropologist he's never met?"

"He's an open-minded type," Bent said. "He's doing research on a Cinasat grant, and I told him about your work. He's interested. We'll set you up with him."

As if he were proposing a date, Duncan thought, rubbing a smudge off the top of his desk. A blind date. "Set me up. Hmm. Never really thought of writing a paper that way."

"I know anthropologists tend to work on their own," Bent said. "But you know in the medical, pharmaceutical fields, collaboration is very common." He pursed his lips. His lips were almost pretty, Duncan thought. There was something feminine about their shape. Bent tapped the pen on the desk. "Our people collaborate quite a bit with top-notch academic researchers. We like to make sure we get into the best journals. Good science is the basis for our drugs. The best science makes the best drugs, we like to say. And lately, people from the humanities, like you—anthropologists, sociologists, even philosophers—have been collaborating with our science folks. I'm sure Hammond told you, we're hiring people who can write well. Persuasively." A loud buzz interrupted him, and a dense-looking black fly landed on the desk.

Bent swiped at it. The fly zipped into a corner of the room. "Looks like Geri needs to get you a swatter," Bent said.

Duncan flipped through the folder. "When do I meet the others? The other anthropologists and sociologists you have on staff?" He had a lot of questions for them. The specifics of what they did at Cinasat, for instance. His nondisclosure agreement had been signed and countersigned, but he still didn't know much more than that he would be writing papers and providing his expertise to the division.

"They have offices here, but they like the flexibility of working from home," Bent said. "One of the perks we offer. Same goes for you, as I said, after you've been with us for two months. You're the only person in this area so far, by the way. You and Geri. The others are in the research division."

"So that's why it's so deserted," Duncan said. His apprehension lifted a little. Earlier, when he'd padded down the silent hallway outside his office, he'd found only closed, unmarked doors. No evidence of life.

"We'll be moving their offices here in the near future," Bent said. "You're at the forefront of a new initiative."

"A marketing initiative?"

"Expecting unprecedented sales," Bent said. He flicked an invisible speck off his gray-clad knee. "Marketing's going to be the key to the whole project. That's what you'll be helping us with. We can go into it in detail later."

"I need a bit more clarity about what I'll be doing," Duncan said. Why were details always being postponed? Was this how it was with all industry jobs? When he'd started at St. Casilda, he had known exactly what he would have to do: teach four classes a semester, advise students, do his own research whenever he had the time. There was something troublingly opaque about this job in contrast.

"As we've said, we need you as an expert consultant. The team will be coming to you with questions. And once you read that"—Bent tapped the folder on the desk with the pen—"we can get you started on a collaboration with Weinberg. We've set up a meeting for tomorrow."

Duncan riffled the pages in the folder. He was expected to read this by tomorrow? Much more rushed than in the academic world. But it was going to be a fine job once he got used to it, he reassured himself, trying to shrug off the heaviness settling over him.

8

GRACE

Tuesday

Four of the vials in rack thirty-eight were rusty brown with adult fruit flies. Grace took one vial out and carried it to the microscope station. She pushed the air pipe down past the cotton wool plugging the top of the test tube and flipped open the carbon dioxide valve. When the flies stopped skittering around, she extracted the cotton wool and tapped a few of the dazed creatures onto a dish. Other faculty left dissections to their research assistants, but she sometimes did them herself. She set the timer for an hour. It helped her to go faster. When her students were not around, undisturbed she could average one fly every two minutes. Thirty per hour. Go.

She held a fly under the microscope with one pair of forceps and ripped its spongy abdomen cleanly with another. The ovaries were so small and pale that she had hardly been able to see them the first time she had tried the dissection. But that had been years ago. Now she was an expert. It took only a few seconds to pull the ovaries free of their ethereal moorings. They were like two small bunches of colorless grapes. Without the microscope, all she could see was a minute drop of semi-transparent mucus clinging to the end of the needle-thin forceps. She smeared it inside the tiny collecting tube she had jammed into a beaker of ice to prevent the tissue from degrading.

She moved on to the next fly, after a glance at the timer's second hand ticking on. Three minutes and ten seconds already, but the first one she did on any day always took the longest.

By noon, she had enough egg sac tissue for the new experiment. Soon she would be able to isolate the protein that gave this strain of fruit flies such thin egg sacs. She turned off her microscope and stood up, feeling the tension in her back release as she straightened her spine. She had less than an hour before she was due to meet Marla in Newark. She stored the ovaries in the freezer and locked up the lab before hurrying to the elevator.

Traffic was light, and she made it to downtown Newark just before one o'clock. Her destination was a tiny Middle Eastern café in a busy area. It was only when she smelled falafel frying that she realized how hungry she was. At the stub of a counter, a hefty woman with a striped bandanna and a sweaty face was shouting orders to two tattooed men in the kitchen. Marla was already seated, sipping a green smoothie.

"Celery-kiwi," she said, tapping the glass. "Sorry I didn't wait. Had to look out for this guy." She touched her belly.

The pale cloud of Marla's hair, when Grace bent to hug her, felt like satin. Marla was sitting well back from the table to give her belly, prominently displayed under a lemon knit dress, sufficient room. Her skin glowed. She looked closer to thirty than forty.

"I only have a couple of hours," Grace said. "I have an appointment. Fertility specialist."

"Duncan's idea?"

Grace shrugged. "Yeah. But he's not as intense after the last miss. After six misses, he'd have to be an idiot to not see something's wrong with the machinery. Has to be a genetic thing. Every miss at the same time."

"Sometimes it just takes trying. And the right vibes," Marla said, taking Grace's hand. Even the skin of her fingers felt silky. "My friend Clara had five miscarriages, and then she had three kids."

"Vibes, I don't know," Grace said. "But trying . . . We buy ovulation kits wholesale. We should buy shares of Procter & Gamble. But it's pointless. And time's running out."

Marla squeezed her hand. "Think positive."

"So are you going to tell me what this is about?" Grace said, dragging her chair closer to Marla. "Why did you want me to come all the way out here?" A loud group had arrived, and she had to raise her voice to be heard.

"I want to go to the funeral, but my doc said I shouldn't fly." Marla pushed her glass aside and leaned close to Grace. "Grace, I can't stop thinking about it. About how I was there with her all night. I wish, I wish. I keep wishing all these things. I wish I had gone hiking with her. Woken up sooner. I wish I hadn't gone to sleep so soon."

The noise inside increased as a small group of chattering women joined the food line. "Do you remember . . . there was a time when you were always going off to Harris to hang out with her?" Grace said. "In senior year. Remember how she used to yell out of her window?" The Harris dormitory had been located on a slight rise above the Woodleigh dormitory, where Grace and Marla had roomed together, and where Marla's mother and father, both schoolteachers, had served as dorm parents. On Friday afternoons after classes had let out, Angie would bellow out of the window of her dorm room, calling Marla's name over and over again until someone alerted Marla.

"I never understood why you didn't like her," Marla said.

"Not that I didn't. We just didn't click. Back then." Grace straightened her back. Angie's message kept scratching at her thoughts whenever she wasn't focused on her work. What if it all came out somehow? Should she tell Duncan? Should she ask Marla what she thought? "But you know—"

"Sheesh," Marla hissed, looking out the smudged glass front of the café. "The ignorance. It really gets to me."

Turning, Grace saw a pregnant woman standing on the sidewalk outside, talking animatedly into a cell phone and wielding a cigarette with the practiced manner of a longtime smoker.

"The smoking? A few here and there don't do that much harm," Grace said. "Think about doctors advising pregnant women to smoke and drink in the old days. To help them relax."

Marla snorted. "When they didn't know any better." She leaned toward Grace, her face screwed up with disgust. Grace could smell the innocent fruitiness of her shampoo. "The other day there was this drunk woman in the booth next to us at Chili's, going on about how she was nearly in her second trimester. The waiter looked like he'd swallowed a stone when he was bringing her third or fourth margarita. I was on the verge of telling her off, but Karl stopped me."

"Pregnant women drink in France," Grace said. "Italy. And other places."

"Please. A glass of wine with dinner, okay. Margaritas one after another? First trimester? Hey, as soon as I found out, I even stopped eating tiramisu. No rum for this one." Marla rubbed her belly. "Or for my first two."

"Too extreme," Grace said. That was always the problem with Marla. Grace sipped her water, trying to smile. It was warm inside the café, with the sunlight beating through the windows and the heat from the kitchen behind the counter.

Their food arrived. Grace said, "So anyway . . . you didn't tell me why you wanted to meet here."

"Didn't want to tell you on the phone. You might have tried to talk me out of it," Marla said, wiping off a thin mustache of green juice.

"Out of what?"

"Going to see a friend of Angie's."

Grace stopped in the middle of chewing a crunchy falafel. "What for?"

"Just to say that she passed, you know. And that Angie had been trying to help her."

"Who's the friend?"

"Her name is Minowa Costa. She lives near here. Off Broad Street." Marla picked a slice of tomato out of her sandwich and put it in her mouth.

"You know her?"

Marla shook her head. "Someone Angie mentioned that night. She was still working when I was trying to sleep. I asked her why she couldn't just finish in the morning, and she said she owed it to Minowa Costa. I told her I had known someone called Minnie Costa in North Jersey, and we were wondering if it was the same person. That's when she said her friend was on Hale Street in Newark. Minowa Lee Costa." Marla blotted her eyes with a napkin and blew her nose. "When I called Angie's mom yesterday, I told her to let this Minowa know, but she didn't know anyone by that name. So I looked her up online. There was no phone number. I thought I would go by and tell her. She was a good friend, Angie said." She looked anxiously at Grace. "You'll go with me, right? I feel like I should do it, you know. The least I can do if I can't go to the funeral. But I feel weird about dropping by."

Typical Marla, Grace thought. She'd always been too impulsive. "It's the middle of a weekday, Marla. She probably won't even be at home."

"We could leave her a note then," Marla said.

"Or we could mail her a note," Grace said, sliding a napkin over some oil from the fries. "That would be less awkward. I mean, what if she gets . . . If Angie knew her well, this could be pretty upsetting for her."

Marla nodded, dabbing her eyes again. "But that's why I thought it would be better if we said it in person."

By the time they finished eating, Grace had given up trying to dissuade Marla. They tramped down to the Hale Street intersection, where an array of not-so-fresh fruits and vegetables was laid out under a grocery store awning. Halfway down the street, just past a nail parlor flashing neon, Marla stopped in front of a six-story brick building. It had a glossy red door with a glass pane set at eye level. The steps leading up to the door were shaded by the valiant branches of a struggling tree planted in a square dug out of the sidewalk. Tied to its trunk with a yellow satin ribbon was a profuse bunch of plastic lilies, some white, some mottled crimson.

"Are you sure you want to do this?" Grace said, but Marla was already climbing the steps, steadying herself against the metal railing. They entered a small hallway with a set of mailboxes. A gray metal door lay beyond, a key card lock indicating its security. An elderly black woman was leafing through a handful of junk mail by one open mailbox. Marla stopped at a panel of doorbells that had handwritten name labels affixed with bits of tape. "There it is," she said, and pressed a button. They waited, but nothing happened. The woman at the mailbox rustled her papers, muttering under her breath.

"Okay," Grace said, taking Marla's arm. She felt uncomfortable. It seemed intrusive, going into some stranger's apartment building, bringing news that probably wouldn't be well received. "She's not there. We tried." It was getting late too, almost three o'clock.

"We should at least leave a message," Marla said, scrabbling in her purse, a bulky zebra-printed affair with many external pockets. She extracted a pen and a small notebook. "What should I write?" Then she looked up again at the panel. "Did I press the right one? Let me try again. Okay. Minowa Costa." She pressed again.

The woman by the mailbox had emitted a surprised grunt. She turned slowly to face them, inching her feet around in shoes with sturdy rubber soles. They appeared to be pinching her ankles, which were heavily swollen under her pale-blue dress. "You looking for Minowa?" she said, squinting at them.

"I don't think she's in," Grace said.

The woman snorted, fixing her with an ornery stare. "She's with the good Lord," she said.

"Er . . . ," Marla said, looking nonplussed. "Is there any way we could leave a note for her? Would you slip it under her door for us . . . ?" Her voice trailed off as the woman rolled her eyes.

"You deaf?" she said. "I said she's with the Lord. Ain't no way she'll be getting your messages."

Grace exchanged a glance with Marla.

"Are you saying . . . ?" Marla said, her eyes widening.

The woman rolled her head slowly, wearily. Her grizzled hair was cut close to her scalp. "Gone to heaven, that one. That's what I said."

"She died?" Grace said, and then realized it had come out as a whisper.

"Knocked down right there. Right outside her own home. Dead of night."

"Jeez, I am so sorry," Marla said. "When did it happen?"

The woman staggered slowly to the outer door, swaying from side to side on unsteady feet, the jumble of mail clutched to her chest. "See that there?" she said, pointing through the glass pane at the street. "Right there was where she got hit. Not been a week. Last Thursday morning in the wee hours." She shook her head again.

"She got hit? You mean by a car?" Marla said.

The woman supported herself against the doorframe. "By the time the ambulance got here, she were already with the Lord, they said. Police been here, but no one seen the car. Those lilies there, for her."

A few of the woman's papers drifted to the floor. Grace crouched to pick them up. "A hit and run?" she said as she handed them back.

"Hit 'n' run, hit 'n' run," the woman said, her head swaying back and forth. "Ain't no justice but with the Lord." She made her way slowly to the inner door.

Grace stood uncertainly with Marla, watching the woman swipe a key card carefully across the lock. She heaved the door open and disappeared inside without another word.

"Jeez," Marla said, her hand to her chest.

Grace took her by the arm and led her back out onto the street. The lilies that had looked whimsical before looked ominous now, hanging there with their plastic stamens dark as if dipped in blood. They crossed the street in unspoken agreement and set off back the way they had come.

"It happened before the reunion," Grace said. "I guess Angie hadn't heard."

"Unless," Marla said. "Unless she had, and that was what her work was about? A report about the hit and run?" She stopped abruptly, causing a man who had been walking just behind her to step swiftly aside with an annoyed glare. "But that wouldn't make sense. She wrote about corruption, immigration, social justice, that kind of thing." She frowned. "But maybe she did write about crimes like this. Especially if a friend was involved. She said she owed it to Minowa Costa to finish the report."

"That could have meant anything," Grace said. "Anyway, if Angie knew Minowa had died, wouldn't she have said? Did she seem upset when she mentioned Minowa?"

Marla frowned. She was holding her belly with both hands. "I don't know. I wouldn't say upset. It was more like . . . urgent. I thought it was that she had a deadline for the article. Also, she seemed reluctant to talk about Minowa."

"What's the point of speculating?" Grace said. "We won't know." The same with the voicemail message. She would never know. Why had

Angie dug up something Grace had tried so hard to forget? *How you both feel.* Why had she wanted to know how they felt?

Marla started walking again. "Did she really have a heart attack? Angie?" She answered herself right away, as if she were trying to convince herself. "She did. She did. After she had the hysterectomy—because of fibroids, three years ago—she was warned that she had an increased risk."

Grace put her arm around Marla's shoulder. *Anyone could just die,* she thought. You could be in the pink of health, and then, the next day, you could be gone. Even Marla, with her baby still inside. The thought made her chest constrict. How easy it was for life to simply end. And what would be left behind to show that you had even existed?

"I wish I had said . . . that . . . I don't know. That she was important to me."

"She called me," Grace blurted, and then wished she could take it back. What if she had to go into the whole thing?

"Angie?" Marla stopped again in the middle of the sidewalk. Her mouth had dropped open. "What do you mean? When?" A young woman with a stroller skirted her, muttering an epithet under her breath.

"That morning, around eight, when I was still asleep. My ringer was off. She left a message on my phone saying she wanted to see me."

Marla frowned. "Wait. You never said . . . all that time when we were wondering when she was going to get back from her hike? And afterward."

"I told Mortensen," Grace said. She was having difficulty meeting Marla's eyes, so she concentrated on taking out her phone and locating her parking spot on Google Maps. "I didn't think it meant anything before. I mean, I still don't think it did. I couldn't hear much of the message. It kept cutting out. I don't know why she wanted to see me. I thought it was . . . like for old times' sake. She said she wanted to meet Duncan."

Looking up, Grace saw that Marla was watching her, still frowning. "Did you keep in touch with her?" Marla said.

"No," Grace said. "That was why I thought it was a bit odd. I hadn't seen her for twelve years. And that was in passing. In Chicago, by accident." *Please don't ask,* she thought.

"Well, that's strange," Marla said. They were walking again, and Grace was grateful that she didn't have to look Marla in the eye. "She never said anything to me about wanting to see you. She didn't mention you at all, although I think someone—Mo?—said something about you and Duncan being there, while we were in the cabin."

"It was probably nothing," Grace said. "Maybe she wanted to make connections with everyone there. People she hadn't seen for a while. Actually, that's probably it. I didn't think of that before. That would make sense."

"I called him, you know," Marla said. "Yesterday. Mortensen." Grace let out her breath. Thank God she'd let it go. "Because it seems so odd," Marla went on. "She was tense about this work thing—maybe it was about this Minowa or something else. But so stressed that she'd have a heart attack? It doesn't seem right. Mortensen said he had been asked to hand the case off to a superior. But he said the medical examiner's report was clear. A heart attack."

"Mortensen came to see us on Sunday night," Grace said. "He was looking into those gunshots we heard. Because it's not hunting season, he said, but he asked us some odd questions. About how well we knew you and some of the others. Whether any of you had a gun."

Marla frowned. "At the camp? Or just owned one?"

"At the camp . . . Well, I don't know. Why would he care otherwise?" Grace eyed Marla. "Do you own a gun?"

Marla nodded. "Sure. Doesn't everyone?"

Grace gaped at her. How nonchalant. "Really?" Marla was the last person she would have expected to own a gun. *You only think you know someone,* she thought.

Marla shrugged. "But why would I—or anyone—bring one to camp?"

"He said Mo had bought ammunition in Ridgeville."

Marla frowned again. "So what? That doesn't mean he brought a gun to camp. If he did, he would have said something if he was going hunting." She shook her head. Her cheeks were flushed. "You know what it is. It's because of his name."

"His name?" What was she talking about?

"Anyone with a Muslim name is targeted. Such bullshit."

"What? That didn't even cross my mind," Grace said.

"I volunteer at a center for Syrian refugees," Marla said, holding her belly as if it were a giant water balloon about to explode. Grace could see how angry she was. "The other volunteers are mostly Muslims. Muslim Americans. All the stories they tell. Forget the ones in hijabs. You can imagine what they have to put up with, right? But everyone else, just because of their names. Job applications. Routine stops for speeding. The police are the worst. Everyone with a Muslim name is a terrorist unless they can prove otherwise."

"I don't think . . . Mortensen?" Grace said.

"You have no idea," Marla said. "Actually, Angie wrote a story on this issue about a year ago. Or at least she contributed to it. She called me to get sources. A colleague of hers interviewed the people at the center."

9

DUNCAN

Tuesday

A company car had taken Duncan to his lunch appointment with Derek Weinberg. The restaurant was called Lyle, and it had the kind of unassuming grandeur that suggested an overpriced menu. The room he entered was high ceilinged and bathed in artificial light that reflected off the gleaming black floor. Streams of light flowed down a black stone wall at one end of the room, mimicking a waterfall.

When Duncan announced his name, he was led to a secluded table, where a man in a crisp cotton shirt and a burgundy tie was seated, examining the menu.

The man looked up at Duncan, pushing his silver-rimmed glasses onto the top of his head. His chestnut hair was thick and brushed back from his forehead. There was no gray in it, although he appeared to be in his sixties. His head looked inordinately large, perhaps because of the height of his hair, but he was still a handsome man, without the sagging neck skin and paunchy belly that so many aging scholars seemed to develop. "Dr. McCloud," he said, extending his hand. "Derek Weinberg. Good to meet you."

Before this eminent academic, Duncan felt a surge of nervousness that reminded him of his early days in his doctoral program. He'd always had butterflies when he'd met with his faculty adviser. He was no longer under anyone's thumb, he reminded himself. This man couldn't tell him what to write, or criticize his research.

"I took the liberty of ordering some wine," Weinberg said.

As if on cue, a waiter in starched linen appeared to pour Duncan a glass.

"So you did your doctoral work at the University of Chicago," Weinberg said as Duncan took a tentative sip, wishing he could stop feeling like a student. He might have been at a no-name college for the past decade, but he had a good publication record, and he knew what he was doing. He set his wineglass down as Weinberg continued speaking. "Anthropology. You knew Adelaide Goetz then."

"I took a couple of classes with her. You worked with her?"

"I knew her from graduate school at Yale," Weinberg said. "Back in the day, of course. We kept in touch over the years. A brilliant scholar. A credit to your field."

Duncan nodded, taking another sip. Something about Weinberg's tone suggested that he didn't think too highly of anthropologists, and that added to his nervousness. He rotated the ring on his finger, trying to relax.

"Bentley sent me your book and a couple of your papers," Weinberg said. "I didn't read the book, but I took a look at the papers," he went on, after a pause during which he'd swirled the wine around in his glass, sniffing its vapors. "I hear *Anthropological Quarterly* is a top journal in your field."

The paper Duncan had published in that journal had been one he'd worked on for more than three years, and Duncan was proud of it. He nodded. "One of the best, actually," he said, and then wondered if that sounded too immodest. But then, he had looked up this man's publication record, and he had hundreds of papers, many in top medical journals. Several had been in the *New England Journal of Medicine* and the *Lancet*.

"Hmm. Well. You read the summary document I sent Bentley?"

"On the placebo effect. Yes. Very illuminating," Duncan said, although he'd found the document tedious to get through. He had spent all the previous day on it, reading until late in the night. It had been a compilation of a large number of studies, many unpublished, comparing various drugs with placebos, for a multitude of conditions. "I thought I knew a fair bit about the placebo effect, just from the popular press and the research I did for an article years ago, but—"

"A 2005 paper? That was the other one Bentley sent. Now that one was quite interesting," Weinberg said.

Duncan gazed down at his wineglass. "You know, anthropologists don't put much stock in scientific explanations for rituals," he said. "What's most interesting are the rituals themselves, and what they mean to the people who do them. Whether or not they work by external standards is not . . . that's not really relevant." The 2005 paper had been one of the earliest he'd had published. It had been in a small interdisciplinary journal that was all but unknown. The anthropologists he knew didn't think much of it, if they'd even read it. But he wasn't surprised that Bent had sent the paper to Weinberg. It had touched on the placebo effect as a possible reason why Sri Lankan exorcism ceremonies might cure illnesses, and Bent had shown a lot of interest in it. In fact, the conversation he'd had with Hammond at the party, and the one with Bent at the reunion, suggested that the paper had a lot to do with why he had been hired.

"You may not be aware of this if you've been working in the usual academic silo, but interdisciplinary work is getting plenty of attention these days," Weinberg said, tapping his wineglass stem. "Even in medicine. Nowadays it's not medicine versus anthropology. It's medicine *and* anthropology. And sociology and psychology. That is why I think a paper pushing an interdisciplinary view of the placebo effect would be worthwhile."

"Not sure how that would play out," Duncan said. "I'd have to hear more about what you have in mind."

"Why don't we order first."

Duncan opened his menu and was accosted with a selection of dizzyingly unfamiliar dishes: grilled oysters with leeks, bacon, and cream; braised rabbit with roasted summer squash and heirloom tomato ratatouille; sautéed veal sweetbreads with wild mushrooms and crispy onions. The mind-boggling prices were equally unfamiliar. He thought of the routine of his childhood, from the time his mother had taken ill, when his dad had cooked his painstakingly recipe-bound meals, rotating through seven casseroles for dinner, one for each day of the week. He wondered what his dad would say if he saw this menu. He wondered what Ms. Logan would have said about this new job. He wished, as he always did when his former teacher came to mind, that she were still alive.

"Cinasat offers a generous expense account," Weinberg said, after their orders had been placed. "One of their many perks. They like to keep their people happy."

"You've consulted for them long?"

"A few years," Weinberg said, and as if Duncan had been too personal, went on rather brusquely, "So, you read the document. As you saw, a lot of the drugs we've been prescribing for years—for depression, for pain, for irritable bowel syndrome, high blood pressure, Parkinson's, countless other things—work no better than a placebo."

Duncan cleared his throat. "All the sources you cited seemed credible, of course, but the extent of it seemed . . . well, I don't want to say overstated, but . . . some of these drugs have to be working, right? I mean, they are being regularly prescribed, after all."

An irritated look appeared on Weinberg's face. "The drugs have an effect, of course. The point is that they have *no more* of an effect than a placebo. In other words, you could just give people a sugar pill, and as long as they believed it would work, it very likely would. This is the same reason nondrug treatments sometimes work. Acupuncture, chiropractic, Rolfing, all of that. Even your healing ceremonies. As you said yourself in your own paper, it's all about context and expectancy. Put people in the right context and get them to believe something will work, and there you go."

"Hmm. Of course you know this subject a lot better than me," Duncan said. What Weinberg was saying seemed implausible, even with all the evidence the document had presented. "But I think it's pretty well accepted that drugs work better than things like acupuncture, all that."

"Do you think people believe more in drugs than in acupuncture?" Weinberg said.

"Here, sure, in general. For most things."

"There you go," Weinberg said. "This is why pharmaceuticals are so powerful."

"Drugs work better because people believe in them more?" Duncan said, trying not to show his skepticism. "Shouldn't it be the other way around?"

Weinberg's smile was cynical. "Of course, it should. But the evidence indicates otherwise." He put up a hand. "Now, to be fair, there are some drugs that are different. I'm no anti-vaxxer. Vaccines work. Antibiotics for infections. Those really do work better than placebos. But for a lot of other conditions, no."

"Well, here's what puzzled me when I was reading your summary," Duncan said. The wine had made him more relaxed, and he felt his tongue getting looser. "Isn't this a huge problem for Cinasat, not to mention any other pharmaceutical company that's producing the same sorts of drugs? Why would Cinasat be passing around this document?"

Weinberg shook his head. "First of all, they are not passing it around. Most of these studies are unpublished. Occasionally some overzealous journalist trying to demonize the pharmaceutical industry gets hold of this or that and puts out a story, but that blows over pretty quickly." He wagged his finger at Duncan. "And you, don't forget, have signed a nondisclosure agreement. I assume you had training sessions before you started. On what you can and can't disclose to people outside the company."

Duncan opened his mouth to speak, but Weinberg went on. "Now, it could become a problem for the company in the long run. If these studies start getting out more . . . But Cinasat, instead of taking this lying down, has decided to be proactive and use the data to their advantage. Make lemon soufflé out of lemons, so to speak." He laughed and pushed his hair back with a gesture that seemed too conceited for a man his age. "Pure genius, I have to say. And that's where you come in."

Duncan was just about to speak when the waiter arrived and, with a flourish, set a plate garnished with edible flowers in front of Duncan. The smell rising from it made his mouth water.

"Why don't we eat first," Weinberg said, picking up his cutlery and setting upon his own dish with gusto. "Then we can talk."

By the time Duncan's plate had been cleared away and he had ordered his dessert, his nervousness had disappeared. He recognized, with surprise, that he'd been much more open about his experiences at St. Casilda than he would usually be in a conversation with a stranger. Weinberg was a sympathetic listener, and the wine had smoothed the conversation further. Duncan had ended up describing the absence of tenure, the limited research budget, the administrative pushback when he wanted time off to write, and the poorly stocked library.

"Well, you are going to have a very different experience at Cinasat," Weinberg said, refilling Duncan's wineglass. "Any resources you need, you can be sure to get."

"But what exactly will I need?" Duncan realized that he still had very little idea about what he was expected to do. "What will I be working on other than this paper with you?"

Weinberg leaned back. "Let me just put it to you straight," he said. "We—Cinasat, that is—may have made the biggest drug discovery in the history of medicine." He paused, evidently waiting for Duncan to react.

Duncan raised his eyebrows politely. *What hyperbole,* he thought.

"We've found the basis for the placebo effect," Weinberg said. He raised his glass triumphantly.

"The basis for the placebo effect," Duncan said, turning the words over in his mind, trying to make them sound less like gibberish.

"Can you imagine what that means? This is going to revolutionize health care."

"Revolutionize?" Duncan realized how dim he must sound, repeating Weinberg's words. "Sorry, I don't quite get what you mean."

Weinberg gazed at Duncan. Duncan saw disappointment, and even exasperation, in his face.

"Right," Weinberg said. "You're an anthropologist." The tone, disparaging, made Duncan wince. "What I mean is, we've found the biological basis for the placebo effect. We've figured out what makes it happen. Or at least we understand it well enough that we've been able to come up with a drug that mimics it."

"A drug that mimics the placebo effect?" Duncan wished he didn't feel so confused. What the hell was the guy talking about?

Weinberg sighed. "Alright. You know a little about the biological research on the placebo effect. Correct? I gathered that from the paper of yours that Bentley sent me. You know about the hypotheses people have been proposing for years. About neurotransmitters being involved in the placebo effect." He turned his gaze on Duncan again.

The waiter arrived with two outsize plates, each with a small, artfully arranged dessert portion. Duncan tried to focus on the delicacy before him. There was no need to get defensive, he reminded himself. Weinberg couldn't expect him to know about research studies in biology. "My knowledge is probably outdated," he said. "I haven't been following the biological research, you know. I'm not a scientist."

"I know, I know. Anthropologists are the furthest thing from scientists." Weinberg skimmed a fork over his own dessert, a black chocolate concoction adorned with shreds of gold leaf.

Again, the disparaging tone, Duncan thought. "Of course, I know neurotransmitters are supposedly implicated," he said, trying to keep his tone neutral. He struggled to remember the details of what he'd written in that long-ago paper. The mechanistic explanations in the biological research literature had always irritated him. All biologists wanted to do, it seemed, was to boil everything down to chemicals and molecules. The most interesting aspects of a therapeutic ritual—the symbols, the words, the gestures, the context—were brushed aside as if they were irrelevant. "I get the idea: when people believe they are going to get well, these brain chemicals are released, and they act on the immune system so that people actually get well. But the problem, as I recall, was that no one knew which neurotransmitters, or how they would act on the immune system in such a broad way that practically any condition would be alleviated. Not much of an explanation there." He allowed disparagement to creep into his own tone.

Weinberg smiled—condescendingly, Duncan thought. "You've got the basic idea. Sufficient for a nonscientist. The problem was that people were focusing on individual neurotransmitters—serotonin, dopamine, endorphins. That didn't go anywhere. What we've found out is that it's the combination of neurotransmitters that matters, not the level of any individual one. And we've come up with a drug that mimics the combination of neurotransmitters. This combination affects the immune system in the same broad way as when people believe they're going to get well. We still have a way to go to work out the exact mechanism, but what matters is that our drug—Symb86—works. We've gone all the way through Phase 3 trials, and we're waiting for final approval to get it to market."

"Phase 3 trials?" Duncan said, and then cleared his throat, realizing he'd parroted Weinberg again. "You're referring to the approval process at the Food and Drug Administration? Sorry, I'm really not familiar with the drug industry at all." He tapped his dessert fork against his plate. "Which is why I was surprised that Cinasat even wanted to hire me."

Weinberg paused. He took a careful bite of his dessert. He glanced at Duncan, his expression more relaxed. "Of course. All this probably seems very foreign to you. That's natural. You don't need to know the ins and the outs of the drug industry to do the job you've been hired to do. In fact, it's better that way, given the proprietary concerns. I can explain whatever it is you need to know." He had another bite and wiped his lips with his napkin. "Our people often each have only a small slice of our information pie. It works better that way. Less room for accidental leaks, so to speak."

He raked his fork across a stream of chocolate. "Let me tell you what you need to know. Phase 3 is just FDA jargon. Basically, we've gone through all the testing to demonstrate that Symb86 works. In the last human trials, we tested people with an assortment of conditions that are considered difficult to treat: irritable bowel syndrome, back pain, asthma, psoriasis, arthritis, ulcerative colitis, and so forth. For every condition, we tested three groups of people. One group got the drugs they normally would get for their condition. The second group got a placebo, and the third group got our drug. The group that got our drug improved much more than the other two groups." He waited, watching Duncan.

Duncan blinked. "But wait, the group that got the drug—what is it, Symb . . . ?"

"Symb86."

"The Symb86 group did better than the group that got the placebo?"

"Much better. Because you see, our drug is like a highly refined placebo. Regular placebos don't work for everyone. No one knows why. Maybe the context isn't good enough to set off the right combination of neurotransmitters, or they don't believe enough that they're going to get better. But we've figured out what's behind the placebo effect, so it works for almost everyone."

"But not everyone?"

Weinberg shrugged. "Real life is messy. Nothing's perfect. No drug is going to work for everyone. But this is as good as perfect. And we've replicated this effect for a number of other conditions, both medical and psychological disorders: depression, anxiety, bulimia, infertility . . ."

"It works for infertility?"

"For several patients, so far," Weinberg said. He picked up a shred of gold leaf with his fork and conveyed it to his mouth. "And also chronic fatigue syndrome. CFS."

Duncan stared at him. "CFS?"

Weinberg considered him with a half smile, only nodding in response.

Duncan pretended to be absorbed in savoring his dessert, turning this information over in his mind. His mother had tried so many CFS treatments over the years. His dad had taken her to physicians as far away as Vancouver and Dallas. He had taken her to chiropractors and acupuncturists. She'd tried stimulants and steroids, hormones and vitamins. Nothing had worked for more than two or three weeks; she'd always returned to her bed, clearly exhausted or in pain. Could this drug really make a difference? How much a cure would mean to her, and to his father. He took a deep breath. *Not so fast,* he reminded himself. No need to get carried away.

"I'm sure you have questions," Weinberg said.

Duncan dragged his mind away from his mother. "How will my work contribute?"

"Well, this is going to be marketed as a broad-spectrum drug that works for a wide array of conditions. We want people to understand its value. You'll not only be writing scholarly papers, but also helping to educate the drug reps and figuring out how to demonstrate the value of the drug. Good advertising is the key, not just for physicians who will be prescribing, but also for the consumers. And you know the drug industry has been getting a bad rap these days. Telling people that this drug acts like the placebo effect is not going to work." Weinberg laughed and shook his head. "The average person understands so little about the placebo effect. Most people think a placebo is something that doesn't work, when it's just the opposite."

"But wait a minute," Duncan said. "This drug will work whether or not people think it will work, isn't that right?"

"Not quite right. It is a real drug and it works, but if people believe it won't work, then it won't be as effective. Any drug is that way. Your belief can work against you just as it can work for you. The nocebo effect. You know this, I gather, from your mention of black magic rituals in your 2005 paper."

Duncan nodded.

"We need to educate people about the placebo effect. Show them that it works. Give them all the data about alternative therapies—you know the National Institutes of Health has been investing in that research for a while—on acupuncture, Reiki, chiropractic. And traditional healing practices like your devil dancing ceremonies. The masses love all that mumbo jumbo. Here's the key: we get people to understand that they all work through the placebo effect. And then we explain how they can get that same effect with this drug. We have people writing papers on all these therapies, connecting them to the placebo effect. A whole woo-woo team. You will be the one writing about devil dancing ceremonies. You persuade people that ceremonies that have been used for centuries, maybe millennia, are working through the placebo effect."

"Woo-woo," Duncan said.

"No need to take offense," Weinberg said. "You can help people see that it's not woo-woo. There is no magic. Context and expectancy release chemicals in your body, and the chemicals are what cure you. And we can give you those chemicals in a nice pill form. You can take the pills in the comfort of your own home. No need to go through these nonsense rituals. Everyone free of woo-woo." He laughed, raising his glass in a salute. "You see, everyone wins. And Cinasat makes a killing."

10

GRACE

Tuesday

Grace tried to return Dr. Chung's smile, to soften the irritation she was feeling. "I have to think about the risks. And the feasibility of the treatment. Such a big commitment of time and effort, isn't it?"

Dr. Chung nodded. Her cheeks were dimpled, even when her smile was only slight. "Reducing your workload might be good anyway. There's nothing like a relaxed lifestyle for promoting a healthy pregnancy."

Grace felt her irritation surge. Dr. Chung had to be barely thirty. Her ideas about working and producing had to be completely different from her own. She wouldn't understand the urgency Grace felt.

"My job isn't always compatible with a relaxed lifestyle," she said. "But honestly, I don't think that's what's preventing me from having a baby. If it were just stress, why would I miscarry at the same point in the pregnancy every time? That suggests there's some biological process going awry, doesn't it? It's like clockwork. Every miscarriage at nine weeks."

Dr. Chung shrugged, the smile now pasted on her lips. "As I said, everything looks normal, and nothing in the exam results suggests you couldn't carry a pregnancy to term. All I can tell you is what the research tells us. High stress is linked to lower rates of conception and higher rates of miscarriage."

"Well," Grace said. "I'll talk it over with my husband. I just don't know if it would be worthwhile, given the risks." There could be a biological problem, even if the tests didn't show it. What if she took these risks and then had another nine-week miscarriage?

Leaning forward to retrieve her purse, she saw a small framed photo on the desk of Dr. Chung by the ocean, arm in arm with a young man. It reminded Grace of a long-ago midsummer picnic at the lake beach in Chicago. She and Duncan had eaten hunks of cheese and French bread, their hands oily from canned smoked oysters and the olives they'd fished from a jar. Two children in Cub Scout uniforms had been throwing sticks for a boisterous dalmatian. Duncan had talked about having children. But fate decided those things. She was not to blame. Life had seemed so relaxing back then, before the fateful breakup that had preceded their engagement. She shook herself mentally. There was no way she could have known the breakup was temporary, she reminded herself for the thousandth time.

11

DUNCAN

Tuesday

Grace edged the dishes aside to make room for the grocery bags and sniffed the roasted garlic and tomato sauce in the air. "Smells good," she said.

She was wearing a patterned blue blouse she'd had for years. Duncan appreciated her thrift. In graduate school, they had survived on a meager budget, buying household items and clothing from garage sales and thrift stores. More than a decade later, they still had most of that old clothing and furniture, and even some of the crockery. They had only recently managed to pay off their graduate school loans and still owed a lot on their mortgage. But he knew that Grace's refusal to spend money on new clothes for herself had less to do with thrift and more to do with her guilt about how meager his St. Casilda salary had been relative to her own. Now they could afford to spend, he thought. They should go shopping, buy her some nice clothes. New briefcases for them both. Start looking for a new car for her. He could manage with his Volkswagen, but her old Honda wouldn't last much longer.

"What made you bring those out?" Grace said.

Duncan gathered the jumble of photographs together and pushed them back into the biscuit tin, a square old one he'd had since childhood, printed with a winter scene. It had been years since he'd taken the tin off the shelf in their bedroom closet.

Grace picked up a photo that had fallen to the floor. It showed Duncan at the age of eight or nine, his arms stretched to catch an orange Frisbee. His mother, in jeans and a bright-pink tartan shirt, had thrown the Frisbee, her mouth open with glee. *How vigorous she looks,* Duncan thought. Not the way she had looked the last time he'd seen her, when he had visited his parents in January. Now his mother's face was lined not only with age, but also her continuing pain and exhaustion. Her sedentary life had thickened her body and sucked the joy out of her eyes.

"Just thinking about what she used to be like," Duncan said. He handed Grace another photo: his mother leaning out of the window of a baby-blue boat of a Chevy, waving, a mischievous grin on her face. "Did I tell you she used to drag race when we were kids?"

Grace blinked. "Actual drag races?"

"No, I mean at traffic lights, she used to look over at whoever was in the lane next to us, and then tell us to watch how she was going to beat them. Sometimes it would be some big macho guy. She'd wait crouched over the steering wheel until the light changed. Then she'd accelerate like crazy into the intersection. We'd look back at the car next to us and tell her how the person reacted. And then we'd all crack up." He sighed, remembering. "Such fun. Things were so different, you know. She was always up for Frisbee and hide-and-seek after Steph and I got back from school. We used to roam around in the woods." He rummaged through the photos in the tin, looking for one he remembered.

"Shall we look after dinner?" Grace said, eyeing the fettuccine tangled in the strainer.

"So what exactly did the new doc suggest?" he said as they sat down to eat.

Grace's fettuccine squelched as she stirred it around in the sauce. "I told you. Aggressive treatments, which she admitted had risks, just to increase the chance of starting a pregnancy. She doesn't understand why the miscarriages are happening any more than all the rest. I think it's time to give up."

Duncan tried not to show his dismay, but he could tell she'd noticed it anyway.

"Not give it all up," she said, sounding defensive. "Just the ob-gyns."

Duncan had been trying not to dwell too much on the new drug since the meeting with Weinberg. Could it change everything? He had to be careful not to build glass castles. But it was hard to choke back the thought that there could be hope, not just for his mother, but also for themselves. That he could play a part in making it happen.

"Tell me more about the hotshot," Grace said, getting up from the table to get a dishcloth from the kitchen counter. "Did he say anything about what Salgado had been doing?"

Duncan knew she just wanted to change the subject. He had already told her a little about the meeting on the phone, when she called him about the doctor. He shrugged. "He had only met with Salgado once, apparently. They had been talking about writing this paper, but Salgado died before it got off the ground. Weinberg was okay. I think I'll get along fine with him. A bit weird to be asked to coauthor an article with someone you only just met. But this isn't academia. Probably happens all the time in industry."

Grace wiped a dribble of sauce off the tabletop. "So what exactly are you going to write about? Do you get to decide?"

"We're meeting again tomorrow. He's going to give me a data set. Or at least that was what he called it. About fourteen hours of film footage. Clips of two different *thovil* ceremonies."

"From?"

"The Galle area, he said. One film is of one group of exorcists doing a ceremony for a patient. The other film is of a different patient with a different group of exorcists."

"Wait," Grace said, frowning. "These are of real ceremonies? With real patients?"

"I know," Duncan said, chewing a charred brussels sprout.

"This was in some village?"

Duncan nodded. He'd been incredulous too.

"But how? People are so secretive about all that. Even in the villages. All the stigma? Who would want to broadcast the fact that they're having an exorcism?"

"That's what I said," Duncan said. When he had lived in Galle, it had taken months to earn enough trust to get the village folk to let him observe the ceremonies. He'd understood their concerns about having a foreigner in their midst. He had been careful to show his respect, remember that he was their guest. "But Weinberg said a local had filmed them, with a camera mounted at the scene."

Grace shook her head, looking unconvinced. "At these things, aren't people really worried about doing the ceremony properly and not getting possessed by demons and all that?"

Duncan pursed his lips, remembering Weinberg's smirk when he'd expressed incredulity at the existence of the films. "Money talks, I guess. Weinberg didn't say exactly that, but that seemed to be the gist of it. They compensated the patients' families and the exorcists. You know thovil are really costly . . ." He smiled, realizing that Grace would have no idea about the cost of an exorcism ceremony. "Okay, right. The exorcists charge for their work, obviously. On top of that, they ask the family for a whole long list of materials for the thovil. All kinds of plants, incense, cloth, a rooster, pots for the offerings. A lot of other stuff. They need coconut leaves for weaving the offering baskets. Plantain tree trunks and coconut leaves for building the structures, the little hut-like things. You know, where the patient sits, where the demons are supposed to be confined. A lot of food has to be prepared, for the exorcists, the guests. Plus they need food for the offerings. All of it cost thousands of rupees, even back then. A lot more now, I'm sure. Anyway, Cinasat paid for all of it."

Grace was still frowning, moving her fettuccine around on her plate. "Is that ethical? To offer so much money that people don't have a choice? How can they refuse, even if they don't like the idea?"

Duncan shrugged. That thought had made him uncomfortable too, at first. "Weinberg said they had ethical approval. They did a scientific study, so it had to go through an ethics review board. His justification is that the patients get to have the ceremony for free."

Grace chewed another mouthful of pasta thoughtfully. "These are whole ceremonies? All-nighters?"

"Yeah. They're long. They're both Mahasona exorcisms." Seeing her expression, Duncan explained, "You know there are different ceremonies for exorcising different demons, right? Depending on the patient's symptoms. Different demons are responsible for different kinds of problems. These ceremonies are for Mahasona, the Great Cemetery Demon. One of the most powerful demons, responsible for a lot of bad stuff." He grinned as she rolled her eyes. When he'd first met her, he had been steeped in the practices he had been observing in the villages near Galle. He had thought it strange that she knew next to nothing about demons and exorcisms, far less than he, a foreigner, did. It was only after he'd spent some time in the city that he realized her family was not unusual in being ignorant of all that, or in their disdain for the rituals village folk considered quite mundane.

"Why do you have to do this?"

"Cinasat wants me to take a close look at the mantra, the songs, the drumming, the dances, and so forth. Seems they're trying to see what aspects of the ceremonies most affect the patient, across cultures. They're also studying ceremonies in Indonesia and Thailand, apparently. I think it's for a longer-term project. I don't know why exactly. I'll be told later, Weinberg said. It all sounds pretty secretive. A bit weird, but it's because a lot of the information is proprietary. But for the moment, I am to just compare these two particular ceremonies."

"But how could this possibly have anything to do with Cinasat?"

"You know I'm not supposed to talk about any of this. That non-disclosure agreement specifically mentioned spouses and partners. You know the penalty. The job, all the sweet benefits, all our stock options . . ."

"Come on, Dunc. You don't really believe people don't talk to their spouses."

"Not that you'd tell anyone on purpose. But what if something accidentally slipped out in conversation? They're apparently really rigid about the nondisclosure thing. That was one of the things Hammond beat into the ground at the party when I was talking to him in his study. We could lose everything."

"As if," Grace said, setting her fork down with a decisive thunk.

How would anyone know if he told his own spouse? It was absurd to expect people wouldn't. "I don't know a whole lot yet, anyway. They're testing a drug. Apparently it does the same thing any healing ritual does."

"I still find it hard to believe that a pharmaceutical company would accept that healing rituals even do anything," Grace said.

"Weinberg said the same thing Hammond said back during the interview. That they have empirical evidence that the rituals do help people. And that the rituals wouldn't have been done for centuries, or who knows, millennia, if they didn't do something for people." Duncan shrugged. "The claim is that all these healing rituals work through the placebo effect, which they say is actually a biochemical reaction. Apparently this wonder drug of Cinasat's takes a shortcut and makes this biochemical reaction happen."

"What the hell?" Grace said. "Is that true?"

"Supposedly. They've apparently tested the drug—Symb86—multiple times, and it works. On a bunch of different conditions. Including CFS."

Grace stared at him, and then at the tin of photos on the kitchen counter. "The photos. That's why you were looking at them."

"I've been trying not to get too hopeful," Duncan said. He took her hand, trying to suppress the excitement he'd been feeling. "But Grace, imagine if it really works. What that would mean for her and Dad. After all these years. It would be like magic."

He could see her skepticism. Grace, the scientist.

"What exactly does the drug do? Biochemically, I mean."

Duncan shrugged. "We didn't get into those details. It wouldn't make much sense to me anyway. Weinberg said something about it mimicking the action of multiple neurotransmitters. But the point is, it works. They've demonstrated that it acts like a very effective placebo. Essentially, they've isolated the mechanism of the placebo effect. A regular placebo might work for thirty to forty percent of people, say. This would work for almost everyone."

"How much evidence do they have?"

"A lot, apparently. They've gone through Phase 3 trials, which is pretty far along in the FDA approval process."

Duncan watched her eyes widen. Evidently she knew more about what Phase 3 meant than he did. She blew out her breath in a long whistle. He could feel her excitement, the tightening of her hand in his. "My God," she said. "Imagine if it is real. This could be the drug of the century. Of the millennium."

"The best drug ever made," Duncan said, grinning. He hadn't been foolish to be hopeful. She saw how amazing this was too. He drummed his hands on the table. "That's what I've been trying to tell you. I'm afraid to believe it, but if it's true, and not just hype, then they've hit the jackpot. *We've* hit the jackpot."

"My God. When's it going to market?"

"Soon, apparently."

"And how exactly is your work going to help?"

"Weinberg wants me to see if I agree that the two exorcisms are the same. These two patients are actually representatives of two groups of patients. One group got a drug that blocks our Symb86." He could hear his own excitement. The drug really was theirs too. They had stock in the company, and he was going to be helping get the drug out. "Apparently, those patients didn't get better. The patients in the other group didn't get the Symb86 blocker, and they got better—most of them. In other words, when Symb86 is blocked, the ceremony has no effect. I think the idea is—that means the ceremony's effect is the same as the effect of Symb86. Weinberg says there are other studies that also show this. But critics are going to say that the group with the blocker didn't get better for other reasons—like they didn't have a convincing ceremony done, not because of our blocker. So Weinberg wants to show—scientifically, he says, as if that's the answer to everything—that both patient groups are having the same ceremony. That would be more support showing that our drug does the same thing that the ceremony does."

"Hmm, okay, I guess if there's already a lot of evidence, this could help clinch it. Can you tell if the ceremonies are the same?"

"Well, I've seen scores of Mahasona exorcisms, and I've studied the order of events in them, so theoretically, yes. But obviously, an experienced exorcist would be in a much better position to tell if the ceremony is being done right. I told Weinberg that, but he says they need someone who can write convincingly about the similarities, someone who can collaborate with a scientist. The problem is that I don't think I can tell from just watching the films. You can't see enough detail. But Weinberg wants me to try, as a preliminary effort. Later, as they said at the time of the interview, I'll have to see some actual ceremonies. In Sri Lanka."

"But that's not for a while?"

"Yeah, not for months. There'll be plenty to do here before that. Everything's moving really fast. I'll probably be putting in a lot of late hours. Every waking hour, probably. After watching these films, I have papers to write, and materials for the marketing campaign."

"I don't know," Grace said, stacking the empty plates and dishes. "It's all too good to be true, somehow. Like there's a catch that'll bring the whole thing crashing down. I'd want to see the data from all the trials. The medical data."

Back down to earth. He could always count on Grace, Duncan thought. Sometimes he wished she would let herself, let them both, dream a little. But it was better this way. He had only been at the company two days. He should be cautious about the prospects for the drug. "There's no way you'd get to see the actual data," Duncan said. "I won't be seeing much of it either. Just what's relevant to what I'll be writing. And even then, just the summaries, probably." The actual data wouldn't mean anything to him, anyway. He didn't have Grace's head for numbers and statistics.

He watched Grace carry the dirty dishes to the sink. "By the way . . . Did you, by any chance, tell Bent about the miscarriages?"

Grace jerked her head around. A serving spoon clanged onto the porcelain of the sink. "Of course not. When would I have done that?"

"I know, I didn't think so. I just wondered."

"Why?"

"I don't know. This guy, Weinberg, he said the drug's been shown to work for a whole lot of conditions, right? He mentioned CFS. And also infertility."

"It works for infertility?" Grace stood still, her hands clenched around the chopping board.

"I just thought it was a bit of a weird coincidence. He just mentioned that in passing," Duncan said. He wondered if he should have brought it up. "I'll have to ask him more about it. I suppose it only works for some types of infertility, though. It can't possibly fix a problem with the actual machinery, but then, so far everyone's said your machinery's fine."

"It couldn't fix a genetic problem," Grace said. "Every miss at nine weeks. How can that be anything but a genetic problem?"

Duncan sighed. The thought passed through his mind again. *Maybe she doesn't want it to succeed.* But she had been so miserable each time she miscarried. It was just that the misses had undermined her confidence, he thought. "All I'm saying is . . . there might be hope," he said.

12

GRACE

Tuesday

"I forgot to tell you. I had lunch with Marla," Grace said, over the clattering of the plates. "And then we found out something—"

The doorbell rang, a single long trill.

"Gordy, I bet," Grace said, trying to order the dishes. No matter how much she tried to divert Duncan from the dishwasher, he always managed to get some dishes in while she was wiping the counters clean. Plates with bits of food still clinging to them were crammed in willy-nilly on the bottom rack. "He's probably going to remind you again that the rear light needs to be replaced on the Honda."

She heard Duncan's surprised greeting. Evidently not Gordon Mann, their next-door neighbor. She wiped her hands and went out into the hallway. Standing on the doorstep was Mortensen, his stubbly blond hair glinting under the entry light. A middle-aged black man sporting a lush mustache and a lavender shirt stood beside him.

"May we come in?" Mortensen said.

Duncan waved the men into the living room. *Again too late for a visit,* Grace thought, glancing at her watch. She said nothing, focusing on trying to quiet the uneasy feeling in her chest.

"We are not disturbing you, I hope," Mortensen said in his soft voice, looking from Duncan to Grace.

The other man put out his hand. "Howie Dyson," he said. "Internal Affairs." Grace shook it, noting his authoritative air. His handshake, firm and a little abrupt, matched his manner.

"Internal Affairs?" Duncan said, looking perplexed. "You're also part of the Ridgeville Police?"

Dyson merely looked gravely at Duncan. His tie, surprisingly for a cop, was patterned with arcs of psychedelic colors, although except for that, he was dressed conservatively enough.

"We have a couple of questions," Mortensen said.

"What about?" Grace said. The uneasy feeling in her chest increased. She didn't like the way Dyson's eyes were resting on her.

"This is about Angie?" Duncan said.

"Our question is for Mrs. McCloud," Dyson said. He made a little bow and corrected himself. "Dr. McCloud, is that correct?"

Grace felt her heartbeat accelerate. This had to be about Angie's message. What was she going to say? She tried to compose herself, focusing on letting her breath out slowly. "Please sit," she said.

Dyson settled on the edge of the sofa, his elbows on his knees. His trousers were gray and crisply cuffed, and his black shoes were polished to a sheen. "What did Ms. Osborne contact you about?" he said, his eyes fixed on Grace's face.

"What do you mean?" Duncan said.

"You didn't know," Mortensen murmured. He had seated himself in one of the striped armchairs, dwarfing it with his height. He opened his notepad.

"There wasn't anything to know," Grace said. Then realizing she sounded defensive, she said to Duncan, "She just left me a message that morning, while I was still sleeping. It must have been after you left for your hike." Standing there with her arms tight by her sides probably made her look defensive too, so she sat down next to Dyson, leaving as much space as possible between them.

"But you never said?" Duncan said, perching on the arm of the sofa. His eyes were confused behind his glasses.

"I forgot," Grace said. "I only remembered later, and then it didn't seem relevant."

"But even after we found her?"

"Then it didn't matter," Grace said, pressing her palms against the nubbly fabric of the sofa.

Duncan seemed to notice that the two men were watching them. He shrugged, although he was still frowning.

"What exactly did the message say, Dr. McCloud?" Dyson said.

Grace could feel her heart begin to pound hard. She wondered if they could hear it. She had never been good at lying outright. "I don't remember the exact wording. Something like she wanted to see me and meet Duncan." She leaned forward to straighten the *New Yorker* magazines lying on the coffee table.

"There was nothing else? No reason given?"

Grace shook her head, trying to push Angie's words out of her mind. *How you both feel.* "I already told Detective Mortensen all this," she said. She tried to still her thoughts. Why did they care? Had they found out something?

"We are verifying some information," Dyson said, rubbing his hands together. Grace breathed deep, trying to focus on the chafing sound his hands made.

"Is this about Angie's death? Was it not a heart attack after all?" Duncan said, looking from Dyson to Mortensen.

"It was ruled a heart attack," Dyson said. His knuckles popped softly as he cracked them.

"Marla said you weren't dealing with Angie's case anymore," Grace said to Mortensen, hoping to divert the conversation.

Mortensen glanced at Dyson, who shook his head slightly.

"Ms. Osborne herself may have been investigating a death," Mortensen said. "That is what we are looking into at present."

"The hit and run?" Grace said. The image of the lilies tied to the tree flashed back to her.

"Huh?" Duncan said. "What hit and run?"

"Mrs. Muller contacted us this afternoon," Mortensen said. He balanced the notebook on his knee and smoothed the page with his pen. "She mentioned you went along to Ms. Costa's apartment."

"I was just starting to tell you," Grace said to Duncan. "Marla and I went to look for a friend of Angie's, but we found out she had died in a hit-and-run accident."

Duncan's frown changed to an expression of horror. He slid off the sofa arm. "That's terrible. But I don't get what that has to do with—"

"Can you tell us what you found out?" Dyson said, massaging one palm with the other.

"About Minowa Costa?" Grace said, relieved to have the focus shifted.

After she'd recounted what had happened at the apartment in Newark, Mortensen leafed through the tiny pages of his notebook. "You mentioned, Dr. McCloud, that you thought it was odd that Ms. Osborne had called you?"

Her heart began to race again. She took in a slow breath. "Yes, because I hadn't been in touch with her."

"The last time was twelve years ago, you said?"

Duncan turned to her. "No, she didn't come to the wedding, remember? So it must have been longer, in high school?"

"I thought I told you . . . I ran into her twelve years ago, in Chicago. Before the wedding. Sometime in the summer, during those three months . . ." Grace met his eyes briefly. He was looking puzzled. She plumped the embroidered pillow lying under her arm and addressed Mortensen. "But it was just a brief conversation. We didn't stay in touch at all. That's why I thought it was odd that she called me. I think probably she was just reconnecting with everyone. She must have called everyone else who came to the reunion, or at least the ones she hadn't seen for a while."

Mortensen's lips tightened. He looked again at his notepad. "Did she say anything at all that was unusual? Something about what she was working on?"

Grace wished she could slow the racing of her heart. "Nothing like that," she said. "Just that she wanted to meet, to talk. The message kept cutting out. I couldn't make out most of it. Just words here and there." She wondered if she should just get up, signal an end to the conversation. But that would seem uncooperative.

"What were the words?" Dyson said. Was there a sarcastic edge to his voice?

Sure Duncan knows. That was a natural assumption for Angie to make. "She mentioned the name of a bar. Where I ran into her. Maybe she was referring to something we talked about back then." Seeing Dyson's expectant expression, she added, "I don't remember much about that conversation. Just personal stuff. About our lives. It was so long ago."

"What was the bar?" Dyson said.

"Sinners," Grace said.

"In Palmer Square?" Duncan said.

Grace nodded. "What does this have to do with Internal Affairs?" she said to Dyson.

Mortensen and Dyson exchanged glances again. Then Dyson said, with a hint of humor, "That has to do with the department. We aren't called Internal Affairs for nothing."

He rose to his feet. Mortensen followed suit, unraveling his immense length.

"Thank you for your time, Dr. McCloud," he said, tucking his notebook into his pocket.

13

Duncan

Wednesday

"There are several hours left of this segment," Derek Weinberg said, when Duncan paused the film after only a few minutes.

They'd been watching the film in Duncan's office, on a large screen Geri had brought in on a rolling cart. On the screen, an *adura* dressed in a spotless white bodice and sarong was frozen in middance, one knee raised, his hands held high, a frill of crimson, white, and black cloth binding his waist. Silver bangles were slipping down his dark, wiry arms, and a necklace with an ornate pendant was swinging across his chest. His eyes glared in his white-powdered face, beneath an elaborate headdress made of coconut leaves and richly colored cloth. Plumes of incense were shooting from a brazier nearby. Other men in bulky silver jewelry and elaborate red costumes were frozen with muscled biceps gleaming and hands poised over their drums. Behind the exorcist, a woman in white, obviously the patient, reclined against a pile of pillows, the whites of her eyes wild and bright against the dark skin of her face. A lily leaf, a coconut, and an iron-ringed wooden pestle were arrayed before her, for protection from demons. The scene was lit by flaring torches, and oil lamps glowed a feeble yellow near them.

"This is part of the midnight watch," Duncan said. "There should be an evening watch before this, and a morning watch after. Do you have those?"

"We have all three parts for each ceremony," Carson Lacey said. He gulped from his coffee cup with an audible slurp. He had been introduced to Duncan as the research coordinator. He was a pasty-skinned man in his midthirties, with a striking cauliflower ear and bulging green eyes that were accentuated by a tendency to stare. His manner was oddly direct, which had made the past half hour of intermittent conversation uncomfortable for Duncan.

"So you can tell which part this was just from watching this," Weinberg said. He seemed impressed. "That's a good sign."

"Sure," Duncan said. "I've seen a lot of these ceremonies. So this was an actual patient? I mean, were the subjects ill in all the ceremonies you studied?"

"Obviously, they had complaints of different kinds. Otherwise why would they have gone for this . . . this?" Lacey had a low opinion of the ceremonies, Duncan could tell. Even during the few minutes they had been watching the video, his contempt had been evident in his snickers and the derisive remarks he'd made about the exorcist's chants.

"What conditions did they have?"

"They were all different," Lacey said. "I don't think you should know the details before you see the videos. It might bias your view."

Duncan wondered what Lacey's qualifications were. He seemed to have a science background. Did he have a graduate degree?

"Carson's right," Weinberg said. "But we did see a difference between the ones who got the blocker and those who didn't, after the ceremonies."

"So just to be clear . . . No one was given Symb86?"

"Correct," Weinberg said. "We were trying to confirm that Symb86 has the same effects on the body as the ceremony. Both groups had the ceremony, and neither got Symb86. One group got a Symb86 blocker—which, as I said, is a drug that neutralizes Symb86, prevents it from having any effects on the body. The blocker prevented the ceremony from having any effects on the body just like it prevents Symb86 from having any effects, so that gives us evidence that the ceremony and Symb86 operate on the same biological pathways."

"How did you manage to give patients a blocker?" Duncan said. "This was a pill that blocks Symb86?"

"Of course it was a pill," Lacey said. "And there was no question of managing to. The patients agreed to take the blocker." He was sitting with his legs spread wide, his feet planted firmly on the flame-colored streaks that ran across the black-and-white rug.

"We told them it was like a vitamin. Obviously, they couldn't be told that the blocker could stop the ceremony from working. They were properly compensated, of course," Weinberg said. "We worked through locals. They followed standard ethical procedure."

Weinberg poured another cup of coffee from the urn Geri had placed on the coffee table. They had turned the lights off in the room to see the video better, and the dark furnishings seemed more somber. Duncan wondered if he should ask how much money the patients had got for agreeing to take the blocker. "Ethically . . . if the ceremony didn't work, isn't that a problem for the patient?" he said.

"We paid for them to have the ceremony done again," Weinberg said, pushing his thick hair back from his forehead. "Without the blocker. A pretty good deal for them, I'd say."

"How do you know if they did or didn't improve?" Duncan said.

Lacey's protruding eyes fixed on Duncan. "The patients were assessed before and after the rituals. Physical exams, interviews with the patients and families." He said it snappily, as if Duncan had attacked him in some way.

"So if the rituals are all the same, but only the ones who didn't get the blocker improved, then that means Symb86 works the same way the ritual does. Hmm. Okay."

"Right, as I said, that's where you come in," Weinberg said. He had unbuttoned the sleeves of his white shirt. Now he folded them back, exposing the weathered skin of his wrists. "We want you to look closely at the videos and compare them. Identify the key steps. Code them as being present or absent."

"But the problem is . . ." Duncan paused and took a breath, making an effort to tamp down his rising frustration. "As I said before, Derek, there's really no way to tell whether the rituals are the same across the board. There are so many specific details that are going to vary from instance to instance. The space it happened in, the decorations, the colors, the way the patient reacts, how the exorcists respond, the audience. These aren't things that can be measured, you know."

"Anything that's real can be measured," Lacey said. He poured himself more coffee.

"That's one perspective," Duncan said, trying not to let his irritation show. "And a particularly narrow one, I would say."

"All of these had the same mumbo jumbo," Lacey said.

Was this guy for real? "So you've already seen them all?"

"I was there at the recordings," Lacey said. "I told you I coordinated the Sri Lankan sessions." There was an edge to his voice, as if Duncan had slighted him in some way again.

"I didn't realize you were actually on-site," Duncan said. How could this guy have been there? He shuddered, imagining Lacey sitting, sneering and smirking, in the crowded scene of an exorcism. How many people he must have insulted with his attitude.

"How would I have had them recorded properly otherwise?" Lacey said. He slurped again from his cup.

"Carson oversaw the experimental setup," Weinberg said. He didn't seem to have noticed anything amiss in Lacey's manner.

"You worked with Frank Salgado?" Duncan said.

Lacey recoiled. "You knew him?"

Duncan nodded, watching him.

"He got the locals involved. Thought he knew everything," Lacey said. *Ah,* Duncan thought. He'd had some conflict with Salgado. Salgado wouldn't have put up with his supercilious attitude.

"We are very sorry to have lost Frank," Weinberg said, looking pointedly at Lacey.

"He's dead," Lacey said, as if conceding. "I was there for two months," he went on. "The team had already been set up by the locals. But someone had to be there to manage everything. Nothing would have got done otherwise." He emitted a short bark that could have been a laugh. "Anything goes there. Third world science." His lip curled in a sneer. "You've been there. You know how it is."

The best approach would be to pretend not to notice the guy's attitude, Duncan thought. "Yes, I know some excellent scholars there," he said. He took off his glasses and polished them on a napkin. "I lived there for months at a stretch, back when I was doing my doctoral work. And my wife is Sri Lankan. A geneticist, actually."

Lacey's green gaze didn't even flicker. "She was trained here then, obviously. But two of the people I worked with had degrees from the University of London, and they still believed in the mumbo jumbo. Spirits and magic. Salgado was no better." He let out another bark of a laugh. "One fellow, a doctor at the University of Colombo, told me some story about how he had once seen a table running down the street. An enchanted table, he said. The owner of the table was running behind it was what he said."

"People believe different things there," Duncan said, trying not to sound defensive. "Why not? Different cultures, different beliefs. Here, we believe drugs work even when they don't. Not much different from believing in a running table."

Lacey's mouth had dropped open a little. With the bulging eyes, he looked like a frog, Duncan thought.

Weinberg closed the binder he'd been consulting and set it on the coffee table. "Duncan here is proud to be a nonscientist," he said to

Lacey, winking. "We need all kinds on our team. That's why his expertise is so valuable. He sees what we don't see. What other cultures value. The emic perspective, isn't that what you anthropologists call it?"

"I just accept that there are other perspectives than our own," Duncan said, shrugging.

Lacey barked again.

Weinberg glanced at him, then tapped the binder. "Okay, so are there any other questions you want to ask Carson before he leaves? The experiment design is clear? Not that you really need to know much about that. Just the basics should give you an idea of why what you're doing is important."

"I think I've got the picture," Duncan said. *You're trying to boil down something as mysterious as belief, and something as complex as ritual, into a set of codes,* he thought. It would be futile. But he only had to do what interested him, to observe. If Cinasat had really done as many research studies as Weinberg had claimed, and they had found that Symb86 worked, this study was only going to be confirmatory, anyway.

"Just to reiterate," Duncan said. "This all depends on the level of detail in the film. It's not like being there. I won't be able to see some features. So this will really be a very basic comparison, which may not be useful because the ceremonies are so incredibly detailed. The requirements are minute, you know. For example, the demon palace—the place to which the demon is confined after it is summoned—has to be constructed out of very specific materials. I can't see that. The offering cup has to contain five metals—gold, silver, copper, iron, and lead. I can't see that. The food offered has to include—"

"We don't care about all that," Lacey said. "The patient isn't going to notice all that, so how could it possibly have an effect?"

"The ceremony wouldn't be a real ceremony if it didn't follow the ceremonial rules," Duncan said.

"It's not like demons were really summoned and banished," Lacey said, his lip curled.

"What Carson means," Weinberg said, "is that we need a broad idea of the similarity. Enough to describe in a paper. All we need to do is generate a table, outlining the steps, and state whether each of the steps is present in both ceremonies."

"You don't seem to understand," Duncan said. "These aren't just steps. You can see, these are more than twelve hours long. They are incredibly intense theatrical events. The space is elaborately decorated, and the costumes are just magnificent. There's comedy and music and chanting. Drums beating, bells jingling, feet pounding, dancers whirling around like demons are after them." He directed his eyes at Lacey, trying to keep his face neutral. "There's a certain atmosphere. Incense smoking, lamps burning, torches heating the place up. The dancers, the drummers, the spectators, the patient—they're all in a trance. What you're asking me to do is boil this all down into a series of steps?"

Lacey snorted and stood up.

"I understand it won't be a complete representation, from your point of view," Weinberg said. "But for our purposes, a series of steps is sufficient."

Lacey jerked his head in what could have been a nod and moved toward the door.

After he had left, Weinberg picked up the binder on the coffee table and put it into his briefcase. "He's very efficient," he said. "A bit brusque, but he knows what he's doing. You can contact him if you have any questions while you're going through the videos."

"What's the time frame on this?" Duncan looked up as a quick buzzing near the door caught his attention.

"Identify the key elements as soon as you can. We need to get this paper out. Time is short. Maybe in the next two weeks?"

"That's much sooner than I had expected," Duncan said. The buzzing sounded again, and a fly zipped past them. Duncan swiped at it and missed.

"Sometimes we end up working overtime," Weinberg said. "But that only happens once in a while." He handed Duncan a thumb drive. "Copies of the films," he said. "They're on our server, but in case you want to work on them at home. But remember the nondisclosure agreement extends to family members and spouses. All our data are proprietary, and that includes the films. Not even your wife can see these." He got to his feet.

The irritating buzzing started up again, low down by the coffee table.

"You need a swatter," Weinberg said, his smile wry. He picked up his briefcase.

"Actually, there's something I've been meaning to ask you," Duncan said. He felt awkward about asking, but it had been on his mind. "About something you mentioned yesterday." He paused. Was this a good idea? Was he just going to seem paranoid?

"Shoot," Weinberg said.

"Well, you said that Symb86 had been shown to work for several conditions. And you mentioned some. I just wondered, did you just mention a few specific ones, or is that the whole list of conditions it works for?"

"Ah, you mean the CFS and the infertility." Weinberg smiled, a little sarcastically, at Duncan's consternation. "I should have been clearer. Yes, we know about your mother and your wife."

Duncan searched for words. *How baldly the man put it,* he thought. As if it weren't a problem that he knew. And was it? Why did it bother him?

"Cinasat always checks out the people they hire," Weinberg said. "And frankly, the fact that you might be interested in finding ways to address those two conditions made you an especially good candidate for the job. Quite apart from your scholarly qualifications, of course, which were judged to be stellar too." This he said rather sourly, Duncan thought. "Cinasat likes motivated employees."

"So they did some sort of background check."

"It probably wasn't that difficult. Medical records, social media . . ."

"Medical records? HIPAA laws," Duncan said.

"There are ways. I don't know what they are," Weinberg said. "But is it a problem that they know? Wouldn't you like to be on the front end of getting the drug? Once safety has been demonstrated, of course?"

"Well, if it worked, yes," Duncan said. "But what kind of infertility did it work on?"

"I'd have to check the details on the patient data," Weinberg said. "But as I recall, all the infertility cases were of the nonspecific variety. The patients and their partners had all undergone tests, nothing was found to be amiss, but they just couldn't carry a pregnancy to term."

Like Grace, Duncan thought.

"A good incentive for you to respect your nondisclosure agreement," Weinberg said, as if he'd read Duncan's mind. "Who knows, maybe the drug will work best for your wife if she comes to it fresh, with no thoughts about the way it was tested, however rigorous those ways were. If she just takes the drug and is confident that it works. No nocebo effects."

Had he ruined the drug's potential effect by discussing it with Grace? Duncan wished he had kept it to himself. But he hadn't said much, and most of it had been hopeful. From now on, if he had any doubts, he would keep them to himself, he thought.

14

GRACE

Wednesday

"It's my fault for agreeing to go looking for that woman," Grace said, her hand clenching around the phone. "That must have really stressed you out."

"I had already decided to go," Marla said. "I would have gone even without you. Anyway, who could have guessed that she'd died?"

Marla sounded like she was getting upset again, Grace thought. She should just hang up and not compound the situation. "Do you have to go back to the clinic?" she asked.

"Jeez, I hope not," Marla said. "They wanted me to rest, but the nurses kept poking and prodding me all night. I told them my first two pregnancies were easy, and this one was going to be fine. But they're taking extra precautions because of my age. Apparently premature contractions are riskier for older women. Did you know we're older women?" There was an effort at a giggle, but she sounded nervous.

Grace heard Karl's voice in the background, calling out, "Marla, who are you calling?"

"Uh-oh," Marla said, sighing. "It's the rest police. He's been harping at me. He wants me to lie down and watch movies all day. For the next two months."

After hanging up, Grace sat down in the small study off the living room, watching the second hand trudge across the white face of the desk clock. All morning, she had been struggling with the niggling worry that she might need to tell the police more about Angie's voice-mail message. They had seemed so suspicious. Could she explain her personal reasons, persuade them that it had nothing to do with Minowa Costa or any story Angie had been writing? Thank God Duncan had been so preoccupied with his own work. After the police left the night before, he had gone back to reading the papers he had brought home, and he had rushed off to work this morning when she was still in the shower. What if she told the police about the message and they told him about its content? She blenched at the thought of his reaction if he found out the whole story. It would be worse if he heard from someone else. Should she just tell him? She couldn't bear to think about it. She had to focus on her work, she thought. Maybe work from home today.

When she opened her university email, the first message in her inbox caught her eye. It had been sent less than an hour ago. The subject line read, *The real reason St. Casilda fired Dr. McCloud.* She blinked, frowning. What was this? The sender was DOG2318@gmail.com.

The message was short. It said, *If you want to find out, meet me at Habib's Café, 119 Springfield Ave, Paterson. 11 a.m. today. Don't tell your husband.* It was unsigned.

It was much too specific to be spam. She emailed back. *Who are you? How did you get my email address?*

She was wondering whether she had been too hasty when a response came back. *Details when we meet. Don't tell your husband. Come alone.* Who was this?

She wrote back, *I can't meet you if I don't know who you are.*

The response was almost immediate. *I know who you are. 11 a.m., Habib's.*

Grace shivered. There was something ominous about that. *I know who you are.* What did it mean? Did it simply mean the person would recognize her? This had to be someone who worked at St. Casilda. Someone who had inside information about the firing decision. A member of the administrative staff? Somehow the email didn't sound like one a faculty member would send. Why should she not tell Duncan if this was about his layoff? It didn't make sense.

St. Casilda's financial problems hadn't been a secret, but the termination letter had come out of the blue, in a mauve envelope carrying the college letterhead. As Duncan read it, his face had gone from confusion to shock. She'd never had the chance to read the letter. He'd ripped it up, flung it in the trash. It was only later, after the news had sunk in, that he had begun asking why. Nobody—not Grace nor his colleagues—could understand why he had been the one to be laid off. His publication record had been unusually good, and he had rave reviews from his students. Even a faculty excellence award the year before. Grace thought that what had been hardest for Duncan was not knowing why he had been singled out to lessen St. Casilda's financial burden.

She read the emails again. Could this person really know something? There would be no harm in going to meet the person, she decided. If she left soon, she would get to Paterson in time.

By a quarter to eleven, her GPS had brought her to a busy part of Paterson. She parked by a shop that sold discount picture frames and set out on foot to the intersection of Springfield Avenue. After turning down the street, she noticed that the area was beginning to look less salutary. Dirty paper cups and empty cigarette packets littered the curb, and shuttered storefronts lurked among shops with dusty awnings, some with "For Lease" scrawled across their front windows.

There weren't many pedestrians about here. Grace hurried across the cracked bricks of the sidewalk, looking around nervously. She passed a trio of young men in hooded sweatshirts hunched near the open doors of an old brown convertible, and then a small unpaved lot choked with weeds, hemmed by a chicken wire fence. Ahead, across a narrow side street, next to a wall defaced with thick swirls of graffiti, she could see a lurid awning emblazoned with the words HABIB'S CAFÉ SHISH KEBABS. She quickened her pace, clutching her purse to her hip.

A sudden burst of sound erupted as a black SUV revved past her. Grace jumped back, startled. The SUV shot forward, and she saw, to her horror, that a black gun was pointing out of the window. Three loud bangs rang out. Glass exploded. Screams pierced the air. Grace froze, an involuntary scream leaving her lips. The SUV zoomed away down the next side street. People poured out of nearby stores. The young men who had been loitering near the convertible rushed past Grace, running toward Habib's, shouting.

Grace realized she was muttering, "Oh my God, oh my God." She stood there, wondering what to do, then ran toward Habib's too. People were pressing toward the doorway. Bits of jagged glass were all that was left of the front window. Shards were strewn across the curb.

"Was anyone hurt?" Grace's voice was lost in the clamor of people shouting and swearing. She pressed forward, but waving arms and thronging bodies blocked her passage.

The shrill sound of sirens shattered the air as two police cars sped forward, skidding across the street. Four uniformed officers rushed out of the vehicles, shouting, "Back, back! Everyone get back." They waved people away from Habib's, clearing a path to the door. Inside, people were shouting. Grace caught a glimpse of toppled chairs and tables, evidently the result of diners having leapt away from the window. No one was seated, but a small group of people was clustered near the back.

"Anyone get a license plate?" one officer shouted.

"No, man. It was too quick," one man said.

"Black Ford SUV," a woman yelled. "Went that way."

Others started chiming in.

"Coming here now doing no good, yo!"

"Where you people when we need you?"

People were getting heated, shouting.

Someone was saying something about gang revenge.

"Move away! Go back to your business! Nothing to see here," one officer said. People started to trickle away, chattering loudly among themselves.

"I was supposed to meet someone for lunch," Grace said to the officer who was posted at the door.

"No one's going in here," the officer said, his tone dismissive. People were yelling inside. He turned away to talk to the restaurant owner, who was gesticulating angrily, shouting in heavily accented English. Grace could only catch a few words: *terrorists, business, America.*

She trudged back down the street. People were still clustered in shop doorways. "Do you know if anyone was hurt?" Grace asked a woman with beaded braids who had emerged from a hair salon.

"Nah," the woman said, her hands on her hips. "No ambulance." She shook her head. "Haven't had a drive-by around here for months. And that Habib's never had a problem."

Grace returned to her car, locked the doors, and leaned her head back, breathing deep. She could have been sitting in there. She could have been an accidental victim, she thought, relief slumping her shoulders.

15

DUNCAN

Thursday

Duncan stepped back to admire the two pictures he had just hung. They were not new drawings—he had not seen Grace draw anything for months.

He turned at a knock on the door. To his surprise, it was Hammond. "I didn't think anyone else would be in yet," Duncan said.

"We start early," Hammond said, a smile hovering on his pale lips. Everyone around here dressed so formally, Duncan thought. Ah, for the casual academic life. He brushed the thought aside. He was lucky to have this job, with all its perks on top of the chance to make a real difference in people's lives.

"I don't usually make it to this wing," Hammond said, straightening the knot of his tie. It was a plain charcoal silk, stark against the white of his shirt. "But today I have a meeting here. Thought I'd drop by. See how you're doing." He cast his eyes from the hammer and nails on the desk to the pictures on the wall. "Decorating." He adjusted the collar of his shirt. "No devil masks?"

No sense in getting annoyed at ignorance, Duncan thought. "Well, those aren't really for decoration," he said, keeping his face impassive. He realized that sounded too critical when there were masks hanging in

Hammond's study and in the Cinasat lobby, so he added, "Because of my work . . . I mean, I think of them more as ritual objects."

He saw Hammond's lips tighten. To change the subject, he pointed at the pictures he had just hung. "Grace did those," he said, inching one upward. The sketches were intricately drawn, in black ink. "When we were out in the Catskills last year."

"An artist," Hammond said, moving closer. His steps were small and neat like the rest of him, his shiny wing tips tapping on the hardwood floor. "Like my wife."

Not much like Ada, Duncan thought, but he only said, "Grace doesn't draw much, actually. Her lab consumes most of her time—she's a biologist. A tenured professor at Dumont University."

Hammond nodded, and Duncan realized that he probably already knew what Grace did.

Hammond reached out to nudge one frame down, apparently dissatisfied with its alignment. "I wonder . . . Do any of her colleagues work for the pharmaceutical industry? One of our competitors, perhaps?"

"I don't think so," Duncan said. "At least, she's never mentioned it."

Evidently responding to his puzzled look, Hammond said, "Faculty often get industry grants for research, as you know. Biologists, particularly. Just a matter of curiosity." He cocked his head, gazing at the pictures. "She's pleased about your new job, I take it?"

"She must be," Duncan said, smiling. "It's not easy to tear her away from her lab, but she went out and bought these frames yesterday, just so I could put the pictures up." He shook his head. "Apparently almost got shot at in the process."

Hammond's scanty eyebrows rose. "Shot?"

"In Paterson. She saw a drive-by shooting,"

"Paterson's not where I'd choose to go for picture frames," Hammond said, stroking the thin line of hair along his jaw with two precise fingers.

You wouldn't go anywhere for picture frames, Duncan thought. The frames around the pictures at Hammond's house had surely not been bought at a frame shop. The pictures themselves had probably cost many tens of thousands of dollars. At least.

"Grace does things her way," Duncan said, shrugging.

"You are close to your wife," Hammond said, his eyes narrowed a little.

Duncan nodded, trying not to show his discomfort. An oddly personal thing for an employer to say to a new employee. There was no way he was going to get into his marital tensions with this man.

"We like that," Hammond said, smoothing his tie. Duncan could see the blue veins that snaked under the thin skin of his hands. "It fits our company philosophy. We believe loyal families make dedicated employees." When Duncan looked at him questioningly, he continued, "When spouses understand that jobs benefit the whole family, employees have more leeway. More support to do their jobs."

"Oh, I think Grace does understand that," Duncan said. "I don't have any worries on that score."

16

GRACE

Thursday

Lydia Delgado stuck her head through the doorway of Grace's office. She was sporting little hoop earrings with beads in them that matched her peach linen shirt. How did she find the time to coordinate her accessories even at exam time, Grace thought.

"How I love grading," Lydia said, indicating the uneven stack of papers on her arm. She groaned. "Is yours done?"

Grace nodded. "But my grant application's due next week," she said. "Still have the analysis to do for that last experiment. Not a chance of getting the grant without those results."

"I thought you did the grant last week," Lydia said.

Grace didn't want to say anything to Lydia about the events of the past few days. There was already too much to think about, and it was interfering with her work. Time to buckle down and get the grant application finished.

After Lydia left, she shut the door. She could usually count on quiet, except for the intermittent clamor from the boiler room by the stairwell. Her office, which adjoined her lab, was the last in the long west-side corridor on the fourth floor of Gannon Hall. When Duncan had worked at St. Casilda College, the view out of her single tall window had been comforting, assurance that her job was not that much better than his. It was a view he would have disliked having, with no trees in sight.

She checked her email. Still no response from whoever it was that had asked to meet in Paterson. She wondered again if the person had got shot. On impulse, she looked up Habib's Café online and dialed the number listed.

After three rings, a thickly accented voice said abruptly, "Habib's, we're closed." There were thumping sounds in the background, other voices calling out in what sounded like Arabic.

"Did anyone get hurt yesterday?"

A pause, and then the voice said sharply, "Who is this?"

"I just . . . I was supposed to meet someone there yesterday, and then there was the shooting," Grace said. "I was just wondering . . . Was anyone shot?"

"No one shot," the voice said. "Tomorrow we open. You come back then." The phone slammed down.

Maybe the whole thing had been a hoax, Grace thought. It was good that she hadn't bothered Duncan with the real reason she'd gone to Paterson. She needed to put these distractions aside. She was about to call Gigi, the graduate student who had carried out the last experiment, when the phone rang.

It had to be Gigi with the information she had requested. But when she picked up the phone, it was Mo's voice she heard.

"You busy? Do you have a minute to talk?"

He had never called her at work before. He sounded pressured, she thought. "Is everything okay?"

"I went to the funeral yesterday," Mo said abruptly.

"I know it hit you really hard. Are you doing alright?"

"It's . . . strange. It's not like I saw her a lot anymore. But she was so much a part of my past . . . I feel like my past died with her. That sounds crazy, I know."

"You two were so close," Grace said. "It's natural you'd feel like that." She could hear the pain in his voice. She wondered why he was calling her. Marla had known Angie so much better than she had. "Did you talk to Marla after you got back?"

"I called, and Karl told me about the bed rest. I didn't want to upset her more." There was a pause, and then, "Something came up that I want to ask you about. I can't get it out of my head. Something odd."

"Odd how?" Grace felt her anxiety return. Had Mortensen told him about the phone call? She should have said something to him. "Something to do with Angie?"

"Well, after the funeral, there was a gathering at her parents' place in Houston . . . Katherine, her mom, wasn't holding up too well. I hadn't seen her for years, but she remembered me pretty well. From when Angie and I were going out." Grace heard his voice quaver a little. Poor Mo. Maybe he had never really got over Angie. "We were talking about the old days, and she took me upstairs to Angie's room. Apparently Angie had visited just three days before she died. A belated birthday celebration. Katherine blames herself. Angie had heartburn the night she left, after dinner, and Katherine had just given her Tums. Now Katherine thinks maybe it wasn't heartburn. A prelude to this heart attack, she thinks."

"How awful. But how could she have known?"

"That's what I said," Mo said. "Angie had heartburn, even in the old days. Spicy food did that to her. I told Katherine, but she kept going on about it. She blames herself for not remembering about the heart attack risk after the hysterectomy."

"But I wouldn't say that was odd, Mo. I can see how her mom would feel that way." Why would he call to tell her about this? She didn't even know Katherine.

"That's not what was odd. I was getting to that. Katherine was showing me stuff in Angie's room: KIS knickknacks, a box full of devil masks from Sri Lanka, old articles she had written. Damn sad, the way they still had her room for whenever she came to visit. I wanted some pictures of her. We were looking through a pile of photos in there. I think she had taken them with her phone and printed them out right there." Again his voice wavered. "There was a selfie Angie had taken with some other woman. You could tell it was inside the Cinasat building lobby because of the logo in the background. I took it and a few others. Later on, when Katherine and I were talking to Bent, I showed the picture to him—the one with Angie and the other woman in the Cinasat building. He said it must have been taken the last time she came to see him in Jersey. He couldn't remember when, he said. I said it looked really recent, but he insisted it was from months ago. He thought at least six months. He hadn't seen her for months before the reunion, he said."

Grace waited for him to go on, but when the silence lengthened, she said, "And so, what was the odd thing that happened?"

"Well, the thing is, I could tell the picture had been taken less than a week before she died."

"How could you tell that? Haircut?"

"She's had the same hairstyle for years. But in the picture she's wearing a pendant that I sent her. For her birthday. That was six days before she died."

"Hmm." It didn't have to be anything more than dedication to an old friendship, Grace thought. If she were a better friend, she would be sending Marla a little birthday present every year. "So the odd thing . . . ?"

"Just that he would say that."

He really was having a hard time, Grace thought. "Maybe Bent just forgot to mention the last time he saw her. Or maybe she went to Cinasat for something else, not to see Bent, and he didn't know she had been there."

"There is no damn way he forgot to mention. I pressed him. He was dead certain he hadn't seen her for at least six months. So the obvious answer would be that she didn't meet him when she went there, right? But the weird thing was his reaction. Shock. I thought he was just upset at seeing her face, you know, but it was almost like he was horrified. And it was odd . . . how vehement he was about her not being there recently. He brought up a mask that was in the picture. It looked like a Sri Lankan devil mask. Not one of the typical tourist ones, bigger. But similar, you know, with the bared teeth and all. Damn strange thing to put in a lobby. He said a workman had accidentally knocked it down and broken it months ago. He said it had been replaced with a different mask. That was how he could tell the picture wasn't recent, he said."

"Okay, then maybe it wasn't. It's probably an older picture, Mo. Lots of pendants might have looked like the one you sent her."

"Not this pendant, Grace." There was a pause, and then he cleared his throat. "Look, let me scan the picture and email it to you, okay? It'll just take a second."

Grace set down the phone and opened her email. She saw that a message from Gigi had just arrived, with an attachment showing the new analysis. She skimmed the message and was about to write back when a ding alerted her to the arrival of Mo's email.

In the picture Mo had sent, Angie was staring into the camera, unsmiling, her face close to that of another, younger, plumper woman. The Cinasat logo was partially visible on the wall in the background. Grace could see the faint sagging of the skin on Angie's cheeks, the crookedness of one eyebrow, the folds of her neck. Seeing her up close, even in partial view, made Grace shudder. How tangible she seemed. And now she was gone. The hollow of her neck, clearly visible there, would have had a pulse. Then, just like that, it had stopped, her hopes stalled, her work unfinished. The nagging question rose again at the back of Grace's mind. Why had Angie wanted to talk about what had happened, so out of the blue? She would have to get used to the idea that she would never know. She pushed the thought away and took a closer look at the picture.

A pendant was dangling from a thin silver chain around Angie's neck. It was an *araliya* leaf, its outline and veins intricately wrought in silver. At the top, where the stem might have oozed a drop of milky fluid, was a small infinity symbol enclosing two white stones that could have been diamonds. *A beautiful piece, though a little off-kilter,* Grace thought as she picked up the phone.

"It's gorgeous, that pendant," she said. "Where did you get it?"

"I had it custom made," Mo said. Grace heard embarrassment in his voice. "Remember that araliya tree in Kandy—the one at the far end of the field, near the pond? It was where we hung out. This was to remind her of the things we talked about back then."

This couldn't just be friendship. What about his marital situation? Grace knew his wife, Mariam. She worked for a nonprofit. Mariam was a staunch feminist. A forceful woman with very definite ideas. Surely she didn't know about Mo giving an old school friend a custom-made, and possibly very expensive, piece of jewelry. What would she have said to that, especially when they had financial troubles? At the reunion, the night before Angie died, Mo had been depressed about some property lease of his company's that was going to be discontinued. He'd said he was expecting a big financial loss.

"I know what you're probably thinking," Mo said. "But there was nothing going on between us. Not anymore."

Grace wanted to believe him, but something didn't seem right. There was something in his tone. Had something been going on during his marriage?

"The pendant—I told her to keep it between the two of us," Mo said. "Otherwise everyone would have thought something was still going on. That's why I couldn't just tell Bent that I knew the photo was recent."

Did Mo know Angie had been seeing Bent twelve years ago? She tried to remember when Mo had got married. At least sixteen years must have passed since his wedding. She'd been at it. His hair had still been thick then. "Bent was probably just remembering another time she came by," Grace said. "Why would he lie about it? There must be a good explanation. Probably she was there recently and he didn't know?"

"Why would she have gone there and not met up with him? And why would he say the thing about the mask? He was so vehement about it, Grace. Protesting too much. It was odd."

How many times he'd said it was odd, Grace thought. He was making such a big deal out of this. She looked again at the photo. In the background, part of a sign was visible, cut off in midword: **OUR MUL**. Underneath it, she could see the devil mask Mo had mentioned. It was large enough to be a real mask, not one of the small gaudily painted curios that were sold to tourists all over Sri Lanka. Even from a distance, she could tell it was intricately carved. Huge black eyes bulged in a green-painted face. Thick crimson lips surrounded bared, pointed white teeth and two downward-pointing tusks. A bright-red tongue hung out of its mouth. A cobra hood, gold and green, reared above its eyes, and two coiled cobras formed menacing ears on either side. Certainly an odd thing to put in a lobby, but to Hammond or Bent, whoever had had it put up, it was obviously just a decoration. "He was probably just trying to help, Mo," she said.

"But I'm telling you, Grace. This picture was taken recently. So why did he keep saying this mask was destroyed months ago? It doesn't make sense." There was a long breath, and then, "Look, I'm sorry. I know I'm going on about this. But I can't get it out of my mind."

"I think," Grace said gently, "that Angie probably went to Cinasat recently, but she didn't meet up with Bent. It's a huge building." She had been there only once, with Duncan. They had driven there when he had got the call from the recruiter, to see the location, to try to get a sense of the company. She had not gone inside the building yet. "There are three wings and lots of divisions. Maybe she went to see someone else. Bent probably didn't know she was there. He's probably misremembering about the mask. Maybe the new one looks similar, and he got confused.

Who remembers things in a lobby anyway? I can't remember the decor in the lobby of my own building."

"Well, that's actually why I called you. I thought you could show Duncan the picture and ask him if he recognizes that mask. Didn't he just start this week at Cinasat? If he recognizes it, then it's a recent picture."

"He said there was a Sri Lankan mask in the lobby, but he said it was an unusual one. He may not remember which one he saw. We are talking about a guy who can't remember where he put his keys. It's worse when he's in the thick of work. Anyway, I don't know what it would prove if he remembers it. Or if he doesn't. Why does it matter exactly?"

"I don't know. Maybe it's just for my own peace of mind. Could you please just ask him?"

"Fine. And I'm sorry, Mo," Grace said. "I can see how hard this has been for you." She wondered if she should tell him that the police had been asking about him and his guns. But he was too distressed already. He didn't need more to worry about.

"I'm coming to Jersey tomorrow. A meeting in Hoboken," Mo said. "Staying overnight. Can you meet up for dinner?"

"You can stay with us," Grace said. "It's been so long since you've come."

17

DUNCAN

Thursday

On the extra-large screen that had been installed for watching the videos, an adura was chanting, his voice high pitched, as he flourished a flaming taper over a clay pot of offerings. Sparks shot from a brazier of burning incense near him. A man was beating a drum feverishly in a corner, his eyes glazed and his muscles rippling. Four dancers, their bodies swathed in ornate crimson-and-white costumes, were leaping around, clearly entranced, their bangles and ankle bells jingling to the rhythm of the drum. Another man was thrusting lighted tapers into holders on a small hut made of coconut leaves, his elaborate headdress bright in the light of the flames. Duncan had watched this particular segment of the video so many times that he almost had the adura's chant memorized.

Watching the film, he could almost smell the musky sweetness of the incense. Almost feel the fire's heat. He clicked on the pause button, and the adura froze, his mask turned toward the camera. The mask, representing the demon Mahasona, was made of intricately woven coconut leaves, with protruding red lips and flaming torches forming tusks. In the background were several structures made of yellow coconut leaves. One structure bore a painting depicting the demon in his horrific power: blue-black, with a bear's head, carrying, implausibly, an elephant across his shoulders.

Duncan gulped the last of his coffee, grown cold. He took off his glasses, sighing, and rolled his head around his shoulders. His neck was stiff from craning too long at the screen. Moving around a little would help, he thought.

Pacing by the window, he saw that the cherry trees bordering the road beyond the lawn had already shed their blooms, carpeting the pavement in faded pink. The sun was lowering in the sky, the slanted sunlight glinting off the skyscrapers in the distance on the New York side of the Hudson. He wondered if Grace had left her office yet for the drive home. He was about to call her when a knock sounded on his office door, a sharp rat-a-tat.

"Yes," Duncan called.

Bent strode in.

He came up to the windows to stand beside Duncan. "Everything going fine?" He glanced back at the computer screen. "Coding coming along, yeah?"

"Sure. It's going to take a while," Duncan said. "You got back today? From the funeral?"

"Early. Been in meetings all day." Bent rubbed at his forehead with his fingers, looking out at the fallen cherry blossoms. Duncan could hear the sound his fingers made against his skin, dry and raspy. "Life goes on," he said. He pushed his hair back with a weary gesture. "Work is what saves us. That was what my grandfather always said. My father disagreed, but he didn't convince me." His eyes were on the grand vista of New York spread before them, the silver-blue might of One World Trade Center rising from the haze of smog below. "My father's dreams were small."

"Does he still work for your grandfather?"

Bent nodded. "But he wanted to be an inventor . . . he was an inventor, I suppose. He wanted to make little things. Things to make kids happy, he used to say. Toys for boys. Twirling balls on ropes, a bit like yo-yos. Peg legs for hopping, like pogo sticks. Puzzles with sliding metal balls. But he could never sell them. They weren't different enough from what was already on the market."

He moved away from the window, shaking his head, and sat down in front of the desk. "I've brought some news that may be . . . a bit of a surprise," he said. "We've had to make a change."

Duncan sat down, waiting to hear more.

Bent crossed his legs and smoothed the crease of his pants over his knee. "I was due to go to Sri Lanka in two weeks, with Janie."

"That KIS summer camp you mentioned?"

"She wants to go. She remembers the best of my stories about my KIS days." He examined his fingernails. They were well kept, with a shine to them. Duncan wondered what his toenails looked like. Grace had once said that Bent had a persistent toenail fungus. How had that come up? He couldn't remember.

Bent looked up again. "You never know what kids retain. I had plenty of complaints about my time there. My family didn't visit. The other kids were always getting food mailed to them, things we couldn't get in Sri Lanka back then: peanut butter, strawberry jam, chocolate sauce, maraschino cherries, Pringles . . . I didn't get any of that." Duncan saw a hint of sadness in his eyes. For a fleeting moment, he looked almost childlike. Then he smiled, suave once again. "But Janie doesn't remember me talking about those things." The evenness of his teeth was impressive, but Duncan remembered that Grace had said something about them too. He had a lot of fillings, she'd said, because he hadn't had much supervision in brushing his teeth when he was a kid. It was strange that he knew so much about his boss, he thought. Things that lay under the veneer.

"KIS isn't the same now, Grace says. Much more modern, from what she's seen online."

Bent nodded. "Patty—my ex-wife—approves of the summer program. A way they're courting new international students, she says."

"You're thinking of enrolling Janie there for school, then?"

"I doubt she'll want to leave her school here, but we'll have to see. Maybe she'll enjoy the summer program so much she'll be clamoring to enroll." He examined the tip of his shoe, a well-polished black loafer. "I'll be doing some work while I'm in Sri Lanka. Seeing some people in Colombo. Some of the researchers who've been working with us."

"They studied thovil? These are researchers at the University of Colombo? Who specifically? Maybe I'll know them, or Grace will."

"They didn't study the ceremonies. They were working on other research. Cinasat's done a number of other experimental trials, over a couple of years, in various locations. Some of it was done overseas, including in Sri Lanka." Bent cleared his throat. "It's easier to get the studies done quickly overseas."

"To test the drug? I didn't realize you could do trials overseas."

"Of course, everything was aboveboard, documented and so on." Bent cleared his throat again. "Anyway, a matter has come up that is of some concern to us here. Some of the studies in Sri Lanka . . . Well, it looks like there may have been some attempts to leak data."

"Leak to whom?"

"This is a proprietary project, of course," Bent said. "I can't really go into all the details. Let's just say we need to keep our data private, yeah? We disclose what we need to, to the FDA and for regulatory purposes. But some things are meant to be kept in-house." He examined his ankle, smoothing the houndstooth fabric of his sock. "We think someone may be trying to sabotage the project."

"Who? What's happened exactly?"

"Any attempt at sabotage is going to be a competitor. This drug is, as you can imagine, a major prize for any pharmaceutical company. A colossal sales opportunity." There was more than a hint of pride in his smile. "We have reason to believe another company has been developing a product along the same lines." He waved his hand dismissively. "But everything's under control. It's being taken care of on our end. We just have to make sure there are no issues in Sri Lanka."

"I'm not sure I understand," Duncan said. "Is there something I can do?"

"That's what I came to see you about. I'll need to get out there, to see what can be done. I can't afford to wait until next week. I'll have to go sooner."

"I see. You want me to take care of something here while you're gone."

"I'd like you to go along."

"Go along?"

"To Sri Lanka," Bent said. "Tomorrow."

"Whoa. Wait," Duncan said. He had only officially begun that week. He had the films to code, a paper to write in a hurry. Was Bent suggesting he drop all that? "You want me to fly to Sri Lanka tomorrow?"

"You know Sri Lanka well. So do I, obviously, but my Sinhala is terrible. Not close to your level. You'll be a big asset."

"But why go there? We could call, surely."

"This is not the kind of thing we can call about. We'll need to meet with a group of researchers there. Also technicians who don't speak English."

"There's always Skype," Duncan said. When Bent frowned, he realized he might be taking this too lightly.

"The internet connection is never reliable enough to Skype with people overseas, we find," Bent said. "And also, this matter is a bit . . . delicate."

"How is that? What will I need to do?" What was he supposed to be? An ambassador of some kind?

"We can talk more about the details later," Bent said. "The most important thing now is to make sure we make the flight."

"And this is tomorrow?"

"We're already booked. The flight leaves in the morning, 8:08," Bent said. "I've informed Janie's school that she'll have to miss her last few days of class." He rose to his feet. "Geri will make sure your laptop is set up with any files you need. You'll be getting an iPhone—also company issue. We'd like you to only communicate on that while we're away, for security. Leave your regular phone at home. All you need to do is go home, pack a bag, and get your passport. Get a good night's rest, and be at the airport by five. Security lines will be long." A faint grin appeared on his face. "Tell Grace you'll be back in a couple of weeks. I'm guessing she won't mind your being away for work."

"You didn't ask if I minded," Duncan said, trying to make his tone light. He hadn't expected to have to fly across the world at a moment's notice. There should have been some advance warning, surely. "What if I'd had some prior obligation, something I had to do on the weekend?"

"But you don't, I'm guessing, yeah?" There was an edge to Bent's voice. Duncan found it annoying. "It's the nature of the job, you could say," Bent added. Duncan thought he saw a shadow cross his face, but then he chuckled, a little dryly. "That's why our compensation packages are so good. Cinasat expects full commitment to the job."

There it was, Duncan thought. The catch he and Grace had wondered about when they found out how much the job paid. For everything there was a sacrifice. But any hardships were not only for the money, he reminded himself. It was for the drug. A drug that could change lives. Not just the lives of people he didn't know. His mother's and Grace's. His own. And really, what was the hardship here? An all-expenses-paid trip to Sri Lanka. It had been three years since he had been back there with Grace. They had talked about visiting later in the summer, but with Duncan's job starting and Grace's grant, they hadn't had time to make definite plans.

"Grace will wish she could have gone along," Duncan said. "But she's in the middle of writing a grant."

Bent shrugged at that, nodding. He picked up the small framed photo Duncan had placed on his desk. It was one Duncan had taken in the Catskills, on the only weekend Grace had been willing to take away from her lab the previous fall. In it, Grace was laughing, her eyes crinkled, her hair strikingly black against a backdrop of fiery oak leaves. "Has she been . . . How is she dealing with the weekend?"

"She's okay." Duncan remembered the police visit they'd had. "We had a visit from that detective twice. Sunday, Tuesday night. Remember Mortensen? He was asking about whether people had guns. Some concern about illegal hunting. And they seem to think Angie was investigating a story. About a hit-and-run accident . . ."

Bent turned the frame over and straightened its stand. "I heard, from Mortensen," he said. "Did they tell you what they had found out?"

Duncan shook his head. "No, but he came with another guy who said he was from Internal Affairs. No idea what that was about. They wouldn't say. They just wanted to find out what Angie was writing about."

"That's what they asked me," Bent said. "Does Grace?"

"Does she what?"

"Know what Angie was writing about? If she was."

"No, she hadn't seen Angie for years. Although apparently Angie called her on Saturday, wanting to meet up. Grace thinks just to reconnect." Every time he thought of Angie, what came to him was the image of her lying among the dead twigs, her tongue hanging out. "Such a sad thing," Duncan said, and then wondered if he should have stayed off the topic.

"Work is what saves us," Bent said. He placed the photo back on the desk and dusted off his hands. "We have to put the weekend where it belongs. Behind us." He was a lot like Grace, Duncan thought, although she would disagree. Work was everything.

The buzzing that had been irritating Duncan all day started up again. It seemed to be coming from under the desk.

"A mystery where these flies are coming from," Duncan said, swatting futilely at the air by his feet.

"Let Geri know, yeah?" Bent said. "She can have the place cleaned out while you're gone." He stepped toward the door. "Okay, off then to pack?" he said, his tone turned businesslike. "Geri will send a car to pick you up." At the door, he turned. "If anything else needs to be done this evening, I'll let you know." He added, "Janie is pleased you're coming along. She's taken a shine to you and Grace."

18

GRACE

Friday

"It's a good thing they gave you a phone," Grace said, pushing a cup toward him. "Otherwise I'd have had to spend an hour switching the cell service to get you covered overseas. Text me so I have your new number?"

Duncan gulped his coffee, standing hunched over the counter. His hair, still wet from his shower, was dripping onto his glasses. "Geri actually apologized for getting us business class seats. Because the booking is last minute, she said. Apparently Cinasat normally travels first class." He grinned at Grace's expression and swung his arms wide, theatrically. "Luxury, baby! We've made it!" He gave her a kiss, reeking of coffee, and made for the door.

It had been a long time since she'd seen him so upbeat. "I forgot to tell you," Grace said. "Mo's coming tonight. He was upset about something that happened at the funeral. No time to go into it now. I think he was blowing things out of proportion. But there was something he wanted me to ask you. Something about what the Cinasat lobby looks like."

Duncan paused on the threshold, looking confused, his wet hair gleaming under the entrance light. It was still dark out, with a bit of moon visible past the black silhouette of the oak in the driveway. The driver of the Cinasat car emerged to take Duncan's bag. "What? Okay, whatever it is, it can wait, right?"

19

DUNCAN

Friday

By the time Duncan arrived at his gate, it was boarding time. Bent was pacing by the gate, scanning the crowd impatiently. Janie, wearing a pale-green Star Wars sweatshirt and weighed down by a bulging purple backpack, was hanging on to his arm.

For the first time in Duncan's life, he was one of the first to board. He stowed his carry-on and sank into his seat, marveling at the size and softness of it, the amazing amount of legroom. There was no way he could watch any of the Cinasat videos on board privately. The thought made him happy. All that week, he had felt too busy. He needed time to relax. That was something he missed about St. Casilda. The pace there had been so much slower.

But he was lucky to have this new job, he reminded himself for the umpteenth time. He extracted his phone and took a picture of himself in his seat, grinning melodramatically, and texted it to Grace with the message: Check out this seat! Wouldn't have happened at St. Casilda. Then he saw that an email had come in from Grace. *Mo's question,* the subject line said. The body of the email said:

Mo wants to know if you've seen this mask in Cinasat lobby. Long story. Will explain later. But he really wants to know. Enjoy business class (maybe even edible food?) and call me from hotel. Remember to call Ma and Appa when you get there.

The attached picture had been taken in the main lobby at Cinasat. The silver Cinasat logo was visible on one wall. Angie's face was leaning close to that of a heavyset young woman he didn't recognize. He emailed back that he'd seen the mask, wondering why Mo cared.

Looking back, he saw that Bent and Janie were already asleep. He took off his glasses, pulled his headrest into place, and closed his eyes.

20

GRACE

Friday

Gannon Hall was always deserted in the days after the end of the spring semester. Summer classes had not yet begun, and even the anxious graduate students who slaved all year in the labs were less in evidence. Grace liked the quiet. She looked in at her lab. There was no one there, of course. She checked to make sure her research assistants had done what was required to keep the experiments going over the summer. Trays of newly sterilized vials, loaded with gelatinous media, had been stored in the large refrigerator. On the adjacent shelf, several racks held vials humming with young flies. The sickly-sweet smell of the yeast used to feed the flies was in the air. No dissections needed to be done yet; the flies were still a little too young. They didn't know they were going to be sacrificed, she thought, and then wondered about these morbid thoughts that sometimes came into her head.

She left the lab and shut herself in her office. She turned on the electric kettle and gazed out the window, waiting impatiently for the water to boil. Only a few students were wandering the street below, their scanty clothing and slackened pace signaling the onset of summer. She couldn't see many people working in the offices across the street either. That was not going to stop her. She started a bag of black tea steeping and got to work. All afternoon, she read and wrote, stopping only to make more tea and eat her tuna sandwich. She managed to enter the silence where nothing mattered but her work. The hum of the air conditioner, the ticking of the clock on the wall, and the occasional clang from the boiler room all faded into the background of her consciousness.

When her cell phone rang, she jumped.

"Hello, is this Dr. McCloud?"

She placed the voice right away. Mortensen again. She felt a wave of anxiety. Was this going to be more about the phone call?

"I wondered if I could ask you a few more questions, Dr. McCloud."

"About what?" She could feel her heart begin its pounding. She clutched the mug of tea on her desk. It had gone cold.

"Just the whereabouts of your husband."

"The day Angie died?"

Mortensen said, "Not that day. We are trying to get in touch with him, but we've been given to understand that he has left the country."

"He left this morning. With Bent. Bentley Hyland."

"Yes, we are also interested in talking to Mr. Hyland."

"What's this about? Angie?"

"We don't know if there is a connection to Ms. Osborne, Dr. McCloud. That is what we are trying to ascertain."

"Connection with what?"

"We just wanted to find out the whereabouts of your husband last evening, Dr. McCloud."

"I don't understand. Late yesterday afternoon, he found out he was going to Sri Lanka with Bent. He came home, and then he was at home until he left this morning."

"Was this a planned trip?"

"No, I just told you. It was out of the blue. He'll be meeting with people there, on Cinasat business. It was a crazy rush getting him packed."

"What time did he come home yesterday, Dr. McCloud?"

Grace paused to take a sip of the cold tea, trying to understand his intentions. "Why are you asking?"

"We are just trying to get some information, Dr. McCloud."

"What for?"

"There's been a death," Mortensen said.

Grace felt her breath stop. "A death! What do you mean?"

"A Cinasat employee. An intern. We are simply asking about the whereabouts of everyone who may have been connected with her."

"How did she die?"

"That has not yet been fully determined," Mortensen said, his tone even. Wooden. He sounded the way he had at the reunion, Grace thought, when she had asked him about the cause of Angie's death.

"Pardon me, Dr. McCloud, but you didn't answer my question about the time of your husband's return home yesterday," Mortensen said. On the phone, he sounded like a robot.

"Probably around six," Grace said. "But what does the death have to do with him?"

"It's just routine," Mortensen said. "We record this information from everyone who may have known the deceased. Were you with your husband all night?"

"I went out shopping for a while. I wanted to buy presents for my family and friends, for Duncan to take with him."

"And how long did your shopping take?"

"I don't know exactly. I was out from about six thirty to maybe nine thirty," Grace said. "No, it was ten when I got back. I stopped at the Rite Aid near our house on the way back, and it was just closing when I left." She wondered if she was explaining too much. Was she just imagining that he sounded suspicious?

"Which stores did you visit?"

"Trader Joe's. Then the Willowbrook Mall. Lord & Taylor, Macy's. And then Toys"R"Us and Rite Aid."

"And your husband was at home meanwhile?"

"Yes. He was packing, getting his files in order. And he insisted on cutting the lawn because he didn't want it to get overgrown while he was gone."

"Do you know if he went anywhere?"

"I don't think so. Otherwise he would have told me. I called him several times while I was out to ask him about things to buy."

"You called him on the home phone?"

"No, his cell. But as I said, if he had gone out, he would have told me."

"But there is no way for you to know?"

"Look, this is crazy," Grace said. "How did this woman die? Surely you aren't suspecting him in some way?"

"No, Dr. McCloud, not at all. This is just a preliminary investigation, and there is no reason to believe there was foul play. We are only asking because two deaths have occurred recently in connection with your husband and Mr. Hyland, and indirectly, you."

"Me? I barely know anyone at Cinasat. Except for Bent. I don't think Duncan knows many people either. We met a few people at a Cinasat party but only in passing. Duncan never mentioned any interns. He's only ever mentioned Bent, a scientist called Derek Weinberg, some research assistant called Carson, and the secretary, Geri. And the CEO, Hammond Gleeson. He didn't know Angie at all. He had never met her."

"This is just standard procedure, Dr. McCloud. As I said, I didn't mean to worry you. You have been very helpful. I won't take up any more of your time."

After Mortensen hung up, Grace lay back in her chair, feeling spent. What the hell had that been all about? What was going on? Why did he keep contacting her?

She sent Duncan an email asking him to call her, even though she knew he wouldn't get it for hours, if not a whole day.

21

Duncan

In Transit

Duncan watched the clustered lights of London recede into the distance below, relieved they'd made their connecting flight. He was pleased that Bent and Janie were sitting several rows back. More time to relax. Duncan's seat was near an older woman with graying, carefully set hair. *Sri Lankan by the look of her,* Duncan thought. She was absorbed in scribbling in what appeared to be a journal. She had barely looked up when Duncan arrived. No conversation would be needed, he thought. This was going to be an easy flight.

He awoke as dinner was being served. The dinner roll smelled as if it had just been baked. The meal was served on deep-pink porcelain, not plastic, and certainly looked better than the ones he was used to eating in economy. Would it taste any better? He wondered what the economy class passengers were being served. It was strange to be cut off this way from the people with whom he identified on the plane. At some point in the trip, he planned to walk down to the economy section on the pretext of getting some exercise. On other trips to Sri Lanka, he had often met interesting people while standing at the back with others who wanted to stretch their legs.

"Doesn't look too bad," the woman in the adjacent seat said, gesturing at the meal before him. She was sipping a glass of red wine and prodding her salad with a fork. "Fresher than I expected." She turned to him with a reluctant smile. Her eyes ran over Duncan's face and then his clothes. Duncan resisted an impulse to straighten his hair. His khakis and blue polo shirt were both already quite crumpled. The woman was stylishly dressed in navy pants, a patterned blouse made of some slippery fabric, and an off-white cardigan. There were large gold-and-sapphire studs in her ears, and two gold bangles on each slim wrist. The folds on her neck and the slightly crepey texture of her skin made her age evident. Early sixties, Duncan guessed. Her eyes had the keenness of youth. Her graying hair had become a little disheveled, and her lipstick had mostly faded from the center of her lips, revealing a maroon outline.

"I am Mrs. Silverine Atukorale," she said.

Duncan introduced himself and began eating his salad, hoping that a long conversation would not ensue.

"Making a connection in Colombo? Or just going to Sri Lanka?" Mrs. Atukorale said, buttering her roll.

Duncan nodded, crunching the head of an asparagus. "Sri Lanka."

"First visit?" she said, politely.

"Oh, no, no. I've been there several times. I lived there for a while. My wife is Sinhalese."

Mrs. Atukorale's demeanor underwent a sudden change. She set down her knife and leaned toward him with a look of marked interest.

"Really? What is her name?"

Duncan sighed inwardly, resigning himself to the long discussion of family connections that would now be inevitable. He knew how it was with Sri Lankans.

"Grace De Silva."

"Ah, De Silva. And from where is she?"

"Her parents live in Colombo, but her father's family is from Negombo and her mother's family is from Kalutara."

"Ah, I see," Mrs. Atukorale said, but Duncan knew that she had only just begun her investigation.

"And her parents are . . ."

"Her father is Lionel De Silva. He's a civil engineer. He used to be in government service, but now he works at LPT Engineering. Her mother is Nalini—her maiden name was Edirisinghe. She's a geography lecturer at the University of Sri Jayewardenepura."

"Ah, right, right," Mrs. Atukorale said. "I have a cousin at the university—in mathematics—maybe he knows her."

Duncan nodded, chewing a bite of peppery chicken and rice. He knew he should ask about Mrs. Atukorale's family, so he said, "You are from Colombo?"

"Yes, yes. I'm coming back from visiting my children in the States. My son is in California, Mountain View. He is at Google."

"A computer scientist?"

"Yes, that was always his passion. Also my daughter-in-law. Both at Google. And my daughter is in Georgia, working for an insurance company. Her husband is American also, a doctor, in emergency medicine at a hospital in Atlanta."

"That must have been nice, visiting them," Duncan said.

"Yes, but unfortunately still no grandchildren!" Mrs. Atukorale laughed. "I told them, they should come home and I will have a *thovile* done." She glanced at him. "A thovile is . . ."

"I know what a thovile is," Duncan said. "Actually, thovil were what I studied in Sri Lanka. I'm an anthropologist by training. I stayed near Galle when I lived in Sri Lanka. A village called Talgasgama."

"Right, right. I was, of course, only joking about the thovile," Mrs. Atukorale said, the words spilling out in a rush. "In the villages, these practices are very common. Not only for barren women. Any ailment, at the drop of a hat, these people will put a thovile. They trust the aduras more than the real doctors. Even more than the *vedaralas*."

At her questioning look, he indicated his understanding of the term, saying, "The native medicine doctors, yes."

"This is all because of the lack of education," Mrs. Atukorale said. "That is why these are so popular with the laborers and villagers." She dabbed her lip with the linen napkin on her tray, her bangles tinkling. "I myself, of course, don't believe in all that. My husband studied in the UK—he got a postgraduate certificate from University of London. And my children, they were at Stanford and Berkeley."

Duncan nodded, wondering what he could say to alleviate her obvious embarrassment at having seemed like a villager.

She removed an errant bit of lettuce from her tray and placed it back on her salad plate. Her nails were short and polished in a conservative pink shade. "My daughter and daughter-in-law—of course there is no question of barren. They are just not yet ready for children. Even though they are in their thirties now. Nowadays career consumes all the young people's time."

"I know how that is," Duncan said. "My wife and I have been trying to have a baby for years now. So far, we haven't been able to. Maybe a thovile wouldn't be such a bad idea for us."

Mrs. Atukorale turned to look at him. "You don't think thovil are backward?"

"I know city people have a low opinion of thovil," Duncan said. "But in Talgasgama and some of the other villages I visited, people were still doing them. Personally, I think they're fascinating practices. I'm interested in what they mean to people."

Mrs. Atukorale was silent. She dipped a piece of asparagus into her chicken curry and chewed thoughtfully. "*Bali thovil, yak thovil*, all these are not proper Buddhism."

"I am not a Buddhist myself, but some of my Sri Lankan friends who are Buddhist seem to believe in things like *yakas* and spirits."

"Well, of course, there are the usual rituals we all do," Mrs. Atukorale conceded. "I have consulted an astrologer a few times myself to find auspicious times for my son's wedding and so forth. And some of these things are traditions for us."

"Do you know anyone who has had a thovile done? I hope you don't mind my asking," Duncan said.

"One or two, I know. Only small ones in the house for important matters." She looked him over, and then leaned close, her voice lowered. "And I have to say that I have also heard of some people getting *hooniyam* done. You know hooniyam . . . ?"

"Sure, black magic, sorcery rituals," Duncan said.

"Yes, you know, no? My cousin's neighbor got paralyzed completely on one side, from here down." Mrs. Atukorale swept her hand from her waist downward. "This happened just after her son got a big promotion, and she was talking about this to everyone. My cousin warned about *asvaha*—you know, evil eye. But the neighbor was not careful. Then the paralysis. Her husband got someone to come and look in the garden, and they found a charm hidden just near the house."

"What kind of charm?"

"A small vial with some hair and nail clippings and ash. The *kattadiya* cut it . . ."

"You mean the hooniyam was returned to whoever put it there?"

"We don't know who it was, but that person must have got the misfortune. That is how it is. It goes back to the source. My cousin's neighbor got a *yantra* to protect her, and she wears that now. You know what a yantra is?"

Duncan nodded. Amulets to ward off malevolent spirits had been common in the village where he'd stayed. "Is she still paralyzed?"

"She is much better now, after the hooniyam was cut and she got the yantra. Almost fully back to normal."

"Did she see any doctors? Western doctors?"

"Of course, of course," Mrs. Atukorale said, starting on her coconut custard. "They are not village people, they got a good doctor. The doctor said it was a stroke and got her to do physical therapy. Who knows if the physical therapy did any good, but."

"She got better . . . ?"

"But," Mrs. Atukorale said, wagging her small dessert spoon at him conspiratorially, "without the hooniyam cutting and the yantra, who knows if any improvement would have come?"

"You don't think it was a stroke then?"

"It might have been a stroke. Must have been a stroke. But question is why did she get a stroke?"

"Ah, I see. You mean without the evil eye, she might not have got it?"

"That is what I'm saying," she said, raising her hand in a triumphant gesture. "You go telling the whole world how successful your son is, how much money, how happy, what can you expect? Someone is going to get envious. That is what my cousin was trying to warn her about."

"Your cousin's neighbor wasn't worried about the evil eye?"

"She was worried, true, but that didn't stop her from boasting. This is the thing."

What about the stroke being the result of worrying, Duncan thought. But he didn't want to seem skeptical after Mrs. Atukorale had opened herself up to him, revealing her penchant for practices that she claimed were beneath her.

Mrs. Atukorale fumbled in her handbag and took out her iPhone. She leaned back in her seat in order to angle the camera and took a picture of the dessert on her tray. "Just a reminder," she said. "Very tasty. I'm going to see if I can reproduce the taste. I am not too bad a cook."

22

Grace

Friday

Mo's eyes had a bruised look, the skin dark around them. His hair looked thinner than it had in the humid air at the reunion, which might have been why she noticed more gray in it. His forehead, below his receding hairline, looked oily. He looked as though he'd had a long day.

"How did your meetings go?" Grace said, taking the bunch of yellow tulips he'd brought. He had said he'd been meeting about a property his company had leased to Novophil, a pharmaceutical giant that had recently begun a new project in Philadelphia.

His forehead furrowed, accentuating the fine wrinkles on his skin. They were all getting old, Grace thought.

"Not good. But I may be able to work something out." He peered around at the spotless kitchen counters, the orange throw folded under the freshly plumped cushions in the living room, the magazines stacked tidily on the coffee table. "Duncan's not here?"

"He had to go to Sri Lanka, with barely twelve hours' notice. Pretty ridiculous." She hauled the big ceramic vase out of the cupboard under the kitchen sink and filled it with water.

When she explained that Janie had gone along, Mo said, "Mariam and I wondered whether to send the girls to the KIS camp. Some time ago." He reached into the pocket of his khaki pants and drew out a slender wallet made of buttery brown leather. He showed her a picture of his wife and three daughters, all in elegant ankle-length dresses and embroidered head scarves. The two teenagers were unsmiling, their arms linked, and the youngest was laughing, her arms wrapped around Mariam's waist.

"Such a long way from home. You wouldn't mind?" Grace said, arranging the flowers in the vase.

"Would have been a good experience. But now it may not happen. With the damn finances . . ." He drew a deep breath, rubbing at the bristly hair along his jawline.

He was eyeing the bottle of wine on the counter. She reached for it, then hesitated at his expression. He'd been alcohol-free for at least a decade and a half, until Angie's death. She knew he did the obligatory prayers five times a day. "Juice instead? Water? Club soda?"

Mo dragged his gaze away from the bottle. "Club soda. And I don't want to talk about it."

Grace poured soda into his glass, and after a second's reluctance, into her own. Mo sat down at the counter separating the kitchen from the living room. Grace laid out plates and the plastic containers of Thai food.

"Are you doing okay?" Mo said. "You look . . . worried."

"Just been a strange day." Grace reached into a drawer for cutlery. "I spoke to that detective today. Mortensen. He called me. He wanted to know about Duncan's whereabouts last night. Someone at Cinasat died."

"What do you mean?" Mo stopped with the fizzing glass raised to his lips, his eyebrows drawn together. "A murder?"

"Why would you think that?" Grace studied him, but he only shrugged, still frowning. "He said there wasn't evidence of foul play," she said. "Just making routine calls was what he said. But do they do that if someone just dies naturally?"

"Maybe," Mo said. "They asked us things when Angie died."

"You know Mortensen asked about you," Grace said.

"Today?"

"The day after Angie . . . on Sunday. He came here. He wanted to know how well we knew you and the others. And about guns."

Mo pushed his glass along the counter, avoiding her eyes. "He and another cop came to see me. Made such a big damn deal about the guns. Like I had committed some crime."

"He talked about deer hunting," Grace said. "And the fact that you'd bought bullets in Ridgeville."

Mo stood up to get a paper towel from the far end of the counter. He rubbed his forehead with it. "How is that a damn problem? I have licenses for my guns. I saw a gun shop, and I bought some ammo. Why does it matter if it was in Ridgeville?"

"Maybe they were wondering why you brought guns to the camp," Grace said, watching him. "I didn't even know you hunted."

Mo twisted the paper towel in his hands. "I didn't bring them to the camp," he said. "They were just in my car. That's not a crime." He went over to the trash basket and flung the paper towel in. "Having guns while Muslim. That's the problem."

"I don't think they were targeting you," Grace said, although she wasn't sure that was true. "Maybe they were just fishing. The same with Duncan. Why Mortensen was asking about him today. Apparently Duncan came up because he was 'connected.'" Grace indicated her skepticism with air quotes. "To two deaths in a short period of time. It's ridiculous to think Duncan's connected. I told Mortensen Duncan didn't even know Angie. He probably doesn't know this person at Cinasat either. He's been there less than a week. He hardly runs into anyone."

"What about Bent? Bent was connected to Angie, and he probably knows this woman."

"Mortensen said they were going to talk to him. But he also asked me about my whereabouts, even though I have no idea who this woman is. Because I'm 'connected' to the two deaths. Me?" She sipped her soda, feeling the bubbles popping against her lips as she watched Mo's face. It was contorted with an expression of grief or worry. "What is it you have against Bent anyway? How come you're so suspicious of him all of a sudden?" Did Mo know that Angie had been seeing Bent for a while? Was there jealousy involved here?

He shrugged, picking up a spring roll. "Sure this doesn't have pork?"

"Only chicken, I checked," Grace said. And then, after watching him for a minute longer, "You said . . ." She didn't know how to ask him without seeming intrusive. "When did you and Angie . . . What I mean is, how come you and Angie didn't get married in the end?" Then she wondered if she should not have asked. The question seemed tasteless, when she'd gone to his wedding. Mariam had come to their own wedding, with Mo and their two oldest girls.

"Not my choice," he said, letting out his breath in a deep sigh. "My father didn't approve, of course."

"It's not like you were religious back then." Mo had been one of the wild ones, a long-haired hippie cutting classes and climbing over the gate to go into town, smoking pot behind the chemistry lab.

He shrugged again. "When I was in high school, he didn't care as much who I dated. Wild oats and all that. He was like that even in his college days. But when it came to me, in college, he felt Angie was a bad influence." He was gazing at the pad Thai he'd spooned onto his plate, poking at it with a fork. He had eaten very little of it. "But really, that wasn't what stopped me. You know how she was."

"A free spirit?" Grace said. She guessed Angie hadn't wanted to commit. She'd probably wanted to travel, to write, to see the world. And other people.

"That she was. But in the end, it was Bent."

Grace looked at him, not sure what to say.

"He had been after her, in college, even when we were together. She said nothing happened. But after we split up, she started seeing him. It was on and off for a long time. A very long time."

Grace frowned. The noodles slithered off the fork she'd raised to her lips. "When did they start . . . ?"

"Not when you were with him," Mo said. "After. Junior year of college. And for years after. It wasn't exclusive. I think the only reason it went on was that Bent didn't want to commit. Angie was like that. Wasn't it Groucho Marx who said he wouldn't want to be a member of a club that would accept him?"

The bitterness in his voice surprised Grace. "But you decided at some point to move on?"

Mo bowed his head, nodding over and over as if to convince himself. "After I met Mariam . . . she reconnected me to the faith. My father approved, naturally. He knew her family. It wasn't arranged exactly. But there were financial reasons for us to marry." He raised his head. His eyes were wet, she saw. "Don't get me wrong, Grace. I love Mariam, my children. But sometimes . . . I think it's more lately, maybe age . . . I think about how life might have been. If Bent hadn't . . . If I had waited . . . Sometimes I feel I might have missed the boat."

"I've always worried that Duncan might feel that way," she said, running her hand against the cold stone of the counter.

Mo glanced at her in surprise, and then nodded, realizing. "Ah, his career?"

Grace nodded. "With his background, his book . . . he could have found a great academic job somewhere if my job hadn't stuck us here."

"But he wanted you to take the job. His choice," Mo said. He shook his head. "And it was my choice to not wait." He stirred his noodles around, his lips twisted. "I don't know if Bent stopped seeing Angie after he married. I could never tell. She stopped talking to me about him. We've barely seen each other the past few years. Maybe they continued on and off. About two years ago, I think she did stop seeing him completely. I think she got over him. That's why I feel . . . if I had waited . . ."

"That's why you seem like you have something against him," Grace said. He was silent. She bit into a spring roll, leaning forward to let crispy shreds fall onto her plate.

"I think Angie had some suspicions about him," Mo said.

"Like what?"

"When we were talking at the reunion . . . After she got there that night—it was late, maybe nine—Suki and Marla and I talked with her in the pavilion for a while, before we went to Marla's cabin. Bent came by for a minute, just to say hi. After he left, someone said something about him. I don't remember what it was. Some casual random thing. And Angie said he had a dark side, that he's not what people think he is. I didn't think anything of it. It was only in passing. But now with everything else, I just have a feeling . . ."

"What do you mean, everything else? You mean that photo you got at the funeral?"

"Not just that. I got an email from Katherine this afternoon." Seeing Grace's puzzled look, he reminded her, "Angie's mom."

Grace waited, chewing her noodles, watching him comb his fingers through his hair. He had still not eaten much of his food.

"Apparently someone broke into their house the night of the funeral service. They had been out, Katherine and her husband—Angie's step-dad, Mel. When they got back, they found the place burgled and the dog dead. Poisoned. It tears me up to think about her having that loss on top of Angie." He wiped his eyes and took a swig of his soda.

"My God. That's terrible."

"I called her," Mo said. "She was pretty broken up. A bunch of things had been taken from the house. Some electronics and some things from Angie's room. And here's the odd thing: she said some pictures had been taken. A pile of pictures on Angie's desk that Katherine and I had been looking through. That's why she had emailed me. To find out whether I had any recent pictures of Angie. All the recent ones she had were in that lot."

"So what does that mean? Why were the pictures taken?"

"Katherine thinks it was just random. Accidental. Someone sweeping things into a bag off desktops and tables. But that doesn't seem like a good explanation. Why would someone want to get into a house enough to poison a damn dog, and then end up taking pictures? There are plenty of valuables in that house. It doesn't make sense."

Maybe he is onto something, Grace thought. Mortensen had been asking a lot of questions. Maybe something really was going on.

"What do the police think, do you know?" she said.

"Katherine says the police are looking into it, but so far, it looks to them like a standard burglary. Whatever the hell a standard burglary is. I just think something is rotten here."

"There's something else we found out. Marla and I," Grace said. "Maybe it's connected to the burglary."

After she had told him about Minowa Costa and the police visit, he said, "Why did they think you'd know if Angie was writing a story? They didn't ask me."

Grace took a deep breath. She had already told Marla and Duncan, she reminded herself. "Because I told them that Angie left me a voicemail before she died," she said. She didn't know where this was going to go, whether she would have to end up telling him the whole story. She had half a mind to, now that he had opened up and said so much about his own disappointments.

Mo looked bewildered. "When? About what?"

"Just to say hi. That she wanted to meet up," Grace said. "I know. Everyone's asking me why I didn't say anything." She tried to make it casual. "Before she died, it didn't seem important. I didn't think anything of it. And then after, I don't know. It didn't seem to matter. I did tell Mortensen when he was interviewing everyone."

Mo stared at her, his eyes piercing. "She said absolutely nothing else?"

"I couldn't make out a lot of the message," Grace said, concentrating on pouring more soda into his glass. "It kept cutting out. She mentioned the name of a bar in Chicago where we'd chatted once. Maybe she wanted to talk about something we discussed then. No idea what. But definitely nothing about any story."

Mo shook his head, frowning. "So the police are investigating this Minowa's death? You think the burglary at Katherine's house was related? Someone was trying to find out if Angie had information about that death?"

Grace realized she had been holding her breath. She let it out, relieved he'd moved on.

"I don't know," she said. "But could be, couldn't it?"

"That doesn't explain . . . I told you how Bent reacted to that picture." He looked sharply at her. "Did you show it to Duncan?"

Grace nodded. "I sent it to him. He emailed me back from the airport. He does remember the mask." She hoped Mo would not make too much of it.

Mo gripped her arm. "He does? That proves it. I knew something didn't make sense." His eyes were fervid as they ran over Grace's face. "If he says it's still there, and he's only been there a few days, it couldn't have broken months ago. That means Bent was lying about when the damn picture was taken. The question is, why?"

"Mo, wait," Grace said, as gently as she could. "The fact that Duncan remembers the mask, the fact that he says he remembers, really doesn't prove anything. He's shockingly absentminded. If you knew how many times a week he forgets where he parked his car, you wouldn't put any stock in this."

"That's a different sort of memory," Mo said. "This isn't about remembering where he put something. This is about recognition. And this is not some random decoration. Devil dancing is his thing. He would notice one of those masks."

"He said he saw a collection of Sri Lankan masks somewhere else recently. At the house of a Cinasat exec. He could have seen this mask there, and not in the Cinasat lobby. I don't think this is a real issue, Mo," Grace said. She understood his sadness about the passage of time, the need to feel that life had been properly lived. And on top of that, he was contending with losing Angie. Grief could be so difficult. She knew what it was like to lose someone. Even a breakup could make a person think and act in ways that were completely out of character. A death would be even harder.

"Look," she said, "even if Duncan is really remembering that mask being there, it's much more likely that Angie visited Cinasat recently to see someone else—maybe the woman she's with in the picture—and didn't meet Bent. Maybe Bent's upset about that now that she's gone, and he can't even admit to himself that she wouldn't have come by to say hello."

Mo shook his head slowly. "No, that just isn't it. I told you, his reaction was odd. Not upset like that, just . . ." He rapped his fingers on the counter and took another swig of his soda. It could have been whiskey, the way he did it, Grace thought. As if he'd conditioned himself to relieve stress with water or soda after he gave up drinking.

He set the glass down decisively. "I know how we can find out. We could go to Cinasat and see if this damn mask is there. That way we don't have to rely on Duncan's lousy memory. And we can ask if this woman works there."

"Just like that, show up at Cinasat," Grace said, closing the containers with the remains of the food.

"Yes. We could go now."

Grace glanced at her watch. "It's after nine thirty. Who's going to be there at this time on a Friday?"

"They probably have a security desk, right?" He stood up, brushing stray noodles off the front of his shirt. They had left small greasy streaks on the pale fabric.

"But I doubt there's anyone there now, Mo. And even if there were, we can't just waltz in and ask—I don't even know who—about this woman."

"We can find someone. And no one's going to prevent us from looking at a mask in the damn lobby, even if Cinasat's all that. A cat may look at a king, right? A man may look at a mask." He chuckled to himself in a way that alarmed Grace.

"This is insane," she said. Then, realizing that *insane* could be a literal description of Mo's behavior at the moment, she said, "Silly, I mean. All this about when a picture was taken. Why does it even matter?"

"It's not just about the damn picture," Mo said. "There was Bent's reaction, and the break-in, and now this Minowa person. And what about this other person Mortensen contacted you about? What if that really is a murder? Not to mention Angie dying in the peak of health, out of the blue."

Grace wondered, with a sinking feeling, whether she should have mentioned Mortensen's call or Minowa. Mo had already convinced himself that something was wrong. With Angie's death and the financial stress he was under, he could be close to . . . what? Some kind of breakdown? All she had done was feed his irrationality.

"Maybe Minowa's death is connected to the break-in, but we don't really know. The rest . . . These could be separate events, Mo. Death happens, sometimes when you don't expect it at all." That was how miscarriages were too. Things happened. "It doesn't mean there's anything suspicious." She paused, wanting to not be too rough on him. "Angie's death has been so difficult for everyone. Especially you. I think maybe you're working everything up into something it's not."

"Grace, I'm telling you, there is something." His breath caught, and he took too big a gulp of soda.

"I'll tell you what," Grace said. She busied herself with transferring the glasses and plates to the dishwasher. "We'll go to Cinasat tomorrow morning. Duncan said some people work there on Saturdays. I really doubt we'll get to ask anyone about the woman in the picture, but you'll see the mask is probably not there, and that'll put your mind at ease. And when Duncan gets back to me, I'm sure we'll find out more."

23

DUNCAN

In Transit

"Good school, KIS," Mrs. Atukorale said, wagging her head. "Now, of course, we have so many international schools. KIS was one of the first, but."

"That's what Grace said," Duncan said. "Academically, it was pretty good. Grace got in because of her exam scores."

"Her parents must have been very proud," Mrs. Atukorale said. Duncan sensed that the conversation could be heading into dangerous territory. Mrs. Atukorale, like every Sri Lankan he had ever met, was interested in family histories. *Better to steer the conversation away from Grace's family,* he thought. He didn't want to risk getting close to the now-forgotten scandal over the bribe that had cost Grace's father his government job. Even though sometimes Duncan wondered about his own reasoning, he felt that long-ago bribe had something to do with Grace's miscarriages. Grace had never got over her guilt about the sacrifice she felt her father had made for her, however much Duncan had tried to point out that her father had made the choice himself. *Without all that guilt, she wouldn't be so focused on her work,* Duncan thought. And if she were more relaxed, who knew whether she would still have the miscarriages?

"I hear nowadays they take a lot of Sri Lankan students, but back then, mostly they had students from abroad," he said. "Diplomats' kids mostly. A big adjustment for her, like getting used to a new culture."

"Must have been the same for you, no?" Mrs. Atukorale said, fixing him with a curious gaze. "Big adjustment for you also to come to Sri Lanka."

"True. I didn't even know anyone from this part of the world when I was growing up."

"Chicago, no, you said? Such a big city." The way she said it, with her eyes wide, made him realize she probably didn't know much about the US, however cosmopolitan she seemed.

"The suburb I grew up in was very provincial," Duncan said. It was only in his senior year at Waterwood High that he'd noticed how white everyone was. In the school gym, the only Asian student in his class, a second-generation Pakistani American named Ali Mustafa, had stood out, his dark arms and legs gleaming under the fluorescent lights amid a sea of pale skin. Skin color had been the only way anyone could have distinguished Al—as Ali had called himself—from the rest of the students. The drawl of his English, his taste for hard rock, and his love affair with McDonald's had all been unwaveringly Waterwood. "The only reason I started learning about different cultures was that I had a teacher—Ms. Logan was her name—who used to tell me stories. She was like a second mother to me."

"Right, right," Mrs. Atukorale said, sympathetically. She was leaning close enough that Duncan could see the pores in her skin, soft and enlarged with age. A faint perfume drifted from her. "That must have been good for you, with your mother being so ill and all. And this Ms. Logan was from abroad?"

"Oh, she was from Chicago," Duncan said. "Born and bred. But she'd traveled all over the world. Taught in Saudi Arabia and Japan. Kenya. Brazil. Also India. She must have been in her early forties then. She wasn't married, she didn't have children. She used to show me

145

pictures and tell me about all the different places, how people lived, what they did. A few times, she brought me food. Tandoori chicken. Stuffed grape leaves and kibbe. Sushi. All very exciting for me. That's how I ended up getting interested in anthropology when I went to college."

"In Ohio, you said?" Mrs. Atukorale said.

"That was also with Ms. Logan's help," Duncan said. He still felt moved when he thought about the drive she'd organized to help pay for his first year at college. He had not had a scholarship in the beginning, and his mother's medical bills had made it difficult for his father to contribute much to his college education. In college, he'd worked in a cafeteria, and in the summers as a janitor, until he finally managed to get a scholarship. "I have a lot to thank her for." He showed Mrs. Atukorale the thin silver ring on his right hand. "She gave me this when I was going off to college." He took it off and showed her the inscription. NIL DESPERANDUM.

"Ah, yes. Never despair," Mrs. Atukorale said. "A good thing to remember." Seeing his surprise, she said, "I took Latin in school. That was one of my best subjects."

She handed the ring back to him. "You didn't meet Grace in Ohio, but? Chicago again, you said?"

"That's where we both went to graduate school. But where I met her was in Sri Lanka, in the Kandy market."

"Aney, really?" Mrs. Atukorale said, with a giggle that was positively girlish.

"I was staying in Galle, but I had gone to Kandy to visit the Temple of the Tooth. A sarong seller was trying to overcharge me, and I was telling him I wasn't a tourist. I'd been in Sri Lanka for two months already by then. I knew how the tourists get charged double, triple."

"Yes, yes, that is the way."

"Grace heard me speaking in Sinhala, and she came over to ask me how I learned to speak it like that."

"Ah, so you speak it well, then," Mrs. Atukorale said, switching to Sinhala.

"Now a little out of practice, but still not too bad," Duncan said, feeling the Sinhala words struggle a little on his tongue. He switched back to English. "Grace didn't try to help me buy the sarong. Actually, she helped the seller get a better price from me."

Mrs. Atukorale laughed. "Good, good, so she helped her countryman," she said, still in Sinhala.

He would have to keep speaking in Sinhala now, Duncan realized. "She invited me to her aunt's house," he said. "She was visiting this aunt, that's why she was in Kandy. Just by chance, at the same time I was in Kandy. Funny how these coincidences happen."

"Yes, yes. There is a right time for everything, no?" Mrs. Atukorale said, smiling. She laid her hand on his arm, her skin dry and soft.

24

GRACE

Saturday

"Hello there, young lady!" Gordy Mann waved, his newspaper in his hand. She saw that he had laid their own newspaper neatly on their doorstep. "Did I do an okay job?" he called as he ambled toward his front porch.

"What did you do, Gordy?" She scrutinized the bushes, but there was nothing noticeably amiss. Gordy wasn't shy about blowing leaves off his neighbors' lawns or even pruning their bushes if he felt they were being too lax about yard upkeep. Grace had once had words with him about her rose bush, which he had pruned to little more than a stump while she and Duncan had been away in Sri Lanka.

He waved his hand at the lawn. "The mowing. I tried to get all the edges."

Neat mower lines covered the lawn, and the scent of fresh-cut grass was still in the air. "You did it?" she called. "Thank you! I thought Duncan did it last night."

"You aren't cracking that whip hard enough, young lady!" He chuckled as he climbed his porch steps. "He should have started earlier. He had the mower out, but then he had to run an errand. He said he had to get on a plane first thing in the morning. So I just did it while he was out. Don't worry, he came by to say thanks when he got back."

"If he had told me, I would have done his errand while I was out," Grace said.

"He said it had to do with work. Too involved with your jobs, both of you. But then, maybe that's a good thing. You won't have a problem paying the bill I send you for the lawn care." He chuckled again and went inside, waving goodbye.

Grace wondered where Duncan had gone. It couldn't have been a quick trip to the Rite Aid down the road if Gordy'd had time to finish the lawn while he was out. It had been a busy night, she reminded herself, shrugging. He had probably not thought to mention it.

The clamor of the coffee grinder greeted her when she went back inside. Mo was at the kitchen counter, putting out cups. He had changed into a clean black polo shirt, and comb lines furrowed his hair. He grunted, rubbing his eyes. "Too many bad dreams."

By the time they'd had breakfast and got to Cinasat, it was after nine. A row of trees bordered the lawn outside the building, which wasn't one of the ugly concrete giants that housed so many large corporations. This building, although sprawling and six storied, aspired to be something more. Its curved front and ridged walls evoked sand dunes. In a small pebbled area outside the front entrance, a fountain spurted hard jets of water. Flower beds full of magenta tulips ran beside a black granite walkway to the front door.

"You're sure it's open on Saturday?" Mo said.

"Well, the cars . . . ," Grace said, pointing out the dozen or so vehicles in the parking lot.

"Let's do it, then," Mo said. He was out and heading toward the building even before Grace had got out of the car.

"I don't even know what we're going to do," Grace called as she hurried after him.

"To put our minds at ease, that's why we are here," Mo said. "Try to look like you know what you're doing."

A faint smell of bleach met them when they pushed open the heavy glass doors. The white-walled lobby was very large and gave the impression of being squeaky clean. The white marble floor gleamed. A man in a navy uniform sat behind a counter paneled in ash-colored wood, under large silver letters that spelled out CINASAT PHARMACEUTICALS.

On the left, next to a bank of elevators, was a smaller Cinasat logo, and near it, a sign that said OUR MULTICULTURAL PARTNERS. Below the sign, several objects hung in two rows, each with a small accompanying sign. They all looked like pieces that could have been in a museum: a dark metal shield, a sword, a dagger with an ornate hilt, an elongated wooden figurine, and three masks. The mask closest to the Cinasat logo was clearly Sri Lankan.

"Look, there it is," Mo said, pointing. "That sign was in the background. And there's the mask! I knew it—Bent *was* lying."

Grace took a step toward the mask, examining it. "No, that's not the same one. The one in the photo had three cobras. And a tongue. But it's pretty similar. That's why Duncan thought it was the same." She felt relieved. "I told you, you can't count on Duncan's memory."

"Are you sure?" Mo said. "Let's check the photo. I have it here." He fumbled with the envelope in his hand.

"Can I help you?" the security guard behind the counter called out.

"No, thanks," Grace said, hoping she didn't sound as uncertain as she felt.

"Are you here to see someone?" the security guard said, his voice rising a notch. "You'll need to sign in." He gestured for them to come forward. He was a fresh-faced young man with spiked red hair. Acne scars marred his cheeks, and a few reddish spots suggested that this was an ongoing problem.

They went up to the counter. "We were actually looking up something," Mo said, pulling a small stack of photos out of his envelope. There were a half dozen or so, five inches by seven.

"Looking up what?" the guard said in a tone that was not too polite.

"This mask," Mo said. The photos tumbled onto the counter. Mo leafed through them and pulled out the photo he'd shown Grace before.

"See," Grace whispered to Mo. "See the tongue?" The mask in the photo had the same bared teeth, but the red tongue hanging from its mouth was missing from the one on the wall. The colors were a little different too. The one on the wall was greener and less menacing. The shape of the ears was almost the same, but on the mask on the wall, each ear was formed from a lotus and several curving leaves, rather than a coiled cobra. It was clearly a different mask.

Mo looked from the photo to the mask on the wall. He turned to the guard. "This mask. It used to be over there, by the elevators. It looks like that one, but see how it's different, with the tongue and the two extra snakes? Do you remember it?"

The guard looked at Mo as if he might be dangerous. "Never seen it before," he said.

"Are there masks on other floors? By the elevators?"

"No, only in the lobby. What is this about?"

"It's a long story," Mo said.

The guard looked skeptical. "What are you? Police?"

"No, no. Actually, my husband works here," Grace said. "We would have asked him, but he's out of town."

"Who's your husband?"

"Dr. Duncan McCloud," Grace said. "He works in the marketing division. He just started working here recently."

The guard typed on a keyboard, peered at the screen positioned beside him, and appeared satisfied. "Okay. Dr. McCloud's office is on the fifth floor . . ." He looked again at the photo. "I don't know anything about another mask. Those are the only ones I've seen down here, but I've only been here a couple of days."

"You're new at Cinasat? When did you start?" Mo said.

"My first day was Thursday," the man said.

"So it could have been here before that?" Mo said, sounding excited. This really was insane, Grace thought. He was feeding his preconceived ideas any way he could.

The guard shrugged. "I don't know. I suppose."

"Do you recognize this woman?" Mo said, pointing to the woman next to Angie in the picture.

"Never seen her. I see everyone passing through, but I don't know very many. All I have to do is look at their badges. Easy work." The guard picked up one of the other pictures that had fallen out of the envelope. "Him, I know. Mr. Hyland. He introduced himself on my first day. And him. He got dropped off by his chauffeur, right at the door. One of the big bosses."

Mo took the picture from him. "Which one is that?"

Grace looked at the picture he was holding. In it, Bent was seated at a table in a restaurant, his face lit by a copper lamp. He was with Hammond and another man, deep in conversation.

"That's Hammond," she said to Mo. "Hammond Gleeson. The CEO."

"Oh, you know him," the guard said, a new note of respect in his voice.

"Sure. A bit," Grace said.

"What is all this about anyway?" the guard said, his expression turning suspicious again. His eyes ran over Mo's polo shirt. "You a journalist?"

"No, no, nothing like that," Mo said. "It's complicated . . . a personal matter." He picked up Angie's photo again. "Are you sure you haven't seen the mask in this picture?"

The guard studied the picture. "Nope. Sure looks like that one on the wall, though. It got stolen or something?"

"Something like that," Mo said. "We're looking—"

Grace grabbed his arm. "We should go," she said, then let go of him to gather up the pictures and stuff them into the envelope. And to the guard, "Thank you for your time." Ignoring the guard's curious stare, she tugged at Mo and propelled him away from the counter.

"What was that about?" she said to Mo as they emerged into the warm air outside the building. "What was that other picture you showed him?"

"I didn't mean to show that one to him. It was just in with the other pictures I took from Angie's room. It was stuck to the back of one of the others." He took the envelope from her fingers and extracted the pictures again.

Grace slid into the driver's seat, irritation rising inside her. She should get to work, and back to the grant. This flight of fancy had gone on long enough. "I'll drive you back to get your car," she said. "Then I really have to get to work."

They traveled in silence for a while.

"Listen," Mo said, as they neared Grace's house. He was holding the two photos in front of him, fanned out against the dashboard. "This is starting to make some sense to me."

Grace nodded grimly. *More of the same,* she thought.

"What if," Mo said, snapping the photos against the dashboard. "What if Angie was writing a story about Cinasat? Maybe there was something she dug up. Maybe that's why she took this picture of Bent and this Gleeson and the other guy. Maybe that was why she was at Cinasat before she died. And maybe that's why Bent doesn't want people to know she was there."

What could she say to this, Grace thought. *Maybe you are losing your mind?* She didn't want to be harsh when he was clearly having a hard time. "Look, Mo," she said. "You're making too many leaps in logic here."

"Think about it," Mo said. "I know Angie was here less than six days before she died. Because of the necklace. The damn mask was here then, so it must have broken after that. Or been replaced. What if Bent had it replaced after I showed him that photo? Because he didn't want anyone to know Angie had been there recently. Maybe he made sure the new mask was similar enough that people wouldn't notice the replacement."

"Please, Mo. Listen to yourself. Bent was grieving, at a funeral. Just like you. He probably just didn't remember the mask. It's a small thing. You're making too much of it."

"I'm not," Mo said with a conviction that was beginning to frighten Grace. "You didn't see his reaction to the photo that day. And then there's the break-in at Angie's house, and the fact that she was here, for whatever reason, and her death. This Minowa. And the other woman who's died at Cinasat. And why did Angie have this photo of Bent and this Gleeson? What's that about?"

"God, Mo. These could all be completely unrelated. You're going by some feeling you had about Bent's reaction. It really is starting to sound as if you're losing it." *There, I said it,* Grace thought.

"Marla said Angie was working on a big story that night," Mo said. He didn't seem bothered at all by what Grace had said.

"I told you, Mo, that could be the story about Minowa. The police are already working on that. It's not connected to Cinasat, or to Bent."

Mo appeared to not have heard. He snapped his fingers. "That's it. Her computer!" He turned to Grace, his expression intense. "What happened to it? Her damn computer? Didn't Marla say she was typing in the cabin?"

"No idea," Grace said. "Someone must have sent it to her mother. There must have been other things, right? Did she come in a rental car? Did she have any luggage? I don't know. It didn't occur to me until now."

"I'm going to call Marla and find out," Mo said. "She'll know."

"Mo, don't stress her out, okay? Remember the pregnancy," Grace said.

"Just drop me off," Mo said. "I'll keep you updated."

25

DUNCAN

In Transit

Bent and Janie had joined Duncan by the galley, where he'd gone to stretch his legs. Janie hopped from one foot to the other, the unbuckled strap of one fluorescent-pink sandal threatening to trip her up.

"Walk to the back of the plane and back," Bent said to her.

"Hang on," Duncan said, stooping to buckle her sandal.

Janie skipped off down the aisle, wagging her head from side to side, her ponytail swishing.

"Sometimes I wonder if I should spend more time with her," Bent said. "Her mother relies too much on babysitters." He shrugged. "The price I pay for my work. But the last thing I want to do is be like my father."

"He didn't spend much time with you?" Duncan said.

"He tried, I suppose," Bent said, his tone grudging. "My parents divorced when I was ten. Dad was in Thailand most of the time when I was a kid. Managing the factory there for Pop, my grandpa."

"Grace said your grandpa has a furniture business," Duncan said.

Bent nodded. "Built it up from nothing. He started in the US, with small wooden chests he made himself. They had inlaid lids—bits of glass or ceramic or stone. He gave Grace one of those early chests once." He twisted his lips. "She probably threw it out. She never liked him much." He shrugged. "She didn't understand him. He can be a bit abrasive, but that's because he came up the hard way. When he was young, he used to go door-to-door with those chests he made. Stack them in his Ford, go driving around the US. Lonely housewives were his best customers, he used to say. My mother thinks those housewives didn't just buy his chests. But she didn't think much of him either. She feels Pop pushed Dad away from her. But I think she and Dad got divorced because she didn't like living in Thailand."

Duncan made a noncommittal sound. He recognized this sudden verbosity of Bent's. Jet lag and lack of sleep, he realized.

"How come you were at KIS? Why not Thailand?"

Bent closed his eyes for a moment. "Pop's idea. He didn't like the international schools in Thailand. He was paying for it, so Dad didn't have much say. Plus Pop was developing some business interests in Sri Lanka." He straightened his shirt. "But it was a good choice. I had a good time there. Mostly. And it made me want to be in a position like Pop's one day. Controlling things." A half smile crossed his face, and then he pushed himself off the bulkhead on which he'd been leaning, his pretty lips thinning. "Got to get back to work instead of standing here going on about old times. I have some things to sort out."

Duncan watched him stride back to his seat and open his computer. He was an eye-catching figure, with his broad shoulders pressed back against his seat. Janie pranced up to him and tugged at his arm. He said something to her, patting her head and pointing at his computer screen. Janie's face fell, and then she came loping toward Duncan.

"Want to play a game?" she said when she reached him. "A race?" She hopped up and down.

"We can't run in here," Duncan said, smiling at her enthusiasm. "How about a guessing game?"

"Boring," Janie said.

The poor kid must be going crazy, cooped up for so long, Duncan thought.

"See who can stand on one leg for the longest," Mrs. Atukorale called out as she returned to her seat. She had spent some time freshening up, Duncan saw. Her hair was neatly pinned and her lipstick freshly applied. "My children always did that when we traveled." At Duncan's mock accusatory look, she laughed. "Very good for the circulation, also."

"You have to do it without laughing," Janie said. She stood on one foot, the other curled up, flamingo-like, and immediately burst out laughing.

It took several rounds of the game to satisfy Janie's demands. When she finally returned to her seat, where Bent was still deep in communion with his laptop, Duncan sank into his seat and stretched out his legs.

"I was watching you and thinking," Mrs. Atukorale said, leaning over to him confidingly. "I was thinking . . . what you were saying about your wife . . . Why keep trying the same doctors if they can't do anything to help? Why not try something else? A ceremony?" Most of their conversation had been in Sinhala for some time now. She seemed to think of him as a native son.

"Grace wouldn't agree to it. She's a scientist. She doesn't believe in all that."

"Scientist maybe, but also Sri Lankan, no? Buddhist, Christian, Hindu, doesn't matter. Some of these ceremonies, we all do," Mrs. Atukorale said. "Not thovil, or any of that. Just simple ceremonies, you know. I myself didn't have children for the first year after my marriage. Only after I poured milk at the foot of the bo tree at our local temple."

"Right, right," Duncan said. She seemed to have forgotten that she had dismissed these sorts of rituals as being villagers' fancies.

"And also I made a vow at the temple. That I would make a pilgrimage to Kandy if I had a child. This is what helped us."

"Grace doesn't even go to the temple now," Duncan said. "I'm pretty sure she wouldn't make a vow."

"At least a *pirit* ceremony, I could organize for her," Mrs. Atukorale said. "That, her family will approve, I am sure."

Maybe her family would agree to an ordinary Buddhist ceremony like that, Duncan thought, *but not Grace.* She didn't believe in karma, let alone that it could be accumulated by chanting or giving alms to monks.

26

GRACE

Saturday

Grace hurried out of Gannon Hall, looking for Mo. His phone call had shattered the elation she had been feeling about all but finishing her grant application that afternoon.

A hard breeze was blowing, turning the air chilly. Grace clutched her cotton cardigan close and headed toward Mo. He was leaning against the hood of his BMW, raking his hands through his hair. His polo shirt was untucked, and he looked agitated.

"Mo, this is crazy," she said. "You have to let it go."

"I think I'm onto something," Mo said. "Get in the car. Please. I'll explain on the way." He climbed in and reached over to open the passenger-side door.

His voice was so urgent that she got in. "I can't believe you went back there," she said. "To bribe the guard!"

Mo brushed this off with a wave of his hand. "It wasn't a bribe. I just asked if he could get me in touch with the guard who worked there before."

"A hundred bucks! Who does that?"

Mo shrugged, accelerating down the road. A small silver unicorn hanging from the rearview mirror swung wildly. "He might not have done it if I had offered less. It's not illegal. This guy is not just a coworker. He's a friend, he said."

"You have to let this mask thing go. I don't know how to . . . Where are we going?"

"Not far. Newark. I know you think I'm barking up a nonexistent tree here, but I want you to hear what I have to say. If I'd just told you on the phone, I was afraid you wouldn't listen."

Grace waited, frowning, feeling faintly nauseated at the smell of the pine air freshener in the car. They were speeding along Route 3. She tried to focus on the looming billboards, pushing back her irritation.

"I called Marla first," Mo said. "Angie's computer is missing."

"How do you know that?"

"Well, she had a computer with her in the cabin, Marla said. A small laptop—you know, the kind you can put in a woman's purse. But it seems to have disappeared. After she died, Mortensen apparently got all the things she had left in the cabin—a backpack with a few things, her car keys—and said he would send it all to Angie's mom. I don't know if he sent the car keys. Maybe he sent that to the rental car company. Anyway, Marla said the computer must have been in the backpack. So I called Katherine in Houston to ask about what was sent to her." He paused and ran his hand over his eyes. "I hated the thought of upsetting her. I just said we were wondering if her computer was in the backpack. I had to come up with a story to tell her because I didn't want her involved in all this speculation."

"You lied to her?"

"Well, I just said that the computer had an essay that I wanted to have."

An essay you believe was on the computer, Grace thought, looking out the side window. The prone body of a dead deer came into view, its legs rigid. Grace winced, turning her attention back to Mo.

"Anyway, Katherine said she got a backpack with a few things, but there was no computer in it."

160

"So where is it?"

"I don't know. But when I spoke to Katherine, she said that Mortensen had called her and asked if she knew of any connection between Angie and Cinasat."

"When?"

"Today."

"I suppose it's because of this other death at Cinasat. Remember I told you he was wondering if there was a connection with Angie? It's not that surprising."

"Well, he also asked Katherine if Angie had been doing any reporting on Cinasat."

"Really?" Grace frowned. Could it be that Mo was actually right about his crazy theory?

"Maybe Mortensen has Angie's computer," Mo said. "Maybe he's found out that she was doing a report on Cinasat."

"Then why would he ask Katherine if she was doing one?"

"I don't know—maybe to see whether Katherine knew anything? Or maybe Mortensen only suspects. Maybe the info on the computer doesn't say enough."

"We don't even know if he has her computer," Grace said.

"That's why we need to contact him, to find out," Mo said. "Although I don't know if he'll tell us. He's pretty cagey. I've left him a message. I'm waiting for him to call me back."

They sat in silence for a while. Grace wasn't sure why she felt uneasy. Maybe because she didn't know what Duncan would say about all of this. It was his employer they were implicating, after all. And the thought of the questions Mortensen had asked made her uncomfortable. She had told Mortensen that Duncan had been home all night before he left, but he hadn't. It was probably nothing, but she wished she knew where he'd gone.

They swerved off the freeway and paused in traffic. Mo was hunched over the wheel, his head thrust forward as if he were watching an invisible scenario unfold on the street before them, although all that was in his view was the back of a large white SUV.

"I wish you had told me before you called Mortensen," Grace said as they lurched forward, the unicorn ornament swaying back and forth.

Mo turned to her, his eyebrows drawing together. "Why? Did you not want me to call Mortensen? I thought you'd want to know what he'd say."

"I just want to talk to Duncan first. If all this has anything to do with Cinasat, that's where we should start. He could probably tell us a lot."

"Well, can you call him? He's probably reached Colombo by now."

"I tried earlier. He hadn't registered at the hotel yet. I'll keep trying."

Mo pulled into a garage, and they went out onto the street, tramping past a dusty construction zone bracketed by orange barrels and temporary barriers of plastic netting. "Right over here," Mo said, shouting over the jackhammer throbbing in the muscled grip of a man wearing a hard hat. They turned onto Market Street. Mo stopped in front of a white high-rise building with **BELLFIELD TOWER** emblazoned above its revolving door. "Come on," he said.

Inside, Grace followed Mo as he approached a young black man sitting at a counter. The man straightened the collar of his navy-blue uniform and smiled invitingly.

"I'm looking for Wayne Durant," Mo said.

"Yeah. That's me," the man said, nodding, a question in his eyes.

"Doug Bratton sent me?" Mo said. "From the Cinasat building? He said you could help us."

Recognition dawned on Wayne's face. "Yeah. Yeah. Sure. He said you wanted me to look at a picture?"

"It's just a quick question," Mo said. He pulled the photo of Angie out of his envelope and handed it to Wayne.

Wayne glanced at it for only a second before he said, "Yeah. What do you want to know about it exactly?"

"You worked at Cinasat?"

"Yeah."

"Did you see that mask in the lobby there?" Mo said.

Wayne nodded. "Yeah. Would've been hard not to. It was right there in front of my eyes every day."

"Are you sure it was that mask? Not just one that looked like that? Did it have three snakes like that? Two at the sides, not just the snake head at the top?" Grace said.

Wayne nodded again. He ran his fingers along the photo. "Yeah, three. And that tongue hanging. I used to look at those teeth and that tongue and wonder who put that up there. Not too friendly."

Mo looked at Grace triumphantly. "See?" he whispered.

To Wayne he said, "When was the last day you worked there?"

"Man, I don't know. Been a while," Wayne said. He scratched at his wiry hair. "Don't know the exact day. Less than a year, though. Maybe six months?"

"What . . . ," Mo said. "Doug said . . ."

"Early November," Wayne said. "Then I was at the Liberty building in Jersey City, then 231 Market, and since then, here."

"But I thought . . . ," Mo said. "Doug said you worked there right before he started."

"Nah," Wayne said. "He said you just wanted to talk to someone else who'd worked there."

Mo slapped the counter, looking exasperated. *What did he expect when he offered a hundred bucks?* Grace thought. Of course he was going to get someone's contact information.

"What's it about anyway?" Wayne said. "Something to do with Ms. Costa?"

"What?" Mo said at the same time as Grace.

"Her," Wayne said, pointing to the woman with Angie. "She was nice. Always stopped to say a few words. Not hoity-toity like some of them."

163

"You know her?" Mo said, just as Grace said, "What did you say her name was?"

"Minowa Costa," Wayne said. "She was in the research division."

Mo was looking from him to Grace, his mouth open. Confusion was clouding Grace's mind. She couldn't make sense of what the man was saying. What was going on here?

"Are you sure that's this woman's name?" Mo said.

Wayne nodded, looking puzzled. "Yeah. Why? She do something?" His eyes widened. "She had something to do with stealing the mask?" He shook his head. "No way, man. She wouldn't have done that. Real straight person, she was."

"No, no," Mo said. "No one stole the mask. That's just . . . Never mind." He ran his hand through his hair. He pointed to Angie. "Do you know this other woman?"

Wayne shook his head. "Never seen her. What's this about?"

"Just something . . . something we're trying to figure out."

"You police?" Wayne said.

"No, no," Mo said again. He pulled out his wallet. "Thanks for your help," he said, pushing a twenty-dollar bill over the counter.

Wayne's eyes widened. He slid his eyes around the lobby before pulling the bill under the counter.

"Now you see," Mo said, when they emerged onto the street. The noise of the traffic seemed very loud, and the number of pedestrians on the sidewalks seemed to have increased. Grace struggled to process what had just happened.

"Do you believe me now?" Mo continued. "It's all connected to Cinasat. Something has to be going on. Mortensen must already know that Minowa worked at Cinasat. He's onto this." He gazed at Grace, his eyes feverish. "Bent is involved in this somehow."

"What's the connection to Bent?" Grace said. "That guy just said the mask was there last November. Bent didn't contradict that."

"Bent works at Cinasat," Mo said. "And something's rotten there. Look, I'm going to call Mortensen again."

While he made the call, Grace walked beside him, trying to make sense of it all. What did this all mean? Duncan would know.

"Not there still," Mo said as they got back to the garage. He looked at his watch. "Damn. Look, I have to get to a dinner meeting. I'll drop you back at your office, and I'll get back to you."

27

DUNCAN

Sunday

It was close to dawn, Sri Lanka time, when Duncan wheeled his bag out of the airport. Beyond the bright lights of the covered porch outside the arrival lounge, a waxing moon hung in a black sky. The humid air enveloped him like a long-awaited friend. Janie's hand was in his, still dry and cold from the air-conditioning inside. The grogginess of jet lag made the surroundings seem oddly far away.

Bent had been preoccupied since they had landed. In the baggage area, he had stood in a far corner, his phone to his ear, his brow furrowed, deep in an animated conversation. Since then, he had been texting incessantly on his phone, pacing about agitatedly. Just something he needed to sort out, he had told Duncan. Duncan had been unable to get his own phone to work since leaving New Jersey, despite repeated attempts.

When the Cinasat car, a shiny white Subaru station wagon, arrived and they had piled in, Janie leaned her head against the backpack she'd plumped down on the seat and promptly fell asleep. Duncan, sitting in front with the driver, found that he could barely keep his eyes open. Turning back, he saw that Bent was still texting in the back seat.

"Anything wrong?" Duncan said.

Bent looked up, frowning. "I'll tell you when we get to the hotel," he said. "Nothing that can't be handled. And Cinasat's tech support is still working on your phone problem."

Duncan tried for a while to take in the familiar landscape, but in the feeble moonlight, not much was visible other than silhouetted coconut trees waving their heads by the side of the expressway. The effort to stay awake became too onerous.

When he awoke, with an ache in his neck, he realized that he had slept all the way from the airport into the city. They were already in the colonnaded porte cochere of the Taj Ocean Hotel. The driver was unloading the bags, and Bent was shaking Janie awake. Through the open car doors, Duncan could hear the roar of the ocean nearby.

"Sit inside with her, would you?" Bent said. "I'll check us in."

Duncan took Janie into the splendid lobby, admiring its gleaming floor of pale marble, its ornate rugs and opulent chandeliers. He checked his phone. Still no connection.

"This is like a palace," Janie said, slumping onto a cream velvet sofa.

"Hotels in Colombo are pretty grand," Duncan said. And such a far cry from the way the people in the villages lived, he thought. Still feeling hazy, he watched Bent register at the reception desk, and then have another long, animated conversation on his phone. Janie had already fallen back asleep, he saw. He could feel his own eyelids drooping. He stretched his legs out and relaxed against the cushioned comfort of the sofa back.

"Duncan!" Bent's voice roused him from his sleep. He put his glasses on, wondering how long he had been sleeping. Not more than a few minutes, surely.

"I need to talk to you," Bent said. "But let's move over here." He gestured to a nearby cluster of chairs. "I don't want to risk Janie overhearing if she wakes up."

Duncan blinked, confused. He moved with Bent to a nearby armchair and sat down heavily. "What's going on?"

"Look, something has happened," Bent said, sitting down across from him. He ran his hand through his hair. The bags under his eyes looked puffier, and his face was flushed. "I've had to make another change in our plans."

"What happened?" There was a dull ache in Duncan's head. He rubbed his temple with his thumb.

"As I told you, we think a competitor is trying to sabotage the Symb86 project." Bent paused. "I might as well tell you. The competitor is Novophil—I'm sure you've heard of the company, yeah? We know we're being sabotaged. There have been leaks . . . and some of our people . . . I don't think I can tell you all the details yet." He eyed Duncan's empty hands. "I assume you haven't contacted Grace yet?"

Duncan tried to suppress his irritation. "How? My phone's still out. I'm not sure whether my laptop will connect now. It didn't when I tried in the airport. I'll try when I get to my room," he said. "I'll need to get a new phone." He scanned the lobby. "There must be a shop in the hotel where I can get one."

"You won't have time for that. I need you to take Janie and go to a safe place. A car is coming—"

"Whoa, what?" Duncan interrupted. "What safe place? What for?"

"I don't want to frighten you," Bent said. "But the situation has become dangerous."

"What situation?" Duncan said. "What are you talking about?"

"There's been a death at Cinasat," Bent said. "The intern who was working on the coding."

"Whoa. She's dead? How?"

"It's being investigated," Bent said. "There seems to be some question of foul play. She may have been involved in the leaks. We don't know. At any rate, it looks like Novophil is willing to go to any lengths to get the information they need. We have evidence that we are all in danger of being abducted here . . ."

"What the hell?" Duncan said, getting up from his seat. What was Bent saying?

"Sit down," Bent said. "We don't know yet who is to be trusted and who is being paid off by Novophil. I'm afraid that Janie might be in danger—if she's kidnapped, they could use her as leverage to get information from me. And I'm afraid you know enough about the project to be valuable to them."

"I don't understand," Duncan said. He had sat back down. The edge of the chair was digging into his thigh. This was going too fast. His head had begun to pound.

"Our security department has worked out a way to keep everyone safe," Bent said. "But time is of the essence here. I need to go and talk to the people here who have been involved in the project, to make sure nothing more is leaked. It's been decided that you and Janie would be safest if you stayed elsewhere, secretly, for a few days, until everything is sorted out. I've called for a car. You'll be taken to a guesthouse in Hikkaduwa. A quiet place, very low-key. I know the manager there, someone I can trust. No one will know you're there. Just lie low, act like a tourist. I'll contact you in a couple of days. Don't tell Janie any of this, of course." He started to rise from his chair.

"Whoa. Wait a minute, Bent," Duncan said. "This makes no sense. I don't understand how the intern died, how that's connected to a leak, what makes you certain we're in danger . . . I don't get any of this. And I can't just go off somewhere right now. I need to call Grace. I have to let my in-laws know I'll be away."

"You can't call them even when your phone is fixed," Bent said. "This is serious, Duncan. Things are happening fast. They're going to try to stop us from getting to market first. We have to assume any communication you have with Grace could be used to track where you are."

"This is crazy. No one is going to be tracking my calls, my emails to Grace!"

"Look, I'm not fucking with you here!" Bent's voice rose sharply. "Listen to me." Duncan saw that he was making an effort to control his volume. "What we are seeing is an effort to get this information at any cost. They have massive resources. Don't forget we are talking about a drug that could be profitable beyond anyone's expectations. Just trust me and go. I'll contact Grace and let her know you'll be down south."

"How do you know she's safe? If there is really this level of interest in getting ahold of me or you . . . why wouldn't they try to abduct her to get to me?"

"We've already thought of that," Bent said. "I didn't want to worry you by mentioning it. We won't tell her, but she'll be under watch to make sure she's fine. It's very important that you not contact her in any way. That might put her in danger."

"My God," Duncan said. He wondered if this was all a dream he was having. A nightmare. Everything felt unreal, much more unreal than was usual for jet lag. He looked out through the wide windows that encircled the hotel lobby. The sun was well up, and the sky was blue, cloudless. There were palm trees outside, surrounding a fountain. Pompous doormen were standing around in their ridiculous livery, and skinny porters with faces burned dark by the sun were scurrying around helping hotel guests with luggage. This was no dream.

"Time to go," Bent said, his voice urgent. He was already standing. He went over to Janie, still asleep on the sofa, and shook her shoulders. "Come on, Janie." When she sat up, he said, "Listen, Janie." He crouched before her. "I just found out that I have to go to a very important meeting. It'll be too boring for you to just stay here. So Duncan is going to take you to stay at a special place at the beach. That'll be fun. I'll see you soon, in a couple of days. Until then, you stay with Duncan, okay?"

Janie rubbed her eyes. Half-asleep, she seemed much younger than her nine years. "We aren't going to stay here in the palace?"

"You can come back later and stay here. But this other place is much more fun. This hotel isn't right on the beach, but the other place is. And it's only for a day or two. Come on now." He tugged her up and beckoned to Duncan.

"The car should be waiting," he said to Duncan, before hurrying off, his cell phone already in his hand.

Duncan picked up their bags and shouldered Janie's backpack. "Come on," he said to Janie. As they neared the doorway, he saw that a young man in a checked shirt and brown pants was waiting by a nondescript black sedan, holding a piece of paper with the word *Cinasat* scrawled in uneven lettering.

28

GRACE

Saturday

Grace called her parents in Colombo. They had found out that Duncan's flight had arrived, but Duncan had not yet got in touch.

"May not be at the hotel yet," her mother said. "Everything takes longer, no, if they are traveling with a child."

"True," Grace said, trying to sound casual. "Could you tell him to call me if he gets in touch with you first? I really need to talk to him about something."

When Grace called the hotel half an hour later, a polite young woman said that Mr. McCloud had checked into room 352. She connected Grace to the room, but no one answered the phone. Grace left a message for Duncan. She called again, at half-hour intervals, with no success. *He probably went directly to some meeting,* she thought. They must have had to take Janie. She probably would not hear from him until the evening, Sri Lanka time. That meant she would have to wait until the morning to talk to him.

She heated the leftover Thai food from the night before and ate dinner with CNN on. A story about another corruption scandal dominated the news. A senior police official had been arrested on federal corruption charges relating to a local political campaign. She sighed, listening to descriptions of the gifts the official had received in exchange for looking the other way as laws were broken in plain view. She flipped the channel, looking for something more positive, but it was the top of the hour, and commercials were on every major channel. A woman dancing through a field of butterflies after taking an antidepressant medication, an elderly man enjoying a romantic date by the ocean after taking a drug to combat erectile dysfunction, a young dad able to play with his infant daughter after taking a decongestant. Then it occurred to her that soon Symb86 would be on these channels too. She'd feel differently about the ads then. She turned back to CNN, where a reporter was describing terrible flooding in Texas.

She turned her computer on and checked her inbox. Still nothing more about Duncan's firing. That had definitely been some hoax. It made her shiver to think that she'd almost got shot on a wild-goose chase.

There was still information she needed to finish the grant application, but there was nothing in her inbox from Gigi. This was the problem with relying on students to get work done. No sense of urgency. Then it occurred to her that Gigi might have emailed her again from her ridiculous Gmail address. The message would have been flagged as junk. She couldn't remember what the email address had been. Something like sillychick71 or hotgirl94. She had told her research assistants repeatedly that graduate students with such unprofessional email addresses would not be taken seriously. She opened her junk mail folder, her jaw clenched with irritation. She skimmed the subject headings. Just the usual spam. Then one caught her eye: *From a friend of Angie Osborne.* She clicked on it, frowning.

The message was from ssam4782@gmail.com. It said simply, *Danibel Garwick knows what Angie was working on. Speak to her privately. The address is 335 Sugarvale Road, Lodi, NJ.* The message had been sent on Thursday evening at six thirty, and Grace saw with a jolt of surprise that it had been sent to both her own and Duncan's work addresses. That had been the evening before Duncan left for Sri Lanka—had he seen it? Who was Danibel Garwick? She was certain she had not heard the name before. She tried Googling the name, but nothing came up. Did it have something to do with Cinasat? She called Mo and left him a message to call back.

He was going to be at his dinner meeting. She could go herself to the address, she thought. She could easily get to Lodi before eight. It wouldn't be too late for a visit.

She took Route 46 to Lodi and, following her GPS, drove down Main Street, past a row of pear trees standing like dark sentries and a deserted strip mall, to a narrow residential street. It was still dusk, the absence of streetlights not yet a hindrance. The houses were small and rather run-down. The area appeared to be a flood zone. She could see the evidence of high water on the discolored walls of several houses. Yards were a little unkempt. When she saw a green metal mailbox with the number 329 painted on it, she parked at an empty spot along the curb, noticing a black sedan double-park half a block behind her, its lights off. Number 335 was only a few doors ahead. The smell of barbecuing meat was drifting down the street. She passed two people conversing in a front yard and approached a bushy rhododendron that hid the front door of number 335 from view. Through the street-facing windows, she could see light inside the house. As she turned around the rhododendron bush, the two people who had been in the yard next door hurried up.

"Are you a reporter?" one said, her tone gossipy. She was a middle-aged woman, rail thin, with protruding collarbones above her hot-pink tank top. "You can't go in."

Grace shook her head, frowning. "I'm just here to see Danibel Garwick. She lives here?" she said, still moving forward. She halted, confused, when the green front door came into view. Yellow police tape stretched in an X across the door. "This is Danibel Garwick's house?" she said again.

The man who had come forward with the bony woman said, "What's your business?" He was elderly, with a stocky body that gave him the air of an aging bouncer. A small black terrier that was on a leash wrapped around the man's fingers pranced over to sniff Grace's shoes.

"I'm a friend of a friend of hers," Grace said. "I'm here about a personal matter."

"You didn't know her, then?" the bouncer said.

"Did something . . . What happened here?" Grace said, looking again toward the door.

"She died," the bony woman said, coming up to stand beside Grace, her skinny arms akimbo, her hip bones jutting through the stretchy fabric of her black workout shorts. She leaned close. "I was the one who found her. Poor thing."

"Police were here half the day," the bouncer said. He pulled at the leash as the terrier stood on two legs to sniff at Grace's hand.

"What happened?" Grace said again, incredulous. Was this really happening again?

The bony woman planted herself more firmly beside Grace. "I went over yesterday morning with her cat," she said. She jerked her head at the house next door. "I live at 333. Dani's cat was in my yard, so I took him back. The door was open. I found her on the living room couch." She shook her head over and over, her eyes glazed. "I can't get it out of my head. The way she was lying there, staring at the ceiling. Her tongue was hanging out." She looked at the man, and he put his arm around her, squeezing her shoulders. "That was the worst part. The way her tongue was dangling out like that."

Grace's breath had stopped. She sucked in a gulp of air. She could feel the warm whiff of the dog's breath on her hand. "Was she . . . How did she die?"

The woman shook her head again. "They don't know. There was no blood or anything. One officer said it was being investigated. They kept asking us if we'd seen any strangers around. But no one saw anything. I heard drumming from over here the night before. She must have been listening to music when she collapsed. She might have had a heart attack, one of the officers said. It must have happened suddenly. There was a glass on the floor when I went in. Orange juice by the look of it. The floor was sticky. Bunch of flies." She shuddered. "Flies all over her."

"Does anyone else live here?" Grace said.

"No, she's . . ." The woman looked over at Grace, examining her closely for the first time. "What's your name? What exactly did you say you came about?"

Grace pushed back an impulse to turn on her heel and run. But there was no reason not to say. "Grace McCloud," she said, hearing the reluctance in her own voice. "It was about something . . . personal. It's not important."

She turned around, ignoring their now-intent stares.

"I'm sorry to bother you," she said over her shoulder as she hurried away. They were saying something to each other. As she reached her car, the woman shouted out, "Hey, wait a minute!"

The man ran out to the sidewalk. "Hold on!" he yelled. The dog started yapping.

Grace got quickly back into her car. They were probably writing down her license number. But why did it matter? She had done nothing. She couldn't make sense of what was going on. How could she come across three unusual deaths in one week? It was statistically improbable. Impossible. Something had to be going on. Was it all connected to Cinasat? Or just to Angie?

She drove back home, her thoughts roiling in a sea of worry. She didn't know why she felt frightened. The lights were on in Gordy's house. Somehow, that was a comfort, even though she had no intention of telling him any of what had been going on. What was going on anyway? She had no idea.

Inside, she tried calling Duncan again, with no success. She logged in to her email and reread the message about Danibel Garwick. The neighbor had said she'd been found the previous morning. Had she died after this message had been sent? Should she call the police and try to find out? Should she tell the police that she'd got this message? Her head was starting to hurt. She wished she could talk to Duncan. There was nothing from him in her inbox. But a new message had arrived, she saw, from someone named Yak Adura. The subject line said, *Vishesha panividayak*. It took her a few seconds to realize that it was not gibberish but transliterated Sinhala. *Important message.* Then she realized that *adura* wasn't some feature of a yak. *Yak adura* was a Sinhala term. Exorcist. An innovative way to avoid the spam filters, she thought, clicking on the message. To her surprise, she saw it was written in formal Sinhala, not transliterated but in Sinhala letters.

> Respected Dr. McCloud,
>
> I am a friend of Angie Osborne. I must speak with you about an urgent matter. Your husband is in danger. Please call me. Do not call from your home or cell phone number. Do not tell anyone about this message. Do not reply to this email. Write down the phone number and delete this message now. Trust no one.
>
> Sincerely,
> Yak Adura

Grace read the message three times, her heart pounding. What the hell was this? It couldn't be a joke or a coincidence. Two messages from friends of Angie? In all the years she had been using email, she had never received a message written in Sinhala. Not even spam. The number below the message appeared to be a Sri Lanka number. The digits were spelled out in Sinhala letters. Why had that been done? For secrecy? Where would she call from at this hour if she couldn't use her phone?

She checked her watch. Twenty-six past ten. Late, but she had to talk to someone. She picked up her phone to call Mo, and then put it back down. *Trust no one.*

She called the Taj Ocean Hotel again. The same female receptionist answered.

"Hello, I think I spoke to you earlier. I'm trying to get in touch with one of your guests, Dr. Duncan McCloud. Could you connect me, please?"

"Yes, please hold the line, Mrs. McCloud." The woman sounded exasperated, Grace thought.

The phone in Duncan's room rang shrilly, but once again, no one picked up. Grace left another message: "Duncan, this is really urgent. Call me as soon as you get this. I need to talk to you right away."

What did the email mean? *Do not call from your home or cell phone number.*

She dialed the hotel again ten minutes later. The receptionist sounded distinctly irritated at hearing Grace's voice.

"Yes, Mrs. McCloud, correct?"

"Yes, hi. I haven't been able to reach my husband, and I need to get in touch with him urgently. Could you put me through to his boss, Bentley Hyland, please?"

"Please hold," the receptionist said, and then, after a pause, "I'll connect you to room 358."

There was no answer from room 358 either. Grace left Bent a message, asking him to call. She wondered if she should call her parents. But what would she tell them? They would worry. *Your husband is in danger.* This had to be linked somehow to all the deaths. Or was she being pulled into Mo's conspiracy theories? Should she call Mortensen? She didn't even know how to reach him. And what would she say? *Trust no one.*

She paced the living room, wondering what to do. She had to call the number, she decided. Find out who Yak Adura was. She could drive to her office and call from there. The drive would be short at this hour, and it would calm her down. Give her time to think. She picked up her purse and keys and walked out into the night.

29

DUNCAN

Sunday

The drive through Colombo was slow even for a Sunday morning. Janie, after complaining half-heartedly about leaving the hotel, had fallen asleep again, her head on Duncan's shoulder. Duncan was exhausted. The conversation with Bent kept replaying in his mind. It still seemed dreamlike. Were they really in danger? From whom? What could happen? He wished he had asked more questions: about the intern, what was known about Novophil, how Bent had got his information. There were too many unknowns.

This was a job that had promised safety, in contrast to the one he'd had at St. Casilda, where there had been no tenure, no financial security. Employees had always been afraid that the college would go under. But now here he was, running for his life. For all the frustration he had felt in his last months at the college, he missed it. He thought of his small office there, the worn blue carpeting, the scratched wooden bookshelves loaded with dusty books, the lumpy upholstery in his chair. Despite its unglamorous fittings, he had felt welcome. And it had been predictable, until the day he received his notice of dismissal. The only unpredictable things that had ever happened were unexpected visits from colleagues wanting to chat or students needing advice. He sighed. The grass was always greener.

This was where he was now, he told himself, twisting the ring on his finger. He would deal with whatever came up. This chaos was temporary. Bent was right. It would all get sorted out. Nil desperandum. He tried to focus on the scene outside the window. They were in an endless stream of cars and tuk-tuks. Motorbikes wove in and out of lanes, ignoring loud honks from car drivers. Pedestrians didn't seem to care much about honking drivers either. The city looked more commercial than he remembered from his last visit three years before. Buildings seemed bigger. Stores seemed taller and closer to the street, and more of them had windows with showy displays. Billboards were everywhere. He didn't remember paint companies—Robbialac, Nippon—advertising so prominently before.

But still, even in the city, Duncan observed the down-to-earth air that he found so attractive about Sri Lanka. Stray dogs lay calmly on the pavement, watching people go by. At bus stops, women stood nonchalantly with umbrellas spread against the sun, which in the midmorning, was already beaming down. Men chatted outside shops, picking their teeth, relaxed. People strolled here. It made the city seem leisurely, even with the bustle of the traffic. As always when he was in Sri Lanka, Duncan was struck by how much less artifice there was here. People seemed more mortal here than in the States. He was always surprised that he didn't find this thought alarming. In fact, he felt lulled by it.

"So much traffic. But once we get out of Colombo, it'll be easy all the way to Hikkaduwa, no?" Duncan said to the driver in Sinhala.

The driver glanced at him through the mirror. "Yes, sir," he said in English, before lowering his eyes to the road again.

Definitely not a talkative man, Duncan thought. He couldn't see the man's face from where he was sitting. His hair was curly and grew over his ears in woolly puffs. There was an alertness to him, in the way he looked through the mirror, and the way he held the wheel. Duncan had made several attempts to engage him in conversation. At first, he had seemed startled at Duncan's fluency in Sinhala, but although he had stared, he had responded only in monosyllables, all in English.

The concern about his present situation began to rear up again. Duncan pushed the worries resolutely aside, adjusted Janie's drooping head against his shoulder, and closed his eyes.

It was only when a rut in the road jolted him awake that he realized he had fallen asleep. The slight stickiness of his skin reminded him immediately that he was in Sri Lanka. They were driving on the Colombo–Galle road, a route Duncan loved. On the left houses stood behind painted garden walls. He could see past the low and latticed ones into gardens with vegetation that looked too green for the seaside. Suriya and araliya trees leaned over oleander bushes, clumps of bamboo, and the occasional bougainvillea. On the right hotels and resorts of varying degrees of luxury eclipsed the view of the ocean with the studied tranquility of their buildings.

Here and there, small stretches of undeveloped land exposed the vast expanse of the Indian Ocean, brilliant blue to where it met a sky of blazing white. Coconut palms, twisted by years of wind into arcs, and groves of screw pines propped on pyramids of roots shaded the smoothly packed sand. Those stretches were what Duncan waited for as the car sped ahead. Each brief glimpse reminded him that the simple splendor of the ocean was right there, free for all to enjoy, just past the businesses that were cashing in on its beauty. Duncan wanted to wake Janie to show her the view, but then he remembered the situation, that he might have explaining to do. He let her sleep.

He glanced at his watch and saw with surprise that it was later than he had thought. They should have been in Hikkaduwa by now. "How much longer to Hikkaduwa?" he said in Sinhala to the driver.

The driver regarded him briefly in the mirror. "Hikkaduwa back," he said in English, gesturing toward the rear window. "Very soon Galle."

"What?" Duncan said, surprised into English. "Wait, wait, we are going to a guesthouse in Hikkaduwa. Didn't Mr. Hyland tell you?"

"Told, sir. Very soon Galle," the driver said. "Five minutes."

"We're going to be there in five minutes?"

"Yes, sir," the driver said firmly.

He could wait five minutes, Duncan thought. If it was the wrong guesthouse, he could have the driver go back. It was only about twelve miles from Galle to Hikkaduwa.

The road curved away from the ocean for a while. They turned and drove along a narrow side lane that sloped up for a short distance past several tall gray garden walls, hedges of hibiscus and oleander bushes, and a couple of uncultivated weedy blocks of land with stray coconut and rubber trees. At the end of the lane, they came to a tall black metal gate set into an equally tall gray garden wall. A squat concrete structure that appeared to be a guardhouse stood to the right of the gate. The name of the house was embossed on a small rectangular brass plate on the wall: THE MAYA. Someone had recently polished the brass. The gate opened at the driver's honking, revealing a middle-aged woman with her graying hair knotted into a meager bun, dressed in a rather shabby brown lungi and a floral cotton blouse. Down a short driveway stood a large whitewashed bungalow surrounded by a portico. Two massive gray urns with flowering bougainvillea shrubs stood by the steps that led up to the portico.

"This is a guesthouse?" Duncan said.

The gate clanged shut behind them as the car crept up to the front steps, the tires scrunching the gravel.

"Right place. Come, sir," the driver said, opening Duncan's door. He went to retrieve the bags from the back while Duncan tried to wake Janie. A line of drool was spilling down her chin. When he shook her shoulder, calling her name, she opened her eyes, grinned, and fell back asleep.

Duncan lifted her gently and stood her on her feet. She wobbled and opened her eyes. "Come on, we're going to go inside and see . . ." He hesitated. He couldn't tell her that he wasn't sure this was the right place. "If there's a nice place for you to sleep," he said.

Duncan could hear the thunder of waves against rocks, but the ocean was not visible from where they stood. They trudged up the stone steps, Janie stumbling in her sleepiness, and entered the cool portico. A man was standing there, in a white sarong and a dingy white short-sleeved shirt. He looked to be in his thirties or forties, with weather-lined skin burned almost black by the sun. His cheeks were hollow and his longish hair oiled neatly back. A neat mustache, curled at the ends, bordered his lip. His eyes were deep set, the whites strikingly bright. He gestured toward the open doorway. A long wooden pestle with an iron-ringed base was leaning incongruously on the wall by it. The door, a heavy wooden one with carved panels, looked like a museum piece. The hall inside was cool and dim and smelled strongly of floor polish. The old-style red cement floor had indeed been recently polished, Duncan saw.

"Is this a guesthouse?" Duncan said, in Sinhala, to the man.

"You are McCloud Sir?" The man replied in Sinhala. The pronunciation of Duncan's name was off—with the stress on the *mac*—but there was no doubt that it was his name the man mentioned. "And this baba's name is Janie?"

Duncan nodded.

"This is the right place," the man said.

Bent had probably not known himself where the guesthouse was, Duncan realized. He had probably been told it was somewhere down south, close to Hikkaduwa. He could call Bent tomorrow and make sure. Right now, Janie was falling asleep on her feet.

"Where can she sleep?" he said to the man.

"Come," the man said. He waved aside Duncan's attempt to help and hefted the bags the driver had set on the portico, the veins standing out on his wiry forearms. He led the way to the back of the house, his bare feet silent on the polished cement floor, his body bowed with the weight of the bags. They walked along a wide corridor with framed paintings on the walls to a spacious bedroom that smelled a little musty. Two beds were set diagonal to one another, each beside a large open window. "This is good?" he said, heaving the bags onto the floor by a tall carved wooden wardrobe.

"Yes, thank you," Duncan said. He led Janie to one bed and tucked her in. "Go back to sleep," he said. "Tomorrow we'll go to the beach."

30

GRACE

Saturday

By the time Grace got to Gannon Hall, it was almost eleven. There were times when she'd left Gannon later, but she had never arrived at such a late hour, and on a weekend at that. The curb was deserted, except for a single gray station wagon parked close to the building entrance. The streetlamp at the end of the block cast little light close to the building, so all was in shadow when Grace got out of her Honda. She could hear nothing except for the muffled sounds of traffic in the distance. She hurried to the front door, readying the key card attached to her car key. *No need to be creeped out,* she told herself. The nagging thought of Danibel Garwick dead on her living room couch kept rising in her mind. With her tongue hanging out. That had been how Duncan had described Angie.

The lights were on in the lobby, but when she stepped out of the elevator on the fourth floor, the hallway to her office was dark. The janitorial staff had already done their work and left, she guessed. The silence was unnerving. She flipped the light switch, entered her office, and shut the door. The wall clock sounded oddly loud. *Ticktock, ticktock.* She pulled out the Post-it on which she'd scribbled the number from the email message. She dialed, wondering what she would even say. The phone rang, but no one answered. *What an anticlimax,* she thought.

Her cell phone rang, making her jump. Mo. He was returning her call at almost eleven? Had something else happened? *Your husband is in danger.*

"Grace, did I wake you?" Mo said.

"No, no, it's fine. I'm in my office, actually. Did something happen?"

She heard Mo draw a deep breath. "I couldn't sleep, and I don't know who else to tell. Mariam knows some of this, but not all. I don't want to say too much to her because Angie—"

"Mo, I found out something," Grace interrupted.

"Did you talk to Duncan?"

"Haven't been able to reach him. But I got this weird email from someone who said I should talk to someone about what Angie had been working on. Danibel Garwick. So I went to—"

"Danibel Garwick? She's dead," Mo said. "She's the one—"

"What? How did you know? You know her?"

"Mortensen said. The one at Cinasat."

"Oh my God. That's the Cinasat intern? I didn't know her name."

When she'd related what she'd found out, Mo said, "That proves it!" His words tumbled out in a rush. "And Mortensen came to see me. He said they don't have Angie's computer. That was one reason he's been suspicious about her death—the fact that they didn't find a computer when Angie had been typing the night before."

Grace's heart sank. Had they found Angie's phone? Otherwise, wouldn't Mortensen have mentioned it to Mo? Did they have some way to find the content of the voicemail message Angie had left?

Mo was continuing, she realized. "I asked him why no one asked us any questions about the computer that night. He said they weren't suspicious then. I don't know what he meant by that. I think it had something to do with the medical examiner, and about why Internal

Affairs got involved. It wasn't clear. He wouldn't go into details. Anyway, in the course of talking about this, I mentioned the mask—"

Grace interrupted. "That mask doesn't prove anything . . ."

"Just listen, Grace. I showed him the picture, you know, with Angie and the other woman. He already knew she was Minowa Costa. And get this. There is a connection between her and Danibel Garwick. Mortensen wouldn't give me details. But they knew each other."

"So what does that mean?"

"Think about it, Grace. Something has to be going on at Cinasat. You have to get in touch with Duncan. Find out whether he knows what all this is about. But . . ." A long breath. "Maybe you should tell him to just come home. We can talk to him when he gets back and then go and see Mortensen."

This would have seemed irrational two hours ago, Grace thought. But now Yak Adura's words were pushing themselves into her mind. *Your husband is in danger.* Could Angie have wanted to talk to her about Cinasat? But then she would have said something in the voicemail. All she'd mentioned was the business at Palmer Square.

"But he can't just leave. He only just got there. What would he tell Bent?"

"He shouldn't tell Bent any of this," Mo said. "I don't know what's going on, but there's something damn fishy, and we don't know who all's involved. But I'm fucking sure Bent is."

"I just can't believe that," Grace said. Should she tell Mo about the second email? *Trust no one.* Would that include Mo? "I have to think about all this, Mo," she said. "I'll keep trying Duncan. He'll have to go back to the hotel to sleep. Tomorrow morning our time. I'll call you when I find out."

She tried Yak Adura's number again. Still no answer. She answered two emailed questions from Gigi, then tried the number yet again. Nothing. She left her office, her footsteps echoing in the empty corridor. Inside the lab, it was eerily quiet, but when she neared the racks of vials, she could hear the flies buzzing. The vials in rack thirty-nine were black now with the growing mass of the fruit flies' vibrating bodies. She'd need to get Gigi started on the batch soon. Maybe she should do some dissections, she thought, to take her mind off everything. She extracted a vial and sat down at the microscope. The flies were swirling madly inside their tiny prison. Her mind kept going back to Danibel Garwick. *Flies all over her,* the neighbor had said. Grace shivered. She sat for a while with the vial in her hand, trying to make sense of it all. It was too late to be doing this, she thought, replacing the vial.

Back in her office, she tried Yak Adura again. No answer. The ticking of the clock caught her attention again. *Ticktock, ticktock.* Had it always been this loud? The boiler room clanged next door, startling her. She was too jumpy.

She turned off the lights and took the elevator downstairs. Someone else had been in the building, she saw as she stepped out. Some of the lobby lights had been turned off, leaving only the one near the front door. She fumbled in her purse for her car key, looking uneasily at the shadowed hallway beyond the elevators. Did something move? She pushed at the door, sighing with relief when the cool night air hit her.

The man appeared out of nowhere, a ski mask obscuring his head and face. Before she had time to cry out, he had seized her arm, one leathery gloved hand clamped against her open mouth. She tasted something sour. The hard leather pushed her lips against her teeth, chafing her skin. Her back was jammed against the man, the smell of cigarettes and sweat overpowering. In a panic, she twisted, clawing instinctively at the air behind her, and felt her car key jab the side of his neck. The man grunted, and the hand across her face slackened. She yanked herself away, hearing a scream leave her mouth. His arms swooped down around her. She spun, jerking her leg upward, and kneed him with all the force she could gather. He hollered and reeled back, doubling over, his hands dropping to cup his crotch. Grace ran to the door and swiped desperately at the lock with her key card. Her hands were shaking so hard she barely managed it. As the man rushed forward, she pushed the door open and slammed it shut behind her. His shoulder thumped against the glass a millisecond after the door clicked shut. It was only then that she realized she had been shrieking, loud gasping sounds reverberating in her ears. She grabbed the emergency phone on the wall by the door and panted, "Help! I need help! Gannon Hall!"

An urgent voice said, "Are you safe?"

The man outside spun around and leapt into a black sedan idling by the curb. He sped away.

Grace slumped against the glass and slid down to sit on the floor, barely hearing the calm voice of the campus security dispatcher telling her an officer was on the way. Her purse was lying on the sidewalk where it had fallen during the fray. She wished it had not been too dark to get the mugger's license plate.

31

DUNCAN

Sunday

Leaving Janie asleep, Duncan slipped out of the bedroom and through the dim hallway, passing several closed doors. On one side of the entrance hall, he found a formal dining room. On an intricately carved eight-seater table, a crocheted white mat held a red tin of Krisco biscuits, a clay water pitcher, and two frosted glass tumblers. A sideboard contained a careful arrangement of china. Through the windows, Duncan could see the glassy blue of the ocean. The house appeared to be set on a cliff.

The adjacent modern kitchen seemed at odds with the living areas, with its black-tiled floor and stainless steel appliances. A cover of fine wire mesh kept a few eager flies away from several curries on the granite counter. Someone was evidently in the process of preparing a meal. Duncan's mouth began to water. It was almost midnight back in New Jersey, and his gut was expecting a long-delayed dinner.

He went back to the entrance hall, past a wooden screen carved with a lotus design, to a sitting room. More carved furniture, some upholstered in dark raw silk. An entertainment center held audiovisual equipment, and a tall bookshelf displayed rows of English paperbacks.

A side door led out onto the back end of the portico, which was visible through the closed windows. The door was locked.

The house looked nothing like the simple, functional guesthouses Duncan had visited while driving around the country, or the modern bed-and-breakfasts he'd seen advertised online. It was more like the private houses of wealthy old Sri Lankans he had sometimes visited. He wandered around, looking for a phone, but none were in sight. He emerged from the front door onto the portico that surrounded much of the house. Three large crows were perched on the white balustrade, their black heads cocked. They barely moved when he hefted the pestle that was still by the doorway, wondering why it wasn't in the kitchen. No one was around.

He descended the three broad stone steps, noting that the garden appeared well tended. A grove of bamboo pressed against the garden wall next to the gate, their leaves hissing in the breeze. He would walk to the main road, he thought. But when he reached the garden gate, he found it secured with a heavy iron padlock. Looking up at the high wall enclosing the garden, he noticed that it was topped with metal spikes set about six inches apart. Between the spikes, pointed shards of colored glass glinted. He was surprised; spiked or glass-topped walls were not uncommon in areas of Colombo where residents feared burglaries, but they seemed unusual for Galle. But maybe Galle had changed now too.

He walked around the house to the left and found that the garden wall ended at a spot that overlooked the ocean below. Two coconut trees stood there, along with a group of screw pines supported by the tangled pyramids of their branched prop roots. A weathered wooden figurine no higher than Duncan's knee stood among the roots, its gray color blending in so well with the roots that it was almost invisible. Bending down to examine it closely, Duncan saw that it was a temple guardian of the kind he'd seen protecting the entrances to Buddhist temples all across the island. The crown of the statue's head was broken, and only a stump remained of one upraised arm, its hand and wrist having broken off, along with the weapon it had presumably once held.

The back end of the portico was above him, with four narrow steps that led to the overlook. The house was situated above a small cove. A rocky path led down to an empty beach. Enormous rocks formed natural walls on both sides of it, isolating the beach from the rest of the coastline. Waves were leaping high into the air like ceremonial dancers. At the sides of the beach, they thrashed the rocks, sending great arcs of spray into the air. Duncan's face was soon damp with it. He could taste salt on his tongue. There was something mesmerizing about the rhythmic power of the sea, the way the waves pounded out their eternal truths. He wanted to stand there, drinking in the view, but he was feeling hungry and thirsty, and he needed to talk to Bent to find out if he was really in the right place. With all of Cinasat's resources, why had his cell phone still not been fixed?

He walked around the garden to the back of the house and found two small brick structures there. One was a garage, with its gray double doors shut. The other was a low-slung building that he guessed was the servant quarters. He heard baila music playing, a jaunty old song he recognized, "Surangani," one that had been popular in the village where he had done much of his research. At the end of the building was a porch that appeared to be an open-air kitchen. A small metal shelf, rusted here and there, bore three chipped ceramic plates, three plastic tumblers, and three teacups. A couple of charred metal saucepans and several clay cooking pots were stacked on the cement counter. Steam was rising from the edges of a clay pot set on a village-style coconut-husk stove, and a mouthwatering smell of curry hung in the air.

An open doorway beckoned at the other end of the building. Duncan approached it.

It was dim inside. An old standing fan was whirring by the door. Duncan spotted two woven straw sleeping mats rolled up near one wall. Next to them, on the floor, was a small black radio, the source of the music.

"Hello?" Duncan said, peering in. He caught a glimpse of something large and red set atop a battered gray cardboard suitcase before a figure appeared in front of him, blocking his view. It was the mustached man who had been in the main house earlier.

"Ah, sir has come here?" the man said, addressing him in Sinhala.

"I didn't see anyone inside," Duncan said, gesturing toward the main house.

"No one is there. My wife and I will look after sir and baba," the man said. He emerged from the building, compelling Duncan to step back away from the doorway. "She is taking a bath. Soon she will finish making your lunch."

"No one else is staying here at the guesthouse?"

"Only sir and baba," the man said, adjusting his bare feet on the scrubby grass.

"What is your name?"

"Jotipala," the man said. "My wife's name is Karuna."

"I am Duncan McCloud. Please call me Duncan," Duncan said, even though he knew that would seem ridiculous to the man. The social gulf between them was wide. Customs about social hierarchies were deeply entrenched. There was no way he would call Duncan by his first name. The most Duncan would get was Duncan Sir.

Jotipala wagged his head, his face still expressionless.

"My boss, Mr. Bentley Hyland, do you know him?"

"I don't know, sir," Jotipala said, looking away at the house behind Duncan. "What I was told was to look after sir and baba."

"Who told you?"

"Fernando Sir sent me a message," Jotipala said.

"Fernando Sir owns this house?"

Jotipala wagged his head. "Fernando Sir lives abroad. He doesn't come here much, but sometimes foreigners come here to stay. When Fernando Sir sends me a message, then I prepare the house for them."

"So you and your wife live here?" Duncan indicated the servant quarters.

Jotipala nodded. There was the sound of a door opening and shutting inside the quarters. Jotipala turned his head back and called out, "Karuna, sir is waiting to eat lunch."

"No, no, no need to rush," Duncan said. "I was just looking for a phone to call my boss."

"No phone, sir."

Duncan realized what Jotipala meant. Obviously the servant quarters would not have a phone line.

"Not here, I know. I mean in the main house," he said.

Jotipala raised his eyes and regarded the brilliance of the sky for a moment, squinting. "There is no phone," he said.

"No phone? In a big house like that?" Duncan couldn't suppress his disbelief. He looked around, and in the distance, through the fronds of the coconut trees, he spotted telephone lines. He pointed. "There, those are phone lines."

Jotipala shook his head. "The line is not working now." He said it firmly, as if their conversation had ended.

Duncan hesitated. He didn't want to assert his authority, but he felt he had no choice. "I have to contact my boss," he said. "I can easily go out to a shop. There must be one not so far away. But the gate is locked."

"Yes." Jotipala nodded.

Was the man a little dense? "Please unlock it."

Jotipala's eyes met Duncan's briefly. Duncan thought he saw resentment in them. "No use," he said. "It is also locked on the outside. There is a police guard."

"What the . . . ?" Duncan said, reverting to English in his consternation. Then he stopped himself. All he had to do was explain. He switched back to Sinhala. "Look, Jotipala . . ."

"For sir's protection," Jotipala said, fingering one curled end of his mustache. "I am just doing what I am told." The resentment was definitely there in his tone.

"This is crazy," Duncan said. "I will be careful, but I have to be able to go outside."

Jotipala said nothing, so Duncan made his way to the gate. It was still padlocked. He found it hard to believe that it was locked on the outside. He tugged at the gate, making it clang.

"Who is it?" a voice called in Sinhala.

"Duncan McCloud," Duncan called back, thinking his name sounded rather ridiculous in response to that Sinhala question. And also in Sinhala, "Is the gate locked?"

There was a silence for a moment, and then, "Can't you see?"

"Open the gate," Duncan called.

Silence again, and then, "The gate has to be locked." The tone of this voice was distinctly different from Jotipala's. This was someone who had more authority.

"Who are you?" Duncan said.

"Police."

Jotipala had come up behind him, with his wife in tow. She was looking anxious, wringing her hands. Her stringy graying hair was dripping onto a frayed towel draped around her shoulders.

"I told sir," Jotipala called out to the person on the other side of the gate. "I explained it is for sir's protection."

"Good, right. The gate has to be locked," the voice on the other side said.

"Then let me make a call," Duncan said. He realized his voice was raised, and that it had turned confrontational. He lowered his voice and said, as calmly as he could, "Someone must have a cell phone."

"No phone," the voice said firmly.

When Duncan turned to Jotipala, the man opened his hands, shaking his head. The whites of his eyes flashed in his dark face. "I don't have a cell phone, sir."

There was a thick silence. Duncan debated his options. Bent had said he would contact him soon, and it was true that he had insisted Duncan not contact anyone. Maybe the danger was greater than Duncan had imagined. An intern had died, after all, and Bent had said something about foul play. He shuddered inwardly. What had he got himself into? And what should he do now?

The question was resolved by the sound of Janie's voice from the big house, calling, "Duncan! Where are you? Duncaaaan!"

"Baba is awake," Jotipala said, relief in his voice.

"I will finish making the meal," Karuna said as she hurried back toward their quarters, toweling the ends of her hair.

Janie appeared on the portico, her hair askew and her T-shirt rumpled. "I've been looking all over for you, Duncan," she said. "Can we go to the beach now?"

Two crows were still waiting on the balustrade, their heads cocked.

32

GRACE

Sunday

The boat was bobbing, engulfed in flames. Grace, running hard, had almost reached it when someone on board began ringing a bell, urgently, persistently. She was close enough to see the dark silhouette of a temple bell mounted on the boat. It was the kind of bell she had often seen in Buddhist temples in Sri Lanka. It was swinging back and forth toward the flames, the ringing reverberating in her consciousness. She jerked awake, thumping the snooze button on her alarm clock, but the noise didn't stop. Groping on the nightstand, she saw that it was only ten minutes after eight. It was Sunday, she remembered. It could only be Gordy at the door, but this was early, even for him.

She sat up, realizing that she had fallen asleep in her work clothes. The events of the night before came back to her. Describing the mugging to campus security had taken a while, and she had arrived home, exhausted, only after one o'clock. She had tried to reach Duncan until she fell asleep. The doorbell rang again. She stumbled downstairs, realizing that the collar of her blouse was soaked with sweat.

On the doorstep was Detective Mortensen.

"I am sorry if I woke you, Dr. McCloud," he said. He edged forward a step. "May I come in?"

Grace let him in, then went to splash her face with cold water and change hurriedly into jeans and a T-shirt. When she returned to the living room, he was appraising a framed photo of Duncan that stood on the mantel. "I understand you have been trying to reach your husband, Dr. McCloud?"

"I still haven't got ahold of him. I will today." The events of the previous day were flooding her mind, making it difficult to think. "He should be back in his hotel room soon. Is there something going on at my husband's company, Detective? At Cinasat?"

"We are investigating every possibility, Dr. McCloud," Mortensen said. He moved his jaw, evidently chewing gum even at this early hour. "We are trying to piece together some information. We would like to talk to him."

"Was Angie writing a story about Cinasat?"

"What makes you say that, Dr. McCloud?" Was there a note of suspicion in his voice?

"Just that you said a Cinasat intern died recently, and if Minowa Costa worked at Cinasat also . . ."

"It was very clever of Mr. Hashim to find that out." Mortensen had taken out his little notepad. "Mr. Hashim is very concerned," he added.

"Mo was very close to Angie," Grace said. "He's having a hard time dealing with her death, I think."

Mortensen glided over to the sofa. "May I?" he said, and when Grace nodded, folded his long body onto the sofa. "You yourself were not close to her, is that correct?"

"No, not really," Grace said, sitting down too. Her heart started to thump. Had they found Angie's phone? Did they know what she had said in her voicemail?

"Is there something you want to tell me, Dr. McCloud?" He looked down at his notepad, to a page scrawled with tiny scribbles, and smoothed an invisible wrinkle on it.

"What do you mean?"

"I could be wrong, Dr. McCloud, but I have wondered for some time whether you have told us everything you know."

Oh my God. They do have the phone, Grace thought. There was no way out now.

"Look, you're probably still wondering why I didn't tell everyone that Angie called me," Grace said. Her voice wobbled, and she took a breath, trying to steady it. "I don't think it's really relevant. But I'm just going to tell you. It's been sticking in my throat for too long."

Mortensen leaned back and put his notebook down on his knee. He said nothing. His jaw moved rhythmically.

Grace took her phone out. "I still have the voicemail Angie sent me," she said. "You can listen to it."

She put the speaker on so that he could hear it.

Hey, I know we haven't talked since that pregnancy test, but I really appreciated that you didn't tell anyone about Bent. And I kept my end of the deal. But speaking of that, listen, I really want to talk to you. And your husband. ....how you both feel about ....for a .... a col.........
I .... keep it secret. The first time, ... miscarried. ....
... . that happened at Sinners...
Palmer...... .... sure Duncan knows.......... let's talk soon. I'll find you.

"And you're saying this was the message Ms. Osborne sent you that morning?"

"Yes," Grace said. She handed him the phone. "See? At 8:19 a.m."

Mortensen examined the phone, and then played the message back. Angie's voice sounded more urgent than Grace remembered. When he looked up, his eyes had narrowed. His voice was sharp. "This . . . Why didn't you say that Ms. Osborne had mentioned Cinasat, Dr. McCloud? What do you know about your husband's involvement?"

Grace stared at him, confused. "What are you talking about? This is the only message she left me."

Mortensen's chewing had stopped. "This is not what you told us previously, Dr. McCloud." He flipped the tiny pages of his notebook.

"You said the message had been about a conversation you'd had at a bar."

"It is," Grace said. "About what happened at Sinners in Palmer Square." She took the phone back and played the message again.

A frown had grown on Mortensen's face. "Sounds to me like she's saying 'that happened at Cinasat Pharmaceuticals.' Something your husband knows about."

"What?" Grace shook her head. "No, no, she's talking about Sinners. The rest of the message . . . She's talking about . . ."

"Why did you say you had deleted the message, Dr. McCloud?"

Grace drew a deep breath. "I didn't want to have to explain about the pregnancy test . . . all of that," she said. "No one knows about that. Except Angie. Only she knew."

"Knew what?" Mortensen said, his voice grim.

"It's difficult to explain, because it's not very clear in my own mind, you know?" She looked at him for understanding.

Mortensen's gaze was on her, his eyes more steely than she'd thought them before.

"It's a long story," Grace said.

"I have time, Dr. McCloud."

"Duncan and I started dating when we were in graduate school in Chicago," Grace said. "We were thinking of getting married, but we broke up. He wanted kids soon, and I wanted to wait until my career was settled. At the time, I wasn't even sure I wanted kids. It was very bitter, the breakup. We both said a lot of things. I was very upset about it. Depressed. About six weeks after we broke up, Bent happened to be in Chicago, and he asked if I wanted to meet up at a bar in Palmer Square. Sinners. We had dated back in high school and college, and we'd stayed friends. When I got to Sinners, he wasn't there—I only found out later that he had left a message for me, canceling. I ran into Angie at Sinners. I thought it was a coincidence at first, but once we got talking, it turned out that Angie was involved with him, although he had recently got married. He had told her he was meeting me for a chat, and she was going to surprise him by showing up—he didn't know she was going to be in town.

"So Angie and I ended up having a drink together. I told her about Duncan, and how difficult the breakup had been. We had something to eat, and it made me sick. I told her I had been feeling nauseated a lot. She suggested I do a pregnancy test, and I agreed. She went out to the drugstore next door and bought a test, and I used it in the bathroom." Grace looked at Mortensen, trying to gauge his reaction. He was watching her impassively.

"I hope I'm not shocking you," she said.

"It is not shocking," he said.

"So I was pregnant, it turned out," Grace said. "I was pretty upset. Duncan was already seeing someone else, you see." She felt like crying. "I don't really remember much after that. Anyway, the next day, I started bleeding, and I had a miscarriage. You know, I had to have a D and C—the whole nine yards. The doctor said I had been at nine weeks." Grace stopped. She had been too personal with someone she barely knew.

After several moments had passed, Mortensen said, "And what did this have to do with not mentioning Ms. Osborne's call at your reunion?"

"When I got her voicemail, I was terrified she would just come up to me when I was with Duncan and say something about that pregnancy. Because she thought Duncan knew. That's what she says in the message. We hadn't been in touch since then, so I don't know if she even knew I'd had a miscarriage. She might have heard from someone that we didn't have kids. I don't know. She could have thought I had had the baby . . . or . . . I don't know what she might have said. Angie doesn't . . . didn't mince her words. She was an outspoken kind of person. I was trying to get ahold of her to tell her not to say anything in front of Duncan."

Mortensen was still waiting, his eyes flicking from her to his notebook, his jaw still moving.

"Duncan and I got back together a couple of months later. I never told him that I had been pregnant." The words kept spilling out. It was as if a box, long locked away, had fallen open. "I was afraid he would think I had done it on purpose. That I had got drunk, knowing that alcohol increases the rate of miscarriage in the first trimester. By a lot. I don't really remember how many drinks I had that night after I found out." She wiped the tears that had begun to fall. "A few years after we got married, we started trying to get pregnant, but we can't. I've had six miscarriages since then. I was afraid that if I told you or anyone else about what she had said, Duncan would have found out about the first miscarriage. If that hadn't happened, we might have a kid by now."

Mortensen walked over to the side table and picked up the box of tissues that lay there. He offered the box to Grace. "I am sorry that this upset you, Dr. McCloud," he said. He patted her knee awkwardly as he sat back down. "I am glad you decided to show me the message. But it's not clear to me why Ms. Osborne would want to bring up an incident that happened years ago."

Grace shook her head, wiping her eyes. "That's what I've been asking myself. I have no idea why."

Mortensen's lips tightened. "It's also not clear to me that what you say is . . . that the entire message is about what you say it is."

"You heard it," Grace said. "She talks about miscarriage. The first time. She wants to know how we both feel about it."

Mortensen glanced at the phone. "'Miscarried,' she says. But that does not have to refer to a pregnancy. She could have been talking about plans. Or justice. And it sounds to me like she mentions Cinasat, not Sinners."

He played the message again. Grace sucked in her breath. Now that Mortensen had put that idea into her head, it sounded different. She pressed the "Play" button again. *That happened at Cinas... Pharma...... .... sure Duncan knows. My God,* she thought. Had she been so worried about Angie contacting her that she'd interpreted the whole message as if it were connected to the pregnancy? Had Angie been contacting her about something that had happened at Cinasat? Something she expected Duncan to know?

She noticed Mortensen watching her. "But what would she be . . . ? Duncan doesn't know anything," Grace said, her voice coming out in a whisper. "What did she mean by 'keep it secret'? Why does she say, 'the first time'?"

"She could have been talking about whatever happened at Cinasat," Mortensen said. "May I ask . . . What made you decide to show me the message now?"

Grace blew her nose and wiped her eyes, trying to grasp the new possibilities. "With everything Mo has been saying . . . He thinks something is going on at Cinasat. Maybe he's right. Maybe I've just been imagining . . . Maybe I've been blind. If Angie was writing a story about Minowa Costa, and she worked at Cinasat . . . God. Maybe that was why she wanted to talk to me and Duncan. Because Duncan was starting there? I don't know." *Sure Duncan knows.* Why had Angie said that? What could he possibly know? *Better not to mention the email about Danibel Garwick yet,* she thought. Mortensen would want to see it. If he saw that it had also been sent to Duncan, he might start barking up the wrong tree, thinking that Duncan was somehow involved. He'd asked her all those questions about Duncan's whereabouts. She needed to talk to Duncan about everything before bringing it up to Mortensen. Then she remembered she had told Mo about the email. Would Mo tell Mortensen? It didn't matter, she decided. She would talk to Duncan soon, and then she could tell Mortensen.

Mortensen was scribbling busily in his book, his face impassive again. She watched him, hoping he would offer what he knew, but he looked away, at the tip of his shoes. "Did Angie really die of a heart attack?" she said.

Mortensen examined her face. "Why do you ask?"

She thought of the bony woman the night before, talking about Danibel. Why had Danibel's tongue been hanging out? "Just with all this going on. Do you know if something is going on at Cinasat?" she said again.

"As I said, Dr. McCloud, we do not have enough information. There are . . . inconsistencies. Questions. We are investigating those. Possibly, someone at your reunion knew something. Possibly more than one person."

"Besides Angie? Duncan doesn't know anything! You mean Bent?"

"Mr. Hashim has a connection to Novophil," Mortensen said.

"Novophil? Yes, Mo is working on a big property deal with them, he said. But this is about Cinasat, isn't it?"

"Novophil is a major competitor of Cinasat's, Dr. McCloud," Mortensen said. "They recently opened a new facility in Montclair. That is the property Mr. Hashim's company has leased. There is some question at the moment about whether the lease will be renewed. That depends on the profitability of a new venture Novophil has initiated, it appears. I am surprised Mr. Hashim did not mention that to you."

"He probably didn't even know it was relevant," Grace said.

"Perhaps," Mortensen said. "Did he mention to you that Ms. Costa worked at Novophil?"

Grace blinked, confused. "No, she worked at Cinasat. We found that out—"

"Ms. Costa quit Cinasat seven months ago," Mortensen said. "Shortly after that, she began working at Novophil. That was where she was working at the time of her death."

Grace struggled to assimilate this information. "Mo didn't know that," she said. "The guard we spoke to said . . . Did he tell you we spoke to a guard who worked at Cinasat?"

"Mr. Hashim took you along with him, he mentioned. He managed to locate a guard who has not worked there since Ms. Costa left," Mortensen said in his wooden voice.

"Wait," Grace said. "Not deliberately. It's not like he sought out someone who had left before a certain date. He was trying to find out about whether a mask—"

"Ah, yes, he mentioned the mask," Mortensen said. "He is very concerned about Mr. Hyland's comments about the mask."

"They do seem odd," Grace said. What was he getting at?

"Of course, we only have Mr. Hashim's word that Mr. Hyland reacted in that way," Mortensen said softly.

Grace shook her head, trying to read his expression. "What are you saying? Mo is lying? Why on earth would he do that?"

"I am not saying anything, Dr. McCloud," Mortensen said. "Other than that there are many things we do not know. At the moment, we are merely investigating all possible connections."

He leafed through his notebook. "It has also come to our attention that Karl Muller frequently carries both Novophil and Cinasat cargo across the US and Canada. Were you aware of that?"

"Who's . . . You mean Marla's husband?" Grace felt her mouth drop open. "God, no, that's just a coincidence. He flies cargo for all kinds of companies. I doubt Marla's even had a chance to talk to him about any of this. She's on bed rest, because of the pregnancy. Karl's out a lot. And he wasn't at the reunion."

"We're exploring every avenue, Dr. McCloud," Mortensen said. "But might I suggest . . . if you have any suspicions, it might be best if you came directly to me. We have some reason to believe that there could be serious danger in this matter. It is best if you, and Mr. Hashim, do not investigate on your own." He pulled out a business card and handed it to her. "And it is important that we get in touch with your husband. Please have him call me as soon as possible."

Grace held the card in her hand, flipping it around in her fingers. Should she tell him about the email from Yak Adura? But if Yak Adura, whoever he was, was in Sri Lanka, what could Mortensen do? And there was the warning. *Trust no one.* Did that include the police? Did it include Mo? Who could she talk to about all of this? Would Duncan be endangered if she asked someone for advice? She felt emotionally exhausted, and it was still so early in the morning.

33

DUNCAN

Sunday

Duncan wasn't surprised to see the message appear again on his computer screen. *No internet connection.* He wondered if he could find a way to make a phone call, despite what Jotipala had said. There were phone jacks on the walls in the dining and sitting rooms. Had the line been disconnected by the phone company? If the phones had only been put away, all he'd have to do would be to find one. He'd not located any in the bedroom or the dining room. He tugged at the doors of the two small cupboards set in the entertainment center, but they were locked. He checked the drawers in the side tables. Inside, there were only a few tourist brochures advertising the attractions of Galle, Hikkaduwa, and the Yala wildlife sanctuary, and some run-of-the-mill office supplies. Nothing really personal, nothing to indicate anyone lived in the house for extended periods. It seemed odd, when the house was stocked with objects that appeared to reflect someone's personal tastes: the fine china in the dining room sideboard, the collection of Agatha Christie mysteries on the bookshelves, the war documentaries among the movies, the classical music CDs.

He was supposed to just wait for Bent to contact him? Expecting commitment to the job was one thing, but this was ridiculous. He should have been given a choice. If Bent had mentioned the lack of phone access, the locked compound, or the need for a police guard, Duncan knew he wouldn't have agreed to coming here. He guessed that was why Bent had not told him. Duncan would have insisted on going straight to the police. Surely that would have been the smartest thing to do. He wondered if Cinasat had concerns about police corruption. Was that why Bent had resorted to having Janie and him sent here for safety rather than taking the matter to the police? Or was it because Cinasat didn't yet have enough information to involve the police? How had Bent got the police to guard this place then? Duncan had tried to find out more from the guard at the gate, but the guard had refused to say anything more than he had already said.

Duncan sighed. He had to look at the bright side. At least he could be sure that he and Janie were not in danger here, with the high garden walls and the guard outside. At least Karuna seemed eager to look after Janie, and the food was good. Thank God Janie wasn't a picky eater. And she had only asked a couple of times about when her dad would arrive. *No sense in worrying,* he told himself. There was plenty to do. He still had videos he needed to watch.

He went back to his computer and opened up a video file of one of the ceremonies. It seemed more appropriate to be watching the ceremony here, with the sun reflecting off the ocean outside, than it had been when he had been in his office in New Jersey. He watched the drummers in their ornate costumes start beating their drums, the rhythm mesmerizing. The drummers' arms and chests rippled, wet with sweat. Their eyes, glazed, appeared to be fixed on the patient, who was reclining against a white pillow nearby. Flames were blazing in a brazier, smoke billowing. An adura came into view, chanting, a long stick over his shoulder. One end of the stick swelled into an arrowhead made of young coconut leaves and areca flowers, symbolizing the eye of Shiva. Still chanting, the adura pointed this object, a potent symbol of divine power, at the patient, drawing it portentously over her body and then flicking it toward the offering baskets nearby. This was intended, Duncan knew, to transfer the demons from the patient to the baskets. The adura's chanting deepened into a hypnotic rumble, rising and falling. Even though the chanting was familiar to Duncan, it still made the hair on his arms rise.

The sound of Janie's recorder intruded into his consciousness. Duncan shut his laptop hurriedly. The video would frighten her. She marched in and stood before him, dressed in a frilly pink swimsuit, playing "Row, Row, Row Your Boat." When she laid down the recorder and took a bow, Duncan applauded.

"Where's Karuna?" she said.

Duncan got to his feet. "Come on, let's go see her."

When they emerged onto the portico, a single large crow on the balustrade flapped its thick wings. Janie reared back, clutching Duncan's arm. Duncan tried to shoo it away, but it only hopped a few steps back, its beady eyes piercing.

"It won't hurt you," Duncan said.

They went down the front steps and into the back garden. A few clouds had appeared, dampening the intensity of the sunlight. Karuna was standing by the door to her quarters, braiding her damp hair.

Janie went up to the door and peered in. "Is this the shed?"

"Where Karuna and Jotipala live," Duncan said.

Janie stepped inside. "Is it alright for her to go in?" Duncan said to Karuna.

She nodded, smiling. "Never mind."

Duncan stood at the entrance, watching Janie. A hint of incense was in the air. The room was small, maybe twelve feet by ten, with a cracked gray cement floor. A shelf on one wall was piled with a few stacks of clothing, an open Ovaltine tin holding some half-burned white candles, and a couple of cardboard boxes, one with a piece of coir rope and a bit of faded fabric trailing from it.

"There are no chairs," Janie said, spinning around. "And where are their beds?"

"They sit on the floor," Duncan said. "And those mats rolled up there, they sleep on those."

Janie frowned. "Like in camp? Are they sleeping bags?"

"Kind of," Duncan said. He felt a little uncomfortable describing Karuna's living situation with her standing there. "She's asking about your sleeping mats," he explained.

Janie had gone over to the suitcase in the corner, on which a large object lay, covered with a red cloth. Before Duncan could stop her, she pulled the cloth off to reveal a long cylindrical drum. It was made of wood and leather, about two feet long.

"A drum! Can I play?"

"Janie! Cover it up again, please," Duncan said. He recognized it as a ceremonial *yak beraya*. He'd seen many such drums played at the thovil he'd attended. A drummer would tie the strings around his waist so that the drum rested horizontally across his midsection, and drum with his hands on both ends.

A shadow fell across the doorway, and Jotipala appeared.

"She was asking about the drum," Duncan said in Sinhala.

Jotipala stepped in and whisked the red cloth back over the drum. "Come, Janie baba," he said to Janie firmly, gesturing to her as he stepped out of the room.

Janie followed reluctantly. "Why can't I play the drum?"

"Only if he wants you to. It's not a toy," Duncan said. He wondered if Jotipala was a drummer who played at ceremonial events. "You are a drummer?" he said to Jotipala.

"Yes, sir," Jotipala said tersely. And then, turning away toward the path that led to the overlook, "The tide is going out. Baba can go to the beach now."

Duncan translated for Janie.

"Yay, yay, the beach," Janie said, dancing down the path.

Jotipala led the way to the overlook, treading confidently on the pebbly surface of the garden path in his bare feet.

"That drum looks like the ones people play in thovil," Duncan said to him. "I knew a lot of people near here who played drums like that. In thovil ceremonies."

Jotipala said nothing.

"In Talgasgama," Duncan said. "That is close to here, isn't it?"

Jotipala glanced at him briefly. "Not very far," he said. Then, after a pause, "When was sir there?"

"A long time ago," Duncan said. "More than ten years ago. I was studying . . . learning about thovil."

They reached the overlook where the battered temple guardian was raising his broken arm in futile warning. The screw pines were swaying on their weathered roots, their mops of spiny leaves shimmying. Jotipala took Janie's hand. "Sir can hold baba's other hand," he said. "The path is risky. Good to be careful." They climbed down in single file. Flat rocks formed shallow steps, making the descent relatively easy, although it was clear that rain or heavy spray would make the steps treacherous. The jagged boulders that loomed on either side of the path provided a few handholds.

When they got down to the beach, Duncan saw that it was a wide tongue of fine sand edged on both sides by huge black rocks. Waves crashed rhythmically against the rocks, misting the air with a salty spray. At high tide, the beach would be completely covered, Duncan realized. At the moment, with the tide out, the waves that rolled onto the beach were gentle, loping toward their legs like playful children before collapsing into a froth of shimmering white.

"It's so warm!" Janie shouted, splashing wildly as the water cascaded past her ankles.

"Not safe after the rocks there," Jotipala said, pointing to the black rocks on either side. "Underwater current."

"Okay, Janie, you can paddle, but you can't swim here, Jotipala says," Duncan said to Janie.

She was already in seventh heaven, Duncan saw, jumping in the waves and laughing, her hair in a tangle around her face. Jotipala had set himself down on a low boulder nearby. When Duncan sat beside him, he got up and settled cross-legged on the sand below, so that Duncan was forced to look down to speak to him.

"Do you drum much nowadays?" Duncan said.

"Sometimes," Jotipala said. "When there is a need. It is what I like to do, but it doesn't bring much money. This job." He gestured up the path toward the house. "This is what gives us our livelihood."

"It must be difficult to find work," Duncan said, choosing his words carefully. It was a sensitive topic. He knew that many Sinhalese considered people who did exorcisms—the aduras and dancers and drummers—to be polluted because of their association with demons. The objects they used in ceremonies were also considered polluted. They were objects to be feared. He knew that was why Jotipala had not wanted Janie to touch the drum.

"It is our good fortune to have jobs here," Jotipala said. His shiny dark forearms, below the short sleeves of his graying white shirt, were wiry. His legs were folded, and his feet were protruding from the edge of his sarong, the heels cracked and calloused.

"Even fifteen, sixteen years ago, when I was in Talgasgama, the drummers and aduras I knew said they couldn't make much money on exorcisms. Now it must be even less."

"True, now fewer people do them," Jotipala said. After a pause during which he dug a small hole in the sand, he said, "Why was sir learning about exorcism?"

"I was writing a book," Duncan said. Trying to describe a doctoral research project would be fruitless. He knew that it was likely Jotipala had not completed a high school education. "I wanted to tell people in America about how people do exorcisms here. We don't have anything like that there."

"This is not something you can learn to do from a book," Jotipala said, digging another hole. "You can only understand by carefully observing and practicing with the community."

"Not to learn to do," Duncan said. "The book was just to describe the customs."

Jotipala looked puzzled, but he shrugged. "I started to drum when I was nine. In the beginning I thought I would be a dancer like my father and my uncle. I danced for some time. I was not very good. My legs are not strong enough." He stretched his legs out, pulling up his sarong to his knees. His legs were burned dark by the sun, but Duncan could still see the raised veins that snaked around the knotty muscles of his calves.

Jotipala scooped out a small tunnel between the holes he had dug, connecting them. "Who does sir know in Talgasgama?"

"I don't know if they will still be there. Ediris, do you know him? He was the adura for many ceremonies in Talgasgama."

"No, I don't know," Jotipala said. "Some of the people have stopped this work. Some of them have gone to the Ambalangoda area, trying to find work. Some of them are working in factories, making little things for tourists. Curios. Masks, bowls, lamps."

Duncan nodded. Even when he had been in Talgasgama, that was the kind of work aduras, dancers, and drummers did, trying to make a living. They were artists. "I also knew Liyaneris. His wife was Muriel Nona."

Jotipala nodded, looking pleased. "Yes, yes, I know. Liyaneris is not drumming now. He has not been well." He raised his hands, demonstrating a tremor. "But his son, Nimal, he is drumming. You know him?"

"Nimal, yes. He was only a small boy when I knew him. Maybe ten years old."

"Now he has a family," Jotipala said. "Two children."

"If you see him, please tell him I remembered him," Duncan said, using the customary way of sending greetings.

Jotipala was chuckling, watching Janie. She had buried herself in the sand up to her waist, waiting for the waves to wash her legs out.

"You have children, you and Karuna?" Duncan asked.

"They are grown now. Three of them. Two daughters are married. I have a grandson. Still a baby. My son is still waiting. He still has no proper job. He is difficult to please. The matchmaker has found good girls. But he has refused. He wants to go to Colombo. I have told him, don't think it will be easy."

"Janie, not so far!" Duncan called, seeing Janie wading out. Janie turned back toward the shore.

"Sir has only one daughter?" Jotipala said.

"Oh, no, Janie isn't my daughter," Duncan said. Until then, he had not realized that had not been obvious. "My boss's daughter. That is why I wanted to get in touch with him."

A shadow passed over Jotipala's hollow-cheeked face. He rose to his feet, shaking the sand out of his sarong. "I have to get back to the house now," he said. "To work on the garden. I will come back later. It is safe down here for sir and baba now. Not like at high tide. Then the water will come right up to the cliff. It will be deep enough here to drown."

He paused, looking up at the screw pines above. "Baba must not come of the house alone," Jotipala said. "It is not safe."

Duncan thought about the garden with its neatly tended croton beds, the jasmine bushes studded between the araliya trees. "As long as she keeps away from the cliff edge, she should be alright," he said.

Jotipala shook his head. "There are cobras," he said.

Duncan felt a jolt of fear. He'd occasionally encountered snakes in Sri Lanka, and even seen a venomous viper slither into a village house once, but never a cobra.

"Only in the past few weeks," Jotipala said. "Several times they have come onto the portico. Two, I killed. After the second one, I keep the pestle by the front door. In case."

He trudged off toward the rock path, leaving Duncan with a feeling of dread.

34

GRACE

Sunday

Grace turned the coffee machine on and checked her email, hoping for a message from Duncan. Nothing. She'd listened to Angie's voicemail message several more times. Now she was convinced Mortensen was right. Angie had been talking about something that had happened at Cinasat. But what? She reread Yak Adura's message for the umpteenth time. Exorcist. Why use that moniker? What should she do? She couldn't try the number again until she got to work. *Your husband is in danger.*

She dialed the Taj Ocean Hotel and asked for Duncan's room. The phone rang, but no one picked up. It was late in the evening there. Could he have gone out to dinner? She thought of calling her parents. But if Duncan had been too busy to contact her, he would not have called them yet either.

She simply had to be patient, she told herself. Once she got to the office, she could call Yak Adura and try Duncan again. She showered and changed, trying to focus on what she needed to do to finish the grant application. She also needed to get Gigi started on the dissections. Thoughts kept pouring through her mind, about Yak Adura's email, what was going on at Cinasat, what Mortensen had said about Mo, how she would tell Duncan about the miscarriage in Chicago. It was only by getting to work that she would be able to deal with it all.

She was on her way out, her briefcase in hand, when the phone rang. Her heart thumping, she picked it up, full of both relief and trepidation. It had to be Duncan.

But it was Bent.

"Bent? Is everything okay? I've been trying to get ahold of Duncan," Grace said.

"I thought maybe he called you," Bent said. There was an urgency in his voice that frightened her.

"What do you mean? Isn't he with you? Where are you calling from?"

"The hotel. We got here this morning. But something came up, and I had a car take him to Hikkaduwa, a guesthouse there. I told him to take Janie along because there would be more for her to do there than here. But now I don't know where he is, or Janie."

"I don't understand. What was he supposed to do in Hikkaduwa? A meeting?"

"I can't go into the details. But it seems there has been some sort of mix-up. The car that took him wasn't the one I had ordered."

"He went in a taxi?"

"No, a hired car." Grace could hear the tension in his voice. "Grace, don't panic, but I think he and Janie have been kidnapped."

Grace's briefcase thudded onto the floor, folders spilling out. "Kidnapped! My God. Who would kidnap them? Are you sure? Could they just have broken down on the way?"

"That's what I thought at first," Bent said. "I called our people who sent the car. That's when I found out the car wasn't ours."

"What? Whose car was it then? Did you call the police?"

"They're working on it. But Grace—"

"I'll call my parents. They can call my uncle. He's a deputy inspector general—"

"Grace, wait, listen. You can't do that," Bent said, his voice insistent.

"What?"

"There's more going on than you know," Bent said. "More than I can tell you right now. We think one of our competitors is behind this, maybe trying to get information from Duncan."

"What competitor? You mean Novophil? Did you tell the police that?"

There was silence for a moment. "Bent? Are you talking about Novophil? Mortensen was here just now. The detective from the reunion. He said something about Novophil being involved. What is going on, Bent?"

"What did Mortensen say?"

"That two people who worked for Cinasat are dead. Did you know about that?"

"I just heard," Bent said. "That's what worries me about all this."

"Mortensen's investigating something at Cinasat. He wanted to talk to Duncan. Has he talked to you?"

"Not for a while. I don't know what's happening," Bent said. "We have to be careful so that we don't endanger Duncan or Janie. You need to keep quiet about this, Grace. I haven't even told Janie's mother. She'll get worked up. I don't want her to get the police involved. I'm doing everything I can. We'll get it sorted out. I wasn't sure I should call you, but I thought I'd better. I know your parents were waiting to hear from Duncan. I didn't want them or you to . . . to get worried."

"How can I not be worried?" Grace said. "What if something happens?" Then she realized what a stupid thing that was to say. Janie was only nine. How worried Bent must be. She couldn't even imagine what he must be going through. "At least Janie's not alone," she said. "Duncan's really good with kids. He'll make sure she's alright, Bent." Unless he wasn't alright himself, she thought. She could feel her heart racing harder, but she tried to calm her voice for Bent's benefit.

"I know," Bent said. "I know he'll look out for Janie. That's my one consolation. Someone's coming over here now, from the team we've put together to help. They're going to track down the car." He sounded on the verge of tears. "Just keep this to yourself, Grace. I'm really sorry to have got you and Duncan mixed up in this. I didn't know . . . It's all so out of control," he said.

"What shall I do? I should tell Mortensen," Grace said.

"No, no, no," Bent said. "That's the last thing you should do. This is too sensitive. We can't risk anything. I just want to make sure they're safe. And there's nothing Mortensen or anyone else can do from there. Please, Grace. I'll call you soon. Just sit tight."

After he hung up, Grace huddled in a corner of the sofa, hugging her knees. What was she to do? Was Yak Adura connected to this? Should she call Bent back and give him the number? But the email had said she should not even use her home phone. *Trust no one. Your husband is in danger.* Should she call Mo? It was ridiculous to think he could be involved. *Trust no one.*

There was only one thing she could do, she realized. She fished her laptop out of her briefcase and looked for the earliest flight to Sri Lanka. There were only two seats left. The price was much too high, but she had no choice. The flight was leaving in less than four hours. She could make it if she rushed. She would call the number Yak Adura had sent when she got to Colombo. It would be better to not call her parents beforehand. Otherwise there would have to be explanations, and she didn't know what she could say.

She lugged a suitcase out of the closet and threw some clothes into it. The KIS sweatshirt she had got at the reunion was lying in a corner of the closet. She tossed it in a carry-on bag with a paper copy of her almost-finished grant proposal. When she finally drove out of the garage, she saw Gordy standing by the fence, trimming a wayward branch off her honeysuckle creeper.

"Gordy," she called out. "Keep an eye on the house, would you? I'm taking a flight out today, to Sri Lanka."

Gordy looked startled. "What, now?" He hurried toward her, the clippers dangling from his hand.

"I have to rush," Grace said. "Plane to catch. To join Duncan for a few days," she added, waving.

"Well, bon voyage, young lady," Gordy said. "You be careful, out there on your own."

Grace watched the house recede in the rearview mirror. She remembered that she had not had time to get Gigi started on the vials in rack thirty-nine. All those dissections still to be done. Soon those flies would be too mature for their ovaries to be of any use. Time would beat her.

35

DUNCAN

Sunday

On the screen, the adura was dancing, rocking from one foot to the other. His head was thrown back, his eyes wild, his painted face contorted with the emotions he was projecting. He passed one of the woven offering baskets over the patient's head. The patient, clearly in a trance, touched the basket and wiped her face, her hands rigid. A relative, his own eyes wide with terror, guided her as she placed flowers, betel leaves, and a handful of rice in a woven tray placed before her, symbolizing both an offering to the demon and her freedom from the demon's will. The adura threw a handful of some substance into the brazier. Orange balls of flame shot into the air, and smoke billowed out in gusts. The adura seized the live rooster that had been a part of the ceremony and held it over the incense burner. The power of the adura's song, in turn terrifying and uplifting, reverberated in Duncan's ears. Duncan had put on his headphones for fear that Janie might wake up. She had passed out on the couch after they had returned from the beach. She'd be terrified if she heard the chanting.

He slid one headphone off to scratch his ear and became aware of the sea calling through the open windows. He would have liked to go down to the main road and walk along the beach. He had been trying to be stoic about being cooped up, but he was starting to feel increasingly angry. Bent should have warned him that he would not be able to leave the compound. He wished he knew more about the danger Bent had mentioned. Why did Bent think he needed so much protection?

His eyes were heavy. Even though it was not yet bedtime here, his body was responding as if he'd just spent a whole night without any sleep.

"Sir is watching a thovile." Jotipala's voice came from behind him. Duncan, taking off the second headphone, turned to see him standing by the carved screen at the sitting room doorway. He looked displeased, even angry, Duncan thought, although he spoke politely. How long had he been standing there?

"Yes, I am watching this for my work . . . for my job . . . ," Duncan said, and then realized how ridiculous that must sound to Jotipala. How could he possibly explain why he was watching a video of an exorcism ceremony?

"Sir knows the woman who is ill?" Jotipala said, his eyes on the video as the patient came into view, her eyes rolled back in her head.

"No, I don't know her," Duncan said. He wished now that he had not been watching the video in plain view. He clicked on the icon to pause the video. The adura froze, his mouth open wide, holding the rooster high above his head.

"Then sir knows the adura? This is part of sir's studies?"

"Part of my studies . . . yes, in a way, but I don't know this adura," Duncan said, hearing the apologetic note in his own voice.

"How did sir get this film?" Jotipala moved a couple of feet forward. There was an accusatory edge to the way he asked the question.

"My boss gave it to me," Duncan said. "He . . . His company had it filmed when the exorcism was happening. The adura gave permission." Surely that was true, Duncan thought. This was part of a scientific study. Ethics boards, in the US and here, would have approved everything. Papers would have been signed. Everything had been above-board, Carson Lacey had assured him.

"Someone must have given him money," Jotipala said. "These things should not be filmed. Nowadays, even the sacred things are not respected. How can the ceremony work when there is no respect?" He shook his head, his eyebrows drawn together in a frown. "The spirits take revenge on such things. This is not a film. These are not film stars to be watching and enjoying."

"I wasn't enjoying like that," Duncan said, horrified. "I would not . . . This is difficult work the aduras, the drummers, the dancers, everyone is doing. I respect what they do."

Jotipala shook his head, his nostrils flared in anger. "This is very dangerous. How can the aduras, all of them, even the patient, be safe when filming is done? The purifications will fail. Sir does not know how terrible the demons are. Their power is great."

Duncan knew about the elaborate purification rituals exorcists did before undertaking a ceremony. People in the villages feared demons and the unearthly havoc they were believed to wreak. During his time in Talgasgama, Duncan himself had seen things that he couldn't easily explain. Once, during an exorcism, he had seen a young man leap impossibly high. The man had been an onlooker standing at the edge of the ceremonial area, by a tall coconut tree. At the climax of the ritual, when the adura had shouted the mantra for driving out the demon, the patient had emitted a shrill scream, and at the very same moment, the onlooker had let out a loud holler and leapt straight up into the air, high enough to touch the dangling fronds of the coconut tree. The coconut fronds had jerked as he touched them. It had happened very suddenly.

Later, Duncan had wondered if he'd imagined it, because he couldn't see how a jump such as that, easily twelve feet into the air, would have been possible. But other ceremony attendees had seen it too, he found out; they'd been matter-of-fact, though frightened. The demon had been driven momentarily into the onlooker, they'd said.

Even now, thinking about it, Duncan had no explanation for what he'd seen, other than to suppose that the power of what the onlooker believed had allowed him to make that superhuman jump.

Now Duncan struggled to find the words to mollify Jotipala. "The adura must have thought it was alright to let it be filmed," he said. "He had a choice." He wondered whether to mention that his work was to help develop a potent drug, but then he thought better of it.

"What choice," Jotipala scoffed. "We make next to nothing doing these ceremonies. It is impossible to make a living doing this. Most of us work in houses or construction to be able to support a family. So if someone comes, some big-shot foreigner, and offers money, what choice do we have?"

Duncan struggled to find something to say. "The company I work for is trying to help people. This was for a good reason. You don't understand . . ."

"Sir is the one who doesn't understand," Jotipala said. "Sir can't understand our life. In England, in America, everyone is rich. No one has to struggle to fill their children's bellies."

"I can't understand what it's like for you, that is true," Duncan said. "But not everyone in America is rich. I wasn't rich when I was growing up. My father had to work hard."

Jotipala scowled at him, the whites of his eyes stark against the darkness of his skin. "The way Fernando Sir works hard," he said. "He sits at a desk and makes money. That is not the kind of work I am talking about."

"My father didn't sit at a desk," Duncan said. "When I was small, he made money by collecting used oil from restaurants. The old oil that was left over after frying food. The restaurants use a lot of oil. When the oil gets too burned, they pour it into big buckets. My father left buckets at the restaurants, and then in the night, he came and collected them. He had enough money to have a truck, it's true. But it was a broken-down old one. I used to go with him to collect the oil. After we collected the oil we used to take it to factories where people made chemicals, dump it into big vats. That was hard work. Our clothes were always dirty from the oil."

Jotipala looked down at his own faded shirt, which was streaked with sweat and dirt from his gardening, and then at Duncan's clean white shirt. Duncan felt like a hypocrite, talking about the hardships he had suffered. Providing access to free higher education, as Sri Lanka did, would be no help to someone too poor to get past eighth grade without having a job.

"I know it must be difficult for you," was all he could find to say. "But we're not so different. It has also been difficult for me, even if it was in a different way."

Jotipala's eyes rested on Duncan's face for a second, and then slid away. "Janie baba must wake up now, to eat dinner. Karuna has made hoppers. If she sleeps any more now, she will be up all night."

36

GRACE

Sunday

Grace had been trying not to think about where Duncan might be, where Janie might be, but images of them locked up in a hut somewhere kept intruding on her mind. Send positive vibes, that was what Marla would say in a situation like this. If only she had Marla's attitude.

She arrived in the chilly departure lounge with fifteen minutes to spare before boarding. She pulled her sweatshirt out of her bag, and only then remembered the chicken curry stain on it. She had forgotten all about putting it in the wash. Then she saw, to her surprise, that there was no evidence of a stain at all. She took it into the light by the windows facing the tarmac and examined it again. Nothing. It looked brand-new, in fact. She pulled it on, and feeling something in the pocket, remembered Bent's card. It was still in there. "Meet me—first bridge, northwest trail. 9 a.m." She had forgotten all about that too. The card was still crisp; the sweatshirt had clearly not been in the laundry.

She thought back to the morning when Angie had died, when this whole mess had begun. She had been standing at the buffet table right next to Janie, serving herself chicken curry. At the first gunshot, her hand had jerked, splattering curry on the sweatshirt. She clearly remembered seeing the top of the *K* in *KIS* stained dark red. How was it unstained now? She lifted the cloth up and sniffed it. No odor. Could this be someone else's sweatshirt? She had tossed it under her picnic bench later that day. Bent had dropped it off at her cabin. But maybe someone else's sweatshirt had been there as well, and he'd picked that up instead.

Had Bent given the card to someone else, someone to whom the sweatshirt belonged? Did that person now have her own sweatshirt?

She looked again at the card. "First bridge, northwest trail. 9 a.m." The northwest trail had been where the shots had been fired that day. Could Bent have met someone the morning of Angie's death? It occurred to her with a shock: could the sweatshirt be Angie's?

She called Marla on her cell phone.

"I'm fine," Marla said, when Grace asked about her health. "Mo hasn't returned my calls. Do you know anything else? Have they found out yet what Angie was working on? Do you want to come over? For dinner maybe?"

"Actually, I'm at the airport," Grace said, trying to keep her voice casual. "Going to Colombo."

"What? I didn't even know . . . You're done with your grant?"

Grace wished she could just open up, tell her everything. "Close," she said, although she hadn't looked at the unfinished application since seeing Mo the previous afternoon. "Duncan had to go to Sri Lanka for work. Unexpectedly. I decided to join him."

"Really, this sudden—"

Grace broke in, not wanting to answer any questions. "Listen, I have to board soon. But I had a quick question for you . . ."

"Yeah?"

"I brought my KIS sweatshirt to wear on the plane, the one I got at the reunion. But I don't think it's mine. Mine had a stain on it. I think I might have picked up someone else's."

"You mean did I get your stained one? No," Marla said. "But why do you care who got it? They'll wash it. The one you have is yours. Good thing there was only one size."

"But actually," Grace said, "I just wondered . . . if it could be Angie's."

"Angie's?" Grace heard the puzzlement in her voice. "Why do you think that?"

"I don't know . . . Well, because obviously if she had one, it might have been left there. Did she have one?"

"She got one, yes, when she showed up to the picnic area that night," Marla said. Her voice had sobered. "And now that you mention it, I don't remember seeing it in the cabin later, after . . . you know. But anyone could have left one and not even noticed. Who was thinking about sweatshirts when we all left there? Mo said he left his. And maybe other people."

Again, she thought of telling Marla everything. *Trust no one.*

After she hung up, her eyes fell on a pay phone stand at the far corner of the lounge. She could try calling Yak Adura from here, she thought. She made her way over to the phones and dialed the number from the scrap of paper she'd put in her purse. It was in the wee hours of the morning in Sri Lanka. Yak Adura was probably asleep. If this was a home number, there could be a response.

The phone rang three times, and then a sleepy woman's voice answered in English, "Yes?"

"My name is Grace McCloud," Grace said.

There was silence for several seconds, then a thump and the clatter of something falling. The voice said, "Yes, yes," sounding newly alert.

Grace fumbled in her mind, wondering what she could say. "I got an email message," she said in Sinhala.

"Yes, yes. This is Yak Adura," the voice said, still in English. "Where are you calling from?"

"The airport," Grace said. "I'm taking a flight to Colombo, leaving in forty-five minutes."

"What's the flight number?" the voice said, suddenly businesslike.

Grace consulted her boarding pass. "Korean Air four seven three arriving in Colombo at 6:20 a.m. Tuesday."

"Does anyone know you are flying here?"

"Only a friend."

"Who is the friend?"

"Marla Muller," Grace said, alarmed at the tone of the woman's voice. "And my neighbor, Gordon Mann."

There was another silence. Then the woman said, "Never mind. When you get to Colombo, I'll meet you. Don't take a taxi."

"How will I know who you are? What's your name? Will you have a name card?"

"No, no. I will wear a . . . no, I will carry a . . . a feather. A rooster feather in my hand. That will be uncommon. Don't go with anyone else."

"What is this all about?" Grace said.

"I'll tell you when we meet," the woman said. "But you should know that you are in danger."

"You said my husband is in danger," Grace said.

"He is in danger because of you," the woman said. "Because you have found out too much."

"What do you mean? What have I found out?"

"I'll explain when we meet. Just be careful. Stay in public view. Don't go anywhere alone until we meet."

"Wait, wait! Do you know where my husband is?" Grace said. "And the little girl?"

"No," the woman said. "But as long as you are out of their reach, he will be valuable to them."

"Who is 'they'?" Grace said.

"We'll talk soon," the woman said. "Look for me. Rooster feather." The line disconnected.

37

DUNCAN

Monday

Duncan sat with his hands clasped around his ankles, his chin on his knees, looking out over the black water. He'd scanned the area for snakes before climbing onto a boulder at the overlook point. To his left, the pale figure of the temple guardian was faintly visible among the equally pale roots of the screw pine trees. Above him, the fronds of the coconut trees rustled. He could hear the mighty rumbling of the ocean and the rush of the waves on the rocks below. A sense of awe overtook him, as it often did when he sat alone in the wildness of nature. Everything was right with the world, somehow. This was the kind of peace he would want to teach his child to experience, he thought. If he ever had one.

When he had woken in the wee hours of the morning, he had lain listening to Janie breathing. She snored a little, soft purring sounds that reminded him of a kitten. He had tried to go back to sleep, but even as he lay there, he knew that it would be futile. This happened to him every time he flew to Sri Lanka from the US. On the first three or four nights, he always woke long before dawn. This morning, the insomnia had been compounded by his frustration at being kept at the guesthouse. When the luminous digits on his watch said it was half past four, he'd given up. He'd dressed quietly and tiptoed out of the house.

Now he waited, watching for the dawn to come. A sliver of a moon had emerged from behind clouds, laying bits of shivering silver across the wide swathe of dark water below. He wished Grace could experience this sense of peace. She was always rushing from one task to the next. Sitting still was not something she enjoyed. He wondered if she was at the lab. In New Jersey, it was late afternoon on Sunday. He hoped Bent had not said anything to worry her when he called. He wished there was some way he could get in touch.

The sound of pebbles clattering startled him. Turning his head, he was barely able to make out Jotipala approaching.

"There is still moonlight and sir is up," Jotipala said, standing beside Duncan.

"I couldn't sleep," Duncan said. "Every time I come here from America, it's the same. I wake up early." He choked back the complaint he had been about to voice, about being stuck here. Jotipala had nothing to do with it. "But this is a good place to be. I like to hear the sea."

"It is inside my heart," Jotipala said. "My whole life I have lived by the sea. I know its moods. Every day, it is different, but underneath, it is always the same."

He sat down on the boulder next to Duncan, and they sat in silence for a few minutes.

"Sir thinks deeply."

"I was thinking about what it would be like to have a child," Duncan said.

"They bring light into life," Jotipala said. After a pause, he said, "Why does sir not have children?"

I wish I knew, Duncan thought. "Who knows the answer to that? Luck maybe."

"The time has to be right," Jotipala said. "The planets have to be aligned properly. And the spirits must be appeased."

Duncan thought of saying that he had not grown up with those ideas, but that could have seemed disrespectful. "My wife . . . she doesn't believe in all that," he said. "Even though she is Sinhalese."

Jotipala's eyes opened wide in surprise. "Sir's wife is Sinhalese?"

"Yes." Duncan fished his new work phone out of his pocket. Since leaving New Jersey, its only use had been as a camera. He opened its photo album to find the selfie he'd taken with Grace the morning he'd left home.

"That madam I know," Jotipala said.

Duncan, surprised, flipped back to the picture he had indicated. It was the one he had downloaded from the email Grace had sent, the picture with the mask that had captivated Mo for some reason.

He pointed to Angie. "You know her?" Angie had gone to school in Kandy after all. He wondered how often she had visited Sri Lanka after leaving high school. It wasn't unlikely that she might have visited Galle. Could she have met Jotipala through Bent?

But Jotipala pointed to Angie's companion. "No, this other madam," he said.

"This one? How do you know her?"

"This madam stayed here. It was not recently. Maybe a year ago. I remember her well. She asked me a lot of questions, but not directly. She could not speak Sinhala. There was a Sinhalese sir who asked me her English questions in Sinhala."

"She was asking about the ceremonies?"

Jotipala shook his head. He didn't seem pleased about his interactions with the woman. "Once or twice, about bali thovil, yak thovil. But what she was most interested in was hooniyam."

"True?" Duncan said. Now he understood why Jotipala seemed displeased about the woman's questions. Most village people didn't want to associate themselves with black magic rituals. "What did you tell her?"

"I told her what I told all of them," Jotipala said.

"All of them?"

"All the madams and sirs who came here to learn about hooniyam."

"There were others? Foreigners?"

"Five or six," Jotipala said. "I don't know from where. America, I think. Some of them came together. I told them I didn't know much about hooniyam. But Fernando Sir said I had to find some *kattadiyas* for them to talk to. I found them two kattadiyas. One was in Henegama and the other one was in Walpola."

"They went to talk to the kattadiyas?"

Jotipala nodded. "The car took them. Many times. I told them I didn't want to go."

"Why did they want to . . . They wanted to get hooniyam done?"

"I don't know what they wanted. They asked me too many questions. In the beginning, I didn't even want to tell them about the incidents I knew about. But Fernando Sir said I had to tell them everything I know. They wrote down what I said. They wanted to know all the details about the incidents I knew about. What the *kattadiya* had done. Did the victims know they had been enchanted. What happened to the victims." He shook his head again. "Not good to ask about these things." He turned to Duncan, his eyebrows drawn together. "Sir is interested in hooniyam also?"

"No, no," Duncan said. "I am only interested in thovil."

Jotipala looked again at the picture on Duncan's phone. "This mask," he said. "Where is this?"

Duncan sighed. "In my office building," he said. "I know it should not be on the wall. People there don't understand what masks are for. They only put the mask there because . . . because it is interesting."

While they had been talking, the sky had lightened to gray. The water shimmered, a darker gray. The rocks below had come into view too, jagged black hulks awash in white foam. On the overlook, the ringed trunks of the coconut palms were visible, and their leaves, dark green against the gray sky, reminded him of a sari pattern.

"A good time to go out for a walk," he said, to change the subject. "Out of the gate to the road. You can go with me if you're afraid I won't be safe."

Jotipala rose to his feet. "I have to see to the garden," he said.

"I'll go then. I'll be careful." He didn't even know what he had to be careful about, he thought. Besides, it was unlikely that anyone would be about at this hour.

"The guard won't let sir go out," Jotipala said, turning away. "He has a gun."

"Maybe he won't be there at this hour," Duncan said.

"The guards come in shifts. When one leaves, another one comes," Jotipala said. "They stay in the guardhouse."

"Then he can come with me for protection," Duncan said. "No one is going to be after me at this time anyway."

Jotipala turned back toward him, and Duncan saw, for the first time, an apologetic look cross his face. "The lock on the gate, the guards . . . that is not to stop anyone from coming after sir," he said. "They are to stop sir from going out."

Duncan frowned. "What do you mean?"

"Forgive me, sir," Jotipala said. "I am only doing my job. To keep sir here, that was what I was told."

"Because someone could harm me or Janie?"

"No one is going to harm sir," Jotipala said. "They are afraid sir will harm them."

"What? What are you saying? Whom could I harm?"

"Aney, sir, I don't know all that," Jotipala said, backing away. "I only know what I overheard when the guard was talking on the phone. We have to make sure sir does not leave here. We were told to tell sir it was for sir's protection." He began to walk off, his head down.

Duncan climbed off the rock and ran behind him. He caught hold of Jotipala's sinewy arm. "Wait, Jotipala," he said. "I don't understand. How can I harm anyone? Do you think I would harm anyone?"

"I don't know, sir. I am just doing my job. If I lose my job, I will have no way to look after my family." Jotipala pulled his arm away and backed down the path. "Forgive me, sir," he said again. He turned and hurried away.

Duncan looked down at the water below, where obedient waves were traveling in orderly lines toward the beach. They came in bearing creamed sand, serving it up to the land like an offering, before slipping back into the sea. The sand they left behind shone like dark glass as the water drained away.

38

GRACE

In Transit

"No more sketching? Not easy to work on a long flight," Ingmar Mankell said, his eyes on the grant application in Grace's hand. "Discipline." He said it approvingly. He had introduced himself earlier. He was an overweight middle-aged man, who, though friendly, was not careful about respecting Grace's personal space. His right leg had been pressed against Grace's for most of the flight, and his arm covered the armrest completely, forcing Grace to squeeze herself toward the center of her seat.

"I don't really think I can," Grace said. She had doodled desultorily for a while in the sketch pad she'd brought along, but her mind kept wandering to the conversations she'd had with Bent and Yak Adura. Those also intruded when she tried to sleep.

"You are returning from a visit to the United States?" Ingmar said.

"No, I live in the US. I'm going back to visit . . . my parents," Grace said.

"Ah." Ingmar eyed her wedding ring. "Leaving the husband at home?"

"He's already in Sri Lanka," she said, a little taken aback by his question. "On business."

"What kind of business is he in?" Ingmar's breath wafted toward her. She could smell something sour in it.

"Pharmaceuticals," Grace said.

"Ah, a chemist."

"Actually, he's an anthropologist." How strange it would sound if she explained that Duncan studied exorcism ceremonies, she thought. "He gave up an academic job . . . actually, he was laid off. Now he's in marketing."

"That's what the drug companies do best," Ingmar said. "Which company is your husband at?"

"Cinasat," Grace said. A week ago, she would not have thought twice about telling a stranger where Duncan worked. Now, she wondered whether this was just a normal airplane conversation or if this man had some ulterior motive.

She stuck her grant application back in the seat pocket, excused herself, and closed her eyes, bringing the conversation, innocent or not, to an end.

39

DUNCAN

Monday

Janie, perky after a long night's sleep, had eaten an early breakfast of coconut-milk rice and treacle, but Duncan had barely touched his food. He sipped the slightly gritty black percolated coffee Karuna had brought him, not knowing what to do with what he had learned that morning. If Jotipala were to be believed, he was a prisoner here. His mind was filled with questions, and he had no answers. Had Bent sent him here under false pretenses? But why? And why would he send Janie along? If Bent had not sent him here, who had? Perhaps this was not the safe place Bent had talked about after all. Had he been brought here by someone else? Whom? And again, why?

He could hear Janie jabbering in the bedroom, talking about her recorder and her Legos, apparently unconcerned that Karuna understood no English. Karuna, by the sound of her replies, was trying to comb the tangles out of Janie's hair.

When Janie burst back into the dining room, her hair was combed and neatly braided. "Come on, Duncan!" she said, tugging at his shirtsleeve. "Can we go back to the beach now?" She looked up at Karuna, who was regarding her fondly. "Can you give us a pail?"

"She's asking for a bucket, to play on the beach," Duncan translated. "An empty biscuit tin would do."

"I will find one and send it with Jotipala," Karuna said, and disappeared through the back door.

On the portico, four crows had already gathered. Duncan wondered what drew them. There always seemed to be at least one there. They were oddly silent for crows.

Janie didn't seem to have noticed them. "Let's go, let's go!" She whirled down the path to the overlook, where the temple guardian waited among the screw pine roots.

"Be careful there," Duncan said, concern startling him out of his reverie. He reached out to hold her hand. They climbed carefully down the path to the beach.

Small waves were tiptoeing in to the shore, as if afraid to rouse the dark swells that heaved like sleeping giants behind them. Duncan walked along the spongy, packed sand, Janie's hand in his, their feet barely leaving any prints in the fine sand. A king coconut lay on the sand in one corner of the beach, its orange color a warning against the black rocks.

"Here comes the tin for the sandcastle," Duncan said, spotting Jotipala descending the path.

Jotipala set down the tin, a rusted red one that had once held Cheesebits biscuits, on the sand, avoiding Duncan's eyes.

"You have to help, Jotipala," Janie said, tugging at his shirt as he turned away.

Jotipala hitched up his sarong and squatted on his haunches, smiling.

With only one tin, it took them a while to build a sandcastle. It was a precarious structure with a prehistoric air, its turrets just fist-size lumps of sand.

"I have to talk to my wife. I don't want her to worry about where I am," Duncan said. Jotipala continued the task Janie had assigned him, scooping handfuls of moist sand into the biscuit tin. Duncan was thankful for Janie's inability to understand what was being said. "I don't even know who sent us here. I thought it was my boss, this child's father, but he would not have us imprisoned here. I have to at least talk to him, to find out. He may not even know we are here."

Jotipala patted the sand into the tin, silent.

"I just need to make a phone call," Duncan said.

Jotipala looked up. "There are no phones, sir," he said.

"A cell phone then," Duncan said.

"Cell phone does not work on this property," Jotipala said.

"You said you heard the police guard talking to Mr. Fernando."

"That was down at the beach road, at the shop," Jotipala said. "On the phone there."

"Then I have to go to the shop and make a call."

"The guard will not let sir leave the compound."

"You can talk to him," Duncan said. "Tell him I am not going to harm anyone. I just need to go to the shop."

Jotipala sighed. "He won't listen to me. He is police. He will be sacked if he lets you leave. The same for me."

"I will make sure he, and you, won't be sacked," Duncan said, although he had no idea how he would do that. "I can explain to your Mr. Fernando. I'm not going to harm anyone." At least he could say that with confidence, Duncan thought.

"Nothing I can do, sir," Jotipala said. He stood up, but Janie pulled at his arm.

"Now a moat," she said, pointing to the furrow she was digging out around the castle.

Jotipala squatted down again, and began to scrape at the sand with his hands.

Duncan looked around at the rocks and the waves lapping against them. "Maybe I don't need to go through the gate," he said. "Can I get past those rocks when the tide is out all the way?"

239

Jotipala sucked in his breath. His eyes were wide with alarm. "No, no, sir, that way is not passable. The power of the sea . . . it will surely kill sir. It has killed before." His voice had turned grim.

"Someone died here?" Duncan said.

"Not so long ago," Jotipala mumbled, his head bowed over the pile of sand he'd dug out.

"Who? Someone you knew?"

"There is no use in talking about the past," Jotipala said. "Sometimes bad things happen. It is our karma." He reached under his shirt and pulled out a knotted yellow cord that was hung around his neck. A small metal cylinder was strung on it. "Since then . . . I have been wearing this yantra. Also Karuna has been wearing one. For the past few weeks, since . . . since the cobras started coming."

"The cobras? What do they have to do with . . . ? They came after the person died?" Duncan said, confused.

Jotipala nodded, silent.

"Who died?" Duncan said again.

"It is in the past," Jotipala said. He was not going to say more about it, Duncan realized. Village people were superstitious about death.

Jotipala dug for a while in silence, following Janie's lead. Then he said, his voice only a murmur, "At dawn tomorrow morning, the night guard will leave. He removes the padlock outside so that Karuna can go to the fish market. The morning guard gets late to come. For an hour there won't be anyone there. Maybe when the night guard leaves, the gate might not be padlocked on the inside. Then anyone who wants to go and come back would have a little time." He rose to his feet and flapped the sand out of his sarong.

"Are you saying—" Duncan started to say.

But Jotipala interrupted. "I have to go and work on the garden, Janie baba," he said, and walked away toward the path to the overlook, leaving a trail of slender footprints.

"Wait, Jotipala! We haven't finished the moat!" Janie yelled after him.

"We'll finish it," Duncan said. "He has to go and do his work in the garden."

He scooped out long streaks of sand with his fingers, considering his options. Which way would he have to go to get to the shop? Would the shop be open at that hour? Maybe he would not even need to go out, he thought. Maybe Bent would send a car for him and Janie before then. He had said they would only need to be away for a few days. But then, Duncan thought, he didn't even know if Bent had sent them here.

40

GRACE

In Transit

"I hope I didn't disturb you," Ingmar said. He set down the two beer cans the steward had just handed him and opened a packet of toasted almonds with astonishing dexterity, given his hamlike hands.

"Don't worry, I needed to wake up," Grace said, opening her own tomato juice can. "The flight always makes me thirsty."

"I mean before, when I was sleeping," Ingmar said.

"I was out cold," Grace said. If Ingmar had snored, she had been oblivious.

"Good, good," Ingmar said. He took a deep swig of his beer. "I always worry on flights whether the twitching will wake people up."

When she looked at him questioningly, he said, "The legs, you know?" He jerked his legs briefly, one by one. "I do this when I'm asleep. That's what my wife tells me. I only notice it when I'm falling asleep."

"Oh, that," Grace said. "That wouldn't wake me. My husband does that all the time. I used to notice it in the beginning, when we first shared the same bed. But now I've got so used to it."

"My wife was like that," Ingmar said wistfully. "For twenty-three years we have been married. She never complained. I have had this all my life. But now she keeps talking about how difficult it is for her to sleep. She is convinced it is restless legs syndrome. You have seen commercials for this maybe?"

"Who hasn't?" Grace said.

"Everyone sees these commercials, and then suddenly they start thinking they, their husbands, wives, have a big problem. Now she is paying attention to it, and so it keeps her awake." He waved his hand in the air. "But what can I do? She is my wife. She needs her sleep. Get separate beds, or take something for it." He gulped from the can, and Grace heard the liquid gurgle down his throat.

"So you take something for it?"

"Not yet," Ingmar said. "My wife, she wants me to take this drug, I don't remember the name." He smiled briefly. "Not your husband's company. Their competitor. Novophil? Now they know how to do marketing." He brushed Grace's sleeve with his hand. "Not that Cinasat is not good . . . Your husband is very good at his job, I am sure. But what I am saying is that Novophil has made my wife so worried about my twitching." He scoffed. "My RLS." He drained the last of his beer. "Now I even have an acronym for it. Isn't that good marketing?"

The second time in less than twenty-four hours someone had mentioned Novophil to her, Grace thought. Was it just coincidence? Novophil was certainly a household name.

"Take ADHD," Ingmar said, snapping open his second can of beer. "So many children being diagnosed. How many really have a condition? Children can't be children now. I could never sit still when I was small. I was always getting into trouble. But no one said ADHD. Now it's different." He crunched a handful of almonds noisily.

"True, ADHD is overdiagnosed," Grace said. This was something she'd read about in the news. "But that's a real condition. I have two colleagues with kids who have ADHD. They're very happy the kids were diagnosed. Ritalin really helps them. And the diagnosis helps the kids get extra help in school."

Ingmar shook his head. He sucked another gulp from his can. "That is the thing. Nowadays, if your child is distracted, hyperactive, you have to medicate. Otherwise, you're neglecting your parental duty." He slapped the tray, flattening the empty almond packet.

"I remember a friend I had," Grace said. "A real tomboy, you know, climbing trees, playing cricket. She couldn't sit still for a minute. Her legs were restless even when she was awake. She was always getting into trouble in school. For not paying attention, blurting things, fidgeting too much. The teachers were always angry at her, but her parents, everyone else, just brushed it off. The naughty girl, that was what my parents called her. Sometimes I wonder if she would have done better if she'd been diagnosed with ADHD."

"Who knows? What happened to her?" Ingmar said.

"I went to a different school later, so I don't know what she was like in high school. But I know she became a lawyer, so she couldn't have done too badly."

Ingmar raised his can triumphantly. "See, she learned to cope with her problems. Other people learned to cope with her." He glugged the rest of his beer, then crushed the can with one squeeze of his massive fingers. The aluminum crumpled as easily as if it were paper. "Extreme cases are different. But other cases . . . How to know if there is a real illness or whether it's being created in people's minds? Once people believe they have a condition, or their kids have a condition, then they have it. Then medication seems necessary. That is what marketing is all about."

"You're against medication," Grace said. She wondered if he was someone who believed in alternative treatment. Chiropractic, Rolfing, acupuncture. Would someone like that take Duncan's drug? Or would they miss out on something that could really help, just because they had a negative opinion of drug treatment?

Ingmar grinned. He leaned close, and his breath, beery now, drifted over to her, making her feel a little queasy. "If I was sure I was sick, I would take medication," he said. "The marketing would have to be very good, for me to believe that."

41

DUNCAN

Tuesday

When the sky had lightened enough to see the outlines of the coconut trees outside, Duncan rose from his chair. He'd been sitting by the open windows of the sitting room for almost an hour, since he awoke, listening to the gossip of the sea. A brisk breeze was blowing. He hadn't wanted to sit at the overlook, although he would have preferred it, because he didn't want to burden Jotipala further. Duncan had tried the night before to ask Jotipala about where exactly the shop was, and whether it would be open at dawn for him to make a phone call. But Jotipala had avoided Duncan's eyes. His only response had been, "I don't know about any of that, sir." Clearly he didn't want to involve himself any further in Duncan's actions. He just hoped Jotipala wouldn't change his mind about leaving the gate unlocked.

Duncan stepped carefully to the sitting room doorway, avoiding the dark shapes of the furniture. He had almost reached the screen when he heard a door bang. Feet skittered across the floor. Janie appeared, hair spilling messily from her braid, one end of her pajama shirt tucked into her shorts.

"Hi, Duncan!" she said. "I'm up!" She threw her head back and stretched her arms wide, emitting a loud, theatrical groan.

Duncan tried to mask his dismay. "It's early. You should go back to bed," he said.

Janie shook her head vigorously. "I'm not sleepy! Let's go to the beach," she said.

Duncan's mind raced over his options. He could tell her to go change and then just slip out by himself. But she would be upset to find him gone. He could just tell her she had to stay, he thought. But she would probably insist on coming with him. What if he left her with Jotipala? But the added complication might change Jotipala's mind about the gate. He sighed. He had no choice here.

"We can't go to our beach," he said. "But I'm thinking of going for a short walk, just down to the road. Do you want to come?"

Janie nodded, jumping up and down.

"Go and change then. And comb your hair. You can only come if you do it quick," Duncan said. "We have to leave in one minute."

She ran back to her room, and Duncan went out onto the portico. He couldn't see the sea from there, but he could hear the whispered warnings of the waves. The sky was a pale gray now, and birds were cheeping urgently in the trees. He had no sooner thought of the crows when a trio of them swooped down onto the balustrade. They paced along it, watching him intently. He backed away, trying to see if the padlock was on the gate. What if Jotipala had changed his mind after all? What would he say to Janie then? He would have to make up some story so that she wouldn't realize they were being held here against their will.

Janie rushed out. She had changed into a yellow sleeveless dress. Her hair was unbraided but a little less messy. Duncan took her hand and hurried to the gate.

He saw, with a burst of relief, that it was unlocked. Jotipala was nowhere to be seen. What if the guard was still outside? There would be a confrontation, and Janie might sense that something was wrong. Duncan put his finger over his lips and whispered in Janie's ear, "Let's be really quiet. Jotipala and Karuna might be sleeping. We wouldn't want to wake them up."

He pulled the latch up carefully, trying to keep the metal from clanging, and inched the gate open. Tire tracks from the police vehicle were etched into the gravel outside, and the weeds at the edge of the road were trampled down. The guardhouse door was open, and no one was around. A sleeping mat, half-unrolled, covered the floor. A grubby pillow lay against the wall. The guard probably dozed sitting up, Duncan realized.

He pulled the gate closed behind them, and they hurried down the sloping lane, which was bordered on either side by *nidhikumba* weeds, leathery bromeliads, and overgrown lantana bushes. Here and there, grass and weeds poked through the packed soil under their feet, suggesting that the lane was not heavily used by traffic. The lane curved after several yards and joined up with a wider, poorly paved road. A metal fence extended along one side of the road, with coconut trees towering over the top. On the other side, they passed several tall garden walls, with no house or resident names posted. The tops of araliya trees and oleander bushes spilled over into the road here and there, their blooms out of reach. They continued downhill and, after some time, came upon a right-angled section of the main road with an esala tree standing guard, its yellow flowers hanging down enticingly. The air was heavy with moisture, and Duncan was sweating a little with the exertion.

On the land side opposite them, a series of painted garden walls blocked the view of houses. No commercial buildings could be seen nearby, but far away to the right, a white balconied hotel loomed above the coconut trees. Immediately next to the road on the beach side was a small thatch-roofed stall for selling coconut, too small and makeshift to have a phone. Farther along, to the right, was a small shop with a corrugated metal roof. Its green-painted metal doors were, to Duncan's disappointment, padlocked.

A narrow footpath led from the shop to a scrap of rocky, undeveloped land with a small strip of sand bordered by a screw pine grove. The sea was close to the road there, which explained why no building had sprung up. Up ahead, Duncan could see another low-slung building. Another shop. They could try there. He checked his watch. Jotipala had said the guard would be back by seven. It was 6:22. There would be time.

Better to go along the beach, Duncan thought. They wouldn't be visible from the road then. They took off their sandals as they hurried forward, skirting bits of fibrous debris fallen from the coconut trees. The breeze was stiffer now, and the waves were in a mutiny, roiling and crossing each other in unruly lines. The water rushed up to drench their legs. A few black crows with glinting eyes swooped down out of nowhere, cawing loudly, and Duncan shooed them away.

"Hurry, we have to keep moving," he said, pulling Janie by the hand. She kept crouching to pick up scallop shells and bits of coral, and he was getting worried about the time. By the time they reached the shop, the pockets of Duncan's shorts were rattling with treasures she had given him to carry.

The road had got busier. Occasional tuk-tuks and motorbikes putted by. At the bus stop, a gaggle of schoolgirls had gathered, the pleats of their white uniforms neatly ironed, their hair tamed into braids and ponytails. More uniformed schoolchildren were drifting out from a lane up ahead, along with a few people in office clothes.

A crimson tuk-tuk was parked next to the shop, and a couple of young men, their dark chests bare and sarongs hitched up to their knees, were standing nearby. They looked around in surprise when Duncan and Janie stepped into the shop.

"Must have come from the hotel," Duncan heard one say in Sinhala.

Burlap bags of rice were stacked near the door alongside plastic crates of bottled drinks and several stalks of king coconuts. Behind the counter were the usual items that wayside shops carried: packets of biscuits, bars of soap, tins of Ovaltine and Milo. In one corner, a small man in a well-worn polyester shirt and khaki shorts presided over two burners, making hoppers. His face glistened with sweat, and the locks of curly hair falling over his forehead were damp. As they entered, he ladled pale batter from a large pot into two small round pans set on the burners. He swirled the pans with an expert motion, cracked an egg into one, and covered both. A small pile of recently made hoppers stood on a plate nearby, their edges crisp.

"Yes, sir?" the shopkeeper standing behind the counter said.

Duncan turned to him. It would be better to buy something first, he thought. "Two hoppers and a Milo," he said hurriedly in Sinhala, and then asked if he could use the phone.

The man looked impressed. "Very good Sinhala," he said. "How is that?"

"My wife is Sinhalese," Duncan said. It was the easier explanation.

"Ah, true?" There were times when local strangers reacted to this proclamation with disapproval, as if he had stolen away one of their own, but this man smiled. He reached behind the counter and produced a phone. "Colombo call?"

"I will pay you," Duncan said. "Do you have a phone directory?"

The man lugged out a hefty directory. It was a good thing directories were still in use here, Duncan thought. He leafed hastily through to the number of the Taj Ocean Hotel. He was about to dial it when he realized he had a problem. How would he talk to Bent about why they were imprisoned at the compound without Janie overhearing? She was munching on her hopper, engrossed in watching the hopper man swirl his batter. The shop was too small for her to not overhear.

He would call Grace's parents, he decided. He could speak to them in Sinhala, tell them to get a message to Bent, to tell Bent that Duncan needed to get in touch. He knew Grace's parents' number by heart. He punched the number in with the shopkeeper watching curiously.

"Hello, Ma," Duncan said, when Grace's mother, Nalini, picked up.

There was a second's silence, and then, "Duncan! I am so happy to hear from you. I've been trying to get in touch with you."

Duncan frowned. "Didn't you hear that I was down south? I ended up in Galle."

"Galle? You were in Galle? Are you calling from the airport now? Has the plane landed?"

"What plane, Ma? What are you talking about?"

"Grace's plane?" Nalini said, sounding confused. "Aren't you picking her up?"

"What? No, I didn't even know she was coming," Duncan said. "When is she coming? When did she call you?"

"She didn't call us," Nalini said. "I don't even know what flight she is on. Even what airline. Tchah." She made an exasperated sound. "How can this be? She didn't even tell you? How can she do this out of the blue?"

"How do you know she's coming?"

"Mohammed Hashim called here last night. You remember that boy from her class in KIS. He was at your wedding. Muslim boy from Indonesia? With the wife wearing the head scarf. They had two small girls running around, remember?"

"Yes, yes, I know Mohammed," Duncan said. "Why was he calling you?"

"He said it was urgent to get in touch with Grace. Something he needed to talk to her about. He mentioned a photo. I couldn't follow exactly what it was about. But he kept saying it was very urgent, that she should call as soon as she landed. That is why I called your hotel, to tell you to get her to call him when you picked her up." She paused. "He sounded very excited. I thought he was upset, to tell the truth. I asked him if there was any problem, but he said no, nothing to worry about."

Did this have to do with the photo Grace had emailed him? She had said Mo had showed it to her. That was the photo of the woman Jotipala had said he knew. *Strange*, Duncan thought. But this could be some other photo. The question was, why was Grace coming here all of a sudden? It was not like her to make a sudden trip. She liked to plan things out.

"Ma," he said. "I'm actually still in Galle. So I can't pick Grace up. She'll probably call from the airport when she gets there. I don't have a phone number she can call me at . . ." Should he ask her to contact Bent? Something didn't seem right, he thought. Why had Bent not conveyed the message that Duncan was leaving Colombo? "I'll call back soon," he said.

"Okay. I'll tell her. Do you know when you'll be back in Colombo?"

"Soon," Duncan said. "I'll call you soon, Ma."

He hung up and paid the shopkeeper, who had been listening with unabashed curiosity. Duncan checked the time. They could hurry and get back to the house before the guard returned. But if they went back, he probably would not be able to get back out to make another call. What was this all about? Why was Grace coming? Did she not know he was down south? If she had known, she would have told her parents. Why would Bent not have informed her as he had promised?

The wind, blowing hard, was whipping Janie's hair back. His own hair was sticky with the moisture in it.

Forget going back to the house, Duncan thought. He needed to get to Colombo, find out what was going on. He'd have to find a car.

One of the men who had been standing by the tuk-tuk was sitting inside it, now with a maroon shirt on. Duncan took Janie's hand and went over to him. "Can you take us to that hotel?" He pointed to the white building in the distance.

"Come, come," the man said as the tuk-tuk shuddered to life.

42

GRACE

Tuesday

The chatter of voices assailed Grace as soon as she exited through the airport door into the sticky humidity of the morning. The covered curb was already crowded with passengers and their families. She looked around at a blur of men in polyester shirts, women with their black hair in braids and buns and ponytails, children in fluffy nylon dresses, bare toes peeping from under lungis and saris and trousers, hard fiberglass suitcases in primary colors, and bulky plastic-wrapped packages tied with pink nylon string. She could smell car exhaust and the sharp reek of sweat. Several men approached her, though tentatively, as if they knew she would not be taking a taxi. "Taxi, miss?" "Going where, miss?" Ignoring them, she tramped down the curb. A middle-aged woman was hastening forward, holding a sign that said **GRACE MC CLOUD**. She was smartly dressed, in a beige short-sleeved shirt and a black skirt that flapped against her calves. Her shoulder-length hair was fashionably cut. The way she was clutching the sign gave her an anxious air. Grace stepped toward her.

"Are you . . . ," the woman said.

"Grace McCloud," Grace said. "And you are . . ."

"Please. Please come this way," the woman said breathily. She hurried down the platform, gesturing for Grace to follow. People were calling out to greet arriving passengers. Porters were shouting as drivers tried to park, and cars were honking as others tried to edge back onto the road. Grace followed the woman, who kept looking back at her urgently. They were almost running, weaving between passengers and their greeters, past a series of cars parked by the curbside. At the very end of the covered area, a man in a dark uniform was waiting, Grace saw, next to a new-looking white minivan.

They were about forty feet away from the van when a dented blue Toyota sedan screeched diagonally into a curbside spot that was just being vacated by a jeep. Its trunk popped open. A sari-clad woman jumped out and grabbed Grace's arm. Grace jerked back, an involuntary shriek escaping her lips.

"Get inside," the woman hissed, pulling at Grace's suitcase with one hand and pushing her toward the passenger door of the car with the other. As Grace resisted, horrified, the woman seized something from her hair bun and waved it at her. It was a gleaming brown rooster feather. "I'm Yak Adura," she barked. "Get in the bloody car!"

The man who had been standing by the van was now running toward them, shoving people aside. Grace leapt into the car, jamming her carry-on onto her lap, and yanked the door shut. Yak Adura heaved Grace's suitcase into the open trunk, slammed it shut, and darted nimbly around to the driver's side, shouting in Sinhala, "That man is a thief! Stop him!"

Grace, looking back, saw the electrifying effect this had on the crowd. There was only one person running, and that was the uniformed man. Several bystanders leapt toward him, gripping his arms as he tried to wrestle free. The woman with the sign was nowhere to be seen. Yak Adura reversed the car, almost hitting passing traffic, and stepped on the gas. Turning back, Grace saw the man gesticulating and yelling at the crowd, an angry expression on his face.

Grace stared at the woman who was hunched over the wheel, concentrating on speeding forward. She was attractive, and in her midthirties, Grace guessed, with a round face and a chin that jutted forward. Her eyes were large and long lashed under straight, rather thick eyebrows. A small black birthmark nudged her lower lip. Her hair was wound into a smooth coil at the base of her neck, and small silver hoops adorned her ears. She was wearing a sleeveless red sari blouse and a nylon sari with a tie-and-dye pattern in white and shaded reds. None of this was what Grace had expected. Although the email message from Yak Adura had been in Sinhala, the phone conversation she'd had in English had not led her to expect a young woman in a sari. In the city, most young women nowadays only wore saris, if at all, to work or to special events. The athletic way this woman had hefted her suitcase, the way she had spoken, and the way she was driving also seemed at odds with the sari and the small stack of alternating red and silver bangles on her wrist. Maybe she was just stereotyping, Grace thought. She was too used to being in the US.

"Sorry, but how do I know you're Yak Adura?" Grace said. "I mean, there was that other woman . . ."

"I sent you an email in Sinhala," the woman said. "And then you called me, from the airport. I told you I would have a rooster feather." She turned to Grace and smiled briefly. There was a hint of mischief in her smile, and it set Grace's mind at rest. "Sorry about the melodramatic pseudonym. I wanted to get your attention. And the rooster feather gimmick," she said. "It was the only thing on my bedside table when you called. I use it as a bookmark. Not something most people carry around, so seemed a good choice." She jerked the steering wheel to avoid a car that changed lanes suddenly, her bangles clinking. "My name is Shalini. Shalini Samaraweera. Better than Yak Adura, no?" She craned her neck to read a large road sign that indicated the various roads permitted for tractors, cars, bullock carts, tuk-tuks, bikes, and pedestrians.

"So what happened back there? Who was that other woman?"

Shalini shrugged. "Don't know, men. Probably someone Cinasat paid to do their dirty work."

"What? What do you mean?"

"Someone obviously knew you were coming. Besides me. You said you told some people, no? Your neighbor, your friends."

"They're not involved in anything!" Grace said. Involved in what, she didn't even know.

"But they may have told someone else," Shalini said. "These bloody people are everywhere, men. You were probably being watched. You don't know the extent of this." She swerved to avoid a car trying to pass. The engine sounded uneven, with occasional loud sputters interrupting its whir. They were driving at a good clip along an avenue pleasantly shaded by the trees that bordered it. Mesh fences secured the road on both sides in this airport area, which was impeccably maintained. Billboards here and there exhorted travelers to INVEST IN SRI LANKA.

"What exactly are we talking about?" Grace said. "I have no idea what's going on. What about Duncan? My husband? Is he okay?"

"I'll start from the begin . . ." Shalini suddenly looked alarmed. "Damn. That bloody van. Is that the van from the airport? Look, look back and see."

Grace looked back. There was a white van gaining on them, but she couldn't see the driver's face. "I don't know. Could just be another white van."

"True. Wait, we can find out," Shalini said. "Watch and see if it stops when I stop." She pulled over onto the shoulder and paused with the engine gasping fitfully. The van passed them, and some distance ahead, it pulled to a stop. "Damn. See that?" She was silent for a moment. "Don't have a choice. When we get off the expressway, we'll stay on the big roads where it's busy." She accelerated, and the car shot forward with a jerk, belching a cloud of black smoke. As they passed the van, Grace saw the uniformed man watching them, his face impassive.

The woman was sitting in the passenger seat with a cell phone to her ear, her neck craned forward to see them, her eyes wide. The van pulled out behind them.

"Why are they following us? What are we going to do?" she said.

"Just hope we don't run out of petrol or break down." Shalini looked anxiously at the dashboard where an indicator was blinking. "This bloody car is useless. That's why I was late getting there. I broke down in Seeduwa and had to get a jump."

They drove on, with Shalini's eyes fixed as much on the van behind them as on the road ahead. "Where are we going?" Grace said.

"Trying to think. I was going to take you to where I'm staying, but now better not," Shalini said. "Most of the evidence I've collected is there. I don't want the place to get ransacked." She glanced at Grace. "It might be time to go to the police." She shook her head. "Problem is, you can't be sure. Who is being paid off, who is to be trusted."

"Is this about Duncan? My husband?"

"Not only him. The whole story, men," Shalini said. She looked back at the van and frowned. "At this point, police may be safest. But who knows?"

"My uncle is a deputy inspector general," Grace said. "We could go to him."

Shalini looked sharply at Grace. "What's his name?"

"Ragu Thangaraja."

"Deputy inspector general? I don't know him."

"He only got into the position recently."

"When?"

"Why does that matter? He's my mother's sister's husband. I've known him all my life. We could go to my parents' house in Colombo, and then we could call him."

Shalini was silent, apparently considering the issue.

"These fellows may already be waiting at your parents' house if they knew you were coming. And this bloody van is following us. What is your parents' house like? Is there a gate, a wall? Are there a lot of people around, or is it out of the way?"

"They live in Colombo 4," Grace said. "Gamini Lane. They're at the end of the lane, right near Immaculate Heart Church. Not many people around usually. There's a wall and a gate. But why are you asking? It's not as if anyone's going to come onto the property."

Shalini snorted. "You really don't know the scope of this, men," she said.

"What is all this about?" Grace said. "I'm worried about my husband. His boss called me. He said Duncan had been kidnapped."

"His boss? Bentley Hyland," Shalini said, her lips pursed grimly. "Yes, I'm sure he said that."

"What do you mean?"

"He's the one masterminding all this," Shalini said.

"What! That's ridiculous," Grace said. "His daughter, Janie, was also kidnapped."

Shalini's head snapped toward her. "How do you know that?"

"Bent told me. She was with Duncan."

Shalini frowned. "That can't be. He must have been lying to you."

"What the hell . . . what . . . Please, can you just explain what you know?"

Shalini looked in the mirror, tapping her fingers on the wheel agitatedly. "We have to get rid of this van before we can even decide where to go." She swerved suddenly and exited the expressway.

"Where are you going?" Grace said, looking around, trying to identify the road. It looked like any other one in the area. Plantain trees grew thickly by the roadside, their broad leaves hanging down to the tangle of bushes beneath. Bunches of bright-orange king coconuts clustered in the palm trees. They passed a rickety lean-to with a thatched roof, where a man in a sarong hitched to his knees was laying out papaws, pineapples, and hands of bananas for sale.

"We'll go to one of the small hotels," Shalini said. "Then we can think about what to do to get rid of this van." She pointed to a sign up ahead. "That one is fine."

The hotel, whitewashed like all the rest of the nearby tourist places, was a low-slung, sprawling building with a tall traveler's palm guarding the front entrance. It was one of the more down-to-earth hotels in the area. There were no liveried footmen to be seen outside. Shalini parked in an unpaved lot that had been cleared of coconut trees, adjacent to the hotel restaurant. A few seconds later, the white van followed and parked at the edge of the lot, facing away from them. "Don't look at it," Shalini instructed, gathering her sari *pota* around her waist. "Let's go inside and see if they follow us in."

Grace climbed out, hugging her purse. "Walk calmly," Shalini said, and Grace slowed her pace, suppressing an urge to look over her shoulder. She heard two car doors slam shut.

They turned the corner. The wide concrete steps of the front entrance were ahead of them. "Wait a little, miss," a male voice called out behind them in a tone that was too menacing for the words he used. Grace heard the sound of gravel scrunching.

The uniformed man was hurrying toward them, the woman a few steps behind.

Shalini grabbed Grace's arm and propelled her forward. "We have to meet someone," she called out over her shoulder.

"Wait, wait, miss," the man said. "Miss's husband said to pick miss up."

Grace slowed her pace, but Shalini pulled at her arm. "He's bullshitting," she hissed. "Tell him you can go with him in half an hour. Tell him to wait here."

"What? Why?" Grace said.

"Just do it. I'll explain."

Grace turned her head. The man was only yards away. "Sorry," she said. "We're late for a meeting. I can go with you when we come out.

In half an hour." She hurried forward, responding to Shalini's tug on her arm.

Grace could hear the two people behind gaining on them. "Come on, Grace," Shalini said loudly in English. "We're already late." They broke into a run, sending gravel flying. They sprinted toward the entrance and up the steps.

"What is going on?" Grace said, trying to catch her breath. She looked out through the glass door. The man and woman were talking at the foot of the steps, underneath the enormous paddle-shaped leaves of the traveler's palm. The man was gesticulating, his face livid, and the woman was shaking her head.

Shalini was rummaging in the scuffed leather purse slung over her shoulder. She pulled out a five-hundred-rupee note that had seen better days. "Just had an idea," she said, looking harried. "I'll come back in ten minutes. You wait here. Don't go with them, whatever you do. If they try to get you to, make a big scene."

"What . . . what do you . . . ," Grace stuttered, but Shalini was already hurrying toward a porter in a red uniform who was loitering inquisitively nearby.

"Trust me. Just wait," she called back to Grace. Grace heard her say to the uniformed porter, "There is a driver and a lady down there, by the steps. Can you make sure they wait right there? We'll be out in half an hour." She pressed the money into his hand. He looked down at his hand in amazement, and then strode purposefully out the front door.

Shalini was hurrying toward a sign at the end of the lobby that pointed the way to the restaurant, the silver-trimmed straps of her red slippers flashing under her sari hem.

Grace stood hesitantly in the middle of the lobby, her purse clutched to her side, confused by this series of events. None of it made sense. What was happening? Why did she have to stay here? She was to trust someone she had just met? What if the van driver was telling the truth, and Duncan had really sent him?

43

DUNCAN

Tuesday

The hotel had an affectedly casual beach cabin air, perhaps to compensate for being on the land side of the road, with no direct beach access. After talking to the man at the front desk, Duncan found out that they were at the outskirts of Galle. He asked for a car to Colombo.

While Janie rinsed the shells she'd collected in a small courtyard fountain, Duncan paced, trying to make sense of everything. Why was Grace coming to Sri Lanka so suddenly? Why hadn't Bent told anyone he was going to the guesthouse? What about what Jotipala had said? It didn't make sense. Why would Bent think Duncan would harm anyone? Was it possible that the guesthouse was not where Bent had intended to send him? Then who had sent him there? Where was Bent? Could Bent have been abducted himself? There were too many conflicting pieces in the puzzle. His head hurt, trying to figure out what was going on.

He looked at his watch. More than thirty minutes had passed since he'd ordered the car. He went over to the desk to check.

"Yes, yes, coming," the young man at the reception desk said, but Duncan noticed that his eyes slid away, not making contact. A little while ago, this same man had greeted Duncan cheerfully, looked him straight in the eye when he paid for the car, and said that a car would be ready shortly.

"Is there a problem?" Duncan said. Maybe he needed to try a different hotel. Galle was full of them.

"No, no, soon it will come. Please sit, no?" the man said, busying himself with the papers on his desk.

They sat down in cane wing chairs in the cool lobby. Janie rustled the thin plastic bag a porter had given her for her shells. Not long after, a skinny waiter arrived with a pot of tea and a plate of assorted sweet pastries that smelled fresh baked.

"On the house, sir," he said, casting an ingratiating glance at Duncan.

When Duncan tipped him, he made a show of turning the pedestal fan on to keep flies away from the pastries, as if the ceiling fan, already spinning above them, weren't enough.

Duncan went again to talk to the receptionist.

"Sorry, sir, car is delayed. Please enjoy the tea," the receptionist said.

Duncan returned to where Janie was sitting. "Mmm, these are good," she said, strawberry jam and cream from a pastry smeared on her lips. Duncan took a pastry, trying to control his impatience.

They had finished the tea and pastries when the receptionist arrived at their side. "Car is here," he said.

The wind was whistling in the coconut trees at the side of the building when they went out to the porte cochere. A white Mercedes with tinted windows was idling there. The young driver standing by the open back door guided Janie inside. Duncan heard her say, "Hi!" To his astonishment, sitting next to her, his pale lips stretched into a smile, was Hammond Gleeson.

"Hammond! What the . . . What are you doing here?" Duncan said, stammering in his confusion.

"I thought we'd give you and Janie a ride," Hammond said. "Get in."

"We're going to Colombo to see Grace's mom and dad! And Daddy," Janie said, rattling the shells in her plastic bag.

Hammond's lips tightened into a thinner line. "That will have to be later, Janie," he said as the driver got in and shut his door. "Right now, Duncan and I have to talk about something important." He crossed his legs, and Duncan saw that a slim black leather briefcase was resting at his feet.

"Hang on, if you're taking us, I'll cancel the car I ordered," Duncan said. "Wait a minute," he said to the driver, pulling at the door handle. "Can you unlock the door?"

"No need," Hammond said to the driver. "Let's get going." As the car jerked forward, he said to Duncan, "Don't worry, the order was canceled."

Duncan frowned. "How did you even know I was here?"

"A shop fellow," Hammond said, pointing in the direction of the hopper shop. "Said you had made a call to Colombo. He was very impressed with your Sinhala."

"But how . . . I didn't even know you were in Sri Lanka," Duncan said, trying to understand. Hammond had to have gone to the house and found that he was missing. Had Jotipala been blamed?

Hammond's nostrils flared. Duncan could see a muscle twitching under the pallid skin of his cheek. "I had the same concerns that brought Bentley and you here."

"The leaks? You arrived today?"

"A couple of days ago."

They drove past the hopper shop and turned into the lane that led to the house. "Back to the Maya?" Duncan said.

Hammond was looking straight ahead, his lips still tight. "There was a reason you were asked to stay there," he said, his voice clipped.

"Stay where?" Janie said.

"So Bent did—" Duncan started to say, but Hammond interrupted, his bony fingers raised to stop Duncan.

He patted Janie's knee. "Karuna will play with you at the house. Duncan and I have to talk. In private."

Duncan polished his glasses on his sleeve. What the hell was going on? Janie was talking excitedly about building another sandcastle when they arrived at the house. There was no police guard in sight. The gate was wide open, pressed against the bamboo leaves. The driver honked, and Karuna and Jotipala came into view, hurrying from the back garden. Jotipala was looking upset, his hollow cheeks sucked in. He avoided Duncan's eyes.

"Tell them to look after the child. Outside," Hammond commanded the driver. The wind was whipping the fronds of the coconut trees, and Duncan could hear the hoarse warnings of the waves down below. Five crows were watching from the balustrade, crouched against the wind. While the driver was talking to Karuna and Jotipala, Hammond led the way into the house, his briefcase held close to his side, his small feet, in expensive-looking loafers, tapping on the cement floor. His pale-yellow short-sleeved shirt had gone limp in the humidity, but his gray trousers were still impeccably creased.

"Something isn't making sense," Duncan said, when he was seated in the sitting room. He clenched his toes in his sandals, which were still gritty with sand from the beach. "I was told . . ." But Jotipala had told him something he wasn't supposed to say, he remembered. "Why was this gate being guarded?"

"There are people who will go to any length to get information," Hammond said, taking a seat by the coffee table.

"So Bent—"

"Leave Bentley out of this," Hammond snapped. "What is important is that you left here, endangering the company."

"Endangering how? How did you know I had left? You were already in Galle?"

"I came here after I found out your wife was being misled," Hammond said.

"Grace? What does she have to do . . . what . . . misled how?" What the hell was he talking about?

"There's no time to go into details," Hammond said. "She's already here in Sri Lanka. As you know from your mother-in-law," he added.

Had the shopkeeper reported his whole conversation? "Where is Grace? I need to talk to her," Duncan said.

"We all do," Hammond said, and when Duncan looked at him, puzzled, he said, "Presumably she's on the way to her parents' house. We need you to call there. If she isn't there yet, tell your mother-in-law to tell Grace that everything she has found out is a lie. That Grace should not, under any circumstance"—Hammond jabbed a finger into the air—"talk to anyone about what she has found out. It is all false. She is being misled. If she talks to a reporter or the police, there could be severe consequences."

"What consequences? The police? Is this about the intern who died? What is going on, Hammond?"

"I don't have time to go into details. Grace is . . . Grace may be with a journalist right now. We need you to make this call immediately." Duncan did a double take, just noticing the phone on the side table by the entertainment center. It was a black modern one, with an array of buttons.

"How . . . ? I thought there wasn't phone access," Duncan said, but seeing Hammond's expression, he knew the answer.

"The phone was put away for a good reason," Hammond said.

Something was very wrong here, but what?

"Maybe we should all just go to Colombo, to Grace's parents' house, and explain everything," Duncan said.

"That will be too late," Hammond said. "If we could get Grace here, that would . . . but we don't know where she is."

How did he have such detailed information about Grace? Then he remembered Bent saying that Grace would be watched for her safety. But even here?

"Fine," he said. "I'll call. Then we can ask Grace what she's found out."

Hammond shook his head. "That won't be possible," he said, his voice pressured. "You will need to be very specific, and say only that everything Grace has been told is a lie, and that she should not under any circumstances say anything to anyone. Say that you will see her soon, and that you and Janie are fine. You can say you don't have time to say more."

"Whoa. Slow down," Duncan said, rubbing his forehead. "Of course I'll have time. I'll need to say more, tell her where we are . . ."

"Absolutely not," Hammond said. When Duncan looked sharply at him, he said, "For the company's security." Then he added, "She is under the illusion that you are in danger. You need to reassure her that you are not." He sighed. It was an exaggerated, impatient sigh. "In fact, you will be in danger only if she is not reassured of that."

"What? What do you mean?"

Hammond looked at his watch impatiently. "I thought we could make this cordial, but time is passing. This has to get done. Let me be plain. If you don't make this call now, if you don't reassure her that her information is wrong, and that you are fine, you—and Janie—will not be safe." He said it with a cold finality that Duncan found alarming.

"Are you threatening me?" Duncan said, incredulous. "I'm not going to say anything without knowing more."

Hammond bent toward the briefcase he'd laid on the coffee table. Two quick snaps and it was open. He reached inside, his eyes on Duncan. When he straightened, his hand held a dull black pistol. Duncan jumped back involuntarily, emitting a shocked yell. "What the fuck!"

"Time!" Hammond tapped his watch with the gun. "I'll explain after you make the call. You can call it a threat or a warning. But this is simply a fact. You and Janie will not be safe unless this message is communicated. Immediately." He strode to the side table and pushed the phone forward.

"What, you're going to shoot me if I don't call?" Duncan's voice wobbled. It was incredible that he was even saying this, he thought.

Hammond pointed the gun at him, his arm steady.

"Do I look like I'm joking?"

I could just grab the gun, Duncan thought. Hammond was a small man. He would be easily overpowered.

Hammond stepped back and braced himself against the entertainment center, the gun still pointed. "In case you're getting any ideas . . . If you make a move, I'll shoot. Whether or not I hit you, the gunshot will be a signal to Jotipala. He will know what to do with Janie."

Duncan rose slowly to his feet. He could see Janie with Karuna and Jotipala at the overlook point, where the tops of the screw pines were whipping around in the wind. Karuna was holding Janie's hand. Jotipala was gazing at the house, although Duncan doubted he could see inside with the windows half-closed.

"What are you, crazy?" Duncan said. "He's going to do what? Fucking kill Janie? Jotipala would never—"

"You think they're your friends? That is why they kept the gate padlocked? That is why they told you there was no phone while they were keeping this"—Hammond jerked his head at the phone on the side table—"hidden in a box in their room?"

Duncan thought about the number of times he'd asked about making a phone call. Jotipala had lied all those times? He'd felt he knew Jotipala.

"Jotipala and Karuna are employees," Hammond said, his lip curled. "With a livelihood to protect. They do as they are told."

"What are you talking about?" Duncan had seen how Jotipala and Karuna treated Janie. "They would never hurt Janie."

"One person has already died here," Hammond said, his face contorted with anger. "Frank Salgado."

Duncan felt the air leave his chest in a great gasp.

"What do you think their role was in that? If they didn't care about a venerable Sinhalese elder, you think they would care about a foreign kid they barely know?"

"Frank Salgado?" Duncan said. His voice came out in a whisper. He was having difficulty breathing. Had Jotipala been responsible for Salgado's death? Was that why he'd seemed upset when he'd said that someone had died recently? Had that been guilt that Duncan had seen on Jotipala's face? "But Salgado wasn't shot."

"He drowned," Hammond said. "You get thrown on those rocks, you don't survive."

Duncan found he was covering his mouth with his hand. "My God. Why? What the fuck . . . ?"

"Time," Hammond snapped. "We can discuss all that after you make the call."

Duncan could feel the wrongness of the situation deep in the churning of his belly. He twisted the ring on his finger, trying to keep his face impassive as he racked his brain.

"Janie's safety is in your hands," Hammond said. "Pick up the phone and move back, away from the base." He put the phone on speaker and poised himself by it, watching Duncan closely, the gun pointed at his chest.

44

GRACE

Tuesday

Grace started when a voice called out, "Hello, miss? Can I help you?" The receptionist who had spoken was leaning across the desk, her face curious.

She needed to call home, Grace thought, and find out what Bent had said to her parents. She paid for a Colombo call and dialed her parents' number, moving as far away from the receptionist as the phone cord allowed.

Her mother picked up during the first ring.

"Grace! There you are! Aney, darling, I've been waiting by the phone for you to call," Nalini said. "Are you calling from the airport?"

Grace frowned. "You knew I was coming?"

"Yes, yes, your friend Mohammed called me last night. He said Marla had told him. I was so surprised to hear you were on the way," Nalini said. "But he didn't know which flight, so I didn't know when to come to pick you up. Why didn't you call ahead, darling?"

"Ma. Ma. Never mind that. Why was Mo calling you?"

"He had to get in touch with you urgently, he said. He wanted you to call him as soon as you got in."

"Is this about Duncan? Ma, did he say anything about Duncan?"

"No, but Duncan called this morning," Nalini said. "Twice. First around seven. Why, you didn't even tell *him* you were coming . . ."

"Wait! Ma? Duncan called you? What did he say?"

"He was calling from Galle," Nalini said. "He didn't have a phone number he could be reached at—probably he is traveling. He said he would call back soon."

"Did he say anything else? Was he with Janie? Bent's little girl?"

"Yes, yes. He called back a second time just now. He was in a rush, so I didn't get to talk much. He said something about you getting wrong information? What information is he talking about?"

"What do you mean, Ma? What exactly did he say?"

"That all the information you found is wrong. He said you shouldn't tell anyone, because it's not true. Very important that you not tell anyone, he said. I asked him what he was talking about, but he said he didn't have time to talk. He said to tell you he and Janie were fine. Not to worry, he said. He told you to tell Ms. Logan that he and Janie would come to see her soon."

Grace froze, clenching her hand around the phone cord. "What? Are you sure that's the name he said? Ms. Logan?"

"Yes," Nalini said. "Who is that? I was going to ask him, but the line got cut off."

Grace could feel her heart pounding. She tried to keep her voice calm. "Did he say where he was calling from?"

"No, but he would see you soon, he said. Where are you? Are you calling from the airport?"

"No, Ma. I'm in a hotel." She was wondering whether to tell her mother more when she saw Shalini emerging from the corridor, running, her sari held off her feet with one hand.

"Grace! Come on!" she called.

"Ma, I'll call you soon and tell you when I'll be there. I'm with a friend," Grace said. She thrust the phone down, ignoring the receptionist's stare, and hurried toward Shalini.

Shalini grabbed her arm. "Hurry up. This way!"

They ran past the courtyard and entered a restaurant whose green walls were striped with sunlight filtering through the window blinds. Diners were crowding the breakfast buffet, leaning hungrily over the open aluminum serving dishes. Grace barely noticed the plates of steaming food, the noise of clinking cutlery, and the mingled smells of bacon, hoppers, and curry as she hurried after Shalini, who had slowed her pace to a fast walk. They passed through to a side door and exited into the parking lot. Shalini started running again, her slippered feet scattering gravel, and Grace followed, her purse slapping against her side. Shalini started the engine as soon as they were in the car.

As they sped through the driveway, Grace saw the van driver turn, openmouthed, then run toward the parking lot, shouting something to the woman.

"Go faster, they're going to catch up," Grace said, but Shalini laughed gleefully.

"Not a bloody chance, men," she said. "Going to take a while to change the tire."

Grace felt her mouth drop open. "My God, you slashed it?"

Shalini rummaged in her purse with one hand and showed her a pocket knife with a pockmarked wooden handle. "Not bad, no?" Her grin was triumphant. "Now we can decide what to do." She looked over at Grace, and her eyes widened. "What? Did something happen? Who did you call?"

"My mother." Grace recounted the conversation. "The thing is, that's impossible. Ms. Logan was one of Duncan's high school teachers. Someone he was close to. She's dead. Why would he say that? I was trying to think whether my mother could have mistaken it for some other name . . . but no. There wasn't anyone he and Janie had been planning to see. Why Ms. Logan? Was he trying to say that he's afraid they're going to die? My God."

"Maybe someone was forcing him to tell you that everything you've found is wrong. Maybe that means you've really found out something incriminating," Shalini said, frowning.

"I don't know," Grace said. "What are we going to do about Duncan and Janie? We have to go to the police."

Shalini shook her head. "We don't know who to trust," she said. "We should go to Galle. He might be at the Cinasat house. Or someone there might know where he is."

"What Cinasat house?"

"I know an address," Shalini said. "From some documents I got recently." She shook her head. "I think a Cinasat consultant might have died there. Or near there." At Grace's confused look, she said, "A professor from Peradeniya who worked—"

"You're not talking about Salgado?" Grace said.

"You know him? Frank Salgado?"

"All I know is that he drowned." Grace explained what Ada Gleeson had said at the Cinasat party.

"His body was found in Galle. There was something fishy about his death. The police closed the investigation, but two friends of his contacted our paper." Shalini studied the dials on the dashboard. They were moving fast, and the car was making fitful rattling sounds.

"You're a journalist?"

Shalini nodded. "Sorry, I haven't even properly introduced myself. I work at the *Daily News*. A few days ago, I got an envelope in the mail. The return address was in Galle. Salgado couldn't have mailed it. He was dead by then. But there are documents with the Cinasat letterhead that show he was there at that address. A house called the Maya. I don't know why the envelope was sent to me. I showed it to one of my colleagues. She's investigating the Salgado death. We did some digging, found out the house is owned by a Mr. Kumar Fernando, but he hasn't been in the country for months. Some big-shot retired venture capitalist—spends most of his time in the States." She gestured at the glove box, her bangles

272

tinkling. "There are two maps in there. Take out the Southern Province one. I know the street address."

Grace peered inside the glove box, which was cluttered with tangled rubber bands, pens, a flashlight, a cracked magnifying glass, a small bottle of Dettol, and an unsanitary-looking roll of gauze bandage. She retrieved the maps under the mess and opened the one for the Southern Province. It was limp and torn at the creases, and she had trouble holding it together in one piece.

"Actually, this is better than trying to get to your parents' house," Shalini said, nodding decisively. "They'll be watching that. We'll take the E01 to Galle."

Grace ran her finger along the map, tracing the way south to Galle. "Why was it fishy, Salgado's death?"

"He didn't swim, apparently, his friends said. He was afraid of the sea, never went out in a boat. They said there was no reason for him to drown. And his body was all bruised and lacerated. As if he had been thrown against rocks maybe."

"Are you saying he was killed?" Another death in connection with Cinasat. There was no way all this could be coincidence. "My God. Duncan and Janie . . ."

"Look, no sense worrying, men. We'll get to the house and see what we can find out. Then we can see how to get help."

Shalini took a look in the rearview mirror and exited the E03 expressway. They drove along Biyagama Road, slowing to a crawl behind a line of noisy lorries, shiny European-made cars, and dusty buses lurching forward. Small shops with gaily painted grimy walls and corrugated metal roofs were open to the road, some with makeshift awnings made of plastic sheeting. Inside their dim interiors, Grace could see familiar wares: baked goods in glass-fronted cabinets buzzing with the occasional fly, soaps and incense sticks arrayed neatly on shelves, luxurious stalks of bananas hanging from ceilings, clusters of orange king coconuts piled by doorways. Inside one thatch-roofed shack, a butcher in a fresh white sarong was sharpening a cleaver near great slabs of red meat that hung from hooks. A shopkeeper was just folding back the metal doors of the adjoining fabric shop, where rolls of patterned cloth were stacked tidily against the walls. Men gossiped in amiable groups on the brick pavement. Drivers relaxed in the shade of their tuk-tuks, watching life go by. The road widened as they passed into a more prosperous residential area, with balconied, terra-cotta-roofed houses, some with high brick garden walls to keep out the rabble.

"All this is . . . What is going on?" Grace said "How are you involved in this . . . all this Cinasat business?"

"Angie Osborne was a good friend of mine," Shalini said. Grace saw her lip tremble a little. "I didn't hear about the death until the day of the funeral. Although I couldn't have gone anyway. The cost of the plane ticket . . ." She shook her head. "I met her years ago in DC when I was in college at George Washington University. Through an internship I did at the *Washington Post*. She was my mentor."

"She was working on a Cinasat story?"

Shalini nodded. "We'd been working on the story together. A couple of years ago, I got some information from a source here about some medical research being done. Studies being done in the village areas. People were going and recruiting poor uneducated folk to take part. Some local doctors were involved. We don't know, still, how many were doing this with good intentions. But at least some of them were taking bribes. Villagers were getting paid to take drugs—bloody big sums they couldn't refuse—and nobody was telling them details about what they were taking."

"These were Cinasat studies?"

"In the beginning, I didn't know that. I thought it was local research. Angie was the one who helped me to find that out. Anyway, in the middle of digging into that story, I came across sources who told me about other fishy things. Research studies getting repeated over and over until they got the result they wanted."

"That happens everywhere," Grace said. They were crossing the rippling green expanse of the Kelani River, few buildings visible through the thick vegetation along its banks. A woman in a dripping *diya redda* was climbing out of the shallows, her long hair clumped into tendrils down her back. "Not ethical, and bad science, but that's not just here."

"True," Shalini said. "But the sources who were talking about that were the ones who led me to a new drug Cinasat was developing."

"Symb86?" Grace said, and then wondered if she should have said the name.

But Shalini nodded immediately. She had obviously heard about it. "While I was digging around here, Angie had been looking into a story in the States about corruption at your FDA. She found evidence that some pharmaceutical companies had a lot of influence on the FDA. Drugs being approved without proper review. Our stories looked like they were linked. The pieces didn't fit, but. We were digging and digging. For a long time. Then Angie got ahold of a woman called Minowa Costa who used to work at Cinasat."

"We found a photo of her," Grace said. "The one who died."

Shalini frowned. "What photo?"

"My friend Mo—Angie also knew him well—he found a photo of Angie when he was at her house for the funeral. This woman, Minowa Costa, was in the photo. It's a long story—how we found out." She explained how the pendant and Bent's reaction had made Mo suspicious, and how they had identified the woman as Minowa Costa.

"Angie definitely didn't know Minowa Costa six months ago, men," Shalini said. "She only contacted Angie about a month ago. She's the one who helped us to connect the dots in the story. She took Angie to Cinasat one night about two weeks ago—that must have been when Angie took the picture, to document that they had been there. Minowa said she had a way to get hold of documents that would prove everything she told us."

"Wait, that doesn't make sense," Grace said, remembering. "How did she get into Cinasat? She wasn't working there two weeks ago. She had already moved to a different company by then. Novophil."

Shalini frowned. "Novophil? I thought Angie said she didn't have a job at the moment."

"That's what Mortensen said. The police officer who's working on Angie's case."

Shalini pursed her lips. "Maybe Angie made a mistake then. Or maybe I'm not remembering. Anyway, doesn't matter, men. She managed to get into Cinasat because she had a friend there, and she knew all the security guards. But then, not long after that—only a few days before Angie died—Minowa died in a car accident."

"I know about that," Grace said. "We just found out—my friend Marla and I—on Tuesday." They were passing a stretch of uncultivated land, lush with vegetation. On the other side, gray buffalo grazed in a field, white egrets perched on their backs. More egrets lurked nearby, pecking at the ground. In the distance, trees grew thickly, drooping plantain leaves and palm fronds standing out against the dark green of teak. How different these vibrant trees looked from the single struggling one that had borne the memorial to Minowa Costa.

Shalini nodded. "You know it was a hit and run? Angie called me. She thought Cinasat had had her killed. I thought that was too far-fetched. But Angie said she was going to talk to Bentley Hyland at your school reunion. She thought he might know something. We'd thought he was involved for a while. She said she was also going to try to talk to you and your husband, to ask how you'd both feel about helping with the investigation. She said she could trust you to keep it secret."

"So that's why she called me."

"You spoke to her about this?"

"No, she left me a message and I tried to call her back, but I never got through to her."

"She wasn't sure Duncan knew anything, but she thought he might help."

Sure Duncan knows, Angie's message had said. But maybe Angie had actually said, *not sure Duncan knows,* Grace thought. "Did Angie really have a heart attack?" she said.

"I don't know, but I just can't believe that, men. I only found out she had died through another friend, someone Angie and I both knew. I called Angie's mother, but I didn't want to say anything about what I thought. It would have been too hard for her mother to bear, no? I tried to get in touch with an intern who worked at Cinasat. Olivia Garwick. Danibel, I mean. She went by Danibel at Cinasat."

"I found out she also died," Grace said. "Someone sent me an email . . ."

"That was also me," Shalini said. "I couldn't get in touch with her, so I was trying to get you or your husband to talk to her. After I found out she died, I didn't want to use that email address again. I think it got intercepted somehow."

"Are you saying Danibel was killed?"

"Don't know, men. That's what I'm thinking. I never met her, but Angie had been in touch with her. Minowa was the one who had referred Danibel to Cinasat, and Minowa had introduced Angie to her. When I found out Danibel also had died, then I really started to get frightened."

"There's a police detective who's investigating all this," Grace said.

"I don't know if that helps," Shalini said. "The police have to be in on this somehow. In the States and also here. Otherwise how would they not see the links to Cinasat? Why are all these deaths being ruled accidents? A few days ago, I got an anonymous email—to the email address I used to contact you about Danibel—warning me to get off the story. A threat, actually. Whoever this bloody email was from, they said you and your friend Mohammed had to stop poking around. They seemed to think you were poking around on my behalf. I've been hiding out here since all the deaths. I got out of my house and went to my parents' house in Negombo for a while. Now I'm staying at a friend's in Colombo. Janice Perera. She's also a journalist, but she's doing a story in Jaffna. This is her car." She chuckled a little. "My car is even worse than this. Anyway, I found out that Bentley and your husband were coming here, and I got worried that they might try to hold your husband as leverage to get you to give up searching for information. That's when I emailed you. I wasn't sure if your emails were being monitored. That's why I emailed you in Sinhala. I thought it would be harder for them to catch it."

"I think I was being followed," Grace said. "I got mugged on Saturday, the night before I left New Jersey. At least that's what I thought. But I've been thinking . . . the guy didn't take my purse. Didn't even try."

"You think he was trying to hurt you?"

"I don't know." Grace shivered, looking out at the landscape beside the road. On one side, a tall cliff of red rock loomed. On the other side, bright saris and sarongs were laid out to dry along a chicken wire fence. Beyond it she caught glimpses of tile-roofed houses set in a thicket of teak trees. Farther away, a plume of smoke drifted up from someone's bonfire. "There was another thing. I don't know how it could be related to all this, but I got an email from someone who said I should meet them. But when I got there, there was a shooting. Not at me. It was in a bad neighborhood so I thought it was random, but I don't know."

"What did the email say?"

"Something about why Duncan was fired." She looked over at Shalini. "I never told Duncan." There was something hovering at the edge of her consciousness, something she had not realized before. Something about an animal . . . A dog? She fished around in her memory, but nothing came up.

Shalini slowed as a lorry, honking loudly, barged into the lane ahead of them. The car sputtered, and Shalini looked anxiously at the dashboard dials. "This bloody car is heating up too much. I hope it can get us there." Something was rattling under the hood. Shalini craned her neck, listening. "I don't know what that is, men. We may have to dump the car."

"Dump it where?"

"I have an uncle near Baddegama. He's bound to be at home. He never goes anywhere these days. It's right on the way. If this rattling keeps on, we'll stop there and see if we can borrow his car."

This seemed far-fetched to Grace. "What if your uncle isn't there? What if the car isn't available? We need a backup plan. We have to get to Duncan."

"Don't worry, men," Shalini said. She patted Grace's arm. "Tell me about Duncan. What does he know?"

"He doesn't know anything. As far as I know. He's been studying some videos of thovil. Apparently Cinasat did research on patients who had thovil done. To test whether the drug works. Symb86."

Shalini snorted grimly. "It doesn't."

"What do you mean? That's the drug they've been testing for years. It doesn't work?"

"This is deception on the grandest scale you can imagine."

"What are you talking about?" Grace said.

"This bloody drug is supposed to mimic the placebo effect. Did you know that? What Cinasat is claiming is that they have found the biochemical basis for the placebo effect. That they've made that into a pill."

"Yes, I knew that."

"But the thing is, men, there is no such drug. Symb86 is essentially a bloody myth. It *is* a placebo. Of course they had a very cleverly designed drug for the purposes of going through the approval process, doing the paperwork. They obviously had to describe the chemistry and so forth. But it's completely inert. And they know that. What they're doing is marketing a placebo, telling people it's a real drug that works on the immune system like a placebo does. Very clever idea but completely unethical."

"That can't be . . . What about all the studies?"

"Some of the studies they only claimed, they never did. Other studies they repeated over and over, until they got enough of an effect to report. Just by chance. True, Symb86 works sometimes, but that's because placebos work. They have done real research, but. To find ways to maximize the placebo effect. That is why they were studying all these ceremonies. To see how to manipulate belief to get the biggest effect. The power of suggestion. That is what they're really studying."

"My God," Grace said, staring blankly out at the verdant paddy fields stretching beside the expressway. A small creek meandered through a weedy field to a patch of towering rubber trees. Up ahead, a long red kite fluttered against the sky, pulled by some unseen child. "How . . . I don't see how they could possibly manage to pull this off."

"Some very powerful people have to be involved. That is the only way they could have got FDA approval. That is why they had to have absolute secrecy, men. They had to make everyone who didn't know the truth believe the drug was real. They are going to market this so-called drug as a cure-all. For all kinds of difficult-to-treat conditions. Can you imagine the bloody revenue? All of it hinges on no one knowing the truth. Only a select few, anyway. Some of the people who know are in danger, probably. Once the drug is on the market, those people could be history."

"My God," Grace said again. She couldn't believe all this could be true. "I'm sure Duncan doesn't know anything about all this."

"Who knows how much he knows? We have to figure out how to get the police, the right parts of the police, involved. Once everything's out in the open, he will be safe."

"What about Bent?"

"I think Bentley is the one masterminding this, but I have no proof still."

Grace shook her head. "I've known Bent since I was in school. He can't be involved. And what about Janie? He wouldn't have his own daughter kidnapped. Put in some risky situation." They were passing a hillside where only stumps of rubber trees were left. On the other side, gargantuan power towers loomed, their orange-and-white girders defacing the countryside.

Shalini drummed her fingers on the wheel. "True. I don't know. Maybe he's only being used. Other people could be the ones . . . Angie said someone at the FDA is also involved, and the head of Cinasat. Hammond Gleeson."

"Him, I know," Grace said. "He, I can—"

Shalini touched her on the arm, veering off the expressway. "Wait, this is the exit. We're going to get off here. My uncle's house is very close."

They drove down a two-lane road that ran first through a small commercial area and then wide swathes of overgrown, uncultivated fields interrupted by copses thick with foliage. Tall grasses and unruly lantana bushes reached toward the road, and huge trees cast patches of shade ahead. Everywhere, coconut trees towered. A few women in pastel cotton dresses were strolling along the narrow pavement, umbrellas raised against the sun, which was already beating down. Very few cars were on the road, although scooters and motorbikes putted by, loaded with packages and passengers. At a corner sheltered by the massive fan-shaped leaves of a talipot palm, Shalini turned down a small lane and into the front yard of a pale-green house. It was built in the old style, set back from the road, its terra-cotta-tiled roof shaded by avocado and jackfruit trees. Only a few clumps of grass were scattered across the packed earth of the front yard, but masses of brilliantly hued crotons grew in a sunny spot by the open front door.

"Wait in the car," Shalini said. "Sorry, but you know how it is. If you come in, we'll have to drink Horlicks and eat biscuits, chat for an hour before we can leave. I'll say we're in a rush."

She ran across the yard and into the house, her sari pota fluttering behind her, calling out "Prema Uncle! Hello, Prema Uncle!"

Grace surveyed the garden, trying not to think about Duncan and Janie. An old white Nissan hatchback was parked at the edge of the yard. Bougainvillea bushes were flowering near the wooden fence, and mynahs were strutting on the low branches of a mango tree. There were mangoes in the tree, still hard and green. Grace realized she was hungry. She was wondering how long it had been since she'd eaten when Shalini burst out of the front door, holding a key aloft, two bottles of Orange Crush and a packet of Lemon Puff biscuits clutched in one arm. "Cheerio, Prema Uncle!" she called over her shoulder.

"Come on, Grace," she said, gesticulating. They took Grace's bags out and loaded them into the Nissan. A man with a head of rumpled white hair emerged onto the small front veranda as Shalini reversed the Nissan out to the road. He hobbled forward in his batik shirt and blue sarong, leaning on a wooden cane. He raised his arm in a wave. "Cheerio! Careful driving!" he called out.

Shalini revved the car down the road, back onto the expressway. "Finally, no need to worry about the bloody car giving up," she said. She jerked her head at the drinks and biscuits that were lying in the pocket between the seats. "Have a drink. We'll be there soon. Tell me what else you found out on your end."

45

DUNCAN

Tuesday

As soon as Duncan mentioned Ms. Logan, Hammond pressed the button that hung up the line. "Who the fuck is Ms. Logan?" he snarled.

Duncan reared back involuntarily, stunned at the venom in his voice.

"I told you not to say anything to—"

"I said that to reassure Grace," Duncan said. He drew a deep breath, trying to ignore the gun pointing at his chest. "If I hadn't mentioned Ms. Logan, she would have thought something was wrong. She knew I had planned to take Janie to see Ms. Logan whenever we had any time to relax. She lives in a flat near the Taj Ocean Hotel."

"Who is she?" Hammond said, his eyes narrowed.

"An old Burgher lady I've known for years. She has a bunch of grandkids. Her flat is a kid's paradise. Plenty of toys for Janie." Thank God he'd thought about what to say in advance, Duncan thought.

Hammond relaxed visibly. "Sit. Over there." He pointed to the sofa. "Any quick moves, I shoot." He showed his teeth in a smile that was more a leer. "Remember that garden out there is dangerous for a kid. Snakes. And most of all, that cliff. One push is all it would take."

They didn't communicate much after that. Hammond made and received multiple phone calls. From Hammond's end of the conversations, Duncan gathered a jumble of information. Hammond was angry that Grace had not been picked up from the airport. He didn't know where she was. A search was going on for her and a journalist named Janice Perera, who had picked her up. The intent was to bring them here, to the house. For what purpose, Duncan wasn't sure. What Grace had found out seemed to involve two Cinasat people who had died. Possibly killed, for leaking information? Duncan twisted the ring on his finger, wishing he knew more. All he had were questions. Did all this have something to do with Mo's photo? Whatever Grace had found out had to be true, if Hammond was going to the length of pointing a gun at him. What was going to happen now? How could he get the gun away from Hammond without jeopardizing Janie?

He kept telling himself that it was unlikely that Janie would be harmed. But could he take the risk, however small? He had to hope that Grace would get the message from Nalini soon. She would know to get help. Cinasat had to be involved in something criminal. Something serious. Had Bent lied to him? What was going to happen? It worried Duncan that Hammond was making no effort to prevent Duncan from overhearing his conversations. Surely he wouldn't just let Duncan go after all this.

Karuna brought in a tray with a cut-glass pitcher of passion fruit cordial, two glasses, and a plate of ginger biscuits, her eyes sliding over Hammond and the gun he was holding. The stringy braid of her graying hair swung forward over her shoulder as she laid the tray on the coffee table. A knotted yellow cord slipped out of the neckline of her blouse. An amulet was hanging from it, like the one Jotipala had been wearing to ward off the cobras, or maybe some other evil. She avoided looking at Duncan. Hammond hadn't been bluffing, he realized. They were on his side.

"Karuna, is Janie alright?" Duncan said.

Her eyes flickered over to him momentarily. They looked watery.

"Enough. Get out!" Hammond snapped in Sinhala.

Karuna straightened and padded away on her bare feet, not looking back.

Hammond continued his phone conversation. "If you don't find them within an hour, we're going to plan *B* . . . Enough. I'll be waiting to hear from you." He set the phone down with a decisive click.

"Look, Hammond," Duncan said. "I need to know what's going on. What has Grace found out? And why is whatever she's found out a problem, if it's false?"

"If we have to prove it's false, we'll have to give away proprietary information," Hammond said, his voice tight. His skin looked even paler than usual and shiny with perspiration. "Do you realize how many millions this project is worth? How long it's been in the making?"

"What exactly are we doing here?"

"We're waiting to talk to Grace and her journalist friend."

"Why not just give Nalini—Grace's mother—this number so that Grace can call us?"

"They will be picked up soon, and then they'll be here," Hammond said. "It's best if you stay away from these questions."

"So what are you going to do after they get here? You're going to let us all go?"

"Don't worry," Hammond said. "In spite of this gun"—he brandished it in the air—"we'll be on amicable terms soon. You'll see." He made an effort to smile, his teeth small and faintly yellow against his pale lips.

The sun was well up now, but the sky was heavy with clouds, the water below a sheet of furrowed slate. The screw pines were tossing their unruly heads, signaling a coming storm. He could hear the booming of the troubled sea against the hissing of the leaves in the wind. The wind gusting in through the side door to the portico brought the sound of Janie's high voice. Duncan couldn't hear what she was saying. She wasn't in sight. He had seen her walk past the windows some time ago with Karuna and Jotipala, on the way to the servant quarters. They were not too far away to hear a gunshot. Hammond had seated himself by the entertainment center. Duncan watched him closely, rubbing his ring, assessing the chances of getting the gun out of his hands.

285

46

GRACE

Tuesday

"There's more. Even harder to believe," Shalini said. "Minowa told Angie—"

"Tell me later. The lane is coming up anytime now," Grace said, her finger tracing the tattered map stretched out on her lap. "We haven't even made a plan for what to do."

"We have to see what the situation is," Shalini said. Her tone was casual, but Grace saw how tensely she was gripping the wheel.

The sky had turned cloudy, and the light was dim under the trees as they drove up the slope of the lane, past lantana bushes and dark bromeliads, to a black metal gate set in a high gray wall. "Spikes and glass," Shalini said, pointing at the top of the wall. "Better hope the gate's not locked." She parked beside a small structure that looked like a guardhouse. No one was about. She pointed to a brass plaque affixed to the garden wall. "Fernando named the place after his daughter. Maya. She's a US citizen. Works for some lobbying firm in the States, we found out."

Grace pushed at the gate. Unexpectedly it creaked open. What if this was a wild-goose chase? What if this wasn't where Duncan was?

They slipped in. The driveway curved to the right, leading to a stately whitewashed bungalow with a long portico around it. Potted bougainvillea bushes were splashed with bloodred flowers on either side of a set of broad stone steps. A line of crows was perched on the portico balustrade. Grace could hear waves crashing nearby. The wind was urgent, stirring the leaves of the bamboo by the gate.

"Let's not just go in," Grace said. "Look, let's go over here by those bushes, away from the house, and we'll think about what to do."

"There are no cars. Maybe no one's even here," Shalini said.

"But what if Duncan's here? What if he's in danger?" Grace said. "Let's hide here for a minute and plan what to do."

She pushed past a cluster of fiery crotons and crouched by the bamboo thicket. Shalini followed. The sun was behind a dark wedge of clouds, and they were in a particularly shadowy corner of the garden under the spreading branches of a breadfruit tree. Ahead, at the back of the house, Grace spotted a garage, and beyond it, a small outbuilding that was clearly servant quarters.

A peal of laughter rang out, and then a child's voice, shouting, "I'm going to show Duncan!" Grace gasped as Janie came into view, running. She was wearing a sleeveless yellow sundress, muddied here and there. Her legs were crusted with sand, her hair flapping against her shoulders in two neat braids.

A man ran out after her, shouting in Sinhala, "Janie baba, Janie baba, wait, wait!" He was barefoot and wiry, dressed in a white sarong and dingy white shirt, with a mustache curling over his lip and oiled hair to halfway down his neck. Janie paused as something she held in her hands fell onto the grassy ground. She stooped to pick it up. It was a tortoise, Grace saw.

A woman emerged from the outbuilding behind the man. She shouted out in Sinhala to the man, "Don't let her go to the house. He's holding a gun to Duncan Sir! Don't let her see!"

The man hurried up to Janie and picked up the tortoise. He guided her back toward the servant quarters, where the woman was exclaiming, her hands against her cheeks, "Aney, aney, poor Janie baba, come, come, we can feed the tortoise."

After they'd disappeared from view, Grace realized that she was clutching Shalini's wrist. "Oh my God. Oh my God. Did you hear that? What are we going to do?"

"We can get the help of those two," Shalini said, but she was looking anxious.

"How do we know? They might not want to get involved," Grace said. "Otherwise, why wouldn't they have called the police already?" She glanced up at the house. No one was visible through the windows, although she could see a ceiling fan whirring in one room.

"We'll have to take a chance and talk to them." Shalini scanned the windows of the house too. "If the guy—whoever it is—has a gun, better not to go into the house."

"But what if he shoots Duncan?" Grace said. "I'm going in. You get Janie away from here and see if you can get help."

"Wait, Grace," Shalini said, but Grace pulled her arm away and charged toward the house. There wasn't time to think about what to do. She'd just have to take it as it came.

A bougainvillea branch scratched her bare arm at the foot of the stone steps, but she barely noticed. She climbed up to the portico, treading as lightly as she could. Why was a pestle lying on the floor? The crows on the balustrade craned their necks, their beaks open, and several flapped their thick wings. She listened, her body flattened against the wall beside the front door. There was drumming inside the house and the rhythmic murmur of a voice speaking in Sinhala, but she couldn't hear it well enough to tell who it was or what was being said. She slipped through the door into a hallway smelling of floor polish and crept forward on the balls of her feet.

Someone was drumming, a mesmerizing, intense rhythm. A man was talking in a soothing voice, but it was English he was using, not Sinhala. It was his cadence that made his speech sound like it was Sinhala. He was describing a scene. Was it a commercial for a resort? Was the TV on? The words were so poetic, and the man was speaking in such a rhythmic voice, repeating the words so musically. It was almost a chant. In the background, there were other voices, murmuring things she couldn't make out. She waited, trying to make sense of what was happening. Someone spoke in a low murmur, and then the commercial started again. Was it being repeated? She crept forward again, placing her feet carefully on the floor.

At the end of the entrance hall, she came upon a wooden screen carved with a lotus design, set by the doorway to a sitting room. The hallway behind her was dim, and the sitting room much brighter. She wouldn't be seen, she thought. She peered through the holes in the intricately carved wood and saw Duncan sitting on a sofa, facing a large TV screen. A man was standing beside the TV. She saw, with a jolt of surprise, that it was Hammond. That slight body, the gecko neck. Then Hammond moved, and Grace saw, to her horror, that the woman had been right. Hammond had a short black gun in his hand, pointed at Duncan. From where Grace was standing, she couldn't see Hammond's expression. She couldn't see what was playing on the screen either. The TV was where the drumming was coming from, and the voices. Duncan was leaning forward on the sofa, facing the TV, his skin shiny with sweat, his shirt unbuttoned and yellow stained. His eyes were glazed and his feet bare. His upturned sandals lay nearby, as if they had been kicked off in a hurry. There were flies on his chest, Grace saw, a small cluster of them. They flitted here and there, but Duncan didn't seem to notice. He was watching the TV intently, his mouth slightly open.

Grace tried to make sense of the scene before her. Why was Duncan looking so . . . She didn't know how to describe the way he looked. Ragged? Feverish? Why was he half-dressed? She was wondering what to do when Duncan spoke, his voice strangely whiny.

47

DUNCAN

Tuesday

"I don't see the point of watching it again," Duncan said. "I don't know what it is you want me to look for. *Unusual* isn't specific enough. What kind of unusual thing should I look for?" He wasn't entirely sure whether he had spoken these words out loud, or whether he had simply thought them. The words seemed very far away from him. Hammond, standing by the video screen with his gun, also seemed far away.

"You'll see it soon," Hammond said, pressing a button on the remote control.

The video started again. Duncan must have watched it more than a dozen times. He'd lost count. He could feel the rhythm of the drums deep inside his body. They were beating in his chest, his belly, his blood. There were many voices in the background, murmuring and running together. It was impossible to take his eyes off the large screen where the video was playing. In it, a young man in a bright-orange short-sleeved shirt lingered at a French window, looking out over an expanse of shimmering blue water, describing it. How cool the water looked, he was saying. Saying, or singing? Duncan couldn't tell. When the man turned away from the window, Duncan could see how pained he looked. How hot it was, the man said. He described the unbearable heat he was feeling, his face contorted with it. His hands fumbled at his shirt, unbuttoning it. He was still so hot. There was a fire running through him, he could feel it. Sweat gleamed on his skin, dripped down his neck in rivulets. The man's hair was wet with it. It curled around his head in sticky-looking tendrils. He fanned himself with a piece of paper, his eyes wild with the heat he was feeling.

Duncan could feel the sweltering heat too. He took another glug of passion fruit cordial from the glass on the coffee table. The drink was too hot. Hot enough to scald. Some dripped down his chin, searing his bare chest. His shirt was open all the way, but that did nothing to soothe the fiery heat of his skin. The cement floor was burning against his bare feet. It was unbearable.

The man in the video turned back to the open window. He stepped through, his bare, burning feet sinking into the grass outside. A breeze blew back the sides of his unbuttoned shirt. It blew through his hair. He walked toward a strip of sand that edged the water, describing the inviting coolness of it, how it would feel on his fiery skin. That was the only way to feel cool again. He had to jump in.

Duncan stood, wanting a view of the water. He could feel the man's pain, the raging heat inside his body. He could see the sea outside the window, stretching to the horizon. Was it calling him? It was cloudy outside, the water gray blue. The side door out to the back of the portico was wide open, and he could see the sea through there too, inviting him. How close by. How cool it would be. The words the man spoke were Duncan's own words. Or were they his thoughts? The man's desire to feel the water was his own desire. He knew it was the only way to calm the heat of his body. He moved toward the door and out onto the portico. He could feel the man's feet on the scorching portico steps, one, two, three, four. He was floating. The breeze blew over him, blew his shirt back. He could feel it in the man's hair.

Then the man's feet were on the grass, pressing the soft blades down as he drifted toward the overlook. He caught a glimpse of something among the screw pine roots, but then his attention fell away. High tide. The water was right below. So dark. So cool. So close. All he had to do was jump.

48

GRACE

Tuesday

Grace watched Duncan walk out onto the portico, his movements oddly slow. He seemed oblivious of Hammond. She could see Hammond's face clearly now. He was watching Duncan silently, the gun still pointed, his expression curious, intent.

Duncan turned to the left and disappeared from Grace's view. Hammond hurried to the doorway, paused, and then stepped out onto the portico. Grace saw him walk forward to the edge of the balcony, the gun still pointed. What was going on? Grace slipped out from behind the screen and tiptoed quickly to the window. Peering sideways through it, she saw that Duncan was poised by a grove of screw pines, next to a broken old wooden statue, gazing down at the sea below. The water swelled and sank in dark waves. She could hear the water thundering on rocks.

What the hell was Duncan doing? In the video, a man had been talking about jumping into the water. The only way to feel cool again. Fear rose in Grace's throat. There was something eerie about the way Duncan had walked out, looking straight ahead. The way Hammond had watched him. Why had Duncan looked so dazed? Why was he standing so close to the edge, so oddly still? Was he about to jump?

She pressed back the scream that rose to her lips, looking desperately around. The only heavy object at hand was the cut-glass pitcher of cordial sitting on the coffee table. She seized it and ran toward the door as a clamor erupted outside. Someone was beating a drum, the rhythm loud and fast. Grace burst through the door and saw that Hammond had spun toward the sound, shock on his face. She swung the cold pitcher hard and high against his back. She heard a loud thunk as it made contact. The pitcher cracked against his shoulder, yellow cordial spurting down his back, and then flew out of her hands. It shattered on the red stone of the portico with a mighty crash. She became aware of herself shouting, "Duncan! Duncan!"

Hammond stumbled, clutching at the parapet, yelling, "Fucking son of a bitch!" He fell to his knees.

The man with the mustache was the one drumming. He was several yards away from the portico steps, his sarong tucked high, a ceremonial drum hanging around his waist. He was leaping back and forth, drumming with astonishing energy, muscles rippling in his wiry arms. Shalini was running toward Duncan, her sari hitched up, screaming, "Duncan! Duncan! Stop!" Duncan had spun around, his face full of confusion, his mouth open.

Hammond was hunched at the top of the steps, his face contorted with rage and pain. The gun was lying on the floor. As Grace lunged for it, Hammond kicked out, hitting the back of Grace's knee. She clawed at the balustrade, trying to keep her balance. A shot resounded, then another. Grace reared back, screaming. Other people were screaming. She didn't know what was happening. She charged at Hammond's back. He flailed, another shot ripping the air, as he crashed heavily down the steps. Grace could hear herself still screaming. Someone was in pain. Someone else was shouting, "Run! Run to the car! Grace, run!"

Looking over the parapet, she saw Shalini running toward the front garden, pulling Duncan. The drummer, his shirtsleeve bloody, was stumbling after her, the blood-spattered drum threatening to topple him. "Grace! Grace! Run!" Shalini shouted.

Hammond was lying at the foot of the steps, his leg twisted at an odd angle, his yellow shirt stained with grime and cordial, his eyes furious, reaching for the gun that had fallen beside him. Flies were swooping on him. He grabbed the gun. Grace leapt away. She heard a shot reverberate as she rushed through the door, thudding against the wall in her desperation. She heard him roaring incoherently as she tore through the house to the front door.

49

Duncan

Tuesday

"Oh my God. Oh my God. We have to stop the blood," Grace was saying as the car revved, veering wildly around the curve in the road. "Duncan, give me your shirt."

Duncan was twisted around in the front passenger seat, struggling to understand what was happening. The noise was chaotic. In the back seat, Karuna was shrieking, "Aney, aney, my Jotipala! Aney, aney!" Janie was whimpering by the window, her arms around Karuna's waist. There was, inexplicably, a tortoise on her lap, with a star pattern on its back. Duncan could feel soreness in his feet. He didn't have sandals on. He pulled at his shirt, trying to remember why he'd unbuttoned it. It was stained with streaks of yellow. It smelled of passion fruit. He remembered cordial dripping on it as he was drinking. Why had the cordial been hot? He had been so hot himself. It had been unbearable. Had he been dreaming? Was he dreaming now? How had Grace appeared?

"Duncan, quick!"

Duncan fought the fogginess in his head. He remembered standing at the overlook. Had he heard the broken temple guardian shout a warning? Or had that been the sea he'd heard? It had only been for a second.

"Duncan! I need your shirt!"

He pulled his shirt off, suddenly realizing the urgency of the situation. Grace grabbed it from him and wadded it. "Keep it pushed hard," she said to Jotipala, pressing it against his shoulder. Jotipala's shirt was soaked with blood. There were crimson streaks on his sarong, and Grace's hands were bloody.

"Why is there blood?" Janie bleated, her voice trembling. Her face was streaked with tears.

Duncan blinked, sitting up straight. He reached back to pat Janie's arm. "Jotipala just got a cut," he said. The sound of his own voice was a relief. He was awake. "He's going to be fine."

He said in Sinhala to Karuna, "Calm down, he'll be okay. Don't frighten the child."

"We have to get him to a clinic," he said to the woman driving, still in Sinhala. The woman was wearing a tie-dyed red sari, and her hair was coming undone from a coil at her neck. She was leaning forward, focusing on the road. They had got onto the main road, and she was driving much too fast.

"Yes, yes. We'll go to my uncle's house near Baddegama. It's close by. He will know where the closest clinic is," she said. "He would have shot you. He would have shot all of us. Poor Jotipala was in the way." She looked in the rearview mirror. "How bad is it, Grace?"

"Not good," Grace said. "Jotipala! Jotipala, keep your eyes open."

"Aney, aney, don't go to sleep," Karuna said, shaking Jotipala's arm. She had one arm around Janie.

"Never mind," Jotipala said breathily. "I am alright." He leaned his head forward with some effort. "Janie baba, look after that tortoise."

Duncan translated for Janie, who rubbed at the tears on her face and hugged the tortoise to her chest. It was not moving. Duncan hoped it wasn't dead.

"Grace, are you sure you're okay?" he said, craning around the headrest to look at her.

"Fine," Grace said. She had her back to the window and both hands pressed to the bloody cloth wadded against Jotipala's shoulder. "Are you? What the hell were you doing on the cliff there?"

Duncan turned back to face the front. "I'm . . . I'm not sure. I was feeling really hot. I thought . . . I don't know if I was dreaming. Maybe I was sleepwalking." They were on the southern expressway, speeding past other vehicles. The landscape was verdant as far as the eye could see, with neat paddy fields giving way in the distance to thickets of tall rubber trees. On the right, a series of white-painted steps emerged from the greenery, leading up to the pristine white dagoba of a Buddhist temple set on a small hill. How halcyon it all looked, he thought. How could all that have happened back there, in a place like this?

"We have to call the police," he said.

"They are not to be trusted," the woman who was driving said.

"What do you mean? You are Janice Perera?" he said to the woman. "The journalist?"

The woman turned, her eyes sharp. "What?"

"I heard Hammond on the phone . . . You picked Grace up at the airport?"

Grace said, "Wasn't that the name you said . . . the owner of the car?"

The woman's eyes widened. "They must have traced the license plate." She said to Duncan, "True, I'm a journalist. But my name is Shalini Samaraweera. I'm a friend of Angie's."

"Angie's? What the hell . . . What is going on?" Duncan said, looking back at Grace.

"A lot. And it's not good," Grace said. Her blouse was stained with Jotipala's blood, and her hair was hanging out of her ponytail in curling clumps.

"First we have to decide what to do," Shalini said. "How to get to the proper authorities."

"We have to contact my uncle," Grace said. "Ragu Uncle, Duncan."

"He can definitely be trusted," Duncan said. "He's family."

Shalini pursed her lips. "Are you sure?" She shook her head. "But we can't go to the police station." She looked at Grace in the rearview mirror. "When we get to Prema Uncle's house, can you call your parents and tell them to get your uncle to their house? Don't give details. Maybe you should say you're worried about the police. Gleeson will put out a search for us. But they don't know what car we're traveling in. At the moment. The sooner we get to Colombo the better, before they have a chance to trace." She tightened her hands on the wheel. "To be on the safe side, but. We should leave the child at Prema Uncle's house, with Karuna." She glanced at Duncan. "What happened back there?" she said.

"Were you kidnapped?" Grace said.

Duncan looked back at Janie. Her arm was linked in Karuna's, and her head was leaning against the older woman. She was stroking the tortoise's shell, saying, "I'll feed you soon. How about some nice leaves?"

They had all been speaking in Sinhala to keep her out of the conversation. "I thought the kid's dad sent me there," he said, not wanting to mention Bent's name.

50

GRACE

Tuesday

Through the open front window of Prema's living room, Grace could see Duncan, bare chested and barefoot, kneeling beside Jotipala, pressing a green towel, already bloody, against his shoulder wound. Grace had helped to get him out of the car, and they had laid him on the porch floor.

Karuna was crouched near Duncan, her arm around Janie. The woman was trying to be stoic for Janie's sake, but tears were running down her face. Grace heard Duncan trying to reassure her. "He will be fine. The doctor who lives down the road here is coming soon, and he will take him to a clinic."

Grace sank onto the cool cement floor in the living room. She didn't want to sit on Prema Uncle's rattan furniture and stain its neat pastel upholstery. She was still wearing the embroidered blue cotton blouse she had put on in New Jersey, but now its side was splotched with blood. Her jeans were stained too. She had washed her hands and face in Prema's small bathroom, watching the water turn pink in the sink. She could hear Prema's horrified questions in the adjoining dining room, and the effort Shalini was putting into making the situation seem less troubling than it was.

She lifted the phone off the side table, her hands still shaking, and dialed her parents' number.

"Grace! Where are you? We thought you'd be here by now."

"I'll be there soon, Ma," Grace said, trying to speak calmly. "We should be there in about an hour and a half."

"So long! Where are you calling from?"

"I'll tell you everything when I get there. But, Ma, I have to ask you to do something. Don't get worried, okay?"

"About what?" Nalini said, a note of worry already in her voice.

"I need you to call Ragu Uncle," Grace said. "Tell him to come over."

"Ragu? What for? You want him to come here?"

"I'm with Duncan and a friend. We're on the way there. Call Ragu Uncle and get him to come there now."

"What's going on?" Nalini's voice was filled with alarm. Grace heard her call out, "Lionel! Lionel! Can you come here?" She heard the resonance of her mother's voice change as she put the phone on speaker mode.

"What?" Lionel's voice said. When Nalini explained, Lionel sounded confused. "Ragu? What for? Grace? Where are you?"

"On the way there, Appa," Grace said. "I'll be there in about . . ." She checked her watch. "A little more than an hour. Tell Ragu Uncle we need him there urgently."

"Urgently? What for?" Nalini said just as Lionel was saying, "What are you talking about, Grace? Are you in trouble?"

Grace broke in. "No, no, not in trouble. Don't worry, but I really can't talk now. I'll explain everything soon."

She hung up and went into the hallway as Shalini hurried out of the dining room, Prema, looking distraught, hobbling behind. He had a batik bush shirt slung over his shoulder.

"We have to go now," Shalini said. "Prema Uncle's doctor friend will be here any minute. He will have to call the police. Gunshot wound, no? We'll have to get out before they start asking questions. Before they see the car we're in."

They ran out to the car. Duncan put on the batik shirt Prema handed him, explaining to Janie that they would be back soon to get her.

"Why? Duncan, why can't you stay? Can I see Daddy?" Janie said, her voice rising in a distressed whine.

"Soon, don't worry," Duncan said. "Stay with Karuna and Prema Uncle, okay? They'll take good care of you."

"Come, come, show me your tortoise," Prema was saying in English as they left. Karuna was tending to Jotipala, who was lying motionless in his bloodied shirt.

51

DUNCAN

Tuesday

Duncan, in the back seat, saw Shalini stiffen as a police siren sounded behind them. He turned, holding his breath. No one spoke. He watched the black police car approach and speed past them. He heard the others sigh as he let out his own breath.

"Never been this afraid of the police," Grace said.

"The whole police force can't be in on this," Duncan said.

"Problem is we don't know who is," Shalini said. "But I think we'll be fine now. We're almost there. They don't know what car we're in, even if they're looking for us."

She took one hand off the wheel to rummage in her purse. After some scrabbling, she produced a cell phone. She pressed a button, squinting at it. "Shall we call your parents to make sure your uncle will be there? Charge is almost gone, but I think enough. I haven't been using it for a while because I've been afraid of getting traced. But maybe we should call."

"Why risk it?" Grace said. "I told them three times. I'm sure they'll get him over."

A cliff towered beside the expressway, bearing mute witness to the way the road builders had torn through the landscape. Nature had now reasserted her authority by covering the cliff with thick vegetation. Duncan rested his head against the back window, exhausted, his mind reeling. They had been trying to piece together what they'd found out. It all seemed impossible: that Symb86 was a placebo, that people could have been murdered, that Grace had been targeted, that he had almost been killed.

"The way Hammond said it . . . I thought Salgado had been pushed," Duncan said.

"Did Jotipala say he actually saw Salgado jump?" Grace said. Duncan could hear the horror in her voice.

Shalini nodded. "He said he was coming toward the overlook when he saw Salgado standing there. And before Jotipala could stop him, Salgado jumped." She shuddered. "It was high tide. Just like today. Jotipala is convinced that Salgado was possessed by a demon. He was going on about how after Salgado died, cobras started coming to the house, crows started hanging around. Because of the dark forces unleashed, he said. You know the village thinking." She shrugged, shaking her head. "But the thing is, right before Salgado jumped, he had been inside, watching a video."

"Alone?" Grace said.

Shalini shook her head. "With a foreigner. Someone called Matison. Someone who'd been there before. Salgado had come to the house the day before Matison came. Salgado had also already been to the house once before, so Jotipala was acquainted with him. Apparently he gave Jotipala some documents he had in his room. He told Jotipala that if anything happened to him, he should mail the documents to me. He had written out my address for Jotipala."

Shalini glanced nervously in the rearview mirror at the road behind them before continuing. "Salgado might have been one of the people who had been leaking to Minowa. That might be how he knew who I was. After he died, Jotipala had been too frightened to do anything. Mr. Fernando had spoken to Jotipala on the phone the night after the incident. He had told Jotipala not to say anything about seeing Salgado jump if the police came, that Jotipala would be blamed for the death. But the police hadn't come by at all. The body had got washed out past the rocks. It wasn't found near the house. But the whole thing had been eating at poor Jotipala's conscience, sounds like. So a couple of weeks later, he mailed the documents. He must have been terrified that the envelope would get traced back to him. Not only because he would have lost his job. He must have been afraid that the death would be put on him. Poor fellow."

"So you're saying Salgado was watching the same video I watched?" Duncan said. He could remember the video, but his memory of the aftermath was hazy. All he had were flashes of images and sensations. Had he fallen asleep watching it?

"Don't know," Shalini said. "Jotipala didn't see the video you were watching. He said the drumming—we could hear it coming out of the back window—sounded the same. He was terrified that you were going to get possessed. When I went back there to the servant quarters, he was already tying on his drum. He had some idea that he could drive out the demon with his drumming. I think he felt he had to do something, and that's all he felt he had the power to do. This was all happening so fast. I told Karuna to take Janie out to the car. He told me about Salgado. Crying. He was so worried it was going to happen again. Then we saw you out there. He got frightened that you might also jump. That's when we ran out there." She shuddered again. "Big risk, now that I think about it. He might have shot us all. But who had time to think? You might have jumped." She looked at Duncan in the rearview mirror. "Were you really about to?"

"It seemed like a good idea at the time," Duncan said. "I wasn't trying to kill myself. I didn't . . . It didn't seem dangerous."

"What was it, some kind of hypnosis video?" Shalini said.

Duncan shook his head. "Hammond said it was a prototype of a commercial that they were going to use. He wanted me to—" He snorted. "That's putting it mildly. He had the gun. I couldn't exactly refuse. See if you notice anything unusual, he said. He wasn't specific. Maybe he just wanted me to focus on it. Over and over."

"I think this is connected to the hooniyam research," Shalini said.

"You mean thovil research," Grace said, sounding confused.

"No, men. Apparently Cinasat was also studying hooniyam."

Duncan leaned forward. "Jotipala said the same thing."

After he'd recounted what Jotipala had said, Shalini said, "That fits with what I found out. That's why Minowa quit the company. Not only because she was unhappy about the ethics, the way all the research was being done. She got frightened after they started talking to the kattadiyas."

Grace was frowning. "About what?"

"Something to do with the marketing strategy," Shalini said. "They've been trying to find out how kattadiyas do hooniyam. Cinasat people don't believe in spirits, all that, obviously. They think what kattadiyas do is manipulate what people believe. Minowa said what Cinasat is trying to do is get ideas about how to do the same thing to market Symb86. Also for marketing other drugs."

"I don't get it," Grace said. "How would hooniyam . . . ?"

Duncan whistled. "The nocebo effect. They're trying to make people believe they're sick. They're probably not focusing on the specific things kattadiyas do. They must be looking at how kattadiyas communicate with people."

"Exactly," Shalini said. "They think what the kattadiyas are doing is somehow hypnotizing people into thinking that they are sick."

"My God. You think that was what the video was doing?" Grace said. "That man going on about . . ." She turned to Shalini. "I told you, there was a man talking about how hot he was feeling, and how he couldn't bear it, how he had to jump into the water. Going on and on. And there was this drum in the background."

"I think I might have been in some sort of trance," Duncan said. "It was like I was dreaming. It was definitely different than just watching a regular commercial. I thought . . . I could feel . . . It was like I was that guy."

"It must have been that bloody drumming," Shalini said. "We could hear it near Jotipala's room."

"Couldn't have only been that," Grace said. "You heard it, I heard it. We didn't want to jump off a cliff. It must have been the whole package. The visuals, the words. There was some chanting or murmuring in the background also. And the fact that you watched it over and over, Duncan." She turned back, her face anguished. "My God. What if we hadn't got there in time?"

Duncan squeezed her shoulder. How could he have been so deluded? He couldn't explain it.

"Minowa said they wanted to use this research—from studying the kattadiyas and also the thovil—to make ads," Shalini said.

"But killing people isn't going to help them sell drugs," Duncan said.

"Maybe they get people to feel they're having some problem, and then offer their bloody drugs as treatment," Shalini said.

"Get people to take a drug to feel better instead of jumping into the water?" Duncan said. "You watch the ad over and over on TV, and then you go out and buy the drug? Go and ask your doctor for the drug?" Was that really what Cinasat was trying to do?

"What a way to sell Symb86," Shalini said. "A drug that doesn't do anything. Convince people they have problems. And then convince them their nonexistent problems will be fixed by a bogus drug."

"What madness," Grace said.

If he hadn't felt the effects of the video, he would have thought the idea was ridiculous, Duncan thought. Had they really been working on this? "What proof do we have?"

"Bits and pieces," Shalini said. "There's a lot we don't know. I don't know if we have enough to pin anyone specific down. The ones in control. Hammond. Bentley."

"We don't have any proof Bent is involved," Grace said. "He wouldn't have risked Janie."

Duncan thought over what had happened. "She wasn't really in danger at any point. If Bent was the one who sent us there . . . The house was guarded by police. She was always with me. If he thought I would take care of her . . . And Hammond only brought the gun out after he had sent her outside with Karuna. It could have all been choreographed to make it look like she was in danger. Which would make it look like he couldn't be involved."

Grace shook her head. "I can't imagine that he would be involved," she said. "It's just not plausible. What if he was only a pawn himself?"

52

GRACE

Tuesday

They'd gone over and over what they knew, trying to understand. Now they'd entered the Colombo city limits, and everyone had fallen silent. The others were as exhausted as she was, Grace saw.

"Almost there. Good thing we came this way," she said. "Traffic is a bit better." Cars were weaving past each other, honking and crossing lanes. A blue bus bulging with passengers raced past, a trio of teenage school boys in white shirts and trousers with dusty knees cheering lustily on the footboard. One of them had only one foot on the bus, the other dangling precariously in the air.

Shalini turned onto Bauddhaloka Mawatha. Grace felt comforted by the familiarity of the place, by the enormous old trees canopying the road, the lush ferns at the edge of the broad brick pavements, the whitewashed garden walls surrounding the buildings they were passing. At the Thunmulla roundabout, they turned onto Havelock Road, where the traffic was heavier. The number of tuk-tuks on the road must have doubled since the last time they'd been in Colombo, Grace thought. There were more billboards than she remembered, competing aggressively with the araliya trees that graced the roadside here and there. She looked out at the pedestrians oblivious to the heat and the blazing sunlight and realized how much she missed being among them. She sighed as they turned down Gamini Lane and moved past a bend in the road. She was ready to be home, to be done with the horror of this whole situation.

"What is this?" Shalini said, her voice rising in alarm.

Grace whipped her head around to see that a wooden barrier had been set up across Gamini Lane. A black police car was parked beside it. Three khaki-uniformed, armed officers stood there, their caps pulled low.

"Haven't seen this since the war ended," Duncan said.

"May be for us," Shalini hissed. "Could be a problem."

"Just act normal," Grace said. "We haven't done anything."

"What can they do? We're just by Havelock Road!" Duncan said.

"How far is it to your parents' place?" Shalini said.

"Less than a quarter mile," Grace said. The officers were moving toward the car, hands held up. She heard a motorbike arrive from the direction of Havelock Road. It slowed down to a chug, its helmeted driver craning his neck inquisitively to look inside the car and then at the road block.

One of the officers, a fleshy-jowled man with light skin, stepped up to the bike. "The lane is closed. No traffic," he said, waving the rider off. The rider turned the bike around and puttered back toward Havelock Road.

"Where are you going, miss?" another officer said in Sinhala. He was middle-aged and stocky, with a bushy mustache shadowing his lips. He bent to look through the window, his eyes stony.

"Just down the lane," Shalini said.

"Your name?"

Shalini hesitated. "Shalini Samaraweera," she said.

"Identity card?"

While the officer was examining the identity card, the third officer peered through the passenger-side window. He was a younger, muscular man, with a nose that looked as though it had once been broken. "Your identity card?"

"I'm a US citizen," Grace said. "Also my husband."

"Passports?"

Grace handed over her passport and said Duncan didn't have his. The officers joined forces, conferring. Grace cracked her window to hear.

"I'll give a call," the older one muttered. "Get them out."

"I'll block the lane off," the fleshy-jowled one said. He swaggered off toward Havelock Road.

Grace could see her own anxiety reflected in Shalini's and Duncan's faces. "What do we do?" she said.

"Doesn't matter if we have to go to the station," Duncan said. "They can't do anything. You can call Ragu from there."

"What if they're not taking us to the station?" Shalini said. "Who knows where?"

"Kindly get out," the younger officer said, his hand on the door. Grace locked it and rolled the window down a couple of inches. "What's the problem?" she said. "We're going to my parents' house, just down the lane here."

"Get out of the car," the older officer said. The handle clanged as he yanked it. He tapped on Shalini's window, one hand on his gun.

Grace covered her mouth with her hand. "Just go through," she muttered. "We're so close. Ragu Uncle will be there."

Duncan leaned forward. He cupped his hands around his mouth so that the officers couldn't see. "Accelerate hard."

The officer on Grace's side yanked the handle again. He was raising his hand to thump the window when Shalini put the car into drive and revved. The car shot forward and tore through the barrier with an explosive crack. Grace caught a glimpse of the older officer's face, his eyes wide, his mouth open. He began running toward the car. When she turned back a few seconds later, she saw to her horror that he was aiming his gun. The barrel was long and black.

"Oh my God! He's shooting!" she shouted. "Duncan, duck! Duck!"

A muffled crack sounded, and then two others, followed by the sound of shattering glass. Shalini screamed. The car veered off to the left and slammed into a lamppost. Grace's head whipped back. When she turned, she saw that Duncan was crumpled in the back seat, blood on his face. Shalini was clutching her side, looking dazed, and blood was oozing from between her fingers.

"Oh my God, you got hit?" Grace shouted, looking from her to Duncan. "Duncan, Duncan, are you okay?"

He nodded, staring at his bloody hands. Behind him, through the glassless back window, Grace could see the older officer running toward them, his gun aimed. On their left was the high red wall of the Immaculate Heart Church. On the other side, a gray garden wall obscured the view of the house owned by the Rodrigos. They'd been away for weeks, visiting their daughters in Australia, Grace knew. The other nearby houses could be unoccupied at this time on a weekday, she realized.

Shalini was turning the key on and off, her face panicked. "Nothing. Not moving." She grabbed her purse and threw it at Grace. "The phone! Call your parents!"

Grace thrust her hand into the purse, scrabbling around for the phone. She grabbed it and tried to dial, her hands shaking. The older officer was almost at the car, shouting, "Get out of the car! Now!"

The younger officer was getting into the police car.

Grace could hear herself shouting something, she didn't know what. She managed to dial the number. "Ma! Ma!" Grace said, as soon as her mother picked up the phone. "Come outside! Now, with Ragu Uncle! Around the bend."

"What? What are you—"

The phone beeped, signaling its imminent death. The police car with the younger officer was speeding toward them.

"Ma, no time! Come out! We're in the lane. Now, now! Run!" Grace found herself shouting.

The officer on foot reached through the open back window and unlocked the back door. He pulled it open and seized Duncan by the shoulder. "Out! Now!" he yelled. The car rocked as Duncan struggled, and then there was a thump as he landed on the ground by the car.

The police car screeched to a halt beside them, and the officer on foot pulled open its door. He hauled Duncan to his feet.

"What, what!" There was a clang as Nalini dropped the phone. Her voice came to Grace faintly, shouting, "Lionel! Come, come! Now, we have to go!" Something thudded.

Grace thrust her door open. "Wait, wait!" she shouted as she leapt out. She heard Shalini shouting something, and the driver's side door banging. The police officer had shoved Duncan into the back seat of the police car, and now he grabbed Grace's arm, hauling her forward. She could hear herself screaming.

Just then, there was a clang up ahead and her parents' voices shouting, "Grace! Grace?" A young man appeared in a khaki police uniform, sprinting. Running behind him was Ragu, followed by her mother, stumbling in a sari, and her father, wearing a white undershirt and holding up the end of his sarong with one hand. A police jeep with three uniformed officers accelerated around the bend behind them.

The officer who had seized Grace by the arm dropped his hand as the police jeep screeched to a halt beside them.

"What the bloody hell is this?" Ragu roared at the officer, his face outraged.

"Aney, aney!" Nalini screamed. "Blood? What happened?"

"Not my blood, Ma," Grace said. "They were trying to abduct us," she said to Ragu. "They shot at us." She could see the confusion on his face. There was going to be a lot of explaining to do. As Ragu turned to

313

the officer in the driver's seat of the police car, shouting orders, she got back into their own car to help Shalini out. The lamppost obstructed the driver's door, leaving a gap too narrow for an exit. Duncan had already climbed out of the police car, the blood on his face adding to the panic.

"What the hell is going on?" Lionel was saying, panting. He propped himself against the hood of the Nissan and clutched his chest.

53

DUNCAN

Tuesday

Duncan laid his head against the sofa back, listening to the chaos of voices in the sitting room. Leela, the elderly cook, was sponging the blood off his forehead, her kindly face bent over him. She had picked out the bits of glass. He felt too drained to join in the explanations. The French windows were open. Leela had removed his glasses, and his vision was a little blurry. He looked out at the sunlight playing on the fronds of the dwarf coconut palm outside, their green iridescent. Croton bushes flamed with color. The jasmine was in flower, its fragrance drifting in through the windows. The air was a little smoky with the bonfire the gardener had going. He was burning some branches that smelled faintly sweet. How had the whole mess happened here in Sri Lanka? How could they have been shot at in the middle of Colombo? In the middle of the day?

Grace had been trying to explain how Cinasat was involved. Duncan realized how unbelievable their story sounded.

"Big drug company, Western fellows, what do they want with hooniyam?" Ragu said, his head cocked inquisitively. He had barely aged since Duncan had last seen him. His hairline might have receded a little, and he had lost a bit of weight, but he still looked fit in his khaki uniform.

Lionel was frowning. He was still in his undershirt. Duncan had never seen his father-in-law so underdressed. "Marketing strategy? What kind of nonsense is that?"

"What, they are going to take kattadiyas to the States?" Nalini said, wrapping a bandage around Shalini's waist.

"No, Ma," Grace said, sounding impatient. "They've been studying what kattadiyas do. Seeing how the kattadiyas frighten people into thinking that they're sick."

"Even our black magic, the Westerners have a way of explaining," Nalini said, her lips twisted sarcastically.

"Not only explaining, using," Shalini said.

"This is all nonsense," Lionel said. "They can't use it. Westerners don't believe in all this. You have to believe in it for it to work."

Ragu loosened the collar of his uniform. "Frightening people? That's not what happens," he said. Then casting an embarrassed glance at Duncan, he said, "At least that is not what people think happens. I'm not saying I believe in all this. But what other people think is that the kattadiya calls on the spirits to attack someone. The person doesn't have to know that the kattadiya has put a spell to get sick!" He looked around defensively. "Someone recently put a spell on one of my sergeants, Kotawatte. He had been having severe stomach pains. He saw plenty of Western doctors—he's not some villager. But nothing wrong. Then he got a kattadiya to come, and that fellow found a charm buried right under the front doorstep. Kotawatte was very upset. He was convinced that his neighbor had hexed him—he and this neighbor fellow had a longtime feud over the boundary between their properties."

"Did the kattadiya do something?" Nalini said.

"He did a ceremony, lime cutting, all of that," Ragu said. "Then a little while later, Kotawatte was fine. But the neighbor got ill. Kotawatte is one hundred percent sure that is because the spirits attacked the fellow. That is what the spirits do when the spell backfires. That is why misfortune affects the one who put the charm."

"Spirits . . . demons . . . Cinasat people aren't interested in all that," Shalini said.

This was not going to make sense unless they explained a whole lot more, Duncan thought. For now, they needed to explain only the basics to get the police investigation started and to charge Hammond. He sat up. "Do we have enough to go on for the investigation?"

Ragu shook his head. "I've got the Criminal Investigation Department involved now. They will get Shalini's records. But my fellow there"—he pointed down the garden path to the driveway, where several police officers were gathered—"he said no one was found at the Maya. Galle, Colombo, everyone is searching for this Hammond fellow. He won't be able to leave the country in a hurry, but we're going to need more to charge him for Salgado. And Bentley Hyland is also missing."

"Just thought of something," Shalini said. "I know what we can do to get the information." She sat up, wincing, and gathered her sari pota, her bangles tinkling.

54

GRACE

Tuesday

They were making the call from Nalini's study. The swaying leaves of the lady palm tree cast dark vibrating shadows over the lily pads floating in the small pond outside. Through the open windows, Grace could hear music from the church. The evening Mass was being celebrated, with the youth choir and the rock band that the young priest there had encouraged. The drums were loud. There was a breeze blowing in, making the chimes hanging by the study window ring like ankle bells. The gardener's bonfire was petering out, but a little sweet-smelling smoke was still in the air.

"Tell me the number," Shalini said. Then she raised a hand. "Wait, must get in the right mindset first. Have to be convincing." She winked, grinning. "Should I say my name is Yak Adura?"

She was taking this too lightly, Grace thought. "He won't even know what that means," she said. "He barely knows any Sinhala." She frowned, looking at the white bandage wrapped around Shalini's midriff. "Are you sure you shouldn't go to the clinic first?"

"Later, men," Shalini said. "Only a flesh wound, no? If we don't do this now, they might all get off scot-free."

"Put it on speaker," Grace said as Shalini dialed the cell number.

"Hello?" Bent's voice said.

"My name is Shalini Samaraweera," Shalini said. "I'm the journalist who picked Duncan up at the Galle house."

There was a long pause before Bent said sharply, "Where is my daughter?"

"You've been in touch with Hammond, it seems," Shalini said, her voice pleasant. She gestured at Grace, mouthing, "Don't worry."

"Is Janie with Grace and Duncan?"

"I'm sure that's what Hammond told you," Shalini said.

Another pause, and then, "What do you mean? Where is she?"

"If I knew, I'd tell you," Shalini said.

Bent's voice rose. "Where are Duncan and Grace?"

"They're at her parents' house. No thanks to you," Shalini said. "But only Hammond can tell you where Janie is. And he's not going to tell you that, because he needs her."

"What? Whose . . . What are you talking about?"

"We already know everything," Shalini said calmly. "The Criminal Investigation Department here is involved. Your friends in the police can try to help you, but they will all be indicted for their part in this. A Sri Lankan citizen has been killed."

"I don't know of any—"

"Look," Shalini said, her voice businesslike. "We know all about Frank Salgado. Also the other deaths. Minowa Costa, Danibel Garwick. Angie. The hooniyam research, Symb86."

"I was not involved—"

Shalini cut him off. "The thing is, right now, Hammond is going to say that he doesn't have Janie. But that's because he's not sure whether his police friends can help him. When the Sri Lankan police, the real ones who don't take bribes, take him in, he's going to implicate you. His story is going to be that you were the only one masterminding all this. That you were the one behind Angie's death. All of them.

Minowa, Danibel, Salgado. And you're going to have to go along with that because he has your daughter."

"Utter bullshit," Bent said, but he sounded frightened. "He doesn't have Janie. I've spoken to him."

"You can believe him," Shalini said. "Or you can be smart and make sure Janie is safe." She tapped her fingers on the phone. "You can verify what I'm saying. Grace and Duncan are here, if you want to talk to them. They'll tell you we don't have Janie. Or you can call your police friends. Their fellows tried to pick us up in Colombo. They'll tell you we didn't have Janie."

"Let me talk to Grace," Bent said.

"Tell us where Hammond is, Bent," Grace said, choking back her reluctance. "The police are looking for him."

"I don't know where he is," Bent said. "Some place where he's being treated for a cobra bite."

Grace gasped. Shalini's mouth had fallen open.

"I couldn't talk to him for long, but he said you had Janie," Bent said.

"Is he going to be—" Grace started to say, but Shalini was gesturing at her, mouthing, "Say you don't have Janie!"

"We don't have her," Grace said, not wanting to talk to him. What if he weren't involved in all this? They'd be putting him through this for nothing. "Shalini's right. I'm worried . . . and Duncan, about Janie. Go to the Bambalapitiya police station. You can get a plea deal if you go forward now. Report Janie's kidnapping so the CID can look for her."

"You better do it before Hammond dies," Shalini said, her tone grim. "I don't know of anyone who has survived a cobra bite. If he dies, you'll be the one who'll get blamed. And we won't know where he put Janie."

55

DUNCAN

Tuesday

"That was Mo," Grace said, coming out to the sitting room after answering the phone call she had received. "Mortensen called him." She took a deep breath. "Apparently Bent turned himself in to the US embassy. That's why Ragu Uncle hasn't heard anything yet. Bent's been offered full immunity in exchange for revealing everything he knows. The FBI is involved now. They must have called Mortensen."

"I'll let the embassy know we have the child," Ragu said, rising.

"Did Mo say anything else?" Duncan said.

"The reason Mo called here trying to reach me yesterday was to say someone from the FDA was involved. He showed Mortensen a photo he had found at Angie's house. A photo with Bent and Hammond Gleeson and another guy, and Mortensen told him the guy was a big shot at the FDA."

Shalini leaned forward. "Christian Nolan? Was that the guy at the FDA?"

"Yes, that's the name Mo mentioned," Grace said. "Do you know who that is?"

"Someone Angie suspected was involved," Shalini said. "But we didn't have proof he was connected to Cinasat."

"This photo's going to help with that," Grace said.

56

GRACE

Wednesday

Duncan emerged from a door at the side of the waiting room and beck-oned to Grace. She had already been interviewed. She'd been waiting in the chilly air-conditioned interior of the US embassy for more than an hour while Duncan was being interviewed.

"They suggested we talk to Bent," Duncan said, taking her arm. "They think it'll help them to get more from him."

They followed a somber-faced young man wearing a black tie down a long hallway. The man swiped a key card through a slot, and they entered a room glaring with fluorescent light. Bent was seated on one side of a long wooden table, facing the door. A formally dressed man with a shock of red hair sat next to him, a tablet computer balanced on one knee. Another man, with a long-jawed, weather-beaten face, sat opposite, a laptop open on the table in front of him. When Grace and Duncan entered, he indicated the two empty chairs beside him. "I'm Garrett Johnson," he said. "State Department." He gestured at the red-haired man. "This is Blue McAllister. He's acting as Mr. Hyland's attorney."

They sat. Bent was hunched over in his chair, his elbows on his knees.

Duncan was silent. Grace waited, not knowing what to say.

"How could you have lied about Janie?" Bent said, raising his eyes to Grace.

"It was the only—" Grace started to say, but Duncan interrupted.

"How can you be asking? All the lies . . . You pretended Janie was kidnapped to show you weren't involved? You let her be involved in all this?" Duncan said, his voice barely controlled.

"I never meant for everything to go this far," Bent said, looking down at his hands. "I didn't have anything to do with any of the deaths."

Grace drew a deep breath. "Was Angie killed?" she said. She closed her eyes. She didn't really want to know the answer, she thought.

McAllister turned to Bent and said, "Don't answer that."

"Who killed her?" Grace said. Her voice came out sounding choked. She couldn't even believe she was asking the question. She couldn't believe that it was Bent she was asking. This was the first man she had ever dated. There was a time she had thought she loved him. She had kissed him, made love to him, slept with him. She had cooked for him, and eaten the food he'd cooked. She had watched him brush his teeth, cut his toenails. How could she have been so intimate with someone, and yet have known so little about him? Or had he changed after she had known him?

McAllister tapped Bent. "Don't answer," he said again.

Bent waved his hand dismissively. "That wasn't my idea," he said. "Look at me, Grace. It wasn't me."

Grace saw that he had tears in his eyes. Were they real?

"You know I was close to Angie once. You think I would have her killed? Let her be killed? That is ridiculous." He shook his head. "She contacted me before the reunion, but I told her I didn't know anything. When she showed up, I knew she was going to try to talk to me. I wanted to warn her to let go of this story. But I never got to do that. She died before I could talk to her. Angie said she was being followed by Cinasat, so I was afraid something would happen. I saw two people on the trail that afternoon who I thought were from Cinasat. Those gunshots that morning. That was me. I was trying to scare them off."

"You brought a gun to the reunion?" Grace said.

McAllister took Bent by the arm. "Don't say any more," he said.

Bent shook off his hand. "It wasn't illegal. I have a permit."

"Did you tell Mortensen all this?" Duncan said.

Bent looked down at his hands. "At the time . . . Look, I had no proof that Cinasat was involved. I talked to Hammond to—"

The attorney touched his arm.

Bent turned to Grace. "I gave Angie a message the night before, telling her to meet me, to warn her. But she never showed up."

"How did you give her the message?" Grace said.

"What does it matter?" Duncan said. "All a bunch of fucking lies anyway."

"I'm not lying," Bent said. "She was talking to people that night, so I couldn't say anything to her directly. I slipped a note into her sweatshirt pocket when I went by to say hello."

Grace fumbled in her purse. Bentley's card, with its handwritten message, was lying at the bottom. "This?" She handed it to Bent.

"How did you get this?" Bent said.

"It was in the sweatshirt you brought me. Remember, from the picnic area that night? You must have picked up Angie's sweatshirt—it must have been lying there."

"This proves it," Bent said to the attorney, to Johnson. He handed the card to McAllister, who read it and passed it to Johnson. "I tried to warn Angie."

"It shows you may have met with Angie just before she died," Johnson said.

"She didn't show up," Bent said. His face had crumpled. "I don't know why. She wanted to talk to me. But she didn't show."

"We have only your word for that," Johnson said.

"What about her cell phone? Her computer? What happened to those?" Grace said. "Was that how Cinasat found out about what she was working on? Who was leaking to her?"

"I don't—"

"That's enough," McAllister said to Bent, his voice firm.

"You thought Cinasat was involved, and you didn't say anything," Duncan said, his voice flat.

"Mr. Hyland has nothing more to say about this," McAllister said.

"What about that phone call I heard you on? At the reunion," Grace said.

Bent frowned. "What?"

"Outside the kitchen building," Grace said. Realization dawned on her. "You *knew* it was Cinasat. You were trying to get them to cover it up." He *was* lying. He had to have known. "Was that how a different medical examiner showed up? Someone Cinasat paid off? Oh my God."

"What the hell?" Duncan said. "Is that even possible?"

Bent said nothing. McAllister was whispering to him, his hand cupped over his mouth.

"Mortensen was suspicious about the whole thing," Grace said. "My God. That was why Mortensen got Internal Affairs involved. Because he figured out the investigation had been rigged. Is that what happened?"

"I don't know what you're talking about," Bent said, but his expression said everything.

Grace covered her mouth, incredulous.

"Mr. Hyland has nothing more to say about Ms. Osborne's death," McAllister said.

There was a thick silence for a moment. Then Duncan said, "The other deaths?"

"I only knew after they happened . . . ," Bent said, trailing off when McAllister seized his arm again.

"You knew about Minowa Costa's accident," Grace said. "So-called accident."

"Only after it had happened," Bent said.

"You thought no one would connect the accident to Cinasat because she quit months ago. That's why you were worried about that photo Mo had. With her and Angie at Cinasat. Because that would show a recent connection between Cinasat and Minowa. You must have known Cinasat was involved in the accident. You tried to cover it up."

"Enough," McAllister said, his eyes on Bent.

"And Danibel Garwick?" Grace said.

"That was not in my hands," Bent said.

"But you knew, didn't you?" Grace said. "Her tongue was hanging out when she died."

"What?" Duncan said.

Grace nodded. "That's what her neighbors said. Just the way you described Angie." She leaned forward. "Was it some special poison that does that?"

"I don't know," Bent said, looking down at his hands.

Duncan said, "Was it a video?"

Bent's reaction was enough for Grace, before he said wearily, "I told you, I was not involved in any of that."

"The deal was based on your providing information," Johnson said, his face grim.

Grace stared at Bent. "My God. A video? It made her what . . . have a heart attack?"

"It wasn't meant for that," Bent said. "We'd been testing the videos in lab studies. We could get people to experience all kinds of things. Simple discomfort. Shame and guilt. Pain and insomnia. Fatigue. Nausea. Cold."

"That was what the hooniyam research was for?"

Bent nodded. "And some of the thovil research on trances. We were getting amazing results. We could get people to feel unbearably cold. Get them to go to a different building to ask for a blanket. Some of the effects lasted for weeks. We were sure we'd be able to get people to go to their doctors, go to the drugstore to get a drug." There was a note of pride in his voice. "It was a brilliant idea. A technological innovation that could have given us unprecedented sales. I didn't mean for it to be weaponized. That was Hammond's . . . He had it tried on Salgado after we found out he was leaking."

"So Salgado was murdered," Grace said. She couldn't believe it still. Duncan had almost been killed.

Bent shook his head. "They weren't murders. Showing someone a video isn't a crime. Salgado felt unbearably hot. He jumped. His own free will."

"My God," Grace said. "That's how Angie had a heart attack. She watched a video? Someone showed her one on the trail out there?"

Bent covered his face with his hands. "Hammond's idea. I had nothing to do with it. After it worked on Salgado, he had the research division design one for a heart attack. I told you. I only found out after it was too late. No one would ever know, he said. Because she had an elevated risk for heart disease. But no one expected the tongue. No one knows why that happened." He sighed. "There's still a lot we don't know. We were still refining the technique . . . Weaponizing was a mistake." He pulled at his hair, angrily.

"All this to market Symb86?"

Bent sighed again. "You're making it out to be something terrible. It's not. Drugs are already marketed this way. Think about all the ads you see on TV. Not just from Cinasat. All the major players use this strategy. All we do is show how our products are useful to people. Show them how we can make their lives better. Men used to think not being able to have sex was normal, yeah? Just a part of getting older. But once they realize there's something called erectile dysfunction, they know they can fix it. That makes their lives better. We're doing people a service."

"Like RLS," Grace said.

"What?" Duncan said.

"Restless legs syndrome. You create disorders," Grace said.

"Nonsense," Bent said. "We create nothing. People already have experiences they'd rather not have, but they put up with them. We point out the emotions that go along with those experiences. That makes people see the experiences are really symptoms, symptoms that can be eliminated."

"So this is all okay? You don't see a problem with using hooniyam?"

"Kattadiyas know how to make people believe. To persuade. We wanted to see what we could learn from them. If people don't believe they have a symptom, how can they believe our drugs will help?" He shook his head. "All we were doing was refining our marketing strategy. I don't see anything unethical about it. We consulted our lawyers. They agreed this was only a refining of what was already being done. That's just what ads do. Evoke strong emotions. Guilt, shame, fear. Then people don't just tolerate discomfort. We show them they don't need to be uncomfortable. Show them how to be happier."

Duncan was looking down at the floor between his knees. His hands were clenched. "With Symb86? A drug that doesn't fucking exist?" he said.

Bent sighed. It was a deep sigh, as if he were trying to breathe out his despair. "It exists. In theory, on paper . . . it could have worked. But our testing . . . We found out it was inert. That's when we decided to use it as a placebo." He rubbed at his forehead, leaving red marks on his skin.

"It would have done nothing for CFS? For infertility?" Duncan said.

"Of course it would have. It could have helped people enormously, yeah. The idea itself, it's genius. The placebo effect is real. People get better when they believe they will. Cinasat was just helping them to believe."

"How could you possibly . . . Why did you think this could be pulled off?" Grace said. "What about the FDA? All those steps to go through to get approval."

Bent shrugged. "Money talks," he said, his lips twisted cynically. "Cinasat knows how to get things done. We know the right people."

"A great company," Duncan said sarcastically.

"This could have really worked out for you," Bent said. "The project was going strong. If not for the leaks . . . Salgado was too fastidious, that was the problem. That was what started everything. Going on about how the locals were being used. Talking about how they had no power. He's the one who corrupted Minowa. And Danibel." He shook his head. "To think I trusted Danibel. She was the one who researched your school . . . You were the first person I thought of when Salgado . . . when we lost him. Your anthropology background, your thovil expertise."

"Wait a second," Grace said, the realization dawning on her. "Did you . . . How did you . . . You got St. Casilda to lay him off?"

Duncan was staring at Bent openmouthed. "You fucking did what?"

"With the best of intentions," Bent said. "You know the college was going under. Cinasat contributed to their renovation project and assured them you would have a great job. You could have got some great publications out of it, with top coauthors. A chance you'd never have got at St. Casilda. It wasn't just self-serving, you know."

"Why not just offer him the job?" Grace said.

"Academics." Bent shook his head. "They don't like jobs outside academia. Grace, cut me some slack here. Think about the compensation Cinasat offered. Something neither of you could have made, even at the very best of universities."

Duncan rose quietly to his feet. "I'm done here," he said to Grace. He opened the door and walked out.

Grace knew who had sent the email about Duncan's layoff. *DOG* something. Danibel Olivia Garwick. She had tried to explain before she'd been killed. "That shooting in Paterson wasn't random," she said.

"No one was hurt," Bent said. "They were just trying to create a diversion, prevent you from meeting Danibel."

"But they did try to get me. Outside Gannon Hall. At Dumont. That wasn't some random mugging."

"I had nothing to do with that," Bent said. "I only found out later. You were interfering in things you didn't understand."

Grace could only gape at him. He was a stranger.

He looked at her pleadingly. "Getting Cinasat to hire Duncan, the hooniyam research, those were the only things I spearheaded," he said. "They weren't illegal. Symb86 wasn't my idea. The deaths, I had no part in those. I only found out afterward." He rubbed at his forehead again. "Look, Grace. I was just doing my job. Marketing, that was all. I did it all for Janie, you know. To do something really great, so that she wouldn't have to think . . . I didn't want to end up a . . . end up like my dad."

End up like a loser. That was what he wanted to say, Grace knew. That was how he had always thought of his dad, because that was how his dad felt about himself. That had always been Bent's goal, to have enough money of his own, and to control it, so that he would not be under his grandfather's control. But now, all that had crumbled. He might be immune from prosecution, but he would surely lose everything.

"I'll make sure Janie is okay," she said, pushing back her chair. She kept her eyes averted from Bent's face as she left the room.

57

DUNCAN

Sunday

"I can't believe you put her up to this," Grace said, watching Leela bring the pitcher down the brick garden path. It didn't seem like a good time to do it either. Black clouds were gathering, threatening a downpour.

"I didn't have to do much putting up," Duncan said, grinning. "I was thinking about what that woman on the plane, Mrs. Atukorale, had said. I just asked Leela what they did in the village when a woman has trouble getting pregnant, and she volunteered the rest." Grace's face tightened, and Duncan wondered if he'd said too much.

Grace had begun to look gradually more relaxed over the past four days. Duncan thought the need to keep Janie occupied until their return to the US was what had changed Grace's attitude. They had taken Janie to the museum, to show her the enormous blue whale skeleton that hung in one of the high-ceilinged halls. They'd bought her a kite and spent hours catching the wind by the beach. Another morning, they had gone boating on Beira Lake; from a flimsy swan-shaped paddleboat they'd watched real swans glide by. They'd taken Janie swimming at the Mount Lavinia beach, among the crowds of other screaming children who splashed in the shallows. In the evenings, guests had been dropping by. Janie had been enthralled with all the attention, so many aunties cooing and pinching her cheeks, so many children to play with. She had only asked once about when her father would be home.

It was only at night that Duncan's thoughts returned to Cinasat. For the past four nights, he'd lain next to Grace's sleeping body, listening to the whirring of the ceiling fan in their bedroom and the croaking of the frogs in the pond outside, and let his mind drift over recent events. He wondered what price Hammond would pay for his greed. When the case went to trial, Hammond would surely lose much more than the hand he'd had to have amputated. He worried about Janie, now that her mother had filed for sole custody. What would happen when she learned the complicated truth about her father's crimes? Would Bent eventually write the tell-all book they'd heard he intended to produce? How would that affect poor Janie?

He thought about Jotipala, with the sea inside his heart. Could Nalini's connections really get him and Karuna new jobs at a seaside hotel? How would the jobs change their lives? Would Jotipala still be able to drum after his shoulder wound healed? He wondered about Mo, still struggling with his grief over Angie. He thought about the turn his own life had taken, and about what the future might bring. Could he have prevented being laid off from St. Casilda? Would he have been happier if he had remained there? How could he not have known something was rotten at Cinasat? Sadness flowed through him at the thought of what he'd lost. Not only a job, but also the hope that his mother would be well again. The hope that he might have a child. But then, his ring impinged on his consciousness, as it so often did, and he remembered: nil desperandum. There was more to come—other doors would open, and he would see what lay beyond.

Now he watched Grace as she reached reluctantly for the small clay pitcher of milk Leela had brought. Grace was dressed in white, at Leela's insistence. He had waited until Grace's parents had taken Janie out for ice cream, not wanting to deal with their skepticism.

"Carefully, right at the base, Grace Madam," Leela said. She stood back, her lungi hitched up, arms akimbo, looking confident but not particularly reverent.

Grace poured the milk on the soil at the base of the araliya tree, splattering a little on the gray bark. They watched the milk run in small rivulets around the tree and seep gradually into the soil.

"May madam be blessed with a child," Leela said as she took back the pitcher.

"That's it?" Grace said, turning away from Leela to roll her eyes at Duncan.

"That's enough," Leela said, wiping a dribble of milk off the pitcher with the edge of her flowered blouse. "Madam will see. The spirits will be appeased."

"Come on, worth a try," Duncan said, after Leela had retired to the kitchen. They walked up the garden path to the coco plum tree. A squirrel was leaping up the tangled branches to where a ripe pink fruit dangled, just out of its reach. "You said you had a much more elaborate puberty ritual. Isn't this like that one a bit?"

"God, no," Grace said. "That was long. Three days sitting in my room with female company only. No fried foods. An elaborate bathing ritual on the fourth day. Neem leaves floating in the bathwater, and a branch of this araliya hanging in the bathroom, dripping sap into the sink. After the bath, I got to break a coconut open by dashing it on the ground. Actually, I only managed it on the third try. Mrs. Gunasiri— the midwife who had arranged the ceremony—didn't seem too thrilled about that. Maybe that was an omen—the miscarriages. You never know." She grimaced sarcastically, shrugging. "That was so long ago. Ma was into all that then, so Appa didn't dare say anything. Now she would agree with him."

"You have to believe a little bit," Duncan said, although he knew she would deny it. "I mean, you grew up with this sort of thing."

"Unconscious belief maybe," Grace said, sounding distracted. She looked up as a streak of lightning brightened the air for a second. A rumble of thunder followed. She drew in a long breath. "Listen," she said hesitantly. "I have to tell you something. I don't . . . It's hard to say it."

Duncan frowned at her expression. "What?"

"It's . . . it's something I should have told you a long time ago."

Duncan felt alarm rising in his throat. Was she ill? Had she got a test result that she hadn't told him about? Cancer?

"I had a miscarriage," she said.

Duncan frowned. He would have known if she had been pregnant again.

"Not now," she added. "When we broke up that time, after the big fight." She was talking fast, the words pressured. "I think I might have brought it on, by drinking."

"Are you saying . . . ? This was someone else's . . . ?" He felt like he couldn't breathe.

"No, no, no. It was yours. But I've been trying to convince myself that I miscarried because of something about my genes or my uterus or my hormones, but I don't think that's true. I didn't want to believe that my body could go beyond nine weeks, because that would have meant admitting to myself . . . I think I did it myself." Tears were falling. He stared, not understanding. "I know I did. I remember what happened. I had a lot to drink after I found out. And I knew that could end the pregnancy." She took a deep breath. "I remember. I hoped it would."

"I don't understand," he said. "What are you talking about?"

He waited while she explained, while the rain came down in hard drops that hit the ground audibly. After she had finished, he could only stand there, staring at her. Why had she not said anything before?

They could have had a child by now. Maybe a girl, only a little older than Janie was now. He would have watched her grow up. Shared with her all the things he loved. The sea, the woods. Taught her about other worlds the way Ms. Logan had taught him.

He thought about how long that argument had lasted, twelve years ago. What they had both said. *Thank God I found out now. I could never marry you.* How firmly he had clicked the door shut behind him.

When he came back to the present, he realized he was getting soaked with the rain streaming past the coco plum leaves. Grace's face was in her hands, her hair dripping.

They trudged through muddy puddles to the porch, their rubber slippers squelching, and sat in their wet clothes on the cane settee.

"If not for that, maybe we'd have a kid." Her voice was so low he could barely hear it. "I took that away from you. And then you gave up everything for me."

Duncan sighed, wiping the water off his face. "You didn't know we'd get back together." What else could he say? There was nothing to be done about it now. That had been a different time. In that time, that was what happened. How strange life was. How little power anyone had to predict the course of it.

Thunder was rumbling in earnest now, and great flashes of lightning cracked the sky. A long time seemed to pass as Duncan watched the rain fall in relentless sheets, pounding against the ground outside the shelter of the trees.

58

GRACE

Weeks later

Duncan was already crouched outside the house, plucking dandelions from the flower beds. He looked at her hiking shoes doubtfully. "Sure you want to go? You're not going to get all worried about your flies in the middle of the picnic?"

"The flies can wait," Grace said. It had been years since she'd been to the botanical gardens.

At the gardens, they walked along an avenue bordered by magnolia trees, swinging their joined hands. Duncan said, "Something's different . . . since we got back home. You seem happier."

How a secret could weigh you down, she thought. Without his forgiveness, she could not have forgiven herself. She hadn't felt this light in twelve years.

He grinned. "A bit odd for someone with a jobless husband."

"You'll get one soon," Grace said. "Plus . . . who knows. It might be good for you to be home."

He stared at her. "Why?" And then, "Whoa. Are you? When did you find out?"

"The week after we got back, but I went to see Dr. Mowad to be sure. Thirteen weeks now."

A small fountain was in sight. Two small children were running along its edge, their parents meandering after them. They looked like they were enjoying themselves. This was what parents did, she thought. They hung around, passing the time with their children.

There were a few birds calling. She had no idea what kind they were. It had been a long time since she'd been outside simply for the sake of it, listening. Another sound too, a quick *rik-triktriktrik*. Frogs? Crickets? Were crickets out at this time? She had forgotten. Some insects with startlingly blue abdomens were zipping low over the water, their wings only blurs. Were they dragonflies? Damselflies? She'd never had time for entomology. The only reason she knew anything about fruit flies was because she needed their ovaries. These flies, whatever they were, looked like they were enjoying themselves. Was this how they spent the whole of their lives?

The vials of flies are waiting. Grace brushed the thought away. If she'd stayed in the lab, this moment would have passed unnoticed. There was something mesmerizing about the constant arcing of water in the fountain, the incessant susurration of it. Up ahead, she could see bushes lush with pendulous lilacs. Their thick, sweet smell was already in the air.

Acknowledgments

I feel fortunate to belong to a nurturing and book-loving family. I owe thanks to two of the most well-read people I know: my brother, Sriyan, who bought me my first computer many years ago so that I could write, and who provided valuable and sometimes hilarious feedback on drafts of this novel, and to my sister, Lilanthi, who could always be counted on to provide thoughtful critiques and suggestions for good books to read. Thanks to my mother, Chandra, for her unflagging confidence in me, and to my late father, Vernon, whose anecdotes and spirit continue to enliven my writing. Thanks to Jon for his kindness in creating my first author website and for maintaining it for many years, and to both him and Susan for their encouragement. I owe much gratitude to my husband, Ben, for his constant support and for feedback on innumerable drafts of this novel, and to both him and Kian for the love that inspires and sustains my writing.

I am grateful to my agent, Shannon Hassan, for seeing the promise in the beginnings of this novel and for her patience and helpful advice, and to my editor at Little A, Vivian Lee, for her able guidance. Thanks also to Irene Billings, Erica Avedikian, and the rest of the team at Little A for all the work they have put into producing this book, and to the designer of my current author website, David Cooper, at Massive Designs, Inc. Finally, thanks to the journal *Literary Mama*, for publishing my 2011 short story, "A Soft Wife," in which I first began developing one of the main characters in this novel.

Glossary

adura—An exorcist

aney—A widely used, versatile exclamation that expresses a range of emotions, such as annoyance, frustration, pity, and hope

Appa—Dad

araliya—Plumeria

asvaha—Evil eye; the negative influence of envy or others' malevolent intentions

baba—A baby or young child; a respectful way of referring to young children

bali thovil—Healing ceremonies performed to negate the malign influence of planetary deities

diya redda—A cloth that a woman wraps around her body when bathing in public

hooniyam—Black magic or sorcery

kattadiya—A sorcerer

men—A word often used when addressing people in Sinhalese English, in a way similar to the usage of *man* in American English

nidhikumba—A touch-sensitive weed common in Sri Lanka

pirit—A Buddhist ceremony involving the chanting of scriptures

pota—The portion of a sari that falls back over the shoulder

thovile (plural: thovil)—A healing ceremony

vedarala—A practitioner of native medicine

yak adura—An exorcist of demons
yak beraya—A drum used in devil dancing ceremonies
yak thovil—Also called devil dancing; healing ceremonies performed to negate the malevolent influence of demons
yaka—A demon
yantra—A charm or amulet

Note: In Sinhalese English, plurals are often constructed by simply adding an *s* to a Sinhala word. For example, *yakas* would mean *demons* in Sinhalese English.

About the Author

Photo © 2018 by John Agnello

Ruvanee Pietersz Vilhauer was born in Sri Lanka and lived in India, Thailand, Canada, and Australia before settling in the United States. She is the 2018 winner of the Iowa Short Fiction Award, and the 2004 winner of the Commonwealth Short Story Competition. Her short stories have been broadcast on BBC Radio 4 and have appeared in many literary journals. This is her first novel. She is a psychology professor in New York and lives in New Jersey with her family.